Shark Bait

A Grab Your Pole Novel

by
Jenn Cooksey

First Printing 2012

This is a work of fiction. Names, characters, organizations, locations, and events that are portrayed in this novel are either products of the author's imagination or are used fictitiously solely for the express purpose of telling an entertaining story and are not to be taken otherwise.

ISBN-13: 9781490330570
ISBN-10: 1490330577

For Davey.
Sorry about the laundry.

Acknowledgments

There are many people without whom this book and the series on a whole wouldn't have been possible. The list is long and the reasons for inclusion are varied, so, let's get to it...

*My husband, *Davey*, and our three minions, *Alison, Faith-dizzle,* and *Erin* – You four have shown me what unconditional love is, seeing as how despite many a night of "on your own dinners," you guys still haven't voted me off the island. You all are my joy and my life would be empty without you.

**Mommy* - Because you know, you gave birth to me and have put up with my shit for the last [REDACTED] some odd years. Not only that, but your genuine love of these stories and your passion for reading them makes me *want* to keep going. And don't worry; Book 4 is on its way. I promise.

**Bapa* -You're my hero.

*My beta-readers: *Alison, Gloria, Miranda, Karen,* and *Becky* - With comments like "Omgosh! So good!" and "This is the best thing I've ever read," I feel I can blame some of you for my inflated ego. Just kidding, I'm honestly just tickled that you guys were gracious enough to share your opinions and your feedback has been invaluable—even if it wasn't always glowing.

*My in-laws: *Suzanne, Jerry, Mike, Kellie,* and *Karen* - You guys go above and beyond, far surpassing what family does. That's all I'm sayin'.

*My BFFs and BFFLEs both past and present and in order of when I met them: *Derek, Billy, Tanya, Rachel, Renee, Becky, Melanie, Mike, Monica C., Karyn, Amy, Jeff, Tisha, Shawn, Stacy, Treena, Karen, Kristina, Cris, Monica S., Crystal, Tonya,* and *Stefani* – Some of you are family, some of you are family in heart, and still some of you I haven't seen or spoken to in what feels like a millennia, but regardless, you have *all* helped to shape me into who I am today. Whether the result of your influence is a good thing or not has yet to be determined. :-p

*My Facebook Poll Participants in no particular order- *Dave, Alison, Faith, Stacy, Stefani, Becky, Karen, Noah, Brooklyn, Tyler, Miranda, Gloria, Brittany, Diana U., Jill, Kellie, Seth, Jon, Natalie M., Diana B., Kristina, Violette, Natalie L., Martin,* and *Sara* – By taking time out of your day to vote on those chapter titles, you all played what might seem like a small role, but it was a vital roll in the production of this book. I hope that by participating in a debut novel this way that you all had fun—I know I certainly did, and I still think some of you are going to be surprised…

*And last but nowhere even close to the realm of least, someone who rightfully belongs in a couple of the lists above, however, she's so incredible, she deserves a special shout-out. *K-E-L-L-Y* – I'm rarely at a loss for what to say, but I honestly don't have the words. Seriously, no one will ever truly understand what a special and integral part you've played in the lives of these characters. We're all better for knowing you...including me. (PS. Here's my official $20 I.O.U. for the sweet find on the cheerleader ornaments.)

So to sum it all up, thanks guys, you're the best.

~Jenn

Prologue

God, I love the beach.

But, I've never given much thought to the perfection of God's creations before now. I gotta tell ya though, He does some damned fine work. I've also never really considered the whole "God has a plan" thing.

Until now…

"Did you hear me?"

"Huh?" I did hear a voice…I'm just not sure who it belonged to. Even though He's never talked to me before, not that I'm aware of anyway, I was kinda thinking God might've been trying to tell me something.

"Jesus, dude, pay attention. I asked if you're ready..."

"Oh, yeah. Gimme a minute though." I am ready. I've been waiting for something like this for a long time.

Unfortunately, I think God was telling me now's not the right time and I have to keep waiting. Which sucks because I'm not all that patient. That's why, if I could get away with it, I'd stay here forever just staring at the aforementioned damned fine work of His creation.

"What for?"

I jerked my chin in the direction of the ocean.

"Oh, that."

Yeah, *that*. I think I'm hooked. I feel like a drug addict. The problem is, I don't know anything about my pusher or when or even *if* I'll get another fix.

"You know if you take a picture it'll last longer."

That's a horrible joke.

On second thought though…it's not a bad idea.

Aim and click.

Beautiful. Now I have Def Leppard's song "Photograph" playing in my head. Not only am I an addict, I'm turning into a stalker. That's just great. And really, it is, because I *am* ready. It just seriously freaks me out to admit it.

I really hope God knows what He's doing…

1.

I "Get" To Be The New Girl

Cancer sucks.

And you know what? It can kiss my almost sixteen-year-old ass.

Now don't get me wrong, I don't swear. It's just not who I am or how I've been raised. I haven't been sheltered or anything like that, I'm just really awesome at self-censoring. See, I'm the good girl. You know, prays before she eats, gets good grades, keeps her room clean, does what she's told, is always polite...that kind of stuff. Yeah, I know. That's me, Cameron Ramsey, AKA: Miss "Goody Two Shoes." I swear Adam Ant wrote that song back in the '80s specifically about me even though I wasn't a twinkle in my dad's eyes yet. Recently though, I've come to understand that, now and then, there are some situations in life that really do deserve a choice expletive.

Like right now. Standing in my bathroom getting ready for my first day of high school, you could definitely say I'm pretty fucking pissed off.

Technically it's not my first day of high school, but it *is* my first day at a public high school. My sister and I were homeschooled until about three weeks ago when my mom's cancer made it too much for her to keep up with...even after the double mastectomy. Her oncologist said they got it all, but the meds she has to take make her really ill and totally exhausted; because you know, losing her breasts—one of the major symbols of womanhood—and facing her mortality at the age of thirty-six wasn't enough.

If all that wasn't just dandy on its own, the icing on the suck-cake was moving last spring. My mom's name is Mandy and she got sick about five months ago but at the time, she was able to keep up with the important things in her life, those things being my sister, Jillian, my dad, Kevin, and myself. However, about a week or so after my mom got the diagnosis, my dad called a family meeting to explain we would be moving back to San Diego. We have a ton of family here and everyone felt it would be easier for them to support us if we came back. Doing so was made possible by the company my dad works for. The head honchos there truly treat their employees like family and when the owner and managers heard what was going on, they totally got on the "Support the Ramsey Family Bandwagon" by giving him a transfer, *and* a cost of living raise.

At first Jillian and I were thrilled to be moving back where we were born. Every time my family visited our hometown, we would whine and complain about having to go back to Arizona; we being my sister and I mostly, but sometimes my parents would join in the grumbling. So that being the case, you'd think we'd be happy with finally having that long-time prayer answered, right? But you have to understand, we're typical girls. Girls are allowed to be fickle. Especially me, since I'm the angst-ridden teenager.

It didn't really sink in until our last day with our homeschool group. I didn't know it was going to be so hard. None of us did. Everything was happening so fast and we were all so excited and busy with packing and stuff, that when it came time to actually say goodbye to our friends and the great people we'd spent the last nine or so years with, Jill and I were totally unprepared for how it would affect us. I guess I did okay. I held my tears back until I was in bed that night and quietly cried myself to sleep. I hadn't done that since I was like six or something. Jillian on the other hand...well, she was a train wreck. She's a twelve-year-old genius and normally has no emotions to speak of, but I haven't seen her bawl like that since the cat she paid for with her own money—the one she actually threw a first birthday party for—got hit by a car when she was four. When it was time to leave the park, my mom had to pry Jill loose from her best friends and carry her to the car. Jillian sobbed the whole way home. She didn't come out of her room for dinner that night and even though her door was shut and the radio was on, we could hear her crying her eyes out. We left the next morning.

The drive from our old house to the new one only took about six hours and by the time we crossed the California State Line, everyone had mostly gotten over the misery of leaving. This was thanks in large part to the seldom sight of lush green grass and being able to roll the windows down in the car. Two things that definitely won't be missed about Arizona are how close the weather resembles the Seventh Ring of Hell and how everything is some shade of beige. Actually, there isn't all that much we'll really miss except for our friends, and thinking about how short a drive it is, it's easy to tell yourself you'll get to visit them all the time.

It was the beginning of May when my dad pulled the U-Haul truck into the driveway of our new house, which so happened to be in the same neighborhood my family lived in before we relocated to the Northwest region of Hades. Honestly though, the move couldn't have been timed better. In Arizona it's usually so hot by May, everyone already has their A/C units cranked up and running 24/7 in preparation for summer hibernation like confused bears. Not in San Diego though. The weather here is just about as perfect as it can get. I can't even begin to explain how awesome it is to have the windows in the house open and being able to breathe the fresh air everyday—like it's some kind of big treat or something. I guess you could say it is for someone who previously risked choking on sweltering heat just walking to the mailbox.

Before we even got settled, my mom sent in the required paperwork so she could continue to legally homeschool us, and she didn't skip a beat in resuming our educational regime. Now, let me just explain something; my mom isn't a schedule kind of gal, so when I say regime or schedule, I just mean we didn't get a moving break or anything like a summer vacation. We did have the chance to do school at the beach when my mom felt up to it though. My parents are big on learning from life and they call those opportunities "teachable moments." We brought books to the beach and talked about tides, the coastal eco-system, and the chemistry of salt water. The highlight for me was getting to drool over all the hot surfer guys. I'd like to go on record right now by saying that in addition to beautiful weather; San Diego also has a *plethora* of saliva producing boys.

That's partly why I'm so mad about going into public school. Sure, I didn't get to see my friends everyday like normal kids, but I really loved sleeping in until 9:00 or 10:00, doing school in my pajamas, and being done with all my subjects by lunchtime. We'd get to learn from experience, too, which is actually lots of fun. Now however, I need a freaking alarm clock to wake me up because my first damned class is at (now get this…) 7:15 in the morning! I mean what are we? Chickens? Seriously, who in their right mind can even *think* straight that early, let alone do math? Not this girl, that's for sure. On top of that, I get to worry about what I'm going to wear so I can fit in with the hundreds of other kids who'll most likely pass judgment on me based on whether I'm wearing last year's nail polish color or something shallow like that. Plus, I won't get home until sometime around 3:30 after being imprisoned in classrooms for seven hours. Oh and here's the kicker; I "get" to do homework. The classes are so crowded that the teachers don't have enough time to ensure every student understands the material during the fifty some-odd minutes of class, so they have to rely on homework and tests to know whether the kids have learned anything from the textbook and their lectures. And it's not like I have any friends here to make all this worthwhile anyway. I was too young when we moved away to have friends I'd remember or who'd remember me now, so here I am…back in sunny San Diego and all alone.

I'm also pretty pissed about my mom being forced to let go of the one thing she loves doing with all her heart and soul; the one thing she and my dad always sacrificed so much for.

When I was born, my parents decided one of them would always stay home with me, which meant we had to live on one income. That's not the easiest thing in the world to do and it got even harder when Jillian was born. My mom and dad made some hard choices and went without a lot of things their friends had or got to do, just so my mom could be home with us. That's also why we moved to Arizona. My parents say that's probably the hardest decision they've ever made, leaving their family and hometown. They felt it was the right thing to do, though, because it was so much cheaper to live. Anyway, after we were there about six months and it was time for me to start first grade, my mom met some women at the park and discovered they homeschooled. Right away she was hooked on the idea. She came home and convinced my dad she should do that with Jill and me and the rest is ancient history, which I've already studied extensively. Heck, my sister and I have even mummified chickens a couple times. And really, even though mummification isn't a skill set one might build a résumé around, it's still pretty freaking cool being able to say you know how to do it.

I *loved* being homeschooled.

So, that brings me back to staring at myself in the mirror, trying to figure out what to do with my hair. I have wavy—okay, maybe it's not so much wavy as it is curly—medium blonde hair that goes just past my bra strap, and I do *not* have bangs. I tried them when I was eleven and discovered bangs look ridiculous on me, and after claiming to have a bad hair day for the more than 365 days it took me to grow them out, I vowed never again. Anyhow, my hair is actually pretty easy to do, but I want to look as good as possible because my new high school has the unfortunately intimidating nickname "Soshmont." From what my parents say, a "sosh" is a stuck-up or conceited person; like they think they're better than everyone else. Most of the kids who go there have money, drive cool cars, and live in huge houses. Then there are the rest of us "poor folk." You know, those of us who live in a two-story house with four bedrooms, four baths, a pool, and a three-car garage. There's a lot of tradition and sentiment attached to the school because it was the first ever in the district and opened sometime in the early 1920s. My parents, who were high school sweethearts, went there and—if you can believe it—their parents before them. To make matters worse, school started four weeks ago in the beginning of September. That means I get to be "the new girl" everyone will gawk at when I walk into my classes. Seriously, *ugh.*

"Hey Camie, you almost ready?" Jillian asked, skipping into my bathroom and taking up residence next to me in front of the mirror.

"Yeah, I guess so. You think Mom and Dad would freak out if I wore some makeup?" From a teenager's point of view, my parents rock and most of the time they rock hard. They're cool about a lot of stuff, but their daughters wearing overly tight clothes and unnecessary cosmetics are two things they are not big fans of.

"Probably. You don't need it anyway…you lucked out with the really dark eyelashes," she said as she ran a brush through her uncommonly long, blonde hair.

As is most often the case, Jillian is right. I have this kind of light Mediterranean skin coloring, and my eyelashes are so dark it looks like I already have mascara on. So according to my parents, essentially all makeup falls into the unnecessary category for me. My sister, however, is allowed some light mascara and blush, although she practically never wears either. She and I share one physical trait and that's our eye color. We both have brown eyes flecked with gold and green, and we get that unusual mix from our dad. I'll have to check the little box next to brown or hazel when I get my driver's license in January, even though neither of those are really right, but whatever.

Now I'm not conceited, but I've been called beautiful my entire life so I don't really worry about my looks, I've just taken everyone's word for it and left it at that. I think I'll blend in okay, though, and be able to make friends in time, but I think Jill's looks will eventually cause problems for her. Most girls will probably be jealous of her, and not just because she's so smart, which she is—scary smart. But the fact is, boys are going to swarm around her like bees on steroids. Seriously. If you want a good idea of what Jillian will look like when she's sixteen, just picture Malibu Barbie.

Physically, Jillian and I aren't all that similar, especially with the difference in complexion, hair and backside. Her—truthfully—slightly wavy, light blonde hair stretches all the way past her cute, perky butt and she has the good fortune of being able to tan amazingly well for being so blonde, just like our mom. I mean I can tan really well, too, but I'm not blonde like she is, so it makes her stand out even more. Anyway, I'm about 5'6" and she's around 5'4" or 5'5", but I think she'll end up being a little taller than me when we're done growing. And at the rate she's going, I bet her boobs will be bigger than mine as well. Seriously, the next time you're in Target, go look at the Barbie dolls…

"I know, but I'm afraid I'm already gonna stick out like a sore thumb. I was thinking maybe if I wear a little makeup, I won't feel so out of place."

"Well whatever, it's your funeral. I don't think you should upset Mom though," Jill said bluntly, this being one of those times she's chosen to be direct, which she does from time to time. I guess I shouldn't complain though; I find her cryptic mode of communication even more irritating.

"Yeah, you're right." Again. "Are you nervous?"

"No. Honestly, I'm afraid I'll be bored outta my skull. I wish Mom and Dad would've let me go into ninth grade like I placed." She sounds totally exasperated—and for good reason.

You see, one of the problems with going into the public school system after being homeschooled your whole life is the likelihood you won't really be taught anything you don't already know, because when you're homeschooled, you tend to learn more at an earlier age and at a faster pace than the kids who are educated traditionally. And trust me when I say that my mom has given us a very thorough education up to this point. In fact, you'll probably find that I lean towards using a vernacular that is more often than not, non-standard in relation to the majority of my peers. More simply put, I know a lot of big words and I like using them. However, I do understand that regardless of their years on this earth, not everyone understands what the hell I'm saying when I feel so inclined as to demonstrate my extensive vocabulary, so, I try making a concerted effort to be understood by toning it down in my everyday speech and talking like everyone else does.

That being said, I'm fairly advanced scholastically, although I'm fifteen going into my sophomore year like I would be if I hadn't been homeschooled, mainly because I don't test well. Not like Jillian. According to her age she should be in seventh grade, but the truth is...she's a flippin' test-taking *genius*. And I'm not exaggerating about the genius thing either. You ever hear of Mensa? Yeah well, she doesn't boast about being a member of that elite group of intellectuals, but the fact remains, she is one.

Now I'm not positive and I'm not about to ask, but I don't think Jillian knows our mom and dad asked the school not to give her any placement tests past the ninth grade. She could've *easily* placed as a senior if not tested out of school entirely. I overheard our parents one night and after talking about it, they decided she isn't ready for high school, but what I really think they meant was, high school isn't ready for her. Jillian is highly confident, exceptionally smart, and she takes great pleasure in her devious tendencies. Not a good mix. And with all that being so, you really want to stay on her good side because she also has a temper. I also think they kept Jill in eighth grade to give me a year on my own. I completely love my sister but after being with her everyday for the last twelve years, a year to myself sounds pretty good to me. We'll see how I feel about that, though, when I'm eating lunch alone.

"I'm not so concerned with being bored...I'm more worried about not knowing anyone." Seriously, I don't know a freaking soul at my school and I'd be lying if I said I didn't find that to be a little scary.

"Yeah... You know, this whole thing really bites," Jillian said, showing what I find to be the proper amount of attitude towards our really crappy lifestyle change.

"I know, especially today. It's gonna be a huge suck-fest...like Buffy meets Twilight," I agreed.

For unto every generation a vampire phenomenon is born, one that girls and even some women will obsess over endlessly. For my mom it was *Buffy the Vampire Slayer*. I get the Cullens. Don't misunderstand me, I enjoyed the books and everything, but just because they both have vampires, it does *not* make them the same. Buffy is just classic. It had everything...cute boys, mass drama, love stories, but best of all, it was freaking hysterical.

"Nice comparison, but it's gonna suck even more if we don't leave right now...we're gonna be late."

I heard my mom calling us from downstairs and then my dad honked the horn. "Crap! Well, good luck Jilly. I'm sure you'll find a way to keep busy today," I told her, giving her a big hug.

"You too, Camie. At least you have one AP class, so that should be interesting," she replied, hugging me back.

Like I said, I don't test well but, I really am sort of advanced. I was able to scrape into a junior level, honors literature class by the skin of my teeth. I'm prepared to be bored in the rest of my classes, though, except for maybe geometry. I hate math. Jillian and I are of like minds about this one thing, but again, she'd probably be in AP calculus if she were in high school.

We grabbed our school backpacks, yet another new thing for us, and flew down the stairs. My mom was waiting, holding the front door open while wearing what was previously normal school attire for my sister and me—pajamas, slippers and a bathrobe.

"Bye Mom! I love you!" Jillian and I said in unison and we each gave her tight, but quick hug. Neither of us wanted to look into her face because we were afraid of becoming emotional.

"Bye girls, I love you too. Oh! Have a good first day!" My mom hollered from the porch as we clambered into the car.

Backing out of the driveway, my dad blew my mom a kiss and I couldn't help sneaking a peek at her. She'd moved onto the front lawn to watch our progress and had the fingers of one hand pressed to her lips and she was waving with the other. Shit. I guess it's a good thing I didn't put any makeup on after all...I'd just end up looking like a clichéd raccoon before the short, five-minute drive to school was over.

2.

Insert Choice Expletive Here

Crossing the street to school with a herd of other kids whose parents dropped them off like my dad had with me, I felt not so much like cattle, but a black sheep. I know most of my trepidation about not fitting in with other kids is only in my head, after all, I *do* fill the requisite teenager status, but there are just so many of them and they all seem like they know each other. They might not all be friends, a perfect example – and one totally responsible for "Welcome to the Jungle" by Guns N' Roses blaring in my head now – is the small group of girls yelling at each other on the front lawn of the campus. But, at least they still *know* each other. I mean seriously, how am I supposed to break into an established group that will accept me as one of their own? I really need to do that, too, if I want to survive my high school experience without needing therapy when it's over. Looking at the somewhat defined cliques around me, I figure that if I don't pick the right group, I'll end up needing professional help anyway.

I don't really care about being popular per se, not that I'd shun the attention, but it has to be good attention, you know? Not the kind that comes from tripping, dropping your stuff all over the quad, and falling flat on your face. No lie; this is what I'm thinking about when a kid next to me does exactly that. And everyone starts laughing.

"Oh my gosh! Are you okay?" I asked and bent down to help gather all the papers escaping his binder. I'm also pretty pissed again. I mean the nerve of all the kids who are laughing and pointing…how would they feel if it were one of them? Mean people just suck.

"Yeah, I'm good. Thanks," he answered and took the papers from me.

His name is Paul Matthison. How do I know that, you ask? Well, I read it upside down on a page of his physics homework. "Hi. I'm Camie. I'm new." This is as good a time as any, right? It's too bad Paul isn't at all cute.

"Oh. Yeah, hi. My name's Paul," he said awkwardly.

He looked embarrassed and then his face flushed even brighter when someone over by "the blue stage" yelled, "Hey new girl! Be careful, Paulitis is contagious!" and a new chorus of vicious laughter spewed forth.

I was trying to screw up my courage to holler some suitable profanity mixed with a nice string of one hundred dollar words from my extensive vocabulary at the offending crowd, but I should've heeded their warning instead. As we shuffled ahead, I hooked the toe of one of my sandals on a crack in the pavement and pitched forward. I would've for sure done a very graceful faceplant but a hand firmly grabbed my arm to keep me from flying to the ground. I was so grateful to him that I was about to throw my arms around Paul's neck and hug him in front of God and everyone—including the disdainful gaggle of teens who'd condemn me to the bottom of the social barrel for sure if I did. I turned to face him and realized with a sizzling jolt of over-active and under-used hormones, it wasn't Paul who was deserving of my intended, full-body expression of thanks.

WHOA. Insert choice expletive here_____, because I got nothin'. In fact, I consciously told myself to close my mouth and then I surreptitiously checked my chin for slobber.

"Hey Paul, you forgot this back there," the most gorgeous real-life guy I've ever seen in all my fifteen years and nine months of life said, brushing against me and causing my skin to tingle as he handed a beat up Isaac Asimov paperback to Paul. Honestly, I imagine that's what a lightning rod might feel like when it's struck.

I'm gonna take a minute here because you seriously need to understand how magnificent this guy is. He's tall—like probably *at least* 6'2"—super tan, and he has sort of long, sun-streaked, light brown hair that's kind of a layered mess, so I'm thinking surfer right about now. This makes sense because he's got a ridiculously powerful physique, but not bulky like a football player's. His chest is really wide and he has well defined arm muscles. And just so you know, I can totally see the outline of his pecs and six-pack abs through his supremely well-fitted H_2O Polo team t-shirt. To top it off, he's got these amazing, sparkling, cerulean blue eyes that are fringed with thick lashes. Truthfully, I've never seen blue eyes like his. I mean he's *YU-UM-MY!*

"Hey, thanks Tristan," Paul said, shoving the book under his arm and looking around us to see if he'd dropped anything else.

"No problem, man," Tristan (OMG!) called over his shoulder as he casually walked away from us, going up and over the blue stage, across the lawn, down a ramp to the lower quad, and out of my most-excellent boy stalking sight.

Other than keeping me from falling, Tristan completely ignored me. But I'm good with that, because hey! He touched me!! I'm chanting that and doing a happy dance in my head when I suddenly thought; damn. Now I really wish Jillian were here. She's totally the go-to girl if you need some reconnaissance done. Since she's not, I'm obviously going to have to fend for myself. So, I focused the kaleidoscope of my Tristan tunnel vision enough to take note of the fact that he waved a lot and called out a bunch of "Heys" to people before he disappeared. No one razzed him when he helped me either, or even when he was talking to Paul.

Hmmm…a smokin' hot guy who's both popular *and* nice? When I get home I think I'll check the weather channel to see if they're ice-skating in Hell. In the meantime, I decided to walk with Paul a bit further and tried my best to covertly learn information about Tristan without sounding like a complete lovesick puppy.

"That was pretty cool of him...you know, returning your book and stopping me from falling and everything," I said as an opener.

"Who? Tristan?" Paul asked, looking at me like I was from outer space.

Hellooo? Alien life form to Paul... YES, Tristan! Did you see anyone else save me from being completely mortified? I didn't. I also noticed you didn't help me either. Thanks for that by the way. "Yeah, whatever his name is," I answered, inwardly rolling my eyes with my sorry attempt at nonchalance.

"Oh. Yeah, he's okay I guess. He can be real jerk sometimes though," he said absently. I was getting the feeling Paul was really uncomfortable talking to a girl. His eyes kept darting all over the place like he was trying to avoid looking at my face.

"What do you mean, a jerk in what way?" Damn it, I am *not* going to let my only source of Tristan Trivia get out of dishing up some goods that easy—Jillian would never let me live it down if I did.

"I dunno. He's usually pretty cool to me, but only because we're cousins."

Oooh…jackpot! I have a *blood* relative to pump for information. "That's the only reason he's nice to you? That sucks." Just as I suspected...Hell is still warm and toasty.

"Well, I guess he's not bad if he's on his own or if you're a girl… I just don't like his friends and the popular crowd he hangs with. Most of them are real assholes," he explained, still looking around.

"Are you guys the same age?" I'm thinking, jeez Paul, you're like Fort Knox with the info, buddy. Then I thought it might be my dreadful lack of skill in giving the third degree with subtlety. I also mentally thanked my dad for not providing a Y chromosome in the making of me.

"No, I'm older. He's a junior," Paul returned with a modicum of smug self-pride. His eyes lit up when a kid with red hair, who's wearing—I'm so not kidding about this—a pocket protector in his plaid button-up shirt, came running towards us. "Hey, I gotta go. Eric and I gotta go over some homework and the bell is gonna ring any time. See ya around," he said and took off at a trot towards the P.P.P.K.—Plaid Pocket Protector Kid, otherwise known as Eric.

Well alrighty then. At least I got some kind of information out of the vault that is Paul. Tristan, my beloved, is a junior, which, I'm afraid, puts him firmly out of reach for me. I think. I don't actually know for sure, I'm just guessing. Add this to the rapidly growing list of things I've never had to be concerned with before.

I sighed and headed into my first class of the day. Much to my substantial disgust, it's geometry. That damned bell went off just as I walked through the door and what did I do? Yes, that's right...I squeaked, and jumped about two feet off the ground. I dropped my backpack, too, which made a loud *thunk!* sound and caused about thirty heads to snap around to stare and snicker at me. Fabulous. While I'm at it, I might as well resign myself to having been inflicted with "Paulitis." I wonder if the school nurse can inoculate me with a shot or something so I don't catch any other social disease.

After calling the much-evil kind of attention to myself in geometry, I made it through the rest of my first four classes without incident, happy to discover my new illness apparently runs its course rather rapidly—I'm thinking it probably needs constant exposure to cause permanent damage. I even made plans to meet up with a girl named Michele and some of her friends at lunch. She seems nice and is in my second period history class as well as my fourth period biology class. And although Michele's moving to Sacramento next month, I was excited about having made a friend on my first day. I was patting myself on the back for that and looking forward to the thirty-minute parole for food when I walked into my honors English class early. I stuttered to a stop and looked around, thinking I had the wrong cellblock (whoops, I meant to say "room") because big, overstuffed pillows in five distinct groups were in place of desks. Thank God I'm early because if I'm in the wrong place, I want ample time to find where I should be...I can*not* be late to an AP class. That would reflect really poorly on me.

"Excuse me. Hello, I'm Cameron Ramsey. Is this Mrs. Henderson's AP English class?" I politely asked the teacher. She's an older woman with a kind and gentle face, and although her gray hair was pinned up in a bun, wild strands had come loose, as if they refuse to be tamed by something so prim and proper. I immediately liked her.

"Yes it is. I've heard wonderful things about you and it's a pleasure to have you join us. Do you like Cameron or do you prefer being called something else? Oh and please call me Dora. I don't care to stand on ceremony in my class," she said with warm sincerity.

"Oh, okay. Thank you. Um, I don't mind Cameron, but everyone usually calls me Camie." How very cool is she?!

"Alright, Camie it is. I have you in a group over here... That makes the last gathering a nice even number. As with ceremony, I don't care for groups of three...someone always gets inadvertently left out," she told me as she led me over to a group of pillows against the wall facing the door. Occupying one of the pillows already was a really pretty blonde girl with gorgeous green eyes who was wearing sunglasses on the top of her head and her hair in a ponytail. When she finished rifling through her backpack and looked up, Mrs. Henderson briefly introduced us. "Kate, this is Camie. She'll be joining you and the boys. Please be kind enough to let her follow along in your book until I can dig up another copy."

"Hi Camie. I'm sorry Dora, I must've left my book at home so we'll both have to share," Kate told the teacher like being unprepared for class was no biggie.

"Alright, the boys should be here soon, maybe they'll have remembered to bring theirs," Mrs. Henderson responded, unperturbed.

What the heck? This *is* a college-prep class, isn't it? I mean I imagined this would be a more rigorous course, but as I considered the unexpected carefree atmosphere, I thought maybe I was wrong. I plunked down next to Kate as the rest of the room's cushions were quickly occupied, and just when that godforsaken bell rang, "the boys" sauntered through the doorway, laughing, and coincidentally, making the phrase *Holy fucking shit!* instantly leap to my mind.

Yeah, yeah. I know I said I don't swear and I seem to be doing it a lot today, but cut me some slack...I've been under a lot of stress lately. And you SO have to give me this one, because Tristan—*MY* Tristan—was one of "the boys" and he was headed straight towards me.

"Hey Katy, who's your friend?" The—*not* My Tristan—guy inquired.

Still chuckling about whatever he and his friend had been previously laughing about, Tristan essentially ignored me again, *but*, the other guy, who I could kiss for doing this and who's also pretty darn cute, sat down next to Kate; *which means*...my future husband had to sit on the pillow next to me! Mental happy dancing ensues...

"Jeff, this is Camie. She's new and you know how much it's been bugging Mrs. Henderson that we have three people in our group, so, we get her," Kate told him in a round about way of introducing me.

"New, huh? I don't remember seeing a new girl on the roster during my office-aid hour this morning," Jeff said more to Kate than to me.

I was kind of getting tired of being treated like I'm invisible so I spoke up and said, "I am new, but my full name is Cameron."

"Ah...okay. You're a sophomore, right? I thought you were a guy," he said and laughed at his mistaken assumption about my gender.

Tristan's ears pricked up when he heard sophomore and he quickly looked me over before laughing about the guy comment and going back to studiously ignoring me. *Oh, be still my beating heart...* I thought to myself in my best sarcastic southern belle impersonation, feeling annoyed. "Yeah, unfortunately I get that a lot," I said with a touch of attitude.

I really like my name, but I hate when people don't take the time to notice that I AM A GIRL!! I'm even bulging out of my 34B cup to prove it! Anyway, you can imagine I'm not all that enamored of "Dear Jeff" anymore. And okay, so I'm not feeling the love from Tristan right now either. Maybe he's just shy? Yeah, let's go with that.

"Yeah, I bet. At least you don't *look* anything like a guy…or a sophomore," Jeff said with a flirtatious grin, his eyes focusing on my boobs a moment longer than they should have.

That's better, I thought, assuming the ogling was either meant to be an apology or a compliment. Beggars can't be choosers and I'll take it either way.

Kate slapped his arm and in a tone that sounded like she was scolding an errant child, she said, "Quit being an ass." That behavior and the physical similarities between the two had an idea forming in my head, but listening to their conversation proved more interesting and therefore I gave my full attention to it. "Do you have your book? I can't find mine and Mrs. Henderson still has to get one for Camie."

"Uh-uh. Besides, I'm not staying. Hey Trist, I'm outta here but that chick, Teresa, wanted me to give you her number again…she thinks you lost it. See ya at practice," Jeff said and leaned across Kate and me to throw a folded piece of paper at Tristan. Then he got to his feet as a messenger handed a yellow slip to Mrs. Henderson.

"Man, you're such a douchebag," Tristan told him, crumpling up the note and throwing it back.

The gods must be in one fantabulous mood, because that blessed piece of paper then bounced off Jeff and landed right on the other side of little ol' me. I couldn't even dream up everything that happened next. Oh and Jeff—bless his heart—is now back in my good graces. Here's why:

Jeff deviously grinned at Tristan and waggled his eyebrows in suggestion, like he was insinuating that either the placement of the note, or the information contained therein gave Tristan some sort of much-desired opportunity. Then he left us to make his approach to the teacher's desk.

"Is he ditching the rest of the day?" Kate asked Tristan across me with a look of irritation on her face.

"I guess, but if he gets caught again, he's gonna get booted off the polo team," Tristan answered as he put his hand on my bare knee and leaned across my lap to pick up the wrinkled paper. YES!! Although I *am* hyperventilating now...

"Well-uh! You're the team captain and his best friend...*you* should be talking him out of doing this crap," she said, like she was charging Tristan with criminal negligence while at the same time, watching him carefully.

"I'm staying out of it. If he gets busted, it's his deal. But if you care so much, why don't you tell him he's being a jackass?" He retorted while making confetti out of Teresa's phone number—God love him.

"If he won't listen to you, he's not gonna listen to me." She narrowed her eyes when she saw what he was doing and then questioned, "I don't get it. Why did you ask for her number when you *know* you have zero interest in calling her? That's messed up."

"What's to get? Come on, you saw her at that party...she was hammered and all over me. I hate it when girls pull that shit. I wanted to tell her she's a skank and to fuck off actually, so it wasn't messed up, it was more like me being polite. Hey, your name's Cameron, right?" Tristan asked and made a face while dusting his fingers off, like the now much abused paper was made out of asbestos or something.

I hadn't even been a minor part of their enthralling dialogue so when Tristan suddenly directed a question at me, all he got was a lame nod and a deer in the headlights look. I did, however, possess the capacity to hear he hadn't used my nickname, so he must've paid more attention to the earlier conversation than I thought. And did you hear what else he said? I'm taking it to mean he's a gentleman...he didn't tell that girl to f-off or call her a rude name even though he wanted to. (Aw, he's just so considerate! Oh, sorry. Back to the story, this is where it gets good...)

"Trade places with me. Since I seem to be the only responsible person in this group with the book, we'll all have to share mine," Tristan said with a butterfly inducing, yet arrogant grin.

Okay, pinch me, please. Or better yet, stick a red-hot poker in my arm so I know I'm not dreaming. You'll understand in a second...

Tristan and I traded cushions but because he stretched out on his back to use the pillow for his head, Kate and I had to do the same. Picture it if you will: She and I are lying there on opposite sides of him like we're the bread of a made to order Tristan sandwich. I mean really, can this class get any better? Mrs. Henderson is oblivious to what's going on and I'm not using sarcasm anymore when I tell my heart to chill out. I swear, it's palpitating so hard and fast it feels like I'm about to experience what I imagine the space shuttle does before it lifts off. Jeff, who I'd completely forgotten about but owe big time, waved from the other side of the door to get Tristan's attention and when he had it, he flipped him the bird. Tristan just snorted and handed his book to Kate. Now get this...he then put his arms around Kate's and my shoulders, pulled us really close against him, and proceeded to stick his tongue out at Jeff. Oh and just so we're clear, I think I'm dying. Every drop of blood in my body must've rushed to my head because all I can hear is the sound of my thundering heart in my ears. And yeah, that freaky tingling is back. Then, Jeff bowed in the hallway as if he was conceding some kind of contest to Tristan, who had an exceedingly smug look on his face as he watched his friend walk down the hall and out of sight.

Let me tell you something, since I'm planning on fantasizing and being stealthy about inhaling the intoxicating scent of Tristan for the rest of class, it's a good thing the book we're supposed to be reading—the one practically no one in class bothered to bring—is *Pride and Prejudice*. I've read it three times and seen both the BBC and the Keira Knightly versions of the movie more times than I can count. It's my mom's favorite. God is SO good. Actually cuddling up with Tristan *and* Mr. Darcy, together in one class? I'm just sayin'…

Anyway, let me see if I can describe what Eau de Tristan smells like… Wow. It's amazing…he smells exactly like fresh-baked snicker-doodle cookies! (I'm totally lying.) Actually, he smells kind of like chlorine, but whatever. I can make chlorine smell yummy in my imagination. *Mmmm, I can practically taste the drop-dead goodness!* Okay, so swimming and eating my favorite cookies will just never be the same again; I don't really give a flying fig right now.

Sigh.

Unfortunately, all good things must end, and the best fifty-five minutes of my entire life ended with the bell heralding the lunch half-hour. I know lunch hour sounds better, but really, it's thirty minutes. I'm not even gonna have time to chew. As soon as he heard the clanging, Tristan swiped his book away from Kate, grabbed the rest of his stuff and took off without a goodbye, a see ya later, or even a backwards glance. In turn, Kate and I gathered our things and walked into the hallway together, and when she met up with a couple of her friends who were coming out of another classroom, Kate turned to me and with a thoughtful, but friendly smile she said, "Bye Camie, I'll see you later."

I floated out of the English building and into the brilliant sunshine on cloud nine, and with the delicious smell of pool water still fogging up my brain, I wandered down to the lower quad to visit my locker and then I went in search of Michele and her friends.

3.

He Might Be A Man-whore

Lunch was not the success I'd hoped it would be.

After I rescued my apple and carrots from my locker and bought myself a soda and something that's called a "big cookie," I finally spotted Michele and her friends amongst the throng of other students who were enjoying their lunch on the grass of the upper quad. When I joined them, Michele introduced me to two of her friends, Lisa and Claire. They seemed okay, but they weren't as welcoming as one would hope. As I started digging into my cookie that I swear is like the size of freaking Jupiter, another girl walked up to sit across from me, and then, to my utter shock—add discomfort if I'm being honest here—Michele introduces her as *Teresa.* I know she's the same Teresa who penned the asbestos laden correspondence to Tristan because that's the first thing out of her mouth. No "Hi" or "Nice to meet you"...nope, she went straight to this:

"So, I gave Jeff Larson a note with my phone number on it for Tristan."

"No *WAY*!! What did he say?!" Claire asked with excessive enthusiasm.

"Jeff promised he'd give it to him last period. I told him I thought Tristan might've lost my number and Jeff said he thought Tristan probably did too. He was really cool about it and said something like 'trust me, I *know* he'll want this so I'll make sure he gets it.' So, that explains why he didn't call or text over the weekend," she explained self-importantly.

"Do you really think he'll ask you out?" Lisa asked with what sounded like awe.

"I'm positive. He's *so* in to me...we would've totally hooked up at that party if he didn't have to drive fuckin' Jeff's drunk ass home," the hussy said with misplaced confidence and a self-gratified smirk.

Yeah, I know. I'm being kind of catty, but I *really* don't like this girl. First off, she was inebriated herself when she hit on my soul mate. Secondly, I know "Dear Jeff" can grate on one's nerves now and then—I know because I've obviously had *so* much interaction with him—but I really don't feel it's necessary to besmirch his good name in such a way because ultimately, he did save her from making an even bigger fool of herself as he could've easily done by informing her of Tristan's true feelings. And lastly...well, she's kind of a bitch. Actually, all these girls aside from Michele are rather bitchy. One positive of this encounter, though, is that

I've discovered a sophomore girl can set her sights on a junior guy and not be thought of as completely insane.

"What did your note say?" Michele asked, sounding only mildly curious as she tossed a half-eaten apple and the crust from her sandwich into the trashcan next to us.

"Oh, just *stuff*...you know, I just gave him some *options* of things we could *do* on our date," Teresa answered with poorly veiled innuendo.

Ew! Ew! EW!

"Oh. My. God. You did not!" Claire said, laughing, and then she gave Teresa a high-five.

"I would've loved to have seen his face when he read it! I wonder where he is..." Lisa commented, looking around the quad for Tristan, whom I'm hoping is well hidden. I mean I wouldn't put much past these three girls anymore as I'm forced to listen to Teresa tell us all what her note actually said. And again I say, *EW*.

Seriously, it's a good thing I'm adept in the fine art of self-censoring because I really, *really* want to put Teresa in her place like she deserves and I have the power to do it. Truthfully, I'd like nothing better than to slap the shit-eating grin right the hell off her face, but let's not kid ourselves—that just ain't gonna happen. Anyhow, in an attempt to distract myself and keep my mouth shut, I looked around the quad and as my gaze traveled over to the blue stage where the socially elite hang out, whom did my eyes almost immediately land on? Yep. The subject of this rather lecherous conversation. Then it dawned on me, I don't want Tristan—or anyone else really—to see me in the company of these girls. So, I was really grateful to Michele when she got up and excused herself just as Tristan's attention shifted in our direction. She momentarily blocked me from his sight when she stood up to leave, and I quickly joined her to beat a hasty escape from becoming a pariah in Tristan's mind.

"Wow. Teresa is *really* something," I said as Michele and I walked back down to the lower quad. I felt safe in saying that to her because it was obvious she wasn't particularly enjoying the lewd lunchtime banter either.

"Yeah, she's had a hardcore crush on Tristan Daniels for years...she's delusional of course."

"Why do you say that?" Hmmm... Maybe my earlier deduction was somewhat premature and a sophomore girl *shouldn't* try for a junior. Crap.

"Because he's Tristan Daniels. I'd guess *at least* a third of the girls in this school and a good portion from a few others have a *major* thing for him. Plus, Teresa thinks she's gonna get him to be her actual boyfriend and he's not the most monogamous kind of guy, you know?"

Her answer does not bode well for me, but, I'm tenacious and probably a glutton for punishment so I'm not giving up on him yet. "Not really.

What do you mean?" I asked just for clarification. I, of course, know what monogamous means, but there's a chance she might be using the term incorrectly. One can hope, right?

"Well for starters, he kinda gets around. Plus, I don't think he's ever had just *one* girlfriend...I mean I can't say he actually cheats on girls because as far as I know, he's never been in an exclusive relationship," Michele explained, having used "monogamous" more or less accurately.

Not to beat a dead horse, but I'm really hoping he's not a complete male slut like she's making him out to be, so I asked, "So you're saying he sleeps around a lot?"

"Umm, I'm tempted to say yes because of how he goes through girls like they're lined up at a revolving door for their chance with him, but I honestly don't know if he bothers to go that far with all of them. I'd imagine he's slept with at least a few of them though...I mean, he *is* a guy and he's totally beautiful. It's just that even though everyone in this school talks non-stop about everyone else's business, I never hear any gossip about him pertaining specifically to sex," she quite generously elaborated for me.

I, Cameron Corinne Ramsey, hereby acknowledge that I've been properly forewarned. However, since I'm already completely infatuated, chances are this disquieting information won't affect me in the manner it probably should, so I moved on to indulging myself in a little gossip of my own. "Okay, you're gonna love this but you have to promise you won't say a thing to anyone else. I'm not usually a gossipmonger or anything, but Teresa bugs the crap outta me and I'm dying to tell someone who might appreciate it."

"Deal. Teresa isn't my favorite person either, but, the four of us have been good friends since elementary school and it's tricky to stay friends with the two I do still like and not the one I don't," Michele told me, giving me some insight into social politics.

I nodded, pretending I understood, and then I looked around to make sure we weren't being overheard before quietly confiding, "I'm in Tristan's and Jeff's reading group during fifth period."

"Nu-uh! You're a sophomore!" She exclaimed in disbelief.

"Yeah, but I tested into junior honors English," I admitted with a sneaky grin, like this just upped my black-ops status somehow.

"Oh my God! That means you were *there* when Jeff gave Tristan Teresa's note!! I'm guessing it didn't have the same effect on him that she thought it would," Michele said, catching on quickly.

"You would be more than correct. I don't think he even read it, but he *did* turn it into mulch in front of my very eyes. He also said some unkind things about her." My mouth was barely closed before I started to feel kind of guilty for talking about someone behind their back like this. I've never done this before and it doesn't exactly feel very good. But then again, this *is* Teresa we're talking about here, and from what I've seen of her, it's not like she'd bat an eye before gossiping about me, or, anyone else for that matter.

"Oh, that's priceless! I wish I could've been there," she said and then sighed in disappointment.

The bell chose that moment to announce lunch was over and the time to move on to sixth period. That would be P.E. for me. Oh goody. Michele and I shared a knowing look when the Trollop Triplets caught up to us, and then the four of them headed off to whatever class they had together. Sullenly, I made my way to the girls' locker room to change for my mandated hour of sweating in the sun. It shouldn't be too bad, though. The temperature is probably somewhere in the low 80°s and I'm so used to 110° weather this time of year that I actually brought a sweatshirt with me to school today just in case. Besides, my seventh period class is dance and I'm looking forward to it. If there's one thing I enjoy and can do well, it's dancing. And as a bonus, dance clothes are extraordinarily flattering on me, which I'd shortly come to appreciate more than I had previously.

Without the benefit of details on the serious fashion atrocity of my new gym clothes and the debacle it was to even find a uniform for me in the first place—I mean one that didn't look as though it was meant for Humpty Dumpty—not to mention how *completely* weird it is to strip down to your skivvies in front like a hundred other girls who are doing the same thing, I'll ask you to just take my word for it when I say P.E. pretty much sucked like I thought it would. The coaches lumped the tenth grade girls and boys together for the next four weeks so we can play co-ed flag football. The upside to this is there are some cute boys in the class and I got to watch them show off for us girls, which is always fun. I mean the boys aren't in the same realm as Tristan cute, but you know…eye candy is eye candy. The downside is that I'm expected to participate. Anyway, I got through it without making myself a laughing stock and I met a few more decent kids, both boys and girls. I was finally starting to feel like maybe I'll get the hang of public high school and it won't be so bad. After all, I have fifty-five minutes in heaven everyday to look forward to and that has to count for something, right? As I was changing into my dance stuff, those musings were pretty much confirmed when I was pleasantly surprised to discover that Kate's gym locker is right next to mine and she's in my class too.

"Hey Camie! I didn't know you danced!" She said, dropping onto the bench next to me.

"Oh, yeah. I've been dancing since I was little…ballet, jazz, and hip-hop mostly, but I've also done a little ballroom and tap."

"Wow, that's great! I'd totally *love* to take a ballroom class!" She enthused before hopping back onto her feet. I like Kate; she's spunky. "Come with me, I wanna introduce you to Melissa. She's in our Lit. class, but she had a student council meeting so she wasn't there today." Before I could even respond, Kate grabbed my hand and dragged me to another aisle of lockers where she planted me in front of a gorgeous girl with long, striking mahogany colored hair and soft blue eyes. "Melissa, this is Camie. She's a sophomore, but she's really cool and she's smart enough to be in Mrs. Henderson's with us."

Little did I know it, but Kate had just handed me my first letter of recommendation that, if properly used, would open the doors to the upper echelons of the social ladder. I was unaware of it at the time so I can say in all honesty that I was just being myself and not trying to advance in the ranks on purpose, but during the next hour I was going to totally hit it off with the co-captain of Varsity Cheer, of which I discovered Kate is a member as well.

After dance was over and instead of changing so we could leave school, the three of us lingered in the open area between the girls' locker room, the pool, and the boys' locker room, still in our dance clothes and I'm gonna learn there's a reason for this. Remember when I said that dance clothes are flattering? Well, I'm not the only brainiac who knows this. Melissa and Kate had positioned us in just such a way as to not be blatantly obvious about it but at the same time, make sure we were very well noticed when the stampede of boys from several locations came thundering back to their locker room to change.

I have to say I really admired these girls' tactical maneuver, especially when they'd put us directly in the path of the guys coming from the gym. Among them was; you guessed it, my favorite womanizer. He definitely took notice, but he opted to view us in all our spandex glory from afar by leaning against the wall of the boys' locker room. He was just opposite from where we were, but that also put an inconveniently wide expanse of concrete between us. However as a consolation prize, we were joined by a couple guys who were both adequately attractive in their own right.

"Check out the new girl," the taller of the two whispered with a nudge to his friend and then to us he said, "Hello ladies."

He really is rather good looking, but his body appears to be on the thinner side; not a big deal on its own, but then you add in his height and he becomes overly lanky, which leaves something to be desired and just doesn't do it for me.

"Hello back," Melissa said and then flirtatiously shoved the shorter guy's shoulder.

Now this guy looks like your typical football player. You know, stocky and a little beefy with "boy next door" good looks, which I'm finding doesn't really do it for me either. But that's cool because I think he might be going out with Melissa. I say that because he picked her up, threw her over his shoulder and gave her butt a playful little smack before setting her down again and all she did was laugh.

"Kate, introduce us," the non-spanker said as he flashed me a grin and then firmly tugged on a lock of my hair. Seriously, what are we? Kindergarteners? I mean really, I imagine that's what a five-year-old caveman would do instead of hitting a girl over the head with a club. Besides, it kinda hurt.

"Oh…yeah…Camie, this is Zack…and that's, uhh, Keith," she said with some distraction as she absentmindedly indicated Zack to be the juvenile Neanderthal and Keith as the spanker.

I was about to issue a greeting to Thing One and Thing Two, and yes, I know calling them that isn't nice, but even though Melissa seems to really like Thing Two and Thing One is super cute and I know he was flirting with me, something about him especially kind of rubbed me the wrong way. Maybe it's because he just moved in front of me, cutting off my view of Tristan, or maybe it's because I'm getting the sneaking suspicion that Tristan didn't come over to talk to us because of these guys. Last I saw, he was still keeping tabs on us but both his facial expression and body language had been screaming "DANGER: Violent Outburst Imminent." Regardless, like I was saying, I was about to issue a greeting to Thing One and Thing Two but right when I opened my mouth to say a version of hello, both Kate and I were given a bone crunching hug from behind. Can you guess by who?

Can you? Can you?

Hooray! Three cheers for my favorite douchebag, "Dear Jeff!" I say this because cave-boy doesn't seem to care for Jeff very much. He gave Jeff, whose eyes are a little red, a dirty look and then he stomped off towards the locker room. I risked a quick glance over at Tristan and was rewarded by seeing he was no longer pissed, but doubled over in laughter. When I looked next to me again, I was totally shocked because Jeff had Kate pressed against the pool's chain link fence and they were in a *full-on* lip-lock.

Although she was alternating between hitting his back and pushing against him in trying to get him to stop kissing her, I'm guessing I can throw my earlier theory about the two of them being related out the window. Remember that semi-formed idea I had in English? Well, Jeff has a different last name than Kate, but he has the exact same shade of emerald green eyes as her, both of them are on the tall side, and aside from his short, almost black hair and being a lot tanner than Kate, they look an awful lot alike so I was thinking they might've been half-siblings or something. After all, Tristan and Paul look less alike than Kate and Jeff and then throw in how condemnatory she was acting in English…well; you can see where I came up with it.

Anyhoo, when Jeff finally relented and pulled away, I thought Kate was gonna lose it but she was laughing instead. Jeez…the mating rituals of teenagers are really quite a confusing concept to grasp.

"You're *such* an ass!" She muttered and finally shoved him away from her with force.

"You know you want me," Jeff teased with a grin, moving close to her again like he was daring her to deny it.

Which she did, just not with much conviction. "Uh, not."

"Love you too, Katy Baby!" Jeff then planted a swift kiss on her cheek, gave me a big smile that I think meant something but I've no idea what, and then he jogged over to Tristan.

Thus began what I'm gonna think of as the Varsity round of showing off…

When Jeff caught up to Tristan, he elbowed him in the ribs. Tristan then went to punch and/or shove Jeff in the shoulder but before he could, Jeff grabbed Tristan's wrist and twisting it behind him, Jeff jumped on Tristan's back and using his hair as reins, Jeff tried to get Tristan to carry him into the locker room piggyback. However, I guess Tristan wasn't cool with that plan because he then flipped Jeff over his shoulder and dumped him unceremoniously on his butt. The wrestling match continued until they weren't visible anymore and unlike the tenth grade boys who'd been showing off in my P.E. class—who could really stand to learn a thing or two from these guys—neither Tristan nor Jeff ever bothered to look back to see if their antics were being appreciated by us girls. And I can't really speak for anyone else, but I enjoyed every second of the show thoroughly.

"I swear, they're like puppies…" Kate said to herself with a silly grin on her face, telling me that she appreciated the boys' performance as well, and hinting that maybe this wasn't necessarily a show, but just how they behave on a regular basis. "Hey Melissa, I'm gonna get outta here. Camie, do you want a ride home?"

"Sure, thanks!" Yeah, like I'm gonna choose walking home over getting a ride with Kate, who I'm rapidly starting to not only like *a lot*, but who I'm also realizing might just be the key to unlocking the treasure chest that is Tristan.

Now, with having just witnessed the whole kissing thing, if I were a cat, I'd probably be dead right now because I was bursting with curiosity about what the deal with her and Jeff was. So, I decided to just be forthright and asked, "So, I'm dying here, what's the deal with you and Jeff?"

"He's my ex," she answered simply.

"Huh. Do all ex-boyfriends kiss their ex-girlfriends like that?" I nudged her with my shoulder. I can totally tell Kate still has a thing for him and I'm guessing she might want to get back together. I think they look good together, so I'm pulling for her.

She laughed. "No, just him. I'm always having to convince myself that I broke up with him for a good reason, but then he does something like that and I find myself admitting just how much I adore him."

"Well, if you like him as much as you do, and I hope you don't mind me asking, but, why *did* you break up with him?" Inquiring minds want to know…

"Because he's a complete jackass, just like Tristan said earlier today," Kate answered and then gave me yet another thoughtful look. "He habitually ditches school, flirts with practically every girl he lays eyes on, and sometimes he gets out of control if he drinks too much or gets high. He was stoned back there…you know that, right?"

"I guessed when I saw that his eyes were all red."

"Yeah, well, Tristan will talk some sense into him and if that doesn't work, he'll beat the shit outta him until Jeff does what he wants," she said and laughed as she unlocked the car doors with her remote. Then, taking her seat behind the steering wheel, Kate clicked a button on the dashboard and looked into the driver's side review mirror, presumably to check her perfect makeup or hair while the convertible roof of her new model, cherry red mustang was lowered. (See what I mean about the cool cars and such?)

"I thought Tristan said he was done dealing with Jeff's crap," I said, sinking down into the cushy leather of the passenger seat.

Before Kate started the car she shot me a sharp glance, making me wonder if I'd just crossed a line or something. "Camie, don't believe everything that comes out of Tristan's mouth. In fact, I wanna talk to you about something I've been thinking about all day, but not here. Let's go someplace where we won't be interrupted," she suggested and as the mustang's engine roared to life and settled into a nice purr, she looked at her side mirror again with a triumphant smirk.

"Okay, sure. Just tell me where we're going so I can let my mom know. I don't want her to worry when I don't show up when she expects me to." My mom would be fine with me hanging out with a new friend, but if I don't check in, she'd probably have the police send out an Amber Alert for me.

"Let's go to the park down below school. It's just below the lower soccer fields..."

"Yeah, I know the one you mean. I used to have big birthday parties there when I was little."

So, as Kate drove us to the park that is actually not too far from my house, I called my mom. I started by asking how she was feeling, and then listened when she told me her doctor appointment had gone really well, for which I was relieved to hear. Then asking her if she needed me home right away, I explained how I'd made a friend and that we wanted to go hang out at the park. Just for good measure I also threw in that Kate and I were going to be doing some homework for our honors class. Although I didn't know it at the time, I should mention that this is not a lie per se. My mom sounded really happy to hear I'd found someone I already clicked with and she told me to take my time and have fun. See? My mom rocks hard.

"Is your mom sick or something?"

"You could say that. She has breast cancer. Everyone, including me, keeps referring to me as new, but actually, my sister and I were born here. We moved back from Arizona in May so we could take advantage of our extended family here," I willingly explained. I don't mind talking about this stuff. In fact, I find talking about certain things like this to be cathartic. Besides, I really like Kate. I don't know why, but I just get the deep-down feeling that Kate is good people.

"Aw Camie, that really sucks, I'm so sorry. But if you guys moved back months ago then how come you're just starting school now?" She asked, politely not pushing for the "other" details.

"Well because my sister and I have been homeschooled our entire lives and my mom insisted that she continue until she absolutely couldn't do it anymore. We actually thought for a while that she'd be able to keep it up and we'd get to stay home, but the chemo and radiation really beat the crap out of her," I admitted, not knowing how Kate would react to the information that I was previously homeschooled. I'm hoping it doesn't make me ineligible to be her friend. I mean I don't know how these things work; there could be a handbook or something that I just haven't been given yet.

"Oh, okay. It sounds like you really enjoyed being home...I bet this place is intimidating as hell," she said, being rather shrewd in her observation. You'll soon discover, as am I, that Kate has wicked-awesome skills at reading people.

"Being homeschooled was really great...I mean that's why I've gotten to take as many dance classes as I have, you know? When you're homeschooled you don't really have P.E. and my parents wanted to make sure my sister and I got plenty of exercise. My sister's a pretty talented dancer, too, but she just never got hooked on any one thing...she experimented with all kinds of stuff like gymnastics, karate, even boxing," I said, leaving out my sister's true talent, which I swear is counter-intelligence. "But I fell in love with dance when I was six and I've been doing it ever since. And yeah, I was pretty freaked out about having to come here. Honestly, I had a long list of reasons why it was gonna suck, but, my classes are pretty easy so far, I still get to take dance, and some of the kids are a lot cooler than I thought they were gonna be so my list is rapidly dwindling," I told her, ending with my own round about way of giving Kate a compliment which she, of course, picked up on and laughed about.

After we stopped laughing though, Kate pulled into a parking space at the very back of the huge park where there was no chance we'd be interrupted. She shut the engine off and shifting to face me, I could see the cogwheels begin to turn in her head as she gave me a long, considering look. And with that look, the energy in the car shifted from being the friendly conversational atmosphere it'd been, to one that felt considerably like it was filled with intrigue and conspiracy. The whole thing felt very clandestine to me, kind of like we were taking part in espionage. Which if you think about all that was about to be imparted, that comparison wasn't very far from the truth. It made me a little nervous and sort of paranoid in the beginning but still, my sister—Jillian the spy—would be so proud of me.

"Thanks, I think I'm kind of awesome too, but now that we're not being watched, let's talk about one of the other cool, or shall we say, *sizzling hot* reasons why going to school at Grossmont doesn't suck as much as you thought it was gonna."

It didn't escape my attention that Kate had just implied we were being watched before, but that little piece of information only aided my sudden suspicious train of thought. I mean, although I'm not all that socially savvy, I'm pretty certain that if I put one foot out of line, the implications could be devastating to my life whilst I'm matriculating at this school. Why I think playing dumb won't damage me even more, I've no idea. I *do* want to trust her but I don't really know Kate yet, and to say that I was questioning the wisdom of admitting how much time I spent thinking about Tristan today would be a gross understatement. What's weird is that I'm not normally suspicious. It's not in my nature. Jillian's, yes, but not mine. I don't know, maybe I've just seen too many movies where the popular cheerleader and her crew befriend the new kid, who of course is blind to the danger of admitting she likes the same guy the cheerleader or one of her friends does, so she falls victim to her new friends' sadistic pranks, which inevitably ends up being more embarrassing than if she were to just trip and fall flat on her face in front of half the school.

So in thinking about all of that and trying—futilely it turns out—to not let on that I know that she knows that I have the hots for a guy who's not only way out of my league, but sounds like he might be a man-whore, *and*, just so happens to be her so-called ex-boyfriend's best friend, I stammered through my lie and tried to not bite my lower lip or fidget in the seat.

"Wh—I don't know what you mean. I umm, I just really appreciate you being so nice to me."

It sounded convincing enough to me, however, I discovered my innocent act was in vain when Kate rolled her eyes and gave me the most elementally "oh please" look I've ever seen. Then seeing my hesitation and guessing at the reason behind it, she gave me a reassuring smile and said, "Camie, if I had a Bible handy, I'd raise my right hand and swear on it…this isn't a setup and I'm not gonna stab you in the back. You can trust me…just, I don't know, tell me what you think about him."

Shoving scenes from the movie *Mean Girls* from my mind and giving up my charade of ignorance, I sighed and took a leap of faith by answering with the naked truth. "What's not to like? I'd be mental if I didn't admit how completely mouth-watering he is. Not only that, but I'd also be lying through my teeth if I said I haven't been thinking about him non-stop since I first laid eyes on him this morning before school and that those thoughts are generally accompanied by the sound of mental wedding bells. Oh and he put the smell of chlorine at the top of my most favorite scents list. Seriously, I wanna go home and beg my dad to swap out the saltwater system on our pool for one that needs chlorine."

I was feeling pretty proud of my fledgling flight with blind trust and honesty, however and unbeknownst to me, Kate was about to reply in kind while at the same time, dropping the biggest bombshell of my teen life squarely on my unprepared head.

"Yeah, I know what you mean, Jeff smells like a pool too. But good news, it fades over time and you get used to it…I don't drool at all anymore," Kate said confidently and winked at me. "Okay, so now that we've established that your olfactory senses are topnotch and you're one hundred percent non-mental, lemme just say this...Tristan is in huge demand and a really tricky guy to figure out, but if you play your cards right and with my help, you might just be able to pull off one of *the* biggest high school coups a girl can hope for."

Crickets. That's what her statement was met with. The sound of crickets chirping away like crazy in my head. I mean, don't get me wrong, this is outrageously great news; I was just *so* not expecting it! I really wasn't…even though it totally fits in with the stereotypical plot of a cruel joke played on the new girl like I was just being paranoid about. And yeah, I know I've been nauseously going on and on about him all day long, but I never really took my ramblings *seriously*. I was honestly just thinking I'd spend the next couple years obsessing meaninglessly over him, so I really don't know how to react or what to do with this information, you know?

"Is that a good thing or bad thing?" I asked, displaying my currently serious lack of brainpower. Of course it's a good thing, I'm just still shell-shocked that's all. It might take me a moment but I'll get there.

This time Kate looked at me the same way Paul did this morning, like I was from outer space. Then, she asked if I was. "Do you live on another planet or something? *If* Tristan Daniels is really and truly interested in you, and I'm not saying he is for sure because he's really hard to read sometimes, even for me, but if he is and you go about it right, not only will it be a very good thing, but you can pretty much call it a miracle."

A miracle? Why a miracle? Is it because I'm not all that pretty, or because I'm younger than he is, or is it something else? For the love of all that is *holy*...tell me *why!* I decided to take a deep breath before I tried again and asked, "Okay, aside from the obvious fact that he's ludicrously hot, I don't get it. So I have two—no, three questions... Why do you think he might even be interested in me in the first place, why did you say it'd be a miracle, and why are you being so nice to me?"

See, I told you I'd get there.

"Thank God! Jeez Camie, I thought you were gonna try to tell me you wouldn't wanna go out with him or something ridiculous like that...I was gonna have to tell the alien freak to get outta my car," she said with a touch of relief before continuing. And when I say she continued, I mean that she more or less ranted an abridged version of *Men Are From Mars, Women Are From Venus* in her explanation of why she was being nice to me.

"And I can understand your skepticism about why I'm taking you in without even knowing you, but I really don't have much of an ulterior motive. It's a little silly really but, I think a lot of girls are jealous of me because I was born into an incredibly tight threesome with two super popular, not to mention gorgeous guys...I mean even when we were little those two were the kings of the playground. All the boys wanted them on their team and all the girls chased them, and I've literally grown up with Jeff and Tristan filling all the roles a best friend would, so, I've never really had that kind of close friendship with a girl. Plus, ever since Jeff and I split up this time, I feel like I've been missing out and I kinda think I might like a best friend who isn't a guy for once.

"You know, someone who understands girl stuff like the fact that when a girl says "rag" it doesn't necessarily mean she's talking about her menstrual cycle. Someone who doesn't need me to explain for the umpteenth time that lavender is *not* the same freaking color as purple, or someone who already understands that not every girl appreciates having her weight broadcast at lunch only to be lifted in the air over and over again to see who can do more reps bench-pressing her body, someone who knows that just because a girl typically keeps gum in her purse and she told you to help yourself *one* freaking time in fourth grade, doesn't mean it's okay for you to rummage through it whenever you want, and that there're *some* girls who'd really rather not rate the crescendo of a burp on a scale from one to ten for crying out loud! I mean, I love them and everything, but they make me nuts. I don't know, Camie, I guess that even though we just met, I feel like we might really get along, and since you're basically new here I thought maybe you'd have an opening in the friend department."

"Wow, Kate, I don't know what to say…I mean who *doesn't* know a girl's purse is sacred? Oh and yeah, I totally have a vacancy," I told her with a big smile. But really, can I just say how relieved I am to know that my initial appraisal of Kate was more than accurate? I can't even imagine how bad it would've sucked to find out she was playing me, and just so you know, paranoia about such things isn't much fun either.

Kate returned my smile with a pearly-white grin of her own and then said, "One time, Camie, I told Tristan to help himself to my pack of gum *one* damned time, like seven years ago, and now whenever he runs out of his own gum, he digs in my purse without permission…I mean who the hell *does* that kind of crap?! Ugh…I could just throttle them both sometimes, but the only one I have any control over whatsoever is Jeff. Although in some ways, that makes his crap even more frustrating than Tristan's...and speaking of, let's move on before I go off on a tangent of crap...seriously, you wouldn't believe some of the crap I've had to put up with over the years and I can tell you all about that later if you want, but right now let's get to the good stuff."

"Okay by me, as long as you promise not to forget to tell me all about the crap later on…I mean crap is important between friends and I wanna hear the crap. No, as your friend, I think I *need* to hear the crap, Kate," I said, teasing her about her mini-outburst and the idea that she could go on endlessly about, well, crap.

"I promise I won't forget. I'll make sure you get a hefty dose of crap daily," she said and giggled with me for a minute before getting serious again. "Okay, now I want you to take what I'm about to tell you with a grain of salt, because I could be way off base here, but I really don't think I am… I believe Tristan likes you. *A lot.* I mean a lot a lot."

Kate then proceeded to say many several things that'll go down in public record as an example of her uncanny perception and cognitive abilities. Well, in my hopeful opinion anyway.

I love Kate.

4.

The Events Of Today Pertaining To Tristan Daniels

"Really?"

"Yeah, really. Your mission, should you choose to accept it, will be to land one of *the* most popular and best looking guys in the school. Let's start with you telling me everything you *think* you know about him," she said, shifting to get comfortable in her seat.

"Well, I've heard he's kind of a womanizing gigolo, but other than that I really don't know much about him..." Then I told Kate everything Paul and Michele had said about him and felt myself fidgeting as I did. I don't know if I'm ready to be getting into such heavy public affairs, it is my first day after all. Plus, all of this is coming from way out in left field and here I am without a glove. I mean aside from having had friends who are girls, I have NO experience with any of this. But this is also "My Tristan" we're talking about here, like I'm gonna pass on the opportunity. Yeah right.

She laughed again and nodding agreement she said, "That's actually a fairly astute observation but doesn't exactly paint him in the best light, now does it?"

"No, not really. I was kinda hoping Michele had missed the mark on him," I said with a little disappointment. I like the guy and he's magnificent to look at and everything, but I don't know him and I don't want to be a statistic either. You know, another notch on the proverbial bedpost. I'd like to think I have more sense and self-respect for that.

"Well, just because she's not far off, doesn't mean he's only looking for a series of one night stands or that he's completely untouchable, because really, he's not...especially in regards to someone who might've unknowingly caught his eye. And, there's a lot more to him than most people realize... As far as the masses are concerned, they're gonna end up languishing away waiting in line, but you've got a few advantages that no one else has. I'm pretty certain he's interested and since he knows nothing about you, that'll work in your favor too."

Apparently Kate has a lot of confidence in me and for some reason, she wants to see this happen, and because of that, I'm feeling a little better about liking him now. I mean I really don't think Kate would lead Camie the lamb to Tristan the wolf for him to play with before devouring whole.

"Okay, so, yay me...but um, tell me why you said it'd be a miracle if I can pull this off."

"Oh yeah, I forgot you asked me that. Okay well, he practically never shows actual interest in anyone. I mean he shows *real* interest in a girl about as often as Haley's Comet passes, if you get my drift. I've known Tristan my whole life and your friend that told you all that stuff about him is only partially right. There *is* a horde of girls who'd kill for a date with him, but the truth is, he really doesn't go out with all that many of them like it may seem...she's right about him never having an honest to God girlfriend though.

"There isn't a girl yet who's been able to figure him out, and he doesn't exactly make it easy for them either. That's partly why they're so attracted to him, you know? He's the epitome of elusive. But, here's where *you're* in luck... Do you remember what he said about that girl, Teresa, today in class?"

"Yeah, I met her at lunch. She's one of Michele's friends," I admitted.

"Camie, I hate to say this, but you might not wanna hang out with them if you want a shot at Tristan," Kate told me with kindness but also, brutal honesty.

"Yeah, I figured. That kinda sucks, too, because I like Michele and I'm not exactly thrilled with having to eat lunch alone until I can find a safer group to hang with." I was afraid of this. I know I can still be Michele's friend while she still lives here, but the other three are really not my idea of the best quality people for me to be influenced by. I'll admit right here and now that I can be somewhat impressionable, and I don't want their personalities to rub off on me in *any* way. I've already gossiped about someone and I'd like to draw the line there, thank you very much.

"Uh, Camie, you and I are friends now, remember? So don't worry about that, you're already in my group. Besides, if you accept the challenge you're gonna be with me at lunch and pretty much all available moments. That being said, one of your advantages is that your new best friend is the one girl who's not after Tristan and who just so happens to know his quirks. For example, unlike almost all other guys, Tristan hates, I mean absolutely *detests* when girls throw themselves at him like Teresa does. And since most girls do exactly that, he wants less than nothing to do with them.

"So that, my friend, is why he doesn't actually date much...I mean he's *really* particular about whom he invests his actual time in. Now let me be clear here, that does *not* mean he keeps to himself, if you know what I mean...but even so, he's pretty selective about who he screws around with casually too. *Unless* he's being self-destructive, which does happen fairly often. Regardless of who it's with though, or how it happens, it's a safe bet his encounters are more or less meaningless to him, but still. In fact, that might be why Michele said he goes through girls like that."

Since I'm truthfully new to this whole world, I'm kind of lost. I know what she meant about him not keeping to himself, but I don't get the other part so I asked for clarification. "I don't mean to be obtuse or anything, but what do you mean about him being self-destructive?"

Kate sighed and then screwed up her face in trying to think of how she could explain. "The best way I can say it is that he's moody as all hell. Most of the time Tristan does a really stellar job of fending off unwanted advances, but I've witnessed many upon many instances when it's like he just doesn't give a shit at the time and hooks up with a girl he'd normally avoid like the plague. He then ends up having to deal with the aftermath of his reckless actions, which of course, pisses him off even more. I'm not sure why, or what makes him do it, but it does seem to happen more than he'd like to admit, I'm sure."

"Okay, I get what you're saying. He's fickle like us girls." In thinking about how Jillian and I felt about moving, Kate's explanation was actually really easy for me to understand.

"Yeah, I guess he is," she said, nodding her agreement once again.

"So, tell me why you think he might be interested in me of all people." I'm really curious about this piece of information and judging from how well Kate knows Tristan; I think I'm safe in believing she might be right about him liking me. Wow. This is totally surreal. I mean, stuff like this just isn't supposed to happen in real life, you know what I mean?

"Okay. Like I said earlier, I've known him my whole life and I'm pretty sure I can recognize the signs when he's considering if a girl is worth his time. I already know for a fact he's attracted to you, that's a given, an—"

"Wait! He's attracted to me?! How do you know he's attracted to me?!" 'Cause in my review of the day, the guy never looked at me twice! Maybe I missed some clue earlier in the day. I thought I'd been paying particularly close attention to everything he did, though... I was, right? God, I really need to learn some pointers from either the most loveable Kate Beaumont here, or my overly observant twelve-year-old sister.

Kate chuckled a little before answering, which she did like she was a sage or something. "Because Camie, I've *seen and heard* things today that you're most likely completely unaware of, and I also know things about how he operates that most don't."

And boy, she wasn't kidding about how much she'd picked up on!

"Liiiike…?" I quizzed her with growing excitement. I mean because the way she said all that made me feel like I was the topic of much discussion among the hierarchy at school today, although I know that's not true. I think I would've heard the buzz if people were actually talking about me. I

have a feeling that'll soon be changing, though, if I decide to accept the challenge like Kate said and if Michele's right about how people talk in this school.

"Alright, first let me just caution you by saying that the events of today pertaining to Tristan Daniels were unprecedented and there was a lot going on that the casual observer would never think of as important. Except they're *hugely important* and every detail counts, especially if you understand there's always meaning behind what this guy does. Basically, it all boils down to the fact that for whatever reason, he's chosen to give you an enormous opening to accomplish what the vast majority of girls on campus dream of. I know I'm being overly melodramatic, but, this is high school and, well…this is the kind of stuff we teenagers live for, you know?" Kate asked rather formally and with a fair amount of suspense in her tone, kind of like we're living in some sort of mystery dinner theater production.

"Yeah. I'm starting to understand there're things at play here that could possibly cause the social dynamics of this school to be thrown into a topsy-turvy kind of upheaval. I never-ever thought I'd be a part of some huge teen scandal, let alone be the cause of it though. I certainly feel honored, but sorta unworthy at the same time." I'm also starting to have a growing understanding of how kids my age take the ins and outs of each other's lives along with the minutiae of those lives so seriously.

And now let's sit back and relax because it's time to pay attention to what Kate's about to tell me. And know this, how she put it all together is nothing short of phenomenal...

"Okay good, you get it. Now, I'm gonna walk you through what I feel to be some very remarkable happenings of today, so let's start at the beginning… I saw how he stopped you from falling this morning. It wasn't like he just happened to be walking behind you two, you know. He literally sprang off the stage and practically sprinted to grab that book his cousin dropped. And this part is pretty amazing in itself and I still can't believe he did it," she said, shaking her head, emphasizing her disbelief. "He then *circled around* so he could come up behind you guys and appear nonchalant in an attempt to not only get a closer look at you, but make sure you noticed him too. And you should understand it's highly unusual for Tristan to draw attention to himself like that.

"Now Camie, I cannot stress enough how important this next tidbit is...*Jeff* witnessed it as well. So, keeping in mind there were a good four hours that passed in which he could've been thinking about you, that brings us to several groundbreaking things that happened in English."

"Oh, you mean the class I've heretofore been referring to as heaven?"

She laughed. "Yeah, that would be the one."

"Okay, just checking. You may continue..."

"Alright well, Jeff is a total flirt, but what he was doing today wasn't so much flirting with you as it was egging Tristan on. This leads me to believe that Tristan either A, said something about you to his best friend, or B, Jeff guessed at his interest like I did.

"Either way, there was enough in his behavior to take notice of. I have a hunch Tristan probably said something though, because not only did they have their heads together for much of first period, but it kinda seemed like they were speaking in code during English, as if Jeff was telling Tristan what he thought of you without actually saying anything. So that could mean Tristan might've asked Jeff's opinion earlier in the day. And let's not forget that Jeff works in the office third period where he could've easily obtained pertinent information about you for Tristan."

"But what about him thinking I wa—"

"A guy? And him not seeing a new girl on the roster?"

I nodded.

"I think that was bullshit. It's my belief that Jeff scripted some of what he said and he did it solely to ferret out a reaction from you. I think he took it upon himself to screen you for Tristan, who was paying very close attention to *everything* being said, even though he did a damned good job of appearing not to be...and judging from the way Tristan looked at you and laughed about what was said, I think Jeff's statement about you being a sophomore took him by surprise.

"Next, Tristan put his hand on your knee when he picked up Teresa's note, making skin-to-skin contact for the second time today, and coming from him, that's a *big* clue that he's attracted to you. He could've very easily reached over you without touching or leaning against you like that, or just not picked it up at all. He didn't *want* the note...I know you saw his face when he shredded it; he was completely repulsed by even touching it! He did all that with intent, Camie, like a test to see how you'd react. You did very well by the way," Kate said with a smile, like she was proud of me or something.

"Why, thank you. I do try to keep my licentious thoughts to myself whenever possible," I replied, feeling kind of proud of myself too. For being someone who doesn't normally test well and having passed the one *he'd* given me without even being aware I was taking it, well, that's pretty much a cause for celebration as anything.

Kate laughed at my humble acceptance of her compliment. "You're very welcome. Oh, and remember what he said as his excuse for asking for her number in the first place?"

"Yeah."

"Well, that was strictly for your benefit, Camie, not mine. He's very well aware that I already understand perfectly just how much he doesn't appreciate being treated like that, but you didn't and he *wanted* you to know. He was point-blank *telling* you what not to do. His tone suggested to me that he could've even been *asking* you not to be like that with him. And then there was that whole thing with the book... Good grief, that was a freaking riot, but *so* completely and totally out of character for Tristan!" Kate said and started to giggle again.

It was several minutes before she regained control of her giggle-fit and was able to continue, and although I found myself grinning and giggling along with her, I'm kind of lost about why this is so funny to her. I kept my mouth shut, though, because Kate can really tell a story. I feel like I'm watching an Agatha Christie movie and the murderer is about to be revealed.

"Sorry for laughing so much, but I mean you just have to appreciate this for what it really was, and trust me when I say it was a *master stroke of genius* how Tristan took outrageous advantage of Mrs. Henderson's kick-back atmosphere and manipulated his environment the way he did! He actually got you pressed up against him with his arm around you under the guise of reading a book you both probably have memorized *and* he did it front of everybody!

"I doubt you noticed this either, but the guy could *not* keep his eyes off you the whole time, or his fingers from playing with a piece of your hair that he could reach without you becoming the wiser. I bet he was just so tickled with himself for pulling that off without being questioned by a soul...I was really impressed actually. And just so you know, I've never seen him do anything like that at school, never-ever!

"He keeps his little affairs not only pretty private, which I'm not too sure how he manages to do with all the gossips in this school, but they're also kept strictly for afterhours events like parties and stuff where people aren't always paying close attention to what he's doing. And not because he's shy, because he's so not. I think it's just that he prefers to keep his personal life out of public view and he considers school to be a very public fishbowl. Plus, he's just not a PDA kinda guy. You know, now that I'm really thinking about that scene in English in conjunction with everything else, I'm positive he's more in to you than even he may realize. Oh! I almost forgot, remember Jeff's shenanigans in the hall?"

I nodded again. And did you hear what she said? He was playing with my freaking hair!

"Well I think he was waiting for a verdict, and Tristan gave it to him with that astounding tour de force of his. I like to think of that part where he stuck his tongue out as being an exclamation point, and once Jeff understood that Tristan had reached some kind of decision, he bowed and went on his way. I think Jeff having that knowledge is important to remember too, especially in light of what happened later. So, moving on… I know you saw him by the locker room and you're also not stupid, but I don't know if you understood his behavior after dance today," Kate said and waited for me to give my interpretation of that more recent event.

"Well, I know he certainly didn't look happy…not until Jeff showed up anyway." Interesting, apparently there's more to that as well. Honestly, I don't know how Kate can figure people out like this, but really, it's mesmerizing to watch her run through her thoughts and then listen to her expound on them.

"Noticed that, did you? Well again, here's what I think was going on... Tristan and Zack don't play well together. Normally, they pretty much avoid each other and that's probably the main reason Tristan stayed so far away from us."

"I knew it!" Man, being right feels awesome!

She nodded, further affirming my correct assumption. "However, I thought he was gonna break that long-standing protocol when Zack started flirting with you by yanking your hair that way. After all, he'd been doing the same thing a couple hours before that, only Tristan wasn't flirting. The way it looked to me, he felt *compelled* to touch you in some way and he'd chosen to give in to that compulsion, but only on the sly because he's still testing the water so to speak…he's not about to lay his cards on the table before you've even thrown in your ante, you know? And I'll bet you money he had a contingency plan in place on the off chance you caught him red handed. You know, like a spider crawling on you or something. But then Zack goes and blatantly shows interest in you…

"Again, this is just my opinion, but watching Zack barely touch you enraged Tristan, because Camie, I was watching him and I'm telling you, he was about to blow. Then when I saw him start cracking up, I knew something was going on behind us and that was right when my stoner ex showed up," Kate explained, shaking her head and rolling her eyes.

And I don't know about you, but Kate has me totally rapt. I'm listening really intently to what she's saying because I'm not only fascinated, but I'm also realizing that I have SO much to learn about the little nuances of people's actions and their motives for doing things. Jeez, when I said Kate was insightful before, I'd no idea how discerning she *really* is.

"Jeff would've totally seen what was going on from where he came from and I'm positive that whatever he did behind our backs, rescued Tristan from having to make a scene, which he *wouldn't* want to do…especially at school and Jeff would know that. As a bonus, it also cracked him up. And another thing Jeff knows all too well is that a laughing Tristan is a happy Tristan, which is important to keep in mind because of that moody issue.

"Jeff's little stunt that he *intentionally* included you in was a statement that Zack read loud and clear. He essentially meant it to say, 'These two are ours, so back the fuck off.' What I'm saying is this, even though he can be a jerk and he's definitely a clown, Jeff was watching over his best friend's interests as well as his own, meaning you and me. That's also how I know Tristan won't abandon Jeff to make rotten choices. The two of them watch out for each other more than the closest of brothers.

"So to break this all down and make it simple, Tristan has displayed some very rare and exceptionally indicative behavior today that I've never seen him do all in *one* day and in regards to *one* girl… He made a concerted effort to make himself known, he shared something personal with his best friend, he dropped a *major* hint on the one thing that really turns him cold, he went out of his way to make an obscene amount of physical contact at school, and the coup de grace…he was *totally* jealous, which I believe is a first for him. So, now do you understand why I think you have more than a snowball's chance in hell?" Kate finished in a flurry, her face beaming with pride.

"Wow, that was spectacular! You could totally be a lawyer or an FBI profiler or something…seriously impressive, Kate," I said after applauding her extraordinarily detailed outline of today's events by clapping and whistling.

She laughed, made a bowing motion and then said, "Thank you. It was actually a lot of fun. I was dying to tell someone about all of this and you were the most likely to appreciate it, seeing as how it all revolved around you. And that's something else…aside from Melissa, there aren't gonna be many girls who'll support your campaign to land Tristan. In fact, if you end up taking him out of the running, one of two things will probably happen. One, you'll be able to write your own ticket socially. Or two, you'll be hated with a passion by every female in this school and many from some other neighboring schools. I can probably get Melissa on board though, and if she backs you, chances are it'll be the first. Are you up to it?"

"Um, I'm not sure yet, and I don't wanna sound rude, but why are you so gung-ho about this? You seem kind of invested." This whole time I've been engrossed in what Kate has been elucidating, and I believe her reason for wanting to be friends with me, but now I'm wondering why she's trying to get her lifelong friend together with a girl neither of them knows. It just seems...odd.

"Well, for a few reasons… I really do like you and think you're cool. You showed compassion to a stranger this morning with Paul, even when you realized being friends with him wouldn't be of great help to you in fitting in. So that means you're brave, too, which you'll need to be if you decide to go for the school's most popular, self-prescribed bachelor. But, the main reason is I care about him. You see, Camie, even though we're not as close as he and Jeff are and our friendship has kinda changed over the years, Tristan is still one of my very best friends and honestly, I don't think he's all that happy. In fact, I think he's sorta lonely, the way he flits from girl to girl, you know?"

I don't really know, but hoping that her question was more rhetorical than anything else, I shrugged my shoulders and nodded anyway.

"It's just that, there're tons of really great looking and popular guys in this school, who date all the time and get involved in relationships, but none of them are as unattainable as he is. He's done it by choice, too, which I think is kinda sad. I mean I know he's remained single on purpose, but I think he deserves to have something special with a girl for once. Try to remember what his voice sounded like when he was tearing up that note, Camie...I swear, the more I think about it, it sounded like he was pleading. Even if it's only on a subconscious level, I think he's desperate to feel valued for more than being a gorgeous face and great kisser.

"For whatever reason, he picked you and I agree with his choice, I think you could be really good for him. And if I'm being honest, I'm kinda hoping if Tristan has a girlfriend he'll settle down, and then maybe Jeff will follow his lead. I mean you've seen him...it's like he's a giant kid and he refuses to grow up. But because they sorta play off each other, they both do a lot of asinine stuff, only Tristan usually knows when to say when. Jeff doesn't and sometimes I think he doesn't even care about the consequences. I guess I'm hoping if Tristan isn't out there ruling the playground with him, Jeff won't be so inclined to play, you know? I just... I just *really* don't wanna see Jeff waste his life...does that make sense?" Kate asked seriously and wiped away a small tear from her cheek.

"Yeah, that makes sense. If you really think I'm the one who can accomplish all this, then I'll give it my best shot. If I've understood everything correctly though, it sounds like it'll be next to impossible," I replied solemnly. Even though I am one, I'd no idea that this emotionally heady current runs unseen in the deep water of a teenager's life. It's pretty sobering to consider.

"Well, I think it's worth a try. If you don't actually land him exclusively, there's still a really good chance he'll wanna be friends, and that's not such a bad thing. Tristan really is a good guy and he can be a powerful ally when it comes to other guys you might be interested in, that is, if things with him don't work out like we're hoping. That's essentially how Melissa and Keith got together. She and Tristan went out a couple times at the beginning of our freshman year and didn't hit it off, but because they're friends, he was more than happy to influence Keith for her when she asked a while back. He's a senior and not only quarterback for the football team, he's the team captain and he's almost as difficult to pin down as Tristan is. I'm not sure how Tristan did that either, but he's responsible for a couple matches that probably wouldn't have happened without his involvement."

Did I mention what an overflowing fountain of information she is? Holy cow! This girl knows *everything*! And now that I've made a decision and I'm armed with a slew of information, I think it's time to get down to brass tacks and figure out what the strategy is for this mission. "Okay. I'm sold. What do I do?"

"Well, this is probably gonna be the hard part, I know I'd have difficulty with it…if you wanna hook him and truly reel him in for good, I suggest you do nothing. He's gotta come to you…it won't work any other way. Oh and you need to be prepared, there *will* be attempts to get away, because I'm sure he's not gonna come quietly. He can be stubborn to a fault and sometimes even to his own downfall."

"His downfall?" Jeez, this guy sounds like he's more complex than the Pythagorean theorem. (Blechk…*math.*)

She laughed and then enlightened me on her meaning once more. "This is just an example, but it's kinda funny… You probably don't know this yet, but both Tristan and Jeff should actually be seniors this year. However, back in third grade Jeff came down with a really nasty case of chicken pox and had to miss almost half the year."

"You're kidding? That's crazy!" I guess I never thought about having to miss school because of illness. It was never an issue, we were already home.

"Yeah, he was super sick. Here's the really crazy part though, Jeff was gonna be held back because he couldn't make up all that work in time, so, because he and Tristan didn't wanna be separated, they came up with a plan that resulted in Tristan being held back too. The downfall came when Tristan missed out on a perfect attendance award he'd been competing for since he'd been in kindergarten," Kate told me, shaking her head like she still couldn't believe they'd done that.

"Um… I don't even know how to respond to that. It's extreme, that's for sure," I said, stunned once again. I think maybe I've underestimated what a best friend actually does…

"Yeah. You know the saying 'blood is thicker than water?' Well, not between these guys. That's partly why Jeff will be key in this whole thing too. It's imperative he does everything he's capable of doing to influence Tristan, but we have to be ultra-careful that he doesn't find out what we're really up to. Since that'll primarily be my job, it looks like I'm gonna be getting back together with the love of my life once again," she said, revealing part of her master plan with a smile.

"Okay, but if I'm not supposed to *do* anything, how am I gonna, you know...do this?" I mean, I really don't understand the inner workings, the machinations if you will, of things like this so I need step-by-step instruction.

"Well, we already know you have his attention…for now. You could say that he's easily distracted so the trick will be keeping his attention and getting him to chase you. Which might actually be the easy part because it was really weird how he totally latched onto you the way he did this morning and I still don't get that. I mean it was *instant.* He actually gasped the second he saw you and froze…that's what had me paying attention in the first place. Even with that though, this whole thing's still probably gonna take time and some planning, but, essentially I think you should just be yourself."

"Just...be myself."

"Yep. Tristan is exceedingly sharp and nothing much ever gets by him so even though he doesn't know you, I'm sure he'd be quick to pick up on any kind of falsity in your character. We can't be obvious about anything, so that leaves out sitting in the stands at the water polo games and swim meets. And if it takes a *really* long time, I don't think going to all his baseball games in the spring will be a very good idea either. However, if you hang with me around the stage at lunch, and I take you to every party and social event that I think he'll show up at, we can put you in his way fairly often without calling too much attention to what we're ultimately trying to accomplish.

"We might even be able to use Zack's interest as bait, but that could be playing with fire…Tristan hasn't ever been jealous before, so his handling of it could go either way. We'll have to see how things play out and make some judgment calls as they unfold. I'll try to dig up some information about what happened today from Jeff, too. I really kinda want you at the football games because the two of them usually go after their polo games. That's also neutral territory and he'd think nothing of it if you were there. The only problem is Melissa and I cheer so we can't sit with you, and you really shouldn't be seen with Teresa and girls like that."

"Yeah, even if being seen with her wouldn't taint me by association, I'd still really rather not hang out with her. I think given the choice, I'd sit alone," I told Kate honestly. I mean I don't care if Teresa likes the same guy I do or anything, but she's just so crass and obnoxious—listening to her speak is like hearing fingernails scraping a chalkboard. So, willingly spending my time with her? Yeah, no thanks.

"I don't blame you... Maybe I can sweet talk Jeff into sitting with you, though, like if I tell him you've never been to a game before and you don't wanna sit alone or something. Ooh…maybe I can hint that Zack has been fishing for information about you and wants to know if you'll be at the game this week. That could work. After today, I'm pretty sure neither of them will want Zack within a twenty yard radius of you at a social gathering," Kate said, laying out the blueprints on how we're to pull off this rather daunting caper.

I have to say, although I'm really excited and giddy about the idea of Tristan being my first boyfriend and that I think I might be able to truly care for him after learning all that I have from Kate, I also understand there are some potentially very serious risks involved and someone could wind up getting hurt.

It's just that I'm afraid it's likely to be me...

5.

That's Real Dedication To The Cause

Kate and I talked strategy a little more while she drove me home and when we got there; I introduced her to my parents. Jillian however was unsurprisingly holed up in her room so that introduction would have to wait. My mom invited Kate to stay for dinner, but she declined by saying that she had more homework to do. I knew that was really her way of saying she was going to put the first part of our plan in motion by getting back together with Jeff, but when her cell phone rang while we were saying goodbye on the porch, we were both surprised by who the caller was.

She looked at the caller ID and gasped, "No way."

I tried looking at the name on the screen. "What? Please say it's Tristan!"

"No, you're not gonna believe this, though, it's Zack…hold on, lemme see what he wants."

Kate tapped a button on her phone and put it to her ear, the picture of serenity, but I was so antsy I was actually bouncing up and down on my toes. You see, after having Kate lay it all out for me, I'm expecting for this to take a long time, but I'm not looking forward to it. I'm not very patient. I'm also trying my best to follow a one-sided conversation and that's pretty annoying. All of a sudden, though, Kate's eyes lit up and her jaw dropped. She looked at me with a big smile in her eyes and then said into the phone, "Listen Zack, I gotta go, I have a call waiting." She then hit the speaker button on her phone and picked up the call that cut her conversation with Zack short.

The following is a kind of transcript of the call Kate graciously allowed me to listen in on:

Kate: "Hi."

Jeff: "Hey Katy. Can we get together and talk?"

Kate: "Um, yeah, I guess…but I'm at Camie's right now."

Jeff: (Awkward pregnant moment of silence and she winked at me.) "Oh. What are you doin' there?"

Kate: "I drove her home from school today and then I was invited to stay for dinner."

Jeff: "Oh. Hold on a second, okay?" (We hear the distinct sound of the mouthpiece being covered up and then what might've been a button being pushed on the phone as the music playing in the background ceased. Kate gives me a silent high-five.) "Sorry, I had to turn the stereo down. You still there?"

Kate: (Pause.) "Yeah, I'm still here. I wanted to step outside to talk so I wasn't being rude to Camie." (She gestures to the porch as if to say that wasn't a lie.)

Jeff: "Oh, right…um, is she cool?"

Kate: "Totally. I really like her. Oh and I'm not the only one who likes her either." (She quietly snickered at this.)

Jeff: *"Huh?!"*

Kate: "Zack called right before you did."

Jeff: (We hear what sounded very much like someone swearing in the background and we both have to cover our mouths so we don't start laughing.) "How'd he get her number?"

Kate: "No, you idiot. He called me. I hung up with him when you called."

Jeff: "Oh, right…okay. So, does she like him?"

Kate: (Silence as she inspects her finger nails.)

Jeff: "Katy? Did you hear what I asked?"

Kate: "No. What?" (She shrugs.)

Jeff: "I asked does Camie like him?"

Kate: "Does she like who?" (She winks at me again.)

Jeff: "Jesus, Katy, you're killing me! Does Camie like Tr—" (We hear the definite sound of paper, like a magazine maybe, flying through the air and a *thwap* as it hit Jeff. Simultaneously, the mouthpiece is covered again. Not well this time, though, because we heard Jeff's smothered *"Quit it, you dick."*) "—Zack or not?" (Both of our mouths form the silent words *Oh My God!*)

Kate: "How am I supposed to know? I literally just hung up with him and answered your call. I haven't had a chance to even talk to her about it."

Jeff: "Well… Oh! Didn't you talk to her about what she thought of him flirting with her today?"

Kate: "Yeah, a little." (She rolled her eyes when she said this.) "How'd you know about that?"

Jeff: "Uhhh…I was there, remember?"

Kate: "Oh yeah."

Jeff: "*Well?*"

Kate: "Well what?"

Jeff: "What did she say?"

Kate: "What the hell, Jeff? You sound like you have a crush on her or something."

Jeff: "*I don't!* God, Katy, you *know* I want you back!"

Kate: "Then why do you care if she likes him?" (She's good, isn't she?)

Jeff: "Uh, I don't. I was just curious, you know?"

Kate: "Whatever. I think it'd be cool if Camie went out with him though." (She shook her head, mouthing the word NO.)

Jeff: "*WHY?* Please Katy, if you love me even a little bit, tell me you won't encourage her to go out with that asshole."

Kate: "Ugh...fine. Hey Jeff, lemme call you later when I get home, okay?"

Jeff: "Oh, um...yeah okay. I love you."

Kate: (Pause and then she sighed.) "We'll talk later, I promise. Bye."

"Well that was unexpected," Kate said and put her phone in her purse.

"What do you think they'll do?" I cannot tell you how grateful I am to be able to learn at the feet of a master like Kate.

"Honestly, I don't know. We'll have to see how this Zack thing sits with Tristan. He may decide not to bother if he thinks you like Zack, or if Zack really starts putting the moves on you. I'm kinda hoping what I told Zack will keep him from being a problem though," she said and then bit her fingernail in thought.

"What did you say to him?"

"Well, it's amusing actually...Zack thinks Jeff is the one who likes you. He missed seeing Jeff accost me. I didn't say one way or the other because he'll find out the truth when Jeff and I get back together anyway. I mean I've never thought Zack was all that bright, but he really is an idiot to think that and then actually ask me about it...Jeff and I have been together for *years*, but whatever. I had to make some things up, though, because if Zack knows it's Tristan who's interested, then he'll probably try to get in the way just to spite him. This whole thing could get really complicated," she told me with a little concern.

"What did you make up?" I asked, growing uneasy myself. I like it so much better when Kate is confident—it's contagious.

"Oh. I told him that you just broke up with your boyfriend and you were taking a break from dating for a while. If he thinks that, then maybe he won't pay so much attention to what you do, *or* how Tristan and Jeff behave. You know, like he won't think of them as competition because he'll think you're not interested in anyone right now," she explained with more certainty.

"Jeez Kate, you're really amazing. I don't think I could've ever come up with some of the things you said to Zack *or* Jeff. I can't believe Tristan was listening in, though, that was hysterical!" I said and unable to hold it in any longer, I let my laughter about that out.

"Oh my God, I *know*!! I thought I was totally gonna blow it a few times!" She started laughing, too, and then continued. "You know what? I think I'm gonna go hunt Jeff down and talk to him in person…if I'm lucky, Tristan will still be with him and I might get some more for us to go on."

"See what I mean? That's so smart! Thanks for everything today, Kate. I really appreciate you being so great." I meant it too. Even though this whole thing could blow up in my face, I think it'd be worth it just to be friends with Kate.

"Hey, no problem! I'm actually really excited about this. Do you know how awesome it'd be if you got Tristan and Jeff and I are together? We'd make the greatest foursome! I'd so love that," Kate said with a big smile, then she hugged me goodbye. "Okay, so I'll pick you up in the morning. Hopefully I'll have some kind of news."

"Sounds good! See you in the morning," I said and watched her get in her car and drive away.

Dinner at my house was a louder affair than it normally is. My dad always has music on, and tonight was no different. A song of The Cult's—my mom's favorite band from when she was in high school—was playing, but my sister and I were talking non-stop with loud excitement about our first day, doing a fair job of drowning out Ian Astbury's hauntingly robust voice. Every now and then during the conversation, my mom and dad would share a bewildered look, like they couldn't believe after all the drama and tears about being thrown into public school that Jill and I both had such glowing reports on our respective days. I didn't share any of what I'm scheming to do, although I did tell them that I'm in love. My mom and dad simply laughed and asked for some details. Again, just another example of how utterly cool they are.

I described Tristan much the same way I had for you, but I left out the part where he should be a senior. I know my parents won't have a problem with me dating or having a boyfriend, *but* I'm not so sure how they'd feel if said boyfriend is almost two years older than me. And I have to admit, I'm a little nervous about it myself. Yeah. Do the math. I'd learned from Kate on the drive home that Tristan is seventeen *right now*, but he's going to be *eighteen* in February. That also means he'll graduate at the ripe old age of nineteen. I can't stress about that right now, though, because if I start to worry about how in over my head I'm probably getting, I won't be able to tread water whatsoever and I'll just end up drowning that much sooner.

Oh, I also asked Kate about what Paul said this morning about being older and whatnot, and I found out Paul is literally only two weeks older than Tristan. Kate says Paul's always been jealous of Tristan because he's both smart and athletically inclined in addition to being popular, and he doesn't have to work hard at any of that so Tristan being a grade below him is kinda like a pride thing I guess, which from what Kate said, Tristan finds funny.

"So tell me what you didn't tell Mom and Dad..." Jillian demanded as she flopped down on my bed that night.

"What do you mean?" Obviously, Jill has been blessed with those same powers of deduction that Kate has. I think I might be a little jealous.

"Gimme a break, Camie. What are you hiding from them and why?" She persisted.

I sighed and decided to just lay it all on the table for her. I really don't want to give my sister any ammunition to turn her super-duper sleuthing skills on me. I'm probably gonna have to be evasive enough as it is, and she'll see right through me anyway. "Okay. You know the guy, your future brother-in-law? Well, Kate and I are kinda stalking him and plotting to make him wanna be my boyfriend."

"So? That's not such a big deal...I mean certainly nothing to keep secret from Mom and Dad. You know they won't care if you have a boyfriend, even *if* you have to plot to get him, sooo, there has to more..." I told you. She's like a mini-Kate, but I know my sister and actually, she's worse.

"Yeah, I know that. Here's the thing though...he's *uber*-popular, most of the girls in school want him, and...he's older than me. Kind of a lot actually," I told her while closing my bedroom door...just in case.

Jillian watched me take that precaution and then studied my face for a moment. "Is he a senior?"

"No...but, *technically*, he should be," I admitted with some anxiety. I'm really hoping to have Jill on my side because if she's not, things could become tricky if she were to decide to throw up roadblocks in the interest of "protecting" me.

She took a minute to absorb what I'd admitted, including everything that might entail. Then she whistled. "Wow, Camie. You really got your feet wet today."

"Yeah, I know, right? Kate really thinks I have a shot and I told her I was in, but, I sorta feel like I'm setting myself up to drown...what do you think?" An almost sixteen-year-old asking advice of her almost thirteen-year-old sister might seem odd, but not only is she as intelligent as she is, Jillian can also be more mature than some adults when she wants to be. Plus, I respect and value her opinions.

"Well, let's think about this for a minute...I'm guessing in scheming, your plans entail going to parties and places where there won't be adult supervision, right?"

I nodded. I seem to be doing a lot of that today...

"Also, there's an expectation factor here if he's that much older and popular... Well, you know you're gonna find yourself in some situations that you've never been in before, which will eventually be the case anyway...unless you simply die an old maid and chances are, that's not gonna happen. So, I guess it all depends on how much you like this particular boy and how wet you think you're ready to get. Like do you think you're ready to get in up to your waist or chin maybe? Or do you think you'd be more comfortable in the wading pool?"

I looked down at my comforter and chewed by bottom lip, thinking.

"All questions you're the only one who can answer, Camie, and you probably won't even truly know until you're faced with having to make a decision, although it would be wise to know your own mind first. Then you won't feel pressured to make rash choices when the time for decisions inevitably rears its head."

She never fails to amaze me with how fast she catches on. She knew immediately what my concerns were. The main one being that I've never even kissed a boy before. Not that I wouldn't relish the chance to kiss or be kissed, but I've just never had the opportunity. Also, like Jillian implied, Tristan's age would indicate that he has a certain amount of life experience and chances are, he'll have certain expectations because of that. Therefore, if I really want him to hang around, I might have to go further than kissing to satisfy some of those expectations.

"Well, from everything I've heard so far, I think I could *really* like him. And I know what you're saying...I've thought about that too. I don't wanna get too ahead of myself, though...this whole thing could be over before it even starts. I just wanted to see if you'd support me." If this whole thing does go south, I'm pretty sure I'll need her shoulder to cry on.

"Oh, I totally got your back, so don't worry about that."

"Cool, thanks..." I heaved a big sigh of relief.

"No problem, that's what I'm here for. Just be careful, okay? You could end up being used *and* never being able to live down a slutty reputation," she replied with sisterly affection.

"Yeah, I'll do my best," I chuckled.

"So how cute is he? Are we talking moderately drool worthy or, 'hey Cujo, you're foaming at the mouth?'" She asked and straightened the ears on one of the bunny slippers she was wearing.

"Jilly, he's Taylor Kitsch hot. In fact, he looks just like Taylor Kitsch with light brown hair and blue eyes. I'm not even kidding."

"Dang, *really?*"

Let me explain. Taylor Kitsch is the king of my "Hot Guy Island." And I really wasn't exaggerating; Tristan actually does look a lot like him. Besides, by using him as an illustration, Jillian can now appreciate how gorgeous Tristan is, too, because I don't compare normal people to my favorite hot actor. EVER.

"Yeah, really, so don't go running for the shotgun when you think I have rabies. Oh. Maybe you can help me with the small problem I have too…I need to figure out a way to go to this Friday's football game without having to sit by myself, or with these girls who won't help my cause *or* my reputation. Both Kate and my other new friend, Melissa, cheer the games and I haven't met anyone who's socially safe for me to pal around with yet. Any ideas?" It's a long shot, but you never know. Jillian is pretty damned crafty.

"Hmm. Even though we both know how *supremely* cool I am, hanging with your family is out because at this stage of the game, you'll look like a dweeb if you do that. *Although…* You know what I'd do?" Okay, now this is what I'm talking about… She has the most devilishly devious look on her face right now so I *know* she's onto something.

"No, what?" I asked and held my breath in anticipation.

"I'd ask Derek," Jillian said, simply, but with a wicked glint in her eyes.

That look is there for a good reason and her suggestion just proves what an evil mastermind she is, too. You see Derek is our cousin. Not only is he a senior at a neighboring school, and even though we're related, I can say he's pretty gorgeous. The girl has style; I'll certainly say that for her.

"Oh Jill, that's brilliant! He got all jealous when this other guy he doesn't like started flirting with me today, so I bet if I show up to the game with some random guy Tristan doesn't know, it'll drive him nuts! I'm gonna call D right now and after that, I gotta get some sleep because after today, I'm beat. I love you, Jilly." I hugged her as she left my room for her own and then, yawning, I thought; if it wasn't for seeing Kate and Tristan tomorrow, I'd probably throw my alarm clock out the window and go on a school strike.

When Kate picked me up in the morning, I could barely contain my curious excitement. She had the goofiest grin on her face and I was hoping that was a sign of good things to come. Unfortunately for me, her good mood really didn't have anything to do with Tristan.

"Morning!" I called from the porch as I made my way to her car.

"Morning, how'd *you* sleep?"

The way she asked that made it sound like she hadn't had the most restful night, but she looked happy and chipper so I didn't really know what to make of it. "Fine I guess. I wouldn't turn down the opportunity for an early morning nap, though. I'm not used to waking up so early and I don't feel like I really got *enough* sleep, you know what I mean?"

I buckled up as she backed out and drove down the street towards school. "Oh yeah. I know. Personally, I'm running on vapors."

"Well, you look good, if that's any consolation," I offered. It wasn't an empty compliment either. She looks great. Actually, she looks *alive.* Sorry, that's really the best way I can explain it.

"Aw, thanks. Actually, I'm super tired...I didn't get much sleep. And I'm sorry, but I don't really have anything new to report either."

"Oh, that's okay. I mean you did try. So, were you not able to find Jeff?" I'm assuming that if she had and Tristan had been there, she'd at least have *some* kind of news.

"Oh, no...I found him alright, but that's why I'm so tired. He was at Tristan's and I didn't think it'd be a good idea to just show up like that right after that conversation. Tristan might've read too much into it."

"Yeah, I can see that. Why are you so tired then?" Even though I've only known her for a day, I'm kind of sensing that Kate is distracted. Normally she explains everything so completely, but this morning she seems a little out of it.

"Well, I was doing surveillance until like 9:00 and then decided to go home. I called Jeff when I got there, but his cell was dead. Anyway, I ended up sneaking out around 1:00 a.m. and went over to his place," she explained, the goofy smile making another appearance.

"Oh. Wow, Kate. Um, that's real dedication to the cause. You didn't get in trouble, did you?" I hope I didn't sound condemning, I'm just really surprised, you know? For one thing, she snuck out on a school night, but the other part...I just don't know how to respond to that.

She laughed. "No. My parents are clueless and I've never been caught."

"What about Jeff's parents?" I'm still trying to grasp the idea that she was in her ex-boyfriend's room in the middle of the night.

"He lives with his dad who acts more like a brother than a father. In fact, I don't have to sneak into his house at all...I have my own key and go in the front door. Mr. Larson was even awake watching a movie with his girlfriend when I got there last night. He asked how I was and actually offered me a soda," Kate told me with a frown.

"*You're kidding?!* So, he doesn't care that you were there *at all?*" I asked stupefied. I mean, *WOW.*

"Not in the slightest."

"Oh my God...I can't even imagine that...I mean I've never had a boyfriend but if I did, I think my parents would completely freak if he randomly showed up and stayed the night."

"Yeah, most parents probably would, but remember, Camie, I grew up with these guys like they're my brothers. The three of us have pretty much always come and gone from each other's houses like they were our own. Our parents swapped babysitting with each other *constantly*, too. When my parents would go out, I'd stay at Tristan's or Jeff's, and then when Jeff's dad or Tristan's parents were gone, it was the same thing...even when we got older and didn't actually need a babysitter. And lots of times, I'd just stay the whole night so it really isn't that big of a deal sleeping over now.

"Of course, everyone knows Jeff and I are together, and I don't sneak out of the house to sleep at Tristan's, so Jeff's dad has to know what's up...I just don't think he cares. But then again, it's not like Jeff and I go around declaring to our parents that we're actually *sleeping* together, so, who knows..." She said, casually admitting that she and Jeff are having sex. Her tone and expression, however, were two very different things as she inspected my face for signs of judgment.

Incidentally, I'm not about to censure Kate for what she chooses to do in that sphere. Like Jillian said last night, everyone is eventually faced with that decision and, sooner or later, I will be, too. However, this *does* sort of go to the theory that if we're successful and I start going out with Tristan, I might have to make that decision on the sooner side of things. And thinking about that possibility, I felt the palms of my hands start sweating.

In an effort to not become obsessive about any of it, I wiped my hands on my jeans and simply accepted her information and moved on. "Huh. So did you guys get back together?"

"Oh yeah. We're *definitely* back together. He was so damned happy to see me when I woke him up that I couldn't even get a word in edgewise...I was too busy being mauled all night. But that's really my fault. I should've known better than to just show up in the middle of the night like that after being broken up. I swear it was like I was a five-course meal to someone who hasn't eaten in weeks. Anyway, that's why I don't have anything new about Tristan," she explained, being satisfied that I hadn't mentally found her guilty of committing some kind of heinous crime. "Oh! But I did talk to Melissa...she picked up on Tristan's unusual display of jealousy yesterday, too, and she's in. She'll be like another pair of eyes and ears for us, so I think our teams are even now."

"What do you mean? Even?"

"Oh that's right...I forgot to tell you. Okay well, I'd totally forgotten about it once we started talking yesterday, but when Melissa and I were discussing the game and who you could sit with, she suggested you sit with Pete and Mike and that reminded me...one of us, and I'm pretty sure it's you, was being watched yesterday."

"What?! Like a stalker?" Now *I'm* being stalked?

"No no…not exactly. I didn't think anything about it during the break yesterday when Jeff and Pete were talking and being all hush-hush because I figured they were just making plans to ditch, you know?"

"Yeah, that would make sense I guess."

"I know, but that couldn't have been what they were talking about because I saw Pete at lunch. However, I also saw Pete by the locker rooms after school, texting. And it's not that that's unusual in itself or a big deal really, but the timing seemed kinda coincidental to me because about the same time he was doing that, Zack was flirting with you, and then Jeff showed up out of the blue.

"Again, it could just be coincidence, but, I also saw Pete in the parking lot before we left and he was definitely watching us that time. So, I *think* Pete might be acting as a spy for Tristan. Unfortunately, there's no way for us to know for sure because we can't ask anyone about it."

"I thought you said Tristan would wanna keep this really quiet?"

"Yeah, he would."

"So why would he involve another person besides Jeff?"

"Well, here's the thing with Pete…he's a really close friend of Tristan's and Jeff's, he's really dialed in to this school, and, he can really keep his mouth shut. Seriously, he's absolutely the most frustrating person in the world to try to wheedle information out of. I don't know anyone who's ever gotten him to say something against his will…blackmail doesn't work either because no one has *anything* on him. So, if someone wanted a little help with something but didn't want anyone to know what they were up to…?"

"They'd go to Pete," I filled in.

"Right. But regardless, we can't ask him for help without knowing for sure if he's already involved or not because if he is, he'll go straight to Tristan. And another thing, Tristan has a lot of friends and he does a lot for those friends, and although it'd be unlikely, it wouldn't be inconceivable for him to maybe call in a favor here and there. Which means directly asking Pete or Mike to sit with you at the game is pretty much out and we can't trust anyone else except Melissa."

"Well, that's okay with me…I think I'd rather not have a ton of people getting involved in this anyway and hopefully, I'll have good news about how to get around sitting alone at the game," I said with some pride in my voice. I'm kind of liking this whole subterfuge thing. It's invigorating.

"Oh yeah?" Kate asked, pulling into her parking space in the back lot.

"Yeah. I haven't talked to him yet, but I left a message for my cousin, Derek, to text or call me about a favor I wanna ask him for. He's a senior at Valhalla and pretty cute, too. What do you think?"

"Ooh. That'll totally throw Tristan off! Especially being that he's *already* jealous…good idea Camie!"

"That's what I thought, too, but I can't take credit for it…it was my twelve year old sister's idea." I mean come on. I have to give credit where credit is due.

"You're kidding?" She asked, halting our progress onto campus to stare at my face in surprise.

"Nope. You'd like her a lot. She's an evil genius," I told her, becoming exceptionally proud of my little sister.

"I guess so. Wow. Well, hopefully that whole thing will pan out. Lemme know when you hear back…okay, so we're gonna have to run to make first period on time…I'll see you later. If we're lucky, *they* will provide more fodder today that we can use in our playbook." Kate took off with a wave. I love how she called Tristan and Jeff "they"—for some reason that cracks me up.

Sadly, nothing else noteworthy happened that day. Or the next, or the next…

6.

Everyone Has A Skeleton Or Two

Over those first few days, Kate was doing her best to introduce me to her peers and I was doing my best to remember their names and faces, while also trying to ignore the feeling that I don't belong. Back when I said I filled the requisite teenagers status, I didn't realize that just because I'm a teen like they are, it doesn't automatically make me a teen *like* them. By just watching some of the interactions and listening to some of the conversations going on around me, it was becoming obvious that I'm on the pathetically shallow end of the life experience pool, and even then, I kept feeling like I was in need of a floatation device.

I kept my insecurities about all that to myself, though, and tried to just focus on the fact that, granted, it's still only my first week and it'll of course take some time, but, I'll eventually be swimming with the big kids. Please understand me, I'm not about to jump in head first by drinking, doing drugs, and having sex or whatnot just so I can have something more in common with a lot of these kids other than saying we go to the same school. My insecurity or self-doubt isn't coming from a feeling of peer pressure to be someone I'm not, it's more that I haven't had any experiences to be able to know who I even am. However, I'll admit that I'm afraid of looking ignorant in *any* way, because in my mind, looking ignorant usually means you are.

Without being obvious about it, I'd been observing Tristan as best I could, too. My findings so far are that he's almost what you'd call larger than life, and everyone seems to worship him in some way. Girls stare and giggle when he walks past them and guys compete for his attention. I never saw him with the same group of people for more than maybe five minutes at a time either. He'd usually acknowledge the giggling girls with a smile or nod, and if he was asked, he always accepted the invitation to play catch during lunch. With that being said, I think it's safe to say that for someone who doesn't care for being in "public view," Tristan's fairly good at being generous with himself. Well, aside from with me that is...

Tristan remained more than aloof the entire week and Kate was attributing his complete avoidance of me to Jeff's slip-up on the phone Monday night. He even foiled our attempts to elicit any kind of interaction in English. Everyday, no matter how early Kate and I tried to get to fifth period; he and Jeff had already beaten us there. By doing that, they were able to pick their seats; Tristan always chose a cushion on the end and Jeff was always next to him. Also, anytime I showed up in his vicinity during the break or lunch, Tristan would wander off to talk to someone and pretend like I didn't exist. Kate and Melissa, both, have assured me that he's still paying attention; he's just doing it remotely. However, since Kate and Jeff are together again, *he's* been around *constantly*. So seeing as how he's been attached to her like glue, and thus to me as well, Kate thinks that Tristan is probably using Jeff as a scout, garnering information about me and then reporting what he's learned to Tristan.

And as far as my maybe stalker goes? Well, the evidence as to whether Pete's embroiled in this is thus far still inconclusive. Melissa's been keeping a casual but close eye on him, and she says there hasn't been anything unusual about his behavior. In fact, I haven't really even heard or seen much of Pete during the breaks or lunch, which makes both Melissa and me think he isn't a player in the game. Even so, Kate still feels it'd be better if we keep our agenda between the three of us.

Anyway, it wasn't until late Thursday afternoon when Kate and I were doing homework at my house that things started to pick up again. We were lying on my bed and working on various pieces of homework when my cell phone started singing, telling me I had a text.

"Who's that?" Kate asked without looking up from her chemistry book.

"Uhh… OH! It's Derek!" I told her with excitement. Since this is the first I've heard from him since I left that message for him Monday night, I'm thinking, *FINALLY!* Jeez, Cuz…thanks for the timely response.

Kate's head snapped up in attention. "Well?!"

I'm just gonna copy the text dialogue for you…it'll take less time.

Derek: hey cuz! whats up?
Me: i need a favor 2morrow nite.
Derek: what kind?
Me: need u 2 take me 2 r f-ball game.
Derek: oooh. dont no.
Me: por favor? es muy importante. (Like my use of Spanish there?)
Derek: por que? (He's pretty quick, huh?)
Me: hot guy!!! :-) (I gotta be honest. I *am* asking him to skip his own game…)
Derek: roflmao!!
Me: well?
Derek: get back 2 u…
Me: incentive: check out r girls! :-p (Can't hurt to throw that in, right?)
Derek: lol we'll see. ttyl

Me: k thx. ttfn. (Yeah, I still like Tigger…he's bouncy, flouncy, trouncy, pouncy, fun-fun-fun-fun-FUN!) (And yeah, I'm a dork.)

"Okay, so I guess we still wait…" I said, frustrated. I mean really, this weekend could be a make it or break it kind of thing. If Tristan is as distractible as Kate mentioned, he might forget that he likes me at all, and it's not like he's done anything to make us think he hasn't already done exactly that.

"Well, at least he didn't say no right off the bat. Let's cross our fingers that the mention of other girls to scam on will do the trick. That was good thinking."

"Thanks. I think you and my sister are corrupting me." Sarcasm. It's not just a form of speech; it's a dear friend.

"Oh, right! You haven't even began to be corrupted, Camie! I'll do my fair share for sure, but just wait until Tristan actually makes a move."

"Humph."

At my discontented and less than confident muttering, Kate lifted her head from her homework again. "Aw Camie…he will eventually you know. I know it's frustrating and seems like it's taking forever, *and* he's being kind of a jerk, too, but I promise, you still have his attention."

"How can you tell, Kate? I swear…I could be a ghost as far as he's concerned." I've been feeling kind of dejected. I know it hasn't been all that long—it *is* only Thursday, and I haven't gone to a single social event either—but still… Even the mention of possibly being "corrupted" by Tristan didn't have its usual nerve-wracking effect on me. This waiting crap is killing me, so now my stance is; if he's gonna do it, then for the love of God, do it already!

"Well, that's exactly it, Camie. Do you really think he'd go from being so in to you on Monday to ignoring you so completely the very next day? I'm telling you, he's just laying low for a bit. I think Jeff's verbal blunder on the phone *really* spooked him and now he's trying to fly under the radar, so to speak. He doesn't want either of us to put together anything that happened on Monday. Poor guy. He doesn't have a clue that he was busted before school even started that morning, *or* that we've joined forces to bring him to his knees," Kate said with a diabolical chuckle and then went back to her chemistry.

I have no other choice except to take her word for it, but let me just say loud and clear that so far, *This. Sucks.*

Friday afternoon rolled around and things were still a very disheartening status quo. I'll be honest; I was in a pretty pissy mood by the time I got to English, too. I had a pop quiz in geometry that morning, which totally bites, and then I also had to bear witness to Teresa mooning over Tristan during our very short, eight-minute break between third and fourth period. Even the fact that—provided they have something to do with the English language—Mrs. Henderson lets us play games on Fridays didn't help my mood much.

Our little group was playing what the guys were calling "Ebonics Scrabble." The rules are simple: Regardless of how it's spelled, if you can use it in a sentence, it counts. *However*, you actually have to use it in a sentence before you can count the points. To help you imagine how completely outlandish Jeff and Tristan got with this game, I want you to think about how many teenagers are so fond of swearing and using crude turns of phrase, as well as how popular "textese" has become. Honestly, Webster would be appalled. And like I mentioned, I think I have a fairly decent vocabulary, but being in the mood I was, I wasn't using it in the most pleasant of ways. Kate kept throwing me looks of concern when I'd spell out my words, every one of them being overtly negative in some way. Then when I used them in a sentence, the words always came out snarky or bitchy. The guys, however, thought it was hysterical.

Now let me preface something here; even though a lot of them do it anyway, kids aren't supposed to use cell phones in class. My parents, however, had explained to the principal that I need mine on at all times because of our family situation. They want to keep a direct line open to Jillian and me in case there's a crisis with my mom so, I'm allowed to have mine on if it's kept on vibrate and I'm not found abusing the privilege. Needless to say, this is the first thing that leapt into my mind when my purse started to dance towards the end of class. I should also briefly mention the three pairs of eyes that darted straight to the bag, which was doing its own version of the funky chicken. I felt beads of nervous sweat develop along my hairline when those eyes then transferred their attention to my alarmed face.

With true panic, I rolled over to dig my phone out. "Oh God."

Kate knew why I get to keep my phone on, but the guys didn't and I started to feel almost sick when she quickly and quietly filled them in about my mom. My hands were shaking by the time I fished my phone out and being too petrified to look at it, I handed it to Kate and held my breath. She slowly took it and almost immediately, her expression went from complete fear to one of relieved joy. She laughed and then showed me the text.

Derek: game on! time?

I swear I thought I was gonna either cry or pass out. Instead, I flopped face first into my cushion, moaning a few obscenities about how he'd scared the living crap out of me. Only I used some much harsher language than crap and didn't actually say "he" or use Derek's name at all.

When I finally recollected myself, Kate handed my phone back and I sent Derek a text informing him when to pick me up. I was not oblivious to the overwhelmingly curious looks passing back and forth between Tristan and Jeff while I did this either. They were both bursting at the seams to know what was going on, but they didn't dare ask. Kate—God love her—didn't say a single word; instead, she just sat there with an essentially blank look on her face. If they can be so damned secretive, then so can we.

All's fair in love and war, right?

Later that evening, Derek and one of his friends, Brandon, showed up for dinner at my house about forty-five minutes before the game was supposed to start. My mom wasn't feeling well so she was sleeping when they got there and my dad played host; something he's been doing more and more since my mom's diagnosis.

We were finishing up our food when Derek—who you just wanna bow down and worship his forethought for this—asked, "Hey Uncle Kevin, what time does Camie need to be home tonight if I'm with her?"

My dad started clearing the table and asked, "What time is your curfew?"

"Oh, well since I'm almost eighteen, I don't have a curfew anymore, but when I was Camie's age, it was midnight. My parents upped it a half-hour each year on my birthday, too." Derek winked at me when my dad's back was turned.

"Makes sense. Alright...it's a little late, but I think Mandy will be fine with that." He came back to sit at the table again and leaned back in his chair, looking at me thoughtfully. "Cameron, your mother and I have already talked about this and we want you to know that we understand how hard it's been for you both, but especially for you, starting high school as a sophomore in a school where you don't know anyone. We know you probably feel like you need to do what you can to fit in....we remember all too well what being a teenager is like and we understand how difficult fitting in can be. *But*, we also know what teenagers do and the things that go on at parties when kids don't have parental supervision. Hell, your mom and I even went to parties where the parents stayed home and supplied the booze.

"What I'm saying is that although we trust you to make good decisions for yourself, we understand you won't have control over anyone else. So, you have two rules to follow. The first being if you think you might not make it home by curfew, or you're having a problem getting your ride to leave, you call me. I know it's hard to be on time when you're not the one with the car keys, so just call and let me know if you're gonna be late...if I need to come get you, that's fine. Which brings me to rule number two…your mom and I want you to know that you can be open with us about anything…we'd much rather have you be *honest and safe*, than put yourself in danger by lying because you think you might get yourself or a friend in trouble. That being said, you are under no circumstances to *ever*, and I mean *never* young lady, get in a car with someone who's been drinking or doing drugs. Do you understand?"

"Yeah, Daddy, I won't. I promise."

"I mean it, Cameron. I don't care if it's *Je*sus himself behind the wheel, if He's been sippin' on His own homemade wine, you call for a ride home," my dad said sternly with a hint of an evangelical tone in his voice. "You have our word that if there's even a need for them at all, any repercussions for misbehavior will be very reasonable, but only if you're honest with us and follow these rules. Are we clear?"

"Yeah. Crystal." A new warmth of appreciation for my parents spread through me. I mean, don't I have *the* best parents a teenager could ever have? And now you see where I get my "most-excellent" witticism from, too. Oh, in case you missed the first one, that was another nod to the movie *Bill & Ted's Excellent Adventure*.

My dad walked us out and told the three of us to be safe and have fun while we piled into Derek's huge, 4x4 truck. As soon as he pulled out of the driveway Derek asked, "Okay Cuz, spill. What's goin' on?"

"Oh, umm, my friend Kate and I have this kind of siege planned for me to land this ridiculously hot and popular guy, and she thinks I should be at the games because it's neutral territory, only Kate cheers and I haven't made too many friends yet. It wouldn't really do me any good to sit in the stands alone, you know? Plus, we both figure showing up with another guy is a bonus."

"Oh, okay. There's two of us though, who's playing the role of the other guy?" He asked, nodding his understanding and agreement.

I didn't even need to look at Brandon in the backseat. He was quiet through dinner and although there's definitely *something* inherently alluring about him, that something also happens to be whispering a subtle warning that I think would be wise for me to just heed without question.

"Um, I think it'd better be you," I told Derek and then turned in my seat to say, "No offense, Brandon…"

"None taken," he said with a single, bored nod, never having shifted his focus from staring out the passenger window.

"Kissing cousins it is, then… So, who's the guy?"

"His name is Tristan Daniels. He's beautiful and I'll hug him, and pet him, and squeeze him, and call him George. Hey! Maybe you can be a groomsman in our wedding," I told my ultra-cool cousin and burst out laughing. I crack myself up sometimes. Incidentally, the whole George thing is from John Steinbeck's Nobel Prize-winning novella *Of Mice and Men*. Or maybe it was from a Bugs Bunny cartoon. I can't remember which.

When the guys quieted their own laughter induced by my snappy repartee, Derek started muttering to himself. "Daniels...Tristan Daniels... Why does that name sound fam—Wait, are you talking about *the* Tristan Daniels, the swimmer?"

"Yeah! You know him?!" I asked with surprise. I don't know why I'm so shocked about this, though. Although this is a big town, a lot of kids' parents grew up together which means most of them still keep in touch with each other, making it common for their children to know each other, too, even if they don't go to the same school.

"Uhhh...kinda. I don't really *know* him, but he's something of a legend in water sports…I think he and I used to swim for Heartland a few years back, but I know for a fact our school has never won a polo game or a single swim meet he's competed in. I mean, he's fuckin' *fast*… Hey Brandon, do you know anything about a guy named Tristan Daniels?" Derek called over his shoulder to his friend who, according to the chirping coming from the backseat, is now playing Angry Birds on his phone.

"Uhh…yeah. Actually, you do too. He's that guy our cheerleaders were all gaga over at that football game against them this year…the pre-season scrimmage one. Remember they all followed him to that huge Grossmont party after the game and we were all pissed about it?"

"Oh *yeah*, you're right! He was! *Ha!* Camie, if you pull this off most of the guys at my school will shout praises for you from the rooftops. There's nothing we hate more than when a shark preys on the fish who live in another guy's sea." Just so you know, I'm not so sure I like being compared to a fish, but I'll take the praise nonetheless.

"Oh I totally forgot to tell you about this, but *he's* the guy who got Samantha to do the things she broke up with Josh for wanting her to do with him…"

"How do you know that?"

"Because Sara never logs out of her phone's email account and she left it at my house one night…I was bored and thought she'd probably have some good reading material in it. Damn, you should've read all the shit Samantha told her about him."

Derek gave me a sideways glance, considering whether he should get the lowdown now or wait until I wasn't around. Unfortunately, he went with now. "Well I know it bugged him that she wouldn't have sex with him, but Josh's bigger pet peeve was that she refused to even let him go down on her or vice versa..." Ahhh!! No, stop there please! I don't think I need to hear any more than that!

"Yeah, well, she didn't refuse *anything* that night. This guy hit a goddamned *grand slam* at that party. Here's the fuckin' funny part though...Josh totally owes him because from what the email says, she doesn't mind doin' any of it anymore and afterwards, instead of getting her number or giving her his, he *actually* talked her into getting back together with Josh! I mean this guy is like my fuckin' hero!" Nice. So yeah, I'm pretty glad I listened to that whispered warning.

"How in *the fuck* did he do *that*?! Dude, I remember when they broke up and she was adamant that it was over...I was totally blown away when they got back together." By the way, I've almost become invisible while they're talking about some cheerleader and my heartthrob—the apparent slut that he is.

"Well, evidently she felt like she could trust him or something and kinda had a mini-meltdown about the break up or some shit...she said he wasn't just a really great lay (kill me now please), but a good listener, blah blah whatever, anyway, he said a bunch of sensitive bullshit and by the time her clothes were back on, it was like nothing happened and she called Josh right then and there. I forwarded the email to myself if you wanna read it." I hate to admit it, but I almost want to ask him to copy me on it as well. *What* is wrong with me?

"Yeah, I want to because *damn*, that's impressive..." My cousin said, nodding his head. Brandon went back to his phone and game, and Derek found a place to park. Then all of a sudden, he remembered how they got on the subject of Tristan in the first place. "Hey Bran, Camie's trying to take him outta the game."

After hearing what Brandon had to say, though, I'm not so sure Derek is as okay with that anymore, however, I'm reconciling myself with this over abundance of information. Honestly, it really shouldn't have come as such a shock. Although I'm sure they're not, it seems like almost everyone around me is having sex. And I mean it's not like I expect Tristan to have a halo and wings, you know? Kate even told me that he hooks up with girls a little more than occasionally; it's just that she used far more tact informing me than Brandon.

We got out of the car and then for the first time tonight, Brandon actually looked at me. Well, it was more than just a look... He *totally* checked me out, his disarming perusal of me ending with a sly tilt of his lips. "I bet she can do it, too."

"Hey! Cut it out, you jerk. That's my little cousin you're leering at." Derek punched Brandon in the arm. Hard.

"*Hey!*" Brandon laughed and rubbed his bicep. Then he looked at me again. "I'm just sayin'…" He left the statement hanging and winked at me.

Aw, that's so sweet…of both of them. My problem now is, though, if Derek's reacting to his own friend like this, what's he going to do if Tristan looks at or even talks to me? *And,* what's Tristan going to do when he sees me with Derek, who isn't so random as I'd thought?

Apparently the answer to those questions is not a goddamned thing. (Ugh…sorry God.)

We arrived at the game kind of late so the stands were already filled with the majority of the crowd's attention engaged on the field. I waved at Kate and Melissa doing a cheer on the track in front of the fans, then the three of us made our way up the metal stairs to find seats in the bleachers. Holding hands and slowly, just to make sure he got a good look; we went right past the row where Tristan was sitting with Jeff and Pete. Although his eyes most definitely zeroed in on my "date" and his face registered some kind of reaction, he didn't do anything else. In fact, the irritating Prince of Passiveness and his previously sex-starved sidekick actually had the nerve to get up fifteen minutes later, leaving Pete and the game altogether.

I sat through the next two and a half hours uninterested in both the game and listening to some girl in front of us literally breakup with her boyfriend via phone; however, I did eavesdrop with half an ear. It sounded like the only reason she did it was because her friends don't think the guy is "boyfriend material" and/or "good enough" for her. Derek shrugged, non-committal, but Brandon rolled his eyes and shook his head, looking like he wanted to smack all four girls upside their heads for their idiocy. Anyhow, when the game was over Derek and Brandon wandered over to the snack bar before it closed, and I moseyed down to the track to meet up with Kate.

"Hey! Wasn't that just an awesome game?!" Kate enthused, bouncing up to me in a flurry of blue and gold pom-poms. I told you, Kate's spunky.

"Yeah, it was a lot of fun except your boyfriend's slutty best friend is a pain in my ass. Did you see them leave?" I asked with a fair—okay, large—amount of annoyance.

"Yeah, I know. He definitely took note of you, though, so that's something," she said in a more upbeat manner than I could appreciate at the time. "But um, why slutty?"

After Kate heard my new intelligence she shrugged her shoulders and grimaced. "Yeah, Jeff told me about her...Tristan was in a *really* big funk when that happened so I think he felt weird or something about that whole thing. Maybe I should've told you, but, he doesn't talk about his sex life,

Camie, and he's bound to have some skeletons…we all do in some way or another."

"Hey! What's up?" Melissa asked as she joined us equally cheerful as Kate had previously been.

I sighed. "Nothing…I'm just cranky and starting to think there's no way he'll wanna waste his time with me."

Melissa frowned. "Why would you be a waste of his time?"

"She just heard about a *massive* conquest…" Kate answered with another grimace.

Melissa's eyebrows rose as her mouth formed a silent "Oh."

"It's not just that…it's…well, it's kinda, I don't know…embarrassing…" I said, dropping my eyes to the ground, my face beginning to heat.

"What is?" They asked simultaneously.

"Well, promise you won't laugh or say anything?" They nodded. "I've never even kissed a guy before…" I shyly admitted and waited for their reactions.

"Really?"

It was Melissa who'd asked and thankfully, without making me wish a hole in the ground would open up and swallow me for admitting my colossal lack of skeletal remains. Kate, however, didn't look surprised one iota. I nodded and then putting her arm around me, Melissa shared a little something about herself to make me feel better.

"He was my first. Kiss I mean… He knew, too, and he was really great about it. He didn't laugh at me or make me feel self-conscious at all. We were saying goodnight after our first date and when he bent down to kiss me, I totally blurted out I'd never kissed anyone. All he said was something like, 'Well, there's a first time for everything' and I remember being so freaking nervous, I thought I might pee my pants or screw it up somehow, but, it was amazing. In fact, I really wish Keith were as good a kisser as Tristan is. Oh and another thing, he's not the kind of guy who expects sex or *anything* like it on a first date."

"That's totally true. Don't stress about this, Camie, he sounds way worse than he actually is…I promise, he honestly doesn't just go around nailing random girls every chance he gets like he did with that other girl. I mean he totally could if he really wanted to, but he just doesn't. Mostly I think he keeps things pretty minor."

Melissa was nodding in agreement and with their combined reassurances, I was able to breathe a little easier. I mean I know he's not a virgin or anywhere close to it—and *now*, thanks to Brandon, I know that for sure—but even so, I just needed to hear someone I trust and who knows him well enough tell me he's not like a sex addict and in need of a twelve-step program or something.

Wanting to move away from "graveyard" talk, I thought to introduce Kate and Melissa to Derek and Brandon, but they weren't within hearing distance yet. They'd stopped on the track on their way back from the snack bar. More accurately stated; they were taking advantage of my "incentive" by scoping out some of the cheerleading squad. I caught Derek's eye and he wandered over to me, but stood so he could keep an eye on MaryAnn, making it clear she's the cheerleader of his choice.

"Okay, so what's our plan for tonight? Keith's going to Megan's so should we go there?"

"Yeah, Jeff wants me to meet him there too, and I'm sure *he'll* be with him," Kate said, eyeing my cousin with some suspicion.

"Yeah, I'm sure where Tweedle-Dee goes, Tweedle-Dum will follow. Oh, don't worry about Derek either…he knows everything and he's in."

"Oh, okay. Seriously though, Camie, you need to chill. I swear you don't need to worry about that other stuff right now, especially since this might take a long time," Kate told me gently but firmly.

"No it won't," Derek chimed in, out of the blue.

Huh?!

"What are you talking about?" I didn't even think he was paying attention…he's been totally busy making some kind of visual love connection with MaryAnn. Now I ask you, why can't my hunk o' good, good lovin' be more direct like that?

"He wants you, Camie. Trust me. Hey Bran, how long do you think before she snags him?" Derek asked Brandon who sidled up next to Kate and handed Derek MaryAnn's phone number. *Damn*, that was beyond fast! I'm *more* than impressed!

"Mmm…I say she sees some kind of action in a week, maybe two," Brandon ventured confidently, crossing his arms over his chest while eyeing some of the football players, who, I think, might've been eyeing him and my cousin first. I swear, sometimes I wouldn't be surprised if guys literally peed on girls to mark them as off limits.

"I'll take that action. I bet it's more like three…four tops. He's a calculating opponent, Camie, but you have this in the bag," Derek informed me with certainty.

"Uh, thanks for the votes of confidence, guys, but how the hell can you lay odds on a freaking time frame?" I was completely mystified yet gratified at the same time. Also, I love my cousin dearly, but I'm hoping Derek loses this particular wager and that Brandon comes out the victor—along with me. You know, my lacking patience and all.

"Camie, we're guys. Anyway, you good? We're gonna hit up a party down at the beach. You can come if you want, but I'm guessing you probably wanna show up wherever the shark's gonna be," my cousin the barracuda said of my ocean dwelling predator.

"The shark?" Kate asked, confused.

"Yeah. Camie'll explain it to you when there aren't so many listening ears." Derek winked at us. You've really gotta appreciate the support of your family, you know? "Hey Bran, you're still DD tonight, right?"

"After that concert last weekend...dude, I won't be drinking for a *long* fuckin' time."

We went our separate ways, Derek and Brandon discussing the concert and what sounded like a possible encounter Brandon had with the missing link. We three girls exchanged an amused look and Kate whispered in my ear, "See? *Everyone* has a skeleton or two..." I giggled and nodded in agreement. Then I started musing about what sort of unpleasantness I'd eventually bury first and who, if anyone, would be attending the funeral with me. Once we were alone though, I explained Derek's shark metaphor to Kate and Melissa as Kate drove us to what would be my first-ever keg-party.

Now I have to say if you haven't been to one of these things yet, I can guarantee your first time will probably shock the crap out of you. At least it did me, unsurprisingly. Upon entering this shindig—or maybe the more appropriate term would be hootenanny...Oz from *Buffy* would know—I immediately pictured the party scene at Jake Ryan's house from the iconic '80s movie classic *Sixteen Candles*. It was unreal. I mean there wasn't a pizza spinning on a record player or anything, but there was just so much chaos my eyes couldn't focus. With this and everything else I've started to learn this week, I'm starting to wonder if maybe I *have* been sheltered up until now. I guess there's only so much knowledge one can glean from watching movies and reading books, you know what I mean?

Kate and Melissa navigated us through the throng of underage alcohol consumers and the occasional patch of noxious fog produced by those who were polluting themselves with cigarettes, and over to the three kegs being manned on the patio in the backyard. We waited for what had to be ten minutes before we were each handed a plastic cup overflowing and dripping with a frothy brew.

When I hesitated on taking the proffered beverage, Melissa leaned in close to my ear and whispered, "Just take it, you don't have to actually drink it if you don't want to. Just think of it as a prop." Interesting. I guess it really *is* all about appearances...

Semi-relieved, I gripped the twelve-ounce cause for all this mayhem and with Melissa bringing up the rear; I followed Kate as she expertly steered a course to where Jeff and Tristan were standing. We made our slow progress through the bodies, being jostled, shoved, and spilled on without ever being apologized to. Or maybe we were apologized to, but music was blaring so loud, I couldn't distinguish what anyone around us was saying. I knew they were communicating, though, because kids would open their mouths wide and lean towards each other, and then indicating they'd heard what had been said; the recipient of the hollering would nod their head.

Tristan and Jeff, along with some other kids I'm sort of familiar with now, were standing in a corner of the backyard when we finally reached them. Somehow, we lost Melissa along the way so I was grateful to have those other kids to shout at because Jeff essentially began feasting on poor Kate the moment we got close enough for her to become ensnared. He only relinquished her once when he went on a beer run for himself and Tristan. Which incidentally, took him a least a half-hour to return from.

The party was such an intense crush I felt like we were in a can of tinned sardines. Sorry. I know that's a horrible cliché, but as I now fully appreciate the meaning behind it, I just couldn't help myself. Honestly though, there are only two things I can say I enjoyed about this whole experience aside from some decent music; 1) Teresa was nowhere to be seen, and 2) Although he didn't shout, holler, or scream a single word to me, Tristan stayed put the entire night. I'm guessing that's because there was really nowhere for him to go.

With my first party experience being what it is, I'm hoping tomorrow night's chosen soiree is more like a shindig, because I'm now definitely certain that Oz would classify tonight's as being a hootenanny. Seriously, watch that above referenced movie. The only thing this party is lacking is a drunk china-man named Long Duck Dong falling out of a tree. And if you happen to have already seen it, try to keep "the geek and the underwear" scene in mind for the future…

7.

Nippley New Girl

Saturday evening Kate and I were standing in her cavernous bathroom in front of the mirror, primping and perfecting ourselves in preparation for round two of the weekend's social circuit. By this time I'm admitting that impatience does not look good on me. I've become pretty saucy, but not in an attractive way. I totally need to cool it with my verbal lashings, too; otherwise I'll probably end up alienating all the people I care about.

That was what I was thinking about when I said, "Hey Kate? I'm really sorry about my venomous tongue lately. I know I haven't been a joy to be around the last couple days."

"It's okay, Camie. I get it. Believe me, I do. I'm a big fan of instant gratification too, but we're making progress so just hang in there. You heard what your cousin and his friend said. Plus, Tristan's strategy last night means we're still moving in the right direction." In the mirror her kind gaze met mine briefly before she returned to touching up her expertly applied eyeliner.

"What strategy? Basically being trapped behind me for the duration of that party was a strategy?"

"Camie, he wasn't trapped. He *chose* to remain rigidly where he was because you were there," Kate told me as if that should've been obvious.

I sighed and tried for more softness in my tone. "Okay, explain. Because from where I was standing, he looked pretty hedged in and since I'm obviously not bright enough to figure this stuff out on my own, you need to give me the play-by-play."

Bending over to fluff her hair, Kate said, "Well, it looked to me like he was doing a couple of interesting things. He could've, and always has in the past, gone to get his own refill, but, he didn't. Instead, he sent Jeff. And I say he sent him, because Jeff was pouting about having to leave. Jeff knew how long it'd take with all those people there, and he didn't want another drink either. He was already pretty buzzed and he ended up pouring his beer out on the grass before he'd even taken a drink.

"I think Tristan was not only being vigilant about keeping you in his sight, but he was using you as cover...like a shield to protect him from other girls. It worked too. When Jeff left and I was able to come up for air for a while, I saw at least two girls make like they were gonna approach him and both times, he shifted directly behind you and closed the gap between the two of you. It gave the almost unmistakable impression that you guys were there together. When the girls saw that and read the message he was sending, they pretty much turned-tail and left."

"How do you *do* that?" I asked, seriously awed once more.

She laughed and put her sandals on. "I don't know. I guess it just comes easy because I've had more experience with this stuff and I've known both of them forever."

"Huh. So, *please* tell me this party isn't gonna be one with wall-to-wall human carpeting like last night...God, that was miserable," I pleaded. Really, it wasn't much fun and Tristan or no Tristan; I've yet to see the attraction to an event such as that.

"Yeah, I know…it really was. Some parties just end up like that, though. Especially the ones after a game because word spreads like wild fire and people from the opposing school inevitably show up, too. Tonight should be better...Mike is usually more selective in his guest list. There'll still be tons of people there, but his house is massive and if it's an indoor-outdoor thing, it won't seem so packed," Kate reassured me with a smile. "You look really pretty, Camie."

"Gee whiz, Kate, thanks. You look great too…I especially like your eyes. They look really fantastic tonight."

"Only because I'm wearing makeup…I *swear* I was born without eyelashes." She swept a big, fat blush brush over her cheeks, giving her fair skin a healthy looking glow. "You know, I wish I could get away with not wearing makeup all the time…it's such a pain."

"I wouldn't know…my parents don't think I need it."

"Well, they're right. Be grateful though, wearing this crap isn't always all it's cracked up to be." Kate then gave her overall appearance one more look in the mirror and finding it satisfactory, she snatched up her car keys and asked, "You ready to go?"

"Yeah, I guess I'm about as ready as I'll ever be…bring on the tinned fish!" I told her genially, trying to get my good sense of humor firmly back in place.

We got to Mike's and although finding a place to park was tricky with all the cars parked bumper to bumper on the long, winding driveway and along the street, I blew out a sigh of relief and mentally thanked God once we entered the house. Kate was right; this gathering was much more on the shindig scale I'd been hoping for. She wasn't kidding about Mike's house being massive either. I mean I thought her place is big, but his is *enormous*. Get this; he actually has his own freaking tennis courts—yeah, plural—a putting green, *and* a hedgerow maze out in the north forty of the backyard.

There were kids ranging all over the place, inside and out, but like Kate had said, the place is so big that you wouldn't notice if half of California were in attendance. Except, of course, when you have to use the bathroom. I learned that at last night's party and I guess it really doesn't matter if there're four available bathrooms or nine, the line will always be uncomfortably long.

Upon arriving, Kate and I went to the backyard to hang out with a tolerable sized group of our peers by a fire pit; one I'd no problem envisioning as the centerpiece of an authentic Hawaiian luau with a big pig being roast in the center. She and I were each sitting on one of the many, cushioned bamboo lounges, both of us listening to and participating in the animated talk going on around us, and we were both keeping an eye out for our men. They hadn't shown up yet and although Kate promised me they would be here, she was starting to have doubts. She kept checking her phone for the time or to see if she had any texts or missed calls. I think the main thing she's worried about right now is if Jeff's okay, so I was about to suggest that she just call him herself when she removed her phone from her back pocket again and took the words right out of my mouth.

"You know, I'm worried. I'm just gonna call him and see what's going on."

I considered getting in line for one of the bathrooms, thinking of it more as a preemptive strike because I didn't have to go yet. Instead, I chose to wait by my friend's side as she listened to "Dear Jeff's" phone ringing while she nervously bit her fingernails. She got his voicemail and left a message clearly stating that if he wasn't dead or dying, he'd better call her back pronto or he could kiss his free meals goodbye again.

"I'm sure he's okay, Kate." I put as much confidence behind my tone as I could. Truth is, though, anything could've happened and she's really starting to freak.

"I know. You're right. Okay, come on…I want a drink. I need to calm down or I'll make myself sick," she said, suddenly standing up and grabbing my hand to haul me out of my seat.

We made our way into the kitchen and while she pounded down two shots of some various kind of liquor, I took in my surroundings. The kitchen was as large and impressive as you would expect it to be in a house this size, but it was a cozy kitchen nook table situated in a corner that captured my attention. Seated all around it; six guys were playing what looked to be a game involving a quarter. For some unknown reason—maybe it's because the coin was so sparkly—I was completely enthralled and went to move closer to better observe what they were doing. However, just as I took maybe a step and a half away, Kate grabbed my arm and showed me that her phone was ringing. Because I didn't know what to say when she was obviously distraught by seeing Tristan's name on the caller ID instead of Jeff's; I took the phone from her and answered it.

"Tristan, what's wrong? Kate is totally frea—Oh! Jeff! Yeah, sh—"

Realizing it was Jeff on the other end, Kate yanked the phone from me and started lecturing her featherbrained boyfriend, who she's undeniably head over heels in love with. So as Kate went off on Jeff about how he needs to learn how to use a phone charger and that he could've called two hours ago to tell her they'd gotten a flat tire on the way home from the beach, I tapped her shoulder, informing her I was going to go to the bathroom. I figure I might as well, since I have time before my personal special someone—who knows how to use a phone charger, but just prefers to be uncommunicative—apparently won't be here for a while.

Aw, crap. This is *so* what I'd hoped to avoid having to endure tonight. I get in line for the bathroom and what do I hear? It's a sound so horrific it makes my stomach clench and I have to cover my mouth to keep from retching on bile...Teresa using foul words to excrete her toxic designs on Tristan. I'm really coming to hate her. She's standing next to Lisa and with just one other girl between us; I can hear everything coming out of her mouth. I'm seriously considering sticking my fingers in my ears and singing la-la-la-la to myself so I don't have to be subjected to her torture, because honestly, my temper's been particularly short lately and I'm afraid I might unleash verbal hell—or worse—on her. At least automotive difficulties are keeping Tristan incommunicado for the time being and maybe once he gets here, he'll find a safe place to hide.

Or, not...

I waited my turn, kept my mouth shut like a good girl, and by the time I got to the front of the line, I had to go. Perfect timing, if I do say so myself. Unfortunately, I can't say much for my timing on exiting the house after using the facilities. I'd just taken barely more than four steps out one of the sliding glass backdoors when, carrying a large pitcher of some kind of red punch and not paying attention to where he was going, a guy clipped the shoulder of a girl who was to my left so that the contents of the pitcher went flying to *completely* drench me. Adding salt to my margarita wound—okay, it isn't a pitcher of margaritas, but it's definitely boozy—is that this whole thing happened right in front of none other than the Trollop Triplets *and* Tristan. I could tell Tristan really wanted to be cracking up and was desperately trying to keep a straight face, but Teresa wasn't nearly as kind. The disparagingly-vapid-malicious-pestilent-bitch immediately pointed at me, first cackling and then, howling in savage laughter.

"*OH MY GOD!!* Hey everyone, *look*!! That's the funniest fucking thing I've ever seen! Sucks to be you!"

"I don't know if *I'd* say that."

If I weren't already so thoroughly stunned, Tristan's disarmingly purred words suddenly coming from *right* beside me would've made me jump out of my skin. My bones may have remained secure, but the look on Tristan's face *is* giving my nerves quite the work out. Plus, my palms are tingling so intensely; I wouldn't be surprised to look and see myself hooked up to electrodes. That being said, I felt his next turn of phrase in my toes...

"While I agree this might not be your best look, I bet you taste pretty good." His eyes locked on mine and, mesmerized, I watched them shift and change into a darker blue than I'd ever known eyes could be. Then—*holy crapolie*—you're *SO* not gonna believe what he did—he slowly ran his finger down my dripping nose, put said finger in his mouth, and sucked the punch stuff right off of it! "Yep...pretty tasty indeed."

OH MY GOD!!

That's all I got. I'm flabbergasted. I mean how am I supposed to react to this?

No really, I'm asking; I wanna know.

I couldn't breathe and my heart had decided it was done pumping so I was just standing there, looking like an asinine court jester who's dripping in alcoholic Hawaiian punch with my mouth slightly ajar, when that @$*& sashayed up way too far into Tristan's personal space. She put a hand on his chest in an attempt to take his focus off me and put it onto her, where she, for some unfathomable reason, thought it belonged. He tried to ignore her and was still looking at me; however, the bimbo was determined to make him notice her.

"Tristan! I'm *so* relieved you're finally here! I was starting to think you were gonna leave me *empty handed* all night, if you know what I mean..." She leaned further into him, oozing vulgarity while her hand intimately moved south, making me want to gag. Actually, I think I threw up a little in my mouth. "You know, you never called me, you naughty, naughty boy."

Yeah. She actually used the word "naughty." Twice. She should be banned from the use of language altogether.

Being that she was practically undulating against him, he was finally forced to look at her. I noticed his eyes lighten back to normal but they were flat, devoid of almost all life. And how she could possibly miss the sheer disdain he regarded with, I've not a clue, but I heard his scorn loud and clear.

"Nope. I sure didn't, did I? I *wonder* what that means..." Looking back at me, the derision began to fade from his expression. Tristan removed Teresa's contemptuous hand from him and then taking mine he said, "Camie, you're a fuckin' wreck, come on..." Then he tugged me insistently along behind him, leaving what's her name glowering behind us.

Hoping to see Kate or a familiar face for some direction, I looked around and discovered I was on my own. Well, not entirely on my own. Tristan, it seemed, was on a mission. Not stopping to chitchat or explain where he was taking me, he led me through the house, up the *Gone with the Wind* staircase, down an endless hallway and then stopped before a locked door. And by the way, I've just been blindly following him, hoping for the best…it vaguely feels like I'm a lamb being led to slaughter.

"Here, hold my cup."

Still holding my hand, making it feel like electric pulses are shooting into it from his, he handed me his cup and reached to the top of the doorframe for a key. I looked into his practically empty plastic cup and thought; if he wants a refill, I can just wring myself out over it. Then, unlocking the door, Tristan turned back to me. He took his cup and proceeded to open the door to a gratuitously huge bedroom…in which a gathering of six people were already occupying. Almost immediately a chorus of greetings to Tristan poured forth from the half-naked group playing cards in the middle of the enormous four-poster bed.

"Hey, you know you guys aren't supposed to be in here." To me it sounded like Tristan *might* have been a little put out.

"*You* shouldn't be either." The good-natured retort came from a guy who was down to his boxers.

"Come on, Tristan, why don't you guys hang with us? Wayne could use the backup…we've already beaten the pants off him and it isn't pretty…" A girl said, casually pulling her shirt off and tossing it on a pile of clothes in the middle of the bed, which left her able to wager her zebra striped bra, socks, jeans, and whatever she is, or, isn't wearing under them. I mean who the hell knows anymore!

The comment was barely out of her mouth, though, before the entire group started to snicker. It took me a minute to catch the smell, but when I did, all I could picture was a particular part of the movie *The Breakfast Club*. Even though it was a hilarious scene and might've *looked* like fun, I'm so not up for reenacting it. However, I'd swear Tristan's eyes sparked as he seemingly unconsciously smoothed his thumb over the side of my hand, giving my face a very brief speculative glance.

"Nah, we're good. Just passing through, but you know Mike's gonna have a shit attack if he finds out you guys are playin' strip poker and gettin' stoned in his parents' room." Tristan's rebuke was promptly and unexpectedly followed by tender concern. "Come on, Camie, over here. Let's get you cleaned up."

I just nodded in response; lost for words with the unforeseen compassion he's showing me. Not to mention I think the sensation of

Tristan's thumb lightly tracing absentminded circles on my hand is beginning to interfere with my cognitive abilities. Thankfully, my momentary ineptitude was limited to speech and I was able to follow along behind him without tripping or making a fool of myself in any other such way as he led me into a bathroom easily twice the size of my bedroom. He dropped my hand to open a cupboard and pull a towel out of it, and I would've thanked him for the towel, as well as for relinquishing my hand, thereby returning normal brain function to me, but...he didn't give me the damned towel. He just stood there, staring at me with a lopsided grin on his face.

"Jesus. Look at you, you're *really* a mess," he chuckled at me in the reflection of the mirror, the tender concern having almost completely vanished.

"Yeah, so I see. Are you gonna gimme that towel or just hold onto it a while longer while this Kool-Aid crap stains my hair?" Kate did tell me to be myself, right? I'm not irritated with him or anything—I really do look pretty damned funny—but the thing is, this is *the* most he's ever spoken to me where I've felt capable of responding, and I don't really know how else to be right now.

He chuckled again, turned the faucet of one of the sinks on and then to my surprise, he shoved my head under the running water.

"*Ack! Grlp!* That's cold!" I complained. Honestly though, I've no idea what the hell I have to complain about. I mean really, the guy I've been stalking for a week has his freaking hands in my hair. Who gives a crap if the water's cold?

"You sound like you're trying to cough up a fur ball, Camie... Would you stop squirming? Jungle Juice *will* stain your hair, so just hold still...lemme make sure it's all out."

I tried to do as I was told, but you try holding still when the guy of your dreams is gently massaging and caressing your scalp; his warm breath whispering down your neck, sending wave upon groundbreaking wave of unprecedented shivers to your toenails. Trust me, it's not so easy!

"Okay, there...you're done, you whiner." He draped the towel over my head unceremoniously, thus punctuating the end of his cosmetology career. Such the gentleman.

"Gee, thanks. Now I just get to walk around all night looking like I'm a front-runner in a wet t-shirt contest. That's perfect," I said with massive sarcasm, staring in the mirror at my disheveled appearance and the soaked shirt unrepentantly clinging to my body.

I'm thinking I shouldn't have called attention to myself that way, though. My palms started to tingle again and Tristan's eyes darkened almost immediately as he gave me the most deliciously wicked look, and then *he* moved way too far into *my* personal space. Of course, my heart chose this moment to make itself known to me again and I swear it feels like it's gonna jump out of my chest like in the movie *Alien,* which would not only be embarrassing, but really gross as well.

When what to my wondering eyes should appear, but the most exquisite sight *ever.* I say it this way because apparently my good-girl ways have finally gotten Santa's attention, and he's about to give me the top item on my depraved wish list!

Standing inches from me, Tristan crossed his arms in front of him, grabbing the hem of his shirt and pulling it off, all in one fell movement. Then he handed it to me and stood there like it was no big deal. My response to Santa's long overdue generosity? Well, naturally, I'm screaming in my head. *Holy Exalted Naked Chest Batman!!!*

Can we just pause here for a station identification break? I need to re-educate myself on how to breathe and somehow or another, I've *got* to pick my jaw up off the floor. I think while I'm down here, I'll pray and thank God for His glorious creation, because seriously, He does some damned *fine* work!! See, when I described Tristan for you on Monday, I honestly had *NO* idea that supremely well-fitted H_2O Polo shirt he wore hid all *this.* Really, OMG, because *he is ripped!!*

Not questioning his chivalry and being careful to not slip in the puddle of drool on the marble floor, I took the t-shirt, still warm from Tristan's body heat. When he just stood there, I twirled my finger and gave him a look, reminding him that gentlemanly etiquette dictates that he should turn his back now. He laughed again while he turned around, allowing me to strip my Jungle Juiced shirt from myself and shrug into his while maintaining at least *some* semblance of modesty.

Although now here's the tricky part; my bra soaked up enough of this stuff to make putting a dry shirt on an exercise in futility, so, it's gotta come off. However, I'm really hoping the fire is still going when we get back to where the party proper is taking place because if it's not…well, with my hair still being wet and the goose bumps Tristan gave me still riding high, I'm gonna look like an idiot with my arms crossed over my chest all evening. The alternative to which is being known from here on out as the Nippley New Girl; a moniker I think I can live without. So while taking a quick moment to study the beautiful and beyond well-muscled specimen whose back is reflected in the mirror, I went through the contortionist act of taking my bra off through the sleeves of Tristan's shirt, then I rolled it into mine, essentially hiding the evidence.

"Okay, I'm done. Thanks for letting me borrow your shirt…I'll give it back on Monday." I don't know why I'm able to do this, but I'm *so* happy I can speak coherently to him and not sound like all I can think about is riding him piggyback through the house. You'd understand the inclination if you were here. He's got a *really* amazing back…

"Just keep it." He meant it to be an offer, although it sounded suspiciously like a command to me.

"Oh. Um, okay, but won't you eventually want it?" I asked, kind of taken aback at the offer of what I'm going to think of as my first engagement present from him.

"It's not a big deal, Camie, it's just an old t-shirt. Look, it's got holes everywhere too." He showed me some minor signs of long-time wear and tear in the fabric, and then he scooped up my wet clothing. "Come on, let's get a bag for this and go back to the party."

He took my hand and pulled me behind him once again, and as I surreptitiously held my breath and politely averted my eyes from the poker game, we left the same way we'd come. This time however, we trekked through the house and into the kitchen where the guys were still playing that game.

Mike looked up from the table. "Tristan, dude…why don't you put some clothes on?"

"Mike, dude…why don't you bite me?" Tristan flippantly answered. It's a good thing he didn't extend the invitation to me; I probably would've.

"Whatever, but don't come cryin' to me when you cause a fuckin' female riot walkin' around like that. I'm just sayin'…"

Ha! I could totally see that happening! Like I said, God does good work and I'm sure I'm not the only girl here who'd acknowledge that fact. The look of understanding that shot across Tristan's face, though, was priceless. I had to work to keep my giggle from escaping when I barely heard him mutter under his breath something like "That'd be a fuckin' nightmare."

"Hey, where does your mom keep empty grocery bags?" My bare chested Adonis asked.

"Under the sink in the butler's pantry. Hey, you wanna play?"

I really wish Kate or Melissa were here to witness, because when Mike asked that, one of the other guys looked up from the game and noticing me for the first time I think, he took a good look at me and then his eyes flashed to Tristan. To me, Tristan's face looked unreadable, but I swear there was some kind of silent communication going on. And who was the guy? Uh-huh…none other than Pete.

Not having any idea what to make of that and trying to act as normal as possible while holding Tristan's hand and considering what the ramifications might be if I were to spontaneously nibble on him, I glanced around the table and noticing that most of the guys were still playing, I became curious again. "Yeah, can I?"

Mike stood up and grandly gestured to the table. Thus I found myself squeezing in between him and Pete, thinking to myself; drat! I didn't take into account I wouldn't be able to hold Tristan's hand anymore if I'm playing some stupid game. Seriously, *ugh.* Anyway, as I got settled, Tristan folded his arms and stood there. Silently and contemplatively, he drummed the fingers of the strong hand gripping his flexed bicep as he looked over the table and the rest of the game participants.

"O Captain My Captain, get her a drink," Mike commanded and then proceeded to explain the rules of the game to me. I'm guessing the reason for Mike addressing Tristan like that is because Tristan is the Varsity captain of both the water polo team and the swim team, although, Mike is only on the swim team, but...whatever.

Tristan grunted but walked over to the counter where rows of bottles and pitchers were lined up and did as our host bid. When he returned with my drink and handed it to me, I looked at the red punch crap. "So what's in this tasty concoction that almost ruined my hair and might've potentially made my clothes look like bad tie-dye?" I'm honestly kind of curious because from what I tasted of it when it was so unceremoniously bestowed upon my person, it's pretty yummy.

"I told you it's good. The main ingredients are coconut rum, vodka, and either a fruit punch, or juice. You got the much-evil (Hey!! I say "much-evil"!!) Kool-Aid blend and I'd say your shirt's new destiny is being part of a hippie costume on Halloween," Tristan told me as he pulled his keys out of the back pocket of his jeans—lucky keys. Then, more to Pete than to me or anyone else, he said, "Okay, I'll be back."

And with that Terminator-esque declaration, he left, taking his magnificent naked chest with him, and leaving me to my own devices with a group of six guys, booze, and a quarter.

Turns out, I'm a whiz at drinking games. When Tristan returned about forty-five minutes later, sadly with more apparel than when he'd left, the game was breaking up. I was only made to drink a few times, but because I'd managed to sink very nearly every quarter, the majority of players were now too soused to continue. I'm very proud of myself. Tristan nodded his approval as well and extricated me from the table. He shared another look with Pete and then, not holding my hand anymore, much to my hearty disappointment, he led me back out to the fire.

We joined Kate and Jeff who were curled up all cozy-like in a lounge chair, in addition to the several other people who were partaking of the warm evening air and pleasantly informal ambience the fire and patio furnishings helped to create. Kate was just taking a sip of her drink when she saw me and practically choked on it.

"*Where* have you been?" She asked, her tone registering more shock than concern. She *had* been worried, I can tell, but apparently my appearance is suggestive of really bad grooming habits. I mean I know I don't look my best after my Jungle Juice shower, but jeez, thanks for the reminder.

"Oh, I was doused with a pitcher of this fruity pirate beverage, so once I got semi-presentable again, I learned a new game in the kitchen," I explained, holding up my cup and souvenir quarter as evidence of both.

Tristan started laughing. "She totally wiped the floor with Mike, Pete, and the rest of those guys...Conner was passed out with his face on the table...it was beautiful!"

"Really?!" Jeff asked with what I think was mild disbelief.

"Yeah, man, really...we should get her in the next beer-pong tourney and bet heavy...she'd kick ass." What an incredibly sweet thing to say! I love him.

Kate was eyeing me, but Jeff started laughing. "That's fuckin' awesome...way to go, Camie!"

"Aw, thanks." My eyes landed on my arch nemesis and my smile at Jeff's genuine compliment faded. "*Ugh.* I *hate* her."

"Who?" Jeff asked.

"*Her,*" I said with menace and pointed to where she was standing.

Jeff looked around, but didn't get it so again he asked, "*Who?*"

"Teresa. You know, of the 'We Hate Teresa Club, of which I am the treasurer,'" Tristan said with a crooked grin.

Hold the freaking phone!

Now seriously, let me just re-play what he said to make sure I didn't imagine it...

HOLY SCHNIKES!! Not my imagination!

I must've had the most utterly shocked expression on my face because the three of them were looking at me like I might've been offended, or ready to be committed. Then Tristan asked, "What? She's a piece of low-grade ass and a simpering bitch on top of that. I thought you were our newest member..."

"*You* watch Buffy," I accused the person with whom I'm now positive I'm meant to spend the rest of eternity. Seriously, that Buffy quote was like a sign from The Big Man upstairs Himself. Not to mention that Tristan used the word simpering and, I'm pretty sure the piece of low-grade ass comment is a quote from the movie *Pretty In Pink.* If so, all of that adds up to the trifecta of MFEO signs.

"How do you know that?" My mate for life asked.

"The 'We Hate Teresa Club, of which you are the treasurer?'" I replied grandly.

"Oh. Huh. I guess I did say that, didn't I? My mom still watches it," he said in answer, as if he was trying to say that he didn't know full well he'd been quoting the show.

I'm not buying it though. No way would someone be able to throw a word-for-word quote out there like that without being a fan. Of course, he replaced Cordelia's name with Teresa's, but still.

The night progressed and although Tristan didn't pay much attention to me after that, he essentially stayed in the group by the fire, and unlike last night's, I found that this kind of party is actually a lot of fun. I socialized and was pleased to discover that I'm getting better at it. I'm also becoming more comfortable with the "in" crowd now, too. Like I belonged with them, I laughed with everyone when Conner was dragged out of the house and thrown in the pool. He also had a Sharpie marker mustache. I filed the scene away in my memory banks as fair warning to never pass out at a shindig like this. Not that I plan on passing out, but you know, one can never be too careful and I don't think a mustache—Sharpie or otherwise—would be all that flattering on me.

It was over before I knew it, though, and a guy named Ian had just finished with an impressive demonstration of talent by touching his tongue to his own elbow when my phone started to vibrate, telling me it was time to think about leaving. "Crap."

"What's wrong?" Kate asked.

"I've gotta get home, it's almost midnight and, no offense, you've been drinking so I need to either find a ride home or call my dad." I don't care if she's been drinking, but Kate is a far cry from *Je*sus so I don't think I should push my luck with this.

"Oh yeah. I'm sorry, Camie, I didn't even think about that…" She apologized sincerely.

"Don't worry about it, it's not a big deal, I just really don't wanna call my dad, so… Hey! Who here is one hundred percent sober and can gimme a ride home?" I hollered to the group at large.

I sighed when everyone just stared at me as if to say, "Duh, none of us is one hundred percent sober." I was about to pull my phone out to call my dad when, having waited until there were no other offers, Tristan raised his hand, indicating he fit the criteria. I'm thinking, yeah right, buddy. As much as I'd love nothing more than to entrap myself with you in your car, I've watched you down at least a half-gallon of Pirate Punch tonight. And yeah, I know Tristan said it's called Jungle Juice, but ever since I was told there's rum in it, I keep thinking about Johnny Depp as Captain Jack Sparrow so I'm just gonna call it Pirate Punch from here on out.

Anyhow, my reluctance to believe him must've been evident in my expression because he handed his cup to me and said, "Drink it…I'm stone-cold sober."

Okay, now you need to understand this is the closest I've ever come to swapping spit with a guy, so I'm kind of excited… Wanting to get as much of Tristan's DNA in my system as possible without looking like a lush, I took a bigger sip than I needed to and realized with a start that it was just plain old cherry Kool-Aid. I downed the rest of it just for funsies and asked, "This is all you've been drinking?"

"Yep. I haven't had a single drop of alcohol all night. Wait. I take that back… If I remember correctly, I'm guilty of having a *few* drops, but still. Do you want a ride home or not?" He asked like he could care less if he drove me home, but when he'd reminded me about the whole finger sucking thing, his tone had been far from ambivalent and his eyes twinkled.

"Uh, yeah, thanks…that'd be great. I really don't wanna have to call home," I said, accepting his offer of being alone in an enclosed space with him for probably at least ten minutes, maybe even fifteen depending on how fast he drives.

"Alright then, let's go. See you guys later," Tristan said first to me and then to the rest of the group as he turned and removed those fortunate keys from his pocket once more.

I should probably take this time to mention that when I started to follow him, I turned around to say goodbye to everyone and tell Kate I'd talk to her later, and in doing so, my eyes caught sight of Teresa shooting daggers at me. I chose to ignore her along with the dark, malevolent laugh that was trying to free itself from my mind by escaping through my mouth. Instead, I finished with my goodbyes and turned back around to realize I'd lost Tristan.

I started looking around for my blessedly beautiful, sober ride home and was just about to throw my hands in the air in defeat when I heard a sharp whistle and my name being called. I peered into the shadows to my left and sure enough, Tristan was standing a ways away holding a gate open. As my eyes adjusted to the dark, I made my way over to him, dodging people and their plastic cups of Pirate Punch as I did. I giggled to myself when Tristan tapped his watch impatiently and mouthed the words "Let's go."

I finally reached him and raised my eyebrows in mock exasperation. "Well? What are you waiting for? Time's a wastin', speedy, let's go!"

He rolled his eyes and on a chuckle he asked, "What the hell were you doing?"

"I was saying goodbye to everyone!" I responded, slightly indignant, and followed him out the gate and down the lengthy, cobblestone path to the front of the house.

"You're such a girl."

Well noted, Captain Obvious. "Are you accusing me or just now noticing?"

He stopped to look at me and gave me cocky half-smile and an answer, both of which had my heart going pitter-patter. "Camie, I'm not blind." Then he reached for my hand and said, "Come on, it's almost midnight. I don't wanna speed to get you home on time."

Hand-in-hand again, I stopped trying to understand why his touch seems to bring my skin and senses alive and just accepted it, giving myself up to the simple enjoyment of the feeling. Thus, we ambled down the street and the long line of parked cars in companionable silence. Our progress slowed and then halted upon reaching a jet black, '68 Chevy Chevelle. I mentally smiled to myself in appreciation, thinking how much my dad and Jillian would *luuuv* his car. And being that I'm sorta familiar with muscle cars of its stature, I'd be willing to bet that it's not only demonically fast, but that it's ungodly loud, too. Then I noticed the license plate; it reads H2OZLIF.

"Water is life, Camie." The words seemed to float in the warm breeze before they settled around me like an embrace, lovingly affirming what I now recognize to be a deep-seeded belief.

Sensing a shift in the previously affable atmosphere and becoming somewhat thoughtful, I stood back while Tristan unlocked the passenger door for me and agreed with him. "It's true…especially when you consider that without it, we die."

He looked at me pensively for a moment, his face barely illuminated by the sparse streetlights. Then he made a minute gesture to the open door for me to get in. I did, feeling as though that in this one simple, reflective moment of time, we communicated more to each other than we had in all the interactions we've had since Monday. And I can't say for sure, but it honestly felt like we'd forged a connection, the level of which I never even knew existed.

Tristan closed my door and rather than immediately going around the other side to get in, he turned his back to me and the car, slid his hands deep inside his pockets and was still. Wholly captured by the sight, I watched him through the window next to me. The moments stretched out as he simply stared up at the clear night sky and the sliver of moon it held. When Tristan finally got in, he looked over at me with a wry, "go figure" tilt to his mouth. Then with a quiet *"Humph,"* he shook his head and started the engine, producing a rumble I not only appreciated, but also felt in my bones—one that comes from the unparalleled power of over 200 harnessed horses pawing the ground and chomping at the bit to be released onto the streets.

"Is something wrong?" I asked, not knowing why he'd gotten so "dreamy" out there or what that look was about, or, in fact, how to take any of it. I was second-guessing myself, as I oftentimes do, wondering if I'd just mistakenly read whatever might be growing between us to be more than what it is.

"No...not wrong. It's just...no one's ever understood it that way before." He sounded almost gratified. Then, adjusting the rearview mirror and looking out the windshield, Tristan quietly asked, "So, where do we go from here?"

The optimist in me thought it sounded like he could've been asking about us in a figurative way and I felt like saying, "I don't care where we go as long I'm with you." My inner realist told him where I live instead.

Aside from that inexplicable feeling that something is happening between us, I don't have anything else to report about Tristan driving me home because basically, nothing happened. We exchanged a *little* small talk, but honestly, that was pretty much it.

When he pulled up in front of my house, I thanked him and gave him a small, but sincere smile, to which he replied with a speaking glance and a short "Yep." As far as goodbyes go, it clearly wasn't much in the way of validating the possible feelings he might have, nor was it all that significant of an interaction. Although, it does seem like we've made some kind of progress. And I'm getting the feeling that if I'm expecting Tristan to be the kind of guy who makes grand gestures and eloquent speeches fraught with meaningful expression, I'll be sorely disappointed. He did, however, wait for me to get all the way inside my house before driving away, proving he does have at least *some* real gentleman-like qualities, for which I'm grateful.

So, overall, I'd say tonight definitely qualifies as a step in the right direction...

8.

A Serious Waste Of Good Lip-gloss

I did a lot of mental reviewing of Saturday night as I spent most of Sunday trying to get in touch with Kate to compare notes and kept getting her voicemail. So, it was with great excitement that I was waiting on my front porch for her to pick me up for school Monday morning. Even though she wasn't present for any of my cardiac arrest moments, I'm sure she'll be able to make *something* out of what I tell her. Besides...even though I've been giving all the dirt to Jillian, I still really want to share all this with my new best friend.

"Camie! I'm *so* sorry I didn't call you yesterday!! I got tossed in the pool after you left the party and my phone got destroyed...second time this year that's happened too. I really should memorize some numbers just in case, huh?" Kate explained with an excited curiosity evident in both her face and voice.

"Please, don't worry about it... Well? I know you're dying, so, go ahead!" I gave her a big grin.

"Oh my God, Camie! I thought I was gonna die when you guys showed up together!! You have *gotta* tell me how that happened! And he drove you home! Did he kiss you?! And how the hell did you end up in his shirt?! Details, now!!" Kate demanded, practically hopping up and down in her seat as we drove to school.

"Alas, there was no smooching to be had..." I told her and proceeded to relay all that she'd missed.

On finishing my re-play for her, we arrived at school. Kate turned the car off and then turned to stare at my face with surprise. "Clarify something...he told you to actually keep *that* shirt?"

"Yeah. I told him I'd return it today and he said, 'just keep it,' exactly like that. Why?" I'm a little confused again. She seems to think my new lingerie is of major importance for some reason. And just so you know, it smells like him so I'm never going to wash it.

"Oh Camie... I think you have him hooked! Two things about what the shirt means...one, parading you all over the house and backyard the way he did while you were in *that* shirt all night was like marking his territory. I mean, Camie, did you actually look at the shirt?" She asked me seriously.

"Uh, yeah…I guess. It's an old swim team shirt…it's a little frayed here and there and has a few small holes in it. What's the big deal?" I'm really not getting the extreme gravity about it. I mean, yes, water and therefore anything to do with it is obviously really important to him, but like he said…it's just an old shirt.

"Camie, that shirt…wow…that shirt is like one of his absolute favorite possessions. He got it when he made the Varsity team our freshman year *before* we even graduated junior high. He was pretty proud of himself for that and it's all torn up because he wears it *a lot.* It really doesn't even fit him anymore, but he still wears it on weekends. Jeez, I really didn't expect that. I mean, I know exactly what he was doing by having you wear it in front of everyone, but he actually gave you one hell of a freaking souvenir!" Kate said, shaking her head in astonishment.

"Oh. I had no idea… Um, explain what you meant about marking his territory though, does everyone know how much he loves it or something? Because that might explain the looks going on back and forth between him and Pete. Oh and I wanted to know what you think about why his eyes change color," I said kind of stunned. I don't know what to say about this…I really don't.

"His eyes change color?"

I nodded. "Yeah, not from blue to brown or anything crazy like that, but different shades of blue…I saw them do it a few different times Saturday night and thought it might be the lighting but I really don't think that's it."

"Huh. I don't think I've ever really noticed that before...I mean I guess they tend to kinda sparkle when he's in a good mood, but other than that, I haven't seen a color change. Then again, I don't spend a lot of time gazing into my boyfriend's best friend's eyes."

"I totally get that. I, on the other hand, was definitely doing a lot of gazing."

"I bet," she said and giggled at me. "Anyway, back to the shirt…no, not everyone knows how attached he is to it, that's kinda just something that people really close to him would know, like me, Jeff, probably Pete and maybe Mike, but it doesn't really matter how many people know how much he loves it. The other very distinguishing feature of that shirt, which you neglected to mention in your description, is that it's got his *name* written in bold lettering on it, which *everyone* would've seen.

"Regardless of *how* you came to be in it, everyone at that party saw you *with* him and *wearing* his freaking shirt! He's not stupid, Camie, he knows how fast rumors spread in this school and if he wanted to keep quiet about being interested, then he would've given you the shirt he had in his car."

That was a really funny shirt, too. It reads, "An awkward morning is better than a boring night." I wonder if it's a personal motto.

"Did you notice that he didn't stay quite so close to you and even left a few times when you were at the fire pit?" She's in almost as good a form as she was on my first day, don't you think?

"Of course. I just thought he was going back to being his standoffish self though."

Kate giggled for a moment and then said, "I'm not laughing at you Camie, honestly. It's just that he's really good at manipulation, that's all. Instead of having you physically close to protect him, he let the fact that you were in what was obviously his clothing do the job, which freed him up to move around more. Plus, it meant he didn't really need to worry about most of the guys there hitting on you while he wasn't around.

"That's what I think the silent communication between him and Pete was about too. They're really pretty tight and Tristan wouldn't worry about Pete or Mike at all, but some of the other guys, like Conner for example, might not have had the good sense to leave you alone in Tristan's absence. Even though I wasn't there to see it, I think he was telling Pete to look out for you for him. Man, when your cousin said he was a calculating opponent, he sure hit the nail on the head!"

"Huh. I remember thinking that Conner was being *kinda* flirtatious, but I really didn't think anything of it. I just figured he's like that and he was being friendly. Do you think that's why Pete kept making him drink every time he sank a quarter?" I asked, feeling like maybe I wasn't so bad at observing details as I'd originally thought.

"Probably. Conner's really an okay guy, but his girlfriend just dumped him. After I got off the phone with Jeff, I overheard him talking about wanting to get trashed and then go after the first cute girl he saw, so if Pete could get Conner blitzed enough to pass out, then problem solved. Well…you know what all of this means, right?" Kate asked.

"Uh-uh, what?" I might be getting better at the observing part, but I still don't know how to put any of it together.

"You could say Tristan's decided to go somewhat public. He chose a slightly more selective venue to do it in, but word will still spread. I wonder how long it'll be before he decides to let you in on it. I don't want you to get your hopes up, because this could still take some time depending on the opportunities he's presented with and how, or even *if* he chooses to take advantage of them.

"I wouldn't expect him to show any interest whatsoever at school yet and that's ultimately what we want. People are pretty used to him having minor escapades that aren't at all serious, so a few parties won't mean much and he might be more inclined to stake a claim out of the public eye.

However, if he develops a *pattern* outside of school…well, that's really the next best thing to checkmate so to speak. It won't be exactly what we want, but it might be the best we can get. I don't know if he'll be willing to enter into an actual commitment," Kate said in all truthfulness.

I know she's worried about me slipping back into my "Bizarro Camie" persona, so I'm going to try really hard to adopt some patience…especially for Kate because I just adore her. "I hear the warning and I'm gonna try to not let the time thing bug me. I'm still just so tickled that he essentially told Teresa off the *way* he did. He was like my knight in shining armor. I didn't have to do or say a thing…honestly Kate, I wish you would've been where you could've seen it."

Giggling, we got out of her car and had barely made it out of the parking lot when the warning bell rang. We looked at each other and took off running. Apparently we'd completely lost track of the time and I now had a good-sized head start on getting my first tardy slip.

You know, let me just say something here; it's not that easy to keep yourself positive and upbeat when circumstances conspire against you. Kate and I had to go to the office for our late slips and since I was already late and still needed to get my math book, I made a frenzied stop at my locker on the way to class. I was in such a hurry, though, I didn't realize my locker had been painted recently. Really recently. I threw myself down on my chair in geometry and when I pulled my supplies out to put them on my desk, I noticed I had paint all over my hands and forearms. Yeah, and it gets better; my teacher passed out last week's pop quizzes. You can imagine that I'm less than pleased with my C- grade.

It didn't look like things were going to improve much as the day moved on either. Michele was absent which left no one for me to really talk to in class, and during the break, both Kate and Melissa were missing, too. As I suspected and even somewhat expected, there's a new buzz floating around school that I'm pretty sure pertains to me, but of course, no one's gonna actually *say* anything to me about it. And I couldn't very well ask anyone in my classes because almost all the people I've been hanging around with are juniors and seniors, and aside from Michele and a few kids in P.E., I really don't know many of the kids in the sophomore class yet.

Also, I've bestowed the title "Bane of My Existence" upon Teresa. During third period, which unfortunately I share with her, and the break right after that, Teresa spent most of her time talking about Tristan with her so very pedestrian grasp of the English language and at the same time, whispering about me behind my back to anyone who'd listen to her. I'm guessing she's informing everyone she can get her claws on about my drink disaster Saturday night. I'm assuming that's what she was doing because she'd cup her hands to cover her mouth and lean in close to a kid and then they'd both look at me and start laughing. Her look has become more nefarious than dirty now, too.

Anyhow, when I showed up to English, Tristan and Jeff were, of course, already there and occupying what I've now come to accept as their traditional cushions. Kate walked in seconds behind me and we both plopped down next to each other. She turned to say something to me and then frowned at my hair like it was offensive in some way.

"What?" Is what I actually said, but I was thinking something along the lines of "It's not like you haven't seen my hair before, Kate! What did it ever do to you? Jeez!"

She reached to touch a piece of my hair. "What *is* that?"

That had the guys turn their attention to our conversation and, naturally because it's just been that kind of day for me, Tristan popped off with, "Jesus, every time I see you, you have some kind of shit in your hair."

"*What?*" I asked a little offended and totally bewildered.

"It looks like paint. How the hell did you get *paint* in your hair?" Kate asked as she scratched at a strand, trying to get it out for me.

"Oh, you have *got* to be kidding me." I pulled a piece of my hair in front of my eyes so I could see. Sure enough, there's paint in my hair and it's the exact same shade as my locker. "Well, that's just swell. So, you know what? This means I've been walking around with paint in my hair *all damned day*! My locker was re-painted and I didn't notice it was wet this morning because I was in such a hurry, remember? I got it all over my hands and arms too," I explained while looking over my clothes to see if I'd missed any other embarrassing patches. Then something occurred to me. "*Aargh!* When are elections for the We Hate Teresa Club? Because I wanna run for freaking president!!"

Jeff's eyes shot to Tristan and then back to me. "You think *Teresa* painted your locker?"

"No. She's just been in rare form today and I thought she'd just been telling half the world about my volcanic ensemble Saturday night, but I was unaware I'd been providing more fodder for her insipid recreational sport," I answered and then crossed my arms over my chest in a huff. Oh, just so you know, on Sunday I watched *Pretty In Pink*—from which I got that witty little dig on my shirt—and I was right...Tristan quoted Steff so my trifecta is indeed quantified.

"Why do you care what Teresa and a bunch of stupid sophomores think?" Jeff asked stupidly.

"*I'M* a sophomore, you *blithering ninny*!!" I said angrily and scrambled across Kate to whack him upside the head a couple of times and punch his shoulder.

"*Ow!* Jesus, I forgot...I'm sorry. Man, you're pretty strong for a girl."

I smacked him a couple more times for that comment, meanwhile, both Kate and Tristan were cracking up at the hole Jeff was digging for himself. He really does mean well; it just doesn't always come across the right way. After physically venting on Jeff, I sat back down on my pillow and decided to get over my irritation with his incentive remarks.

"I'm sorry. I have a *bit* of a temper and she's been pushing it since my first day."

Tristan broke from his laughter to say, "A *bit*? Remind me not to piss you off!" Then he started laughing again and while wiping at his tears, he looked at Jeff. "Sorry man, but that was damned funny!"

Kate, Melissa, and I spent lunch looking like monkeys. They had me seated on the stage a step below them while they scraped and scratched as much of the paint out of my hair as they could. Melissa hadn't been at Mike's party because she'd been obligated to help her parents with a formal dinner party they were hosting, but through the grapevine she'd heard about the punch being spilled on "some girl" and then also, about me wearing Tristan's shirt. It's interesting...there's still a buzz going on with the upperclassmen but it's much more subtle. I'm not really sure why that is, but I'm kind of grateful I belong to this group rather than where my grade level would rightfully place me. The only problem I can see with that is; what am I gonna do when they all graduate and leave me behind?

The following day Michele was back in school and I learned something from her that *really* pissed me off. From what she said, Teresa *did* have something to do with why my locker had wet paint on it. Michele had overheard Teresa in the girls' locker room pouting about how her vandalism was never seen by anyone else in school. Apparently, she and her two I'm with Stupid gal pals had snuck onto campus in the early hours of Monday morning and used permanent marker to write on my locker what I can only imagine were tasteless things about me. She'd been complaining that they shouldn't have gone back home afterwards because then they could've just re-vandalized it before school started. Here's where she's lucky; I'm not about to get into some immature war with her even though I'll applaud anyone else who beats her to the ground.

After English, I shared my new intelligence with Kate and Melissa on our way to lunch and they both had looks of disgust on their faces by the time I finished my tale. They consoled me by saying they hadn't heard a peep about it, so chances are no one had seen what was written and the whole thing would most likely just blow over.

However, I was still fuming on Friday when I arrived at Derek's school with my family for the football game my school was playing against his. My mom was feeling pretty good and wanted to go, so I decided to ride with them and then knowing I probably shouldn't sit with Derek again, not only that, but it wouldn't do me any good to be on the other side of the field, I figured I'd find one of my new safe acquaintances to sit with. We were just getting out of the car when the Trollop Triplets pulled up and parked several spaces away from us.

"Jill, that's Teresa," I whispered to my sister, to whom I'd confided my serious loathing of Teresa.

"Which one?" She asked, intently looking over the three girls.

"The one getting out of the passenger seat."

"Is that…? No. Oh, for the love of God, that's just crude…have at least *some* self-respect! Why does she think anyone needs to see she's wearing a thong? What a serious waste of good lip-gloss," Jillian ranted when her eyes picked up the unmistakable sight of a red lacey thong riding high above the waist of Teresa's low-rise short-shorts, which also showed more of her butt cheeks than I'll ever care to see. Her too short and too tight tank top didn't help.

"Classy, isn't she?" I agreed as we continued walking out of the parking lot.

"Who's the guy that drove her?" She asked as she studied the foursome in front of us.

"Her brother, Mark. He's a senior and that's how she gets to all the parties, too. I don't know him more than to know what his name is though. Oh, wait. You know what, that's not true. He's a jerk. I forgot, but Kate told me he's the guy who made that rude comment when Paul fell my first day."

On hearing that, Jillian let loose a disgruntled "*Humph.*" She's not a big fan of people who pick on those who are weaker than them.

We got to the field and parted ways. Jillian went to sit with Derek and a few of his friends, who were totally cool with having a kid sit with them, and I walked with my parents to the guest side, totally trying to avoid catching any glimpse of the Norsemen's cheerleaders. Once there, I left my mom and dad and located a few people to watch the game with. I ended up sitting with Mike, his girlfriend Kristen, Pete, and a guy named Justin. They all welcomed me and the whole event was very comfortable.

The Dynamic Duo didn't make an appearance at the game, but that's okay. I had a good time with the people I was with, Mike especially. He's got kind of a wry sense of humor, but he always says what's on his mind and I can appreciate that. Pete was still relatively quiet and actually, he ended up taking off before halftime, presumably to get things set for the party he was to have after the game. Which was actually sort of exciting.

Both teams had done such a good job of keeping each other out of the end zone that the score was 0-0 until like the last fifteen seconds of the game. Keith set up the offensive line like they were going to go for a field goal, but instead of positioning the ball for the kicker after the hike, he made a blind lateral pass which was caught and then ran in for a touchdown, making it impossible for Derek's school to even the score in the game's remaining few seconds. When the excitement was over, I met up with Kate and Melissa and then the three of us fell in with the rest of the crowd walking back to the parking lot.

"Camie, do you have all your stuff for tonight?" Kate asked, making sure I was packed and good to go for the sleepover Melissa and I were having at her house.

"Yeah, it's all here," I replied, holding my bag up.

"What is all *this* commotion about?" Melissa asked as we approached a group of people hovering around a car in the lot. "Wait for me, I wanna see what this is about."

She jogged over to where the "commotion" was taking place and then disappeared amongst a couple dozen kids as she squeezed in to join them. She came running up to Kate's car about five minutes later, laughing hysterically.

"Oh my God! You guys won't believe what I just saw! Mark Austin's car…oh oh!"

"Okay Melissa, get a hold of yourself. Spit it out." Kate put her hands on Melissa's shoulders in an attempt to calm her laughter. Her mascara was starting to run because of the tears streaming down her cheeks and Kate gave me a look that said, "See? Makeup is a pain."

"All the tires were taken off and one was put in each of the seats…buckled up!! And there's black stuff like shoe polish or something on the windshield that says…that says…" She promptly burst into another lengthy gale of laughter, one that lasted some minutes before she could finish. "It says, 'FYI, I'm not contagious anymore, the rash is almost gone, so the ointment is working' Oh, I'm dying…I can't breathe!"

Wiping at her face, Melissa dragged us over to see the carnage for ourselves and we in turn laughed about it the whole way to Pete's house for his party. It's kind of poetic, don't you think? And yes, it *could* be a coincidence, but I'm going to text Derek right now to ask about my little sister's whereabouts during the game just in case.

9.

An Open Invitation To Take My Clothes Off

Thanks to the vandalism and people choosing to loiter in the parking lot to look at and/or share it with the world via Facebook, we got to Pete's before a ton of other people did, which was kind of nice. I'd found out shortly after that first party I went to that aside from a special occasion here and there, Melissa doesn't drink. That being the case, she'd offered to be designated driver tonight. In turn that meant Kate was free to indulge, and because I wasn't going home tonight, I decided to join her. I'm not planning on going nuts, but I figure I can let my hair down a little bit. I mean, I seriously doubt having a couple of beers at a party is going to be a bury-able event, you know?

We were sitting in Pete's kitchen playing the quarter game again and although I was still more than pleased with my skills, the others were playing pretty well, too. By the time my fiancé showed up an hour and a half later, I was a good ways done with my third beer. And you know what? I actually felt fine. I can't imagine how much of this stuff kids have to consume to wind up behaving like out of control lunatics, but, it must be a lot.

Kate and I abandoned the game when the guys showed up and we went to socialize outside with them and the rest of the raucous partygoers. There were several other events taking place so there weren't as many people as there'd been at that first party or at Mike's and because of that, the environment was more—for lack of a better word—intimate. Although that really doesn't describe it well. People were catapulting themselves off the roof of the small-ish guesthouse into the pool and someone; I actually think Pete himself is responsible for this, put Mr. Bubble in the hot tub. It seemed like Tristan was acting kind of wishy-washy and, of course I could be way off base about this, I got the feeling he was vacillating between wanting to pay attention to me, finding another girl to play with, or hiding. I gotta say, it's a little annoying.

God, Fate, Destiny...whatever you want to attribute what happened next to, forced him to make a decision—at least for a time.

I'd gotten kinda warm so I'd taken my hoodie off and left it, along with my cell phone, on a lounge chair by the pool. The four of us were standing amongst a larger group of people; I had my back to the pool, and even though he wasn't really paying attention to me or even facing me for that matter, Tristan was on one side of me, Jeff was on the other, and Kate was opposite us, making it like a little clique within a clique.

"Hey Camie, you have a text," Kate said, hearing my general text ringtone which just so happens to be the song "Please Mr. Postman" by The Marvelettes.

"Oh, who is it?" I asked.

"It's from Derek."

All of a sudden, Tristan went rigid, almost like he was on full alert. A sinister laugh echoed in my head as having forgotten all about the question I'd asked Derek earlier, I suddenly realized the potential promise this opportunity held before me...if I dared take it. I mean why not? Let's do a little experiment, shall we?

I mentally crossed my fingers. "Read it, what's his answer?"

She giggled and then said, "It says 'Yes. 30 min or so. Luv u shark bait.' Does that make sense to you?"

"Yes." With a huge grin, I watched Kate put my phone back in my sweatshirt pocket and tried my absolute best not to give anything away.

God, I so love my cryptic cousin!! You see, the question I'd asked went something like this; did Jillian disappear during the game, and if so, for how long? However, Derek's answer wasn't quite the most informational text in the world, and it could've easily been misconstrued by someone who might think my cousin and I have a thing going. Especially when you add in the ringtone, which is pretty much a doo-wop love song. I just happen to find it funny as a ringtone for text messages. And I just love the term of endearment he used for me, don't you? Not to mention he threw in the "I love you" part which just makes it so much more intriguing.

Just when I was being questioned about the meaning by both Jeff *and* Tristan—intriguing in itself—a couple of other party attendants tried to walk through the narrow space between the guys, Kate, and myself. They bumped into Tristan first, then when they turned around to apologize to him, their shoulders shoved me and I was forced to take a few steps backwards, placing my heels right on the very edge of the pool.

So I'm teetering there and circling my arms for balance—yeah, I looked like a dork—and then a third idiot tried to push past Tristan, which had him turning sideways to face me. He was pretty stable still as he reached his arm around my waist to keep me from going in, but I guess I pulled him off balance. His body weight pushed me over the edge and into the pool I went, with him on top of me. Yes, I couldn't have *been* happier with the result. The splash we made was large enough to get Jeff, Kate, and the three troublemakers all wet, too. At least we weren't the only ones in the pool, though, because then I would've really stood out when I started stripping my clothes off.

Tristan and Jeff were laughing about the fall and Kate had a skeptical look on her face as her eyes kept going back and forth between Tristan and me. Although when I gained my footing in the pool and pulled my shirt off over my head and then went to tug my jeans off, all sounds of laughter coming from Tristan and Jeff abruptly ceased. Their laughter was replaced however, by Kate's with Melissa joining her hilarity, as she'd been watching the whole event unfold from the other side of the pool.

Tristan's eyes practically popped out of their sockets when he saw me remove my shirt; he got right next to me, hovering almost protectively like he didn't want anyone to see me, and then he bent to whisper, "Jesus, Camie! You made me turn around last weekend and now you're putting on a *damned show?!*"

My jeans had become stuck around my thighs and I was tilting, so I steadied myself by putting one hand on his rock hard bicep, which I'm pretty damned sure I felt jump and then flicker under my touch, like his muscle was trying to maintain its composure. "Hardly. If you'll take the time to notice, you'll see I'm wearing a bathing suit."

He looked down and instantly saw that I was speaking the truth and through touching his arm, I felt him begin to relax as he muttered to himself "Thank God." I had to swallow more than once to get my heart to return to its proper place, because touching him like that...? Well, I ain't got the words. I certainly got a reaction out of him, though, didn't I? Yes, I'm pretty pleased with myself, too.

"Why are you wearing a bathing suit?"

"Because if you'll recall last weekend, I didn't fair so well in the clothing department and you have yet to return my bra. Since I don't wanna lose another one, and in preparation for stuff like this happening to me, I thought I should adopt a new motto...wanna hear it?" I asked he who makes my heart go rat-a-tat-tat like a snare drum in a marching band.

Oh yeah, didn't I tell you to remember "the geek and the underwear scene" from *Sixteen Candles* for the future? Well, guess who played the role of the geek who gave a girl's underwear to the studly jock. Yeah, that would be me. I'd completely forgotten he took the bag with my clothes in it with him to his car and I only remembered once I was getting dressed Sunday morning. Not only could he have reminded me to take it when he drove me home that night, but he hasn't, in a week of opportunities, returned my clothing. Kate and Melissa like to think of it as if he's taking scalps. You know, like a trophy of some kind.

Tristan gave me a lopsided, teasing grin and with dancing eyes he nodded that, yes; he'd very much like to hear my new motto. "Okay, you're gonna love this... My new motto is 'hope for the best, but plan for the worst.' I even have a change of clothes in Kate's car... Crap, I'm stuck. Take my jeans off, please," I said as I started to tilt in the water again.

I know. I didn't really mean to give him an open invitation to take my clothes off, but having done exactly that, I guess I deserved the utterly heart-stopping and rather cocky look of consideration that crossed his face. It quickly changed to more of an "I don't need to be told twice and just so you know, you asked for it" kind of look as he reached under the water to help me wiggle out of the denim Chinese yo-yo that my jeans had become. The whole process would've been laughable if wasn't for the shared intensity which made it highly intimate.

Once we fell in, the novelty of the spectacle we'd become wore off fairly quick so no one other than Melissa, Kate and Jeff were paying much attention to us in the pool anymore. Tristan finally managed to yank my pants off and as he went to throw them on the deck, he realized Kate had been laughing the entire time and still was. I didn't have time to warn her when I saw the gesture Tristan made with his chin to Jeff before he took Kate's arm and launched her into the pool, doing a canon ball after her. She smacked him when he resurfaced and then tried to swim away. She didn't get too far, though, because both Tristan and Jeff being in their element, jumped at her and shoved her back under the water. I giggled, watching them torture poor Kate for a few minutes, and then I swam over to join the group in the hot tub turned bubble bath.

I was feeling like I'd done a pretty good night's work, so, I didn't decline the plastic glass of champagne that Pete offered me. Apparently, the game inside had broken up already and Pete was being a magnanimous host to those of us in the uncommonly large Jacuzzi. The Three Musketeers eventually joined me and we all stayed there for the rest of the party. Happily, Tristan and Jeff, both of whom had already been in shorts, had done away with their shirts, too. But, the even bigger bonus was that Tristan chose to sit next to me in the hot tub! I know, right?! I mean it wasn't like he made an attempt to get familiar with me under the bubbles or anything, but still. I felt it warranted a quick mental happy dance anyway.

Having me next to him also made it easy for him to lean close and whisper to me when Jeff began to regale us with much animation, the story of his heroics last weekend when his Jeep had gotten the flat tire. Somehow the whole thing started when Kate said something about how Jeff should be grateful that she hadn't had her new phone on her when he tossed her into the pool earlier. Then she started in on him about how she'd appreciate it if he'd take some responsibility for his actions and grow up. So, with Tristan whispering in my ear to give me the *real* story in hilariously matter of fact asides, this is how it went:

"Grow up?! I'm plenty grown up! In fact, if it wasn't for me and my extremely mature handling of our flat tire last weekend, Tristan and I would be dead right now," Jeff declared.

Kate rolled her eyes. "Gimme a break, babe, it was just a flat tire..."

"Oh that's what you think, but I'll have you know that it wasn't *just* a flat tire...it was a full blowout *and* it was on the freeway no less!" He exclaimed, waving a finger in the air dramatically to illustrate his point.

"Yeah, but still...it's not like a flat or even a blowout is that big of a deal."

"Well, wait...that can be kinda dangerous, Kate, I mean even without a flat, aren't a lot of Jeeps prone to tipping?" I asked, happy to be able to participate in a conversation and not sound like I had no clue about what was being discussed.

Jeff's eyes lighted on me and with a mischievous grin and a flourish, he grabbed the bottle out of Pete's hand and refilled my cup with more bubbling champagne. "Ah, yes indeed they are, my young Padawan learner... So you see, without my lightning fast reflexes and superhuman strength, the death-defying feat of keeping all four wheels on the ground would've been nigh impossible. Thus I saved the lives of both myself, my apprentice here, and countless others on the road."

Tristan snorted and scoffed. "And exactly how did you do that again?"

"Well, as you'll remember, we were tooling along at a nice clip of speed—"

And thus began Jeff's tall tale. This was also when Tristan leaned over to me and began his interjections with hilariously deadpanned amusement.

"We were at a stop light waiting to get on the freeway."

"—and then suddenly! We heard an explosion that would make most men tremble in their shoes...not I however—"

"He screamed like a four year old girl."

"—No, not I. I was a rock of steady calm and with amazing strength, I gripped the steering wheel—"

"He drank too much chocolate milk at the beach and his tummy hurt so I was driving."

"—to regain control and kept the beast from toppling end over end, which would've of course killed us both instantly. Then immediately knowing the danger wasn't over, I leapt from my seat and with stone and flint, I produced a blazing fire in which to divert the frightened civilians from the wreckage—"

"I hit the hazard lights."

"—then I single handedly and with sheer brawny might, hefted the Jeep from the ground to replace the shredded remains of the tire with a new one—"

"His spare was flat too, so he called Triple A."

"—Once that was accomplished with unheard of speed, I calmed my distraught and mechanically useless compatriot—"

"I laughed as he totally blew chunks. Oh and he doesn't know a socket wrench from a fuckin' coat hanger."

"—Then I discovered the beastly Jeep wouldn't come to life, but never fear! I applied my knowledge and skill to solve that as well and now here we are, alive and celebrating amongst our fellow countrymen and women! Huzzah!"

"He had Triple A tow us to my house so I could spend my Sunday working on his piece of shit Jeep."

Jeff then looked at Tristan and whined like a petulant child. "She is *not* a piece of shit! You take that back!"

"She *is* a piece of shit, but only because you don't take care of her and the only reason she's running at all is because I do the maintenance…and you're lucky I haven't had to keep her together with JB Weld and fuckin' duct tape, so you're welcome!" Tristan told him with his eyebrows raised high, comically defying Jeff to deny any of what he'd said.

"You just can't let me have anything, can you?" Jeff asked and threw a soapy beach ball at Tristan's head, which he saw coming but didn't make a single move to miss being hit with.

"I let you have Kate, *and* I let you beat me at chess," Tristan replied while wiping the suds off his face.

"No you don't!" Jeff laughingly accused Tristan.

"Yeah I did…remember that one time when you had strep throat?"

"Oh, *one* time and I was on my death bed… You know, one of these days, you're gonna play the game with someone who's gonna make you bleed and I'll be there, buddy boy…oh yes, make no mistake… The king *will* fall and I'll be there, rooting your opponent on."

Next to me, I felt Tristan's body tense but he just chuckled and simply said, "We'll see…"

The whole dialogue was hysterical and I'd been giggling throughout most of it, but at that point—and I'm not exactly sure what it meant and as it would turn out, the whole thing would be forgotten—I noticed Kate staring intently at Jeff, like she maybe thought he wasn't talking about Tristan losing a game, chess or otherwise. But then, like they'd planned it, both Tristan and Jeff splashed Kate in the face with bubbly water to first distract her, and then they each got one of her hands and feet and swung her so that she went flying into the pool. Including our host who was still wearing his clothes, many of the hot tub occupants joined Kate of their own volition and the evening's frivolity pressed on.

Even more than Mike's, the party was a ton of fun; I really didn't want it to end, but end it must. However, for me, it didn't end how I would've preferred it to. Not by a long shot in fact. All told, I had at least four beers and three-ish—maybe more?—glasses of champagne and by the end of the evening, I was *not* feeling well. I don't think I was behaving all that different so I'm not sure if anyone could tell how pickled I was, but I will say this; I'm *so* relieved no one actually saw me throw up.

We'd gotten out of the hot tub and Pete had given us towels to dry off with; however I had dry clothes to put on, too, so I got Kate's keys and went to get my bag out of her car by way of the back gate. I could tell it was gonna happen and there was no way I'd be able to make it to a bathroom, let alone wait in a line. With that in mind, I looked around to make sure the coast was clear, stepped up on the short, block wall that put my head higher than the side fence, and just as my insides decided they would prefer to be on the outside, I bent my head over the fence. It was ugly. I mean really, really hideous. And thus I buried my first "life experience skeleton." I didn't know it at the time, but I'd soon discover that I'm sort of a lousy crypt keeper...

I woke up at Kate's Saturday morning with the most hellacious pounding in my head that made every sound feel like shards of glass were piercing my eyes.

"Oh my God…what in the name of all that is holy is that appalling sound?" I moaned as I rolled over and tried to sit up. When I did this, though, my stomach lurched. I wasn't going to be sick again, but it was like my stomach was reminding me of what I'd put it through last night and it was *not* happy with me about it.

"The birds chirping their obnoxious good morning song," Kate answered, a little too chipper for my state of being.

"Can't you shoot them? Oh. No, don't do that…I think the sound would put me in a coma," I said miserably.

"You need some juice or breakfast, Camie," Melissa suggested, already dressed and in the process of brushing out her gorgeous head of hair. Next to Jillian's, I think Melissa's hair is probably the longest and prettiest hair I've ever seen on a real-life person, and where Jillian's extraordinarily long, blonde hair reminds me of Lady Godiva and her selfless bravery, Melissa's flowing locks of deep mahogany lend her an air of soft spoken sensuality.

"NO. No food. Juice maybe, but my stomach doesn't want solids." I groaned at the thought.

"Well, on the bright side, last night went really well. You know he let you guys fall in, right? He totally had his balance, but made a snap decision to get you in the pool with him. I really admire his technique, you know?" Kate said, quietly giggling in an attempt to distract me from my abominable condition.

"I was wondering about that. I thought he was steady too, but then I just thought I pulled him off balance… You guys? Did I make a fool out of myself at any time last night?" I asked, trying to remember the details of my behavior through a thick haze of post-inebriated forgetfulness.

"No, I don't think so," Melissa answered. "You were pretty much yourself, maybe a little unsteady on your feet when we left, but not in a way anyone would think anything of. And by the way, the bathing suit thing was very well played. You completely blew his mind with that...I mean he totally didn't know what to do! He kept looking around trying to make sure no one was watching you take your clothes off, and then he'd look back at you all conflicted and I'd swear there was a mighty battle being waged in his head. It was actually kinda painful to watch, poor guy." She stuck her bottom lip out, displaying what was obviously false sympathy for Tristan's predicament last night.

I got up slowly and went hunting for my stuff so I could get dressed. "Yeah, well, I didn't actually plan any of that so maybe I'm just getting better at manipulation like he is. You know he actually sounded hurt when he accused me of putting on a show after having made him turn around in the bathroom last weekend. He didn't deny keeping my clothes either, although he could've forgotten about them like I did, so I won't count that."

"Hey, I almost forgot...what was that text from Derek about? The only part I understood was why he called you shark bait."

"Oh yeah. I forgot about that too. Actually, when you told me it was from Derek, I was hoping he'd be vague enough to provoke some kind of reaction from Tristan...that's why I had you read it out loud. It worked; I just don't know what his reaction meant...he totally went stock-still." I shrugged, still not knowing what his reaction meant. "Anyway, Melissa, you'll especially wanna hear what the text really meant. My cousin was answering a question I'd asked him earlier about my little sister, Jillian. Kate, you remember what I told you about her, right?"

Kate nodded.

"Well, on the way to the party last night, I sent Derek a text and asked him if Jillian had disappeared during the game and if so, for how long," I said and looked at the two of them to see if they were picking it up.

I could see the wheels in Kate's head spinning, but Melissa didn't get it. "I don't see the connection. I mean, I don't know your sister so why would I be so interested in where she was during the game?"

"NO!!" Kate gasped; putting it all together quickly after Melissa's question jogged her own hung-over memory. "But how in the world could she do it?"

"You see, Melissa, my twelve year old sister is a criminal mastermind, much in the same way as *Artemis Fowl*, just without the monetary funds to back her."

"I still don't get it," she said, looking back and forth between Kate and me.

"Melissa, Jillian is responsible for the retribution put forth on Mark's car," I said simply.

"*What?* Why and *how* is that even possible?" She asked with disbelief ringing in her voice.

"Yeah. I can totally believe she *would* do it, but I don't see *how* she could."

"Well, you guys, Jill's not your ordinary girl for one thing. She's kind of a gear-head and actually enjoys working on things in the garage with my dad...she helps him with car stuff all the time. When my dad rotates the tires, he always lets her take 'em off…I've seen her do it and she's pretty quick.

"That whole thing last night reeked like something she'd do. I'd pointed Teresa out to her when we were in the parking lot before the game and also happened to tell her that Mark was the jerk who made fun of Paul that day. My sister took it upon herself to exact a little revenge."

"Okay, but how did she get into the car to put the tires in there? And where did the shoe polish come from?" Kate asked with wide eyes.

"Oh, I'm sure she picked the car lock. I'm also pretty sure something like window markers or actual shoe polish would be a staple in her bag of tricks, along with a camera of some kind, a handheld telescope or binoculars, and other various pieces of spy equipment. I'm telling you guys…you do *not* wanna mess with my sister. You'll come out the worse for wear every time." Seriously, I wasn't kidding about wanting to stay on her good side. If she uses her powers for good, she's an exceedingly valuable asset, but if you've pricked her temper, she can be an unsurpassed menace.

Kate was shaking her head. "Wow, Camie. I don't know what to say…that's just shocking. It's completely awesome of course, but still…shocking."

"Well I love it! I can't wait to meet her!" Melissa said enthusiastically.

"That's all fine and good, but it might not be the best idea to encourage her. That little prank was nothing compared to what I'm sure she's capable of and I'd hate to see someone get hurt or Jill get in trouble, although I doubt she'll ever get caught at anything. In fact, I don't think I'm even gonna mention that I know it was her. I will however, peek in her backpack to see if there's any evidence. Who knows, maybe she kept a lug nut or something as a souvenir." I started to giggle about that which, of course, made my head feel like it was going to split down the middle.

"Okay, so let's talk about our plans for the rest of the weekend... Since we have Monday off for that teacher in-service thing, we should try to squeeze as much as we can in, don't you think?" Kate asked, now prepared to move on after having accepted the unbelievable.

"I wish, but I can only go out tonight...my parents are co-chairing some charity event at their country club so I'm playing the dutiful daughter again all Sunday..." Melissa sighed, resigned and sounding somewhat melancholy.

"Aw, that stinks...but we're all going to that bonfire at the beach tonight, right?" Kate again asked, walking into her bathroom.

"Yeah, I guess. I'm actually supposed to go down there today with Jill and my cousins...Derek promised to take all of us non-driving folk. I feel like a Mac truck plowed into me, though, so maybe I'll just play tonight by ear, you know? If you don't hear from me by like 5:00 or 5:30, call me."

I really want to go because it sounds like a blast, but I do feel like garbage so I might take the night off. Even though things are progressing so well with Tristan and I don't want to lose an opportunity, I might not be at the top of my game in time for tonight. So, we'll see.

"Okay, sounds good. Camie, Melissa's right, you should get something in you. It'll probably make you feel better. Here, at least take this," Kate directed, handing me some aspirin and a glass of water.

Even that was hard to get down, but I managed. At least now I can appreciate Melissa's reluctance to drink outside of a celebratory toast from time to time. You know though, I honestly thought that when something happened to me that I didn't really want other people to know about, I'd have a decently justifiable reason for why it happened. But no. No such reason exists aside from being just plain stupid and that's not even a reason. That's just stupidity...

10.

Water Is Life Indeed

"Hey, I'm sorry if all that stuff Brandon said about the shark weirded you out," Derek said as we spread our towels and blankets out on the sand. He sounds concerned, but I kinda don't want to talk about it today.

"Whatever. Now I know what I've gotten myself into, right?" Wow, that sounded really bitchy.

"True. Um, I don't wanna get all in your business or anything but, he hasn't tried to get you to do anything you don't wanna do, has he?" *Ugh.*

"Nope."

"Okay, good. You know Samantha wasn't at all pressured, but still…I kinda got worried about that. So if he does, I'll kick the shit outta him for you, but only if you want. " And again I say, *ugh.*

"Thanks for the offer, D, but I'm sure that won't be necessary." Derek is really pretty built but Tristan is way more cut. I also think he might outweigh Derek, too, which leads me to think my cousin would have his hands pretty full defending my honor. Not that it needs defending. Even something like a freaking toy slingshot would prove to be overkill at this point. *Ugh, ugh, ugh.*

"No really, it might be fun just to see..." He mused aloud with a chuckle.

"*Humph.*" What is it with guys beating their chests to see who deserves to be the Alpha?

"What's wrong with you? It seems like something's buggin' you. That's kinda why I asked if he'd done anything…"

I'm still feeling really lousy. Even though we're having a warm spell today and the sun feels good, I'm tired, my head is killing me, and my stomach is still protesting the violation of its rights. And the only reason I feel this way is because I was stupid, and even without the physical repercussions I *hate* being stupid! "Well he hasn't. He's been a perfect (well maybe not perfect) gentleman, and I'm sorry for my slightly bitchy state of being today."

"What's goin' on?"

I sighed. I don't think he's gonna let this go…I might as well just tell him and get it over with. "Don't tell anyone, but I have *the* worst hangover…" I replied, feeling sheepish. I'm really disappointed in myself, too, you know? Maybe Adam Ant didn't write that song "Goody Two Shoes" about me after all.

"Ooh. That sucks. Did you take anything? I have Excedrin if you want it," Derek offered sympathetically. Clearly that song wasn't written about him either.

"No thanks. I've been popping Tylenol like Pez since I woke up. I think I'm just gonna lay here and close my eyes…maybe take a nap," I told him as I stretched out on my abused tummy.

"Okay, I'll try to keep the kidlets out of your hair then." He then turned around to face all the other kids swarming around us and asked, "So who's up for some Frisbee?"

All told, Derek has three younger siblings of his own, and counting Jill and two of our other cousins; he's got six kids under the age of fifteen to keep track of today. I wish him luck.

I lay on my towel feeling the warm sand below and with the sun ministering to me from above; I found that being here at the beach seemed to help make me feel better. The sound of waves crashing against the shore then the water rushing back, along with the cries of sea gulls was soothing. I listened to it all, allowing the ocean's lullaby to infuse me with peace and after a time, I drifted off. I must've been more asleep than I realized, though, because I woke with quite a start when I felt several drops of water hit my back and a foot gently nudge my rear-end.

"Go. Away," I growled and made a shooing gesture with my hands. How dare they? Really, the nerve of some people…can't these kids see that I'm trying to nap? Not to mention that the water is cold, and now I probably have sand on my butt as well.

"Has anyone ever told you that your manners are kinda shitty?"

My eyes popped open and even though he was on the other side of me and I couldn't see him, I *knew* that voice. He'd asked the question with amusement too, so I didn't have a problem picturing the lop-sided grin he was most likely wearing as well.

"They are not. I'll have you know that my manners have been widely acclaimed by many. What do you expect when you not only drip water on someone's bare back, but wake them up too?" I grumbled in reply while holding my position.

I didn't turn my head to look at him and I'm still too out of it to pretend like I'm in perfect health, so, Tristan gets to see the real me today. Unfortunately for me, that could go either way with Mr. Moody here. I could end up coming off really snotty and he could be offended, or he could actually like me for who I am. Let's hope for the latter.

He chuckled and I heard something hit the sand. "Who are you here with?"

I pointed towards the water where my family was frolicking about. "My family. Well, my sister and cousins."

I turned my head to look at him then and saw he was wearing a wet suit and sitting on the sand next to a surfboard. Beads of salt water were dripping from his hair and I don't think I've ever seen him look as happy…no, that's not right; maybe the word is euphoric…as he did in that moment. Water is life indeed.

"Your family? You're *related* to Derek Bailey?" He asked with some surprise.

"Yep. He's my cousin," I admitted. I'm not in the mood for games, and besides, I'd have lied if I said no. I don't want to lie to him. Mislead from time to time in the interest of keeping him chasing me, maybe, but not outright lie.

He started laughing and then looked at me for a moment before saying, "Zack's been telling everyone that Derek was…or, *is* your boyfriend."

"That figures."

"Why?" He asked, making it obvious he'd held a fair amount of his own misapprehension on the topic.

Then I realized what that meant. I had been a topic of conversation, one that he'd been a part of. Not that I didn't know before now, but hearing it confirmed in words that came straight from his mouth is different somehow. I sighed and smiled to myself in what felt like long awaited satisfaction...and relief.

"Because Kate told him I'd broken up with my boyfriend recently and then I showed up at the football game holding hands with Derek. It wasn't that far of a leap if someone didn't know the relation. Don't get me wrong, I really love my cousin, but I don't *love* my cousin…I'm pretty sure God frowns on that sort of thing too. And just so we're clear about *my* thoughts on the subject, EW," I explained and closed my eyes again.

He chuckled. "I think you're right, God probably takes issue with that sort of thing." Once again, we shared a quiet moment that wasn't awkward; rather it was familiar and, easy. Then, Tristan broke the affable silence by saying, "So, I'm guessing you've got a killer hangover."

I wish he wasn't so accurate about that. I opened my eyes to look at him again and even though I'm pretty sure he's laughing at me, I have to be honest…he's got the most ridiculously gorgeous grin on his face and if I felt better, I'd be hard pressed to not tackle him on the spot. I'm already wondering if his wet suit is as hard to get off as my wet jeans were. Oh my God...seriously, *what* is wrong with me?

"You would be correct." Like I said, no lies today. Besides, he was there last night so I'm sure he knows just how much I drank.

"Did you puke?"

"Boy howdy, did I... Oh God...that poor dog," I gasped, suddenly remembering the whole grotesque scene.

"*What?*" The surprise and confusion about how a dog would have anything to do with me tossing my cookies was entirely understandable.

"I threw up on Pete's neighbor's dog. I didn't mean to and I didn't even see him down there until it was over... I wonder if I should go back and leave a sorry note and cash for a good grooming though." Wow, I'm not holding anything back, am I? I guess my motto for today is "what you see is what you get."

Tristan started cracking up and I have to say, his laughter was a better balm than the hypnotic sounds of the ocean. "Oh that's awesome! Pete hates that dog, it's always barking in the middle of the night."

"Well then, I'm glad to have been of service. However, my days of vomiting on yappy dogs are over...I'm never drinking again."

"It was the combination of beer, champagne, and the hot tub," he told me, still chuckling.

"What was?" I asked and rolled over to get some sun on the flip side. Thank God my sunglasses are pretty dark or this would be excruciating for my eyes.

"Why you got so sick. First off, sitting in a Jacuzzi will dehydrate you pretty quickly if you don't replenish what you sweat out and alcohol makes dehydration worse, but there's also the rule...haven't you ever heard the rhyme or been told not mix certain kinds of alcohol?" He asked as he ran his eyes over me. How do I know he's doing that? Well duh, I'm watching him through my lashes...

"No, I must've missed that part of the lecture in my teenage alcoholism dos and don'ts 101 class," I replied flippantly.

"I kinda aced that class...you want me to help you feel better?"

What kind of question is that? Like I'm gonna say; "No, I want you to leave me alone." I just have no idea what he could do aside from sitting vigil next to my death towel to make me feel better.

"Are you gonna kill me and put me out of my misery? I'd love nothing more than if you did..." After all, I already feel like I'm dying so his work is partially finished.

"Well, that's no fun, so no," he said with a smile and stood up.

"Really, I'd be forever grateful." I closed my eyes again.

"You have no sense of adventure..."

"Uh, I beg to differ...if you want proof, though, you can go see for yourself. I believe you'll find remnants of my sense of adventure on the side yard of Pete's neighbor's house."

"Yeah, I think I'll just take your word for it." He chuckled again and then grabbing my hand to haul me up he said, "Come on...ups a daisy."

"*Ugh*. I don't *wanna* go in the water," I whined, dragging my feet through the sand as he pulled me towards the ocean. "Can't you just let me die on the beach like a whale?"

"Nope. Trust me, Camie, you'll feel better," Tristan told me as we reached the water's edge.

"*Oh, hell no!*" I shrieked emphatically, having felt the frigid water with just the tips of my toes. Then I turned to go back to dry land.

"Oh, you're goin' in!" He said firmly, grabbing both my hands to prevent my flight.

We struggled for an all too brief moment, playing a kind of tug of war, which Tristan won hands down. I yelped when he picked me up and threw me over his shoulder. Then he carried me, kicking and screaming, out into the surf.

Now, you have to understand something here; I'd be more than thrilled to be thrown over this guy's shoulder any day, hung-over or not—Hey, that was a kind of pun, wasn't it? Ha!—but have you ever felt the Pacific Ocean in October? I don't care how warm it's been, that water feels like the freaking polar icecaps have melted into it! Although I guess since I didn't have a choice about it anymore, I should just be grateful that my bikini stayed in place when he tossed me into the waves.

I came up spluttering and hollered, "And you said *my* manners are shi—"

I couldn't finish yelling at him, though, because a tower of salt water crashed down on me from behind. I lost my footing with the unexpected force, the wave catching me up and sweeping me forward. Right as I was about to go past him, a jubilantly laughing Tristan grabbed me around the waist and pulled me to him with my back against his chest. He held me there for a charged moment filled with anticipation until another surge came, then we fell backwards together into the swell. His eyes were dancing as the backwash of the wave began carrying us towards the shore. Then he pulled me up with a big beautiful grin on his face and led me back out to repeat the process.

A quick word of advice: Regardless of the temperature, if you ever have the good fortune of being given the opportunity to play in the ocean with an incredibly gorgeous guy...do it.

"See? You get used to the temperature," he said as we stood waiting for another breaker to roll in.

"Easy for you to say, you big cheater...you're wearing a wet suit," I retorted and held my breath just as the sea pushed me over.

He was laughing again when he wiped the water from his face and shook his hair out at the same time, sprinkling my face with delicious drops of Tristan-ized saltwater as he did.

"True. I'd take it off just to be fair, but I'd get arrested for indecent exposure."

OH.

Well *that* was entirely unexpected. I wasn't sure how to respond to that remark and I hope he didn't see the light bulb moment I had right before I was rescued from commenting by another wave. The current of this one, however, rushed me on a collision course to slam bodily into him. Tristan caught and steadied me in his arms and let me just tell you; I'm not the *slightest* bit cold anymore. Quite the opposite in fact as the impact created so much energy and electricity between us; I swear Ben Franklin would've been jealous about how easy we made it look. And I thought he might've been about to kiss me, but unfortunately, the ocean had other plans and we were separated by another whitecap.

Tristan and I played in the water for a little while longer, sadly, without experiencing any more close encounters. Then I noticed my family on the beach beginning to pack things up. Crap. The whole afternoon has been like a page out of a fairytale for me and I really don't want to read those last two words: The End.

"It's time for me to leave, but I had a lot of fun. Thanks." Reluctantly, I made my way against the current to the shore.

"You're not going to the bonfire?" He asked, coming up next to me.

"Um, I told Kate I'd play it by ear...I wanted to but, I didn't really think I'd be up for it, you know?" Now I'm even more irritated with myself. Stupid alcohol rules.

"That doesn't answer the question. How do you feel now?"

"Oh. Um...huh. I do feel a little better. My headache's totally gone...I didn't even realize it." I'd been having so much fun cavorting in the water with my Prince Charming that I completely forgot how crappy I'd felt and now my headache really is gone. Maybe Tylenol or Excedrin can bottle the beach and market it as a hangover cure. I bet they'd make qua-trillions.

"*Sooo?* Bonfire?" He prompted.

I guess I'm still not at the top of my game, though, seeing as how I've *yet* to answer the original question. I mean really, good lord, I have *got* to get it together!

"Yeah, I suppose I will. Provided that by the time Kate picks me up, my steamroller of a headache hasn't come back to reiterate the message it was getting across so well earlier." I really hope it doesn't…I *so* want to see him again tonight.

"How about if I just hold you hostage down here and then even if your headache does come back, you won't be able to stay home…bonfires are usually a lot of fun, Camie."

Exsqueeze me? Did he just ask me to stay here the rest of the day and go to the bonfire *with* him? That's what it sounded like to me, too.

"Oh. Umm…I'd have to clear it with my parents. I don't *think* it'll be an issue, but if Derek shows up at my house shy one of their daughters…well, that probably wouldn't go over very well." I immediately began praying that my parents' cool factor would extend to letting me stay at the beach all day and evening with a guy neither of them has ever met.

"Okay, so call 'em. It seems kinda like a waste of time for you to go all the way home only to turn around in a few hours and come back out here," Tristan said realistically.

Hmm, I'm not sure how to take his offer now. Is he being practical or does he want to spend more time with me? Kate?! Where are you when I need you?

Wait a minute. Why do I care what his motives are for asking me to stay? Honestly, it's not like it makes a difference. Tristan time is Tristan time, right? And this would be even better because it would be *alone* time! Woohoo!

When we made it to the sand, I stopped him and decided to preface the introductions. "Okay, I'm gonna have to introduce you to my family, but you see the girl that looks like an adolescent Barbie doll?"

Tristan laughed at my description. "Yeah. I assume she's your sister."

"Yeah, she is, but I just wanna warn you…you wanna be nice to her."

I have no idea what to expect from Jillian after the prank she pulled last night and I'm really hoping that got her trickery out of her system for a while.

Tristan laughed again and I got the impression he didn't fully appreciate what I'd told him, so I gave him more truth. "No, I'm dead serious. You wanna stay on her good side, Tristan. Did you see Mark Austen's car last night?"

"No. I heard about it, though. Why?"

"You're looking at the twelve year old sadistic deviant responsible for that. She heard about Mark making fun of Paul and, of course, I've told her all about how much I loathe Teresa. So she uh…gave them a taste of their own medicine with the first opportunity presented to her. I'd just really hate to see anything happen to you or your car if she were to take something you do or say the wrong way," I said seriously and watched his face for a reaction.

His eyes widened and he looked back and forth between Jillian and me for a moment before chuckling. "No shit? Thanks for the heads up."

I love that he didn't even question a girl's ability to pull off what my sister did. Because really, changing out a tire isn't a big deal and besides, if men can be ballerinas, girls can be grease monkeys. Any other belief is quite simply chauvinistic in my mind.

When we reached where everyone was shaking sand off the towels and packing up, I introduced Tristan. The younger kids were more interested in his surfboard than him and he, of course, already knew Derek a little so that actually went pretty well. Derek didn't pound on his chest even once, for which I'm relieved. Jillian remained more or less observant, just listening to him talk with Derek and studying him in general while I was on the phone with our mom. When I saw her reach into her backpack, however, I gave her an "I'm begging you" kind of look. She just opened her eyes innocently at me, pulled out a tube of Chap Stick and held it up for me to see. Knowing her, though, I wouldn't be surprised to find out that it wasn't lip balm at all, but a microphone or some other tool of the trade.

"Okay! I'm good. My mom even extended my curfew half an hour because of the drive." My mom was in a *great* mood, so I'm thinking my parents might've had a really good day together without any children home to—ahem—"bug them."

"Okay, cool. Uh, Camie, can I talk to you really quick?" Derek asked and motioned for me to join him a few feet away from everyone.

Ugh. I so do not want a lecture from my cousin about Tristan right now...that would totally irritate me. I'm over the cheerleader so he needs to be, too. I swallowed the bitchiness I could feel rising, though, and simply asked, "What's up?"

"I just wanted to make sure it'd be okay for me to date MaryAnn now. I've been holding off because I didn't wanna blow it for you, but now that he knows I'm your cousin, it's cool if I ask her out, right?" Aw, how great is he? He put his dating life on hold just for me. MaryAnn had better appreciate what a good guy my cousin is.

"Oh, totally. Date away!" I told him with enthusiasm, more than happy to be completely wrong for once.

Tristan and I said goodbye to my familial entourage, and then I pulled my t-shirt and shorts on before we walked to his car so he could get out of his suit and put his surfboard away. I stopped short when he approached not his Chevelle, but a lime green, VW Westfalia bus that I'm pretty sure was made some time in the 1970s, the personalized plate of which reads: 4THZTMZ.

"I'm confused," I admitted, watching him open the barn-type doors of the "surfari" van, revealing a kitchenette inside.

"Oh, this is just more practical for carting surfboards around. Plus, it comes in handy for those times when I shouldn't be driving home. I don't normally drive my car to parties...last weekend was a fluke and it's also why I wasn't drinking," he explained with a wink when he understood what I meant by the look on my face.

Again with the practicality, but I can see his point. His bus is decked out with a table, sink, ice box, a two burner stove, and is complete with not one, but two beds. The bench seat folds into one and there's a pop-up sleeping compartment, too. It's *so* cool! I love it. I love everything about it, including the color. The interior is a green plaid that matches the paint and the curtains on the windows.

I climbed in to look around. "How fun is this!"

"Yeah, it's a blast and it makes little camping trips easy," he agreed while yanking the zipper on the back of his wetsuit down.

Ummm. Excuse me, Tristan? What about that indecent exposure thing?

So, yeah. I was pretty much panicking, seeing as how he'd pulled his arms out of the wetsuit and was proceeding to remove the damned thing right in front of me. Seriously, he's standing here, gloriously naked from the hips up, and for the life of me, I can't *not* watch. So when he wrapped a towel around his waist and continued to more modestly shed his second skin, I didn't know whether to thank him for keeping my virtuous eyes from being sullied, or pout and complain that he *didn't* sully them. By the way, have you ever seen a surfer do this? If not, then trust me when I tell you; it's *quite* the sight to behold.

He finished putting his clothes on which, incidentally, I aided him in doing like a nurse in surgery. I kind of felt like Hot Lips in *M*A*S*H* every time he asked me to hand him an article of clothing...minus underwear. I'm not sure if he's just not wearing any or if they were wadded up in his shorts because I didn't think to check before I handed them over. I'm going to try not to obsess on that right now though, and thankfully, his question totally helped me in that.

"Are you hungry?"

"Are you trying to be funny? I think if I eat anything you'll have to search out an unsuspecting pooch for me about thirty seconds after the food hits my stomach." No food for me, thank you very much.

He laughed at me again. "Well I am. There's a really good pizza place down by the roller coaster. Come on, we can walk."

Awesome. Food and a roller coaster...just what I need.

11.

Oh, No He Isn't!!!

As we walked along the boardwalk, we talked about the usual kinds of things kids do when they're getting to know each other. You know, music, movies, how much we hate school...stuff like that. I was sort of surprised to learn that Tristan and I have a lot of similar tastes in the music department, which is just one more hash mark for the MFEO checklist I have going in my head. And since I honestly feel that music plays an important part in peoples' lives, I was relieved to find that we not only like a lot of the same kinds of popular stuff, but that he has a fondness for the oldies, too. Not oldies as in music from the '50s, but the '70s and '80s. I also found out that Tristan *really* knows his music. For instance, when I made a random comment referring to that first party I went to that held the phrase "teenage wasteland," he knew the correct title of The Who song to be "Baba O'Reily," and really, not many kids in my generation know that. I was actually very impressed.

When we got to the pizza joint and he received his two *enormous* slices of Hawaiian style pizza, which I count as just one more item to go in the pros column, Tristan ended up force-feeding me about one fourth of his meal. I tried to resist, honestly I did, but it smelled really good and he insisted I eat something. And since he was right about the ocean helping me feel better, I figured I should just take his word for it. Not surprisingly, he was right and, along with Mission Beach's canine population, I could breath easy once again.

During the hours we spent together, we learned a lot about each other and I found out that we actually have more than just music in common. For instance, we like a ton of the same movies, that like mine, his parents were high school sweethearts, and that aside from spiders; he likes all kinds of animals and even has his own horse. He not only reads, but likes it, and he happens to be just as well read as I am if not more so. I mean how hot is that? I also discovered that Tristan is exactly, give or take a few hours, one year and eleven months older than I am. My birthday is January 15th and his is on February 15th. Oh, he also admitted to being a fan of Buffy. He's not quite as avid as I am, but I learned he does have a memory like a steel trap, which is why he can quote things the way he does.

In the not so much in common category is the fact that he has no problem with math or tests, he's kind of a morning person, and he's an only child with very few rules. From what I gather, Tristan and his parents have a very relaxed and open relationship with each other and he's essentially treated as an adult, if not an equal in the family.

Another difference between us is that along with a lot of the kids I go to school with, his family is totally loaded. From what he said, the family money comes from his dad's grandparents owning a *ton* of land in San Diego from way back when that his grandparents and parents have now either leased or developed in some way, and then there's some property in Texas, too, and that land has oil rigs on it. And incidentally, I didn't get this information because he was bragging about how much money he has; it came from him explaining what his parents do and why they do it, because even though neither of them need to, both of his parents work. And they work only because being pilots for the same airline, they get to be together all the time and they deeply love what they do.

While we were talking about our families, my mom's cancer came up and that's when I told him I'd been home schooled. He asked what that was like and when I told him how much and why I'd loved it, Tristan asked me how I was adjusting to the change. I was honest and told him I was still trying to get used to the dynamics and meeting so many new people all at once, and also, my utter dislike of already having an enemy in Teresa, as well as my desire to just fit in as soon as possible. Then he made an attempt at empathy by telling me not to worry about it, that I'd be one of them and feel at home in no time.

"Yeah, easy for you to say...you've been going to school with these people forever and every single one of them loves you," I said in response.

"No...not everyone," he corrected.

"How do you figure? I mean, from what I've seen it seems like they do..."

He shrugged. "Zack won't be shedding any tears at my funeral."

"Oh, okay...*one* person...that doesn't exactly make you a social outcast."

"I think one person is enough."

His tone suggested he might be bothered by Zack disliking him so I ventured to find out. "Does that bother you? That you and Zack aren't friends?"

"Nope. The feeling's mutual...he's my Teresa. It's just that our war has a brutality to it that yours and hers doesn't."

"What do you mean?" A brutality? Eesh...

"When we fight, we fight dirty, Camie," he told me with a wink.

"You guys don't *really* fight, do you?" I asked, remembering that Kate had said he and Zack avoid each other, and other than my first day, I haven't witnessed even the smallest altercation between them whatsoever.

He looked at me then with a seriousness I couldn't quite place and said, "Oh we fight alright...just not constantly. We sort of ah...take turns throwing punches and it's not my turn right now. But if you stick around, I'm sure you'll get to see it."

I dropped the subject after that, thinking if he wanted to expand on his answer, he would've, and also, that I'd very much like to stick around with him as long as possible.

That previous, fleeting feeling I'd had when he drove me home from Mike's party—that there's *something* happening—was becoming more and more pronounced as we continued on, talking about other random things. And although there was an unexplained energy surrounding us, by the time we made the long walk back to his bus, I was feeling fatigued. My misadventure from last night has really taken a toll on me, not to mention being in the sun all day. So when we stopped next to the bus and I waited for him to pull his keys out, I couldn't keep myself from squinting up into the sun and yawning.

"Camie, you look really tired. Why don't you take a nap?"

"Actually, that sounds really good, but what are you gonna do? I don't wanna force you to hang around and listen to me snore," I told him in jest. I totally don't snore. I don't!

"I'll probably lay down too. You're not the only one who woke up feeling like shit this morning," he admitted. Huh. You would've never guessed. Obviously he's had a lot more practice than I have and therefore knows the stupid rules, but still.

Now are you ready for this next little scene in my fairytale day? Tristan opened the windows and pulled the drapes closed, then he plugged his iPod into some battery operated speakers, unfolded the couch—or bench seat if that's what you want to call it—and then like today wasn't already a dream come true for me, we stretched out together and took a nap. Honestly, this is a gazillion times better than when I got to cuddle with him and Mr. Darcy that day in English. I was so giddy I didn't think I'd actually fall asleep, but I'm pretty sure I was out like a light because I don't remember hearing anything after the first song.

I woke up some time later to find it was just starting to get dark outside and heard a frustrated Tristan saying, "Jesus, Kate, what in God's name is so fuckin' important that you have to text and call every ten goddamned minutes? —*Because she's asleep!*"

"Not anymore," I grumbled and looked over to see that Tristan was talking on *my* phone.

"Here, talk to her yourself. You can apologize for waking her up, you pest," Tristan said to her and then handed me my phone.

I took the phone and gave him a "what the hell is going on" look. Then I told Kate what'd transpired to have Tristan able to answer my phone. Of course I had to be selective in the details and in how much enthusiasm my voice held, but Kate was smart enough not to grill me, knowing that Tristan was most likely sitting right there.

I hung up with her and then tossing my phone back on the little shelf next to me, I turned back to him and asked, "What was that all about?"

"When your phone first went off I was worried it might be something about your mom so I checked the caller ID and saw it was Kate. She's been either texting or calling practically every ten minutes or so, it was making me nuts. I was about to tell her off when you woke up." He sounds a little testy but I'm super glad he didn't question my choice of ringtone for her; it's the theme song from Mission Impossible.

"I'm sorry, that's probably my fault…I should've told her I was already down here. This morning I told her to call if she hadn't heard from me by now and she's been ready to go but she didn't wanna leave me behind," I told him through a yawn while I stretched my arms.

"Did you get a good nap?" He asked while gazing down at me. Good grief…he is *so* very beautiful…

"Mm-hmm. Did you?" I asked with a smile. His hair is kinda messy. It's so cute.

OH CRAP! If his hair is messy, what does *my* bed head look like?! I wonder if there's a mirror anywhere in here…

"Sorta…Kate woke me up though," he pouted.

"Aww, poor baby. Are you gonna be cranky now?" I teased and giggled at him.

Laughing, he took his pillow and smooshed it in my face. "Look who's talking. You practically bit my head off when I woke you up earlier."

"Yeah, get over it, 'cause I'm not apologizing. That's who I am...take it or leave it," I said quite bluntly, although I really didn't mean it to come out like that.

Tristan grinned at me for a minute and then his eyes started to sparkle. "So, I'm assuming since you picked up on the whole 'We Hate Teresa Club' thing the way you did and being kind of a fan, you're pretty familiar with the show." How's that for a drastic change of subject?

"Again, you'd be correct. Even though it's not on anymore, it holds the number one position in my top three favorites as far as TV goes." I'm not sure where this came from or where he's going with it, but I'm more than curious.

"Sooo, you'd probably know what to say if I said... 'I'm going to ask you to go out with me next weekend.'" Oh, no he isn't!!! "—'And I'm kinda nervous about it actually. It's interesting,'" he said with the most irresistible lopsided grin ever.

This is truly unreal. Just so you understand; he's using a scene from Buffy to *ask me out*!!!! Oh, hold on. That's my cue...

"'Oh! Well, if it helps at all, I'm gonna say yes,'" I replied, saying the next lines with a huge grin on my face and hoping he didn't notice that I was having heart palpitations again.

His eyes got even brighter when I picked it right up and then he continued with the lines. "'Yeah, it helps. It creates a comfort zone... Do you wanna go out with me next weekend?'"

"I hope you're not expecting the rest of the lines because I'm just gonna say yes and be done with it."

Oh my God! He asked me out! He asked me out! He asked me out! I'm doing the Snoopy happy dance in my head and wondering if this day could possibly get any better than being asked out on my first date ever—by Tristan no less, who used quotes from my favorite television show do it. I really kinda doubt it.

Oh man! Was I ever wrong about *that*!

I didn't even have the chance to get nervous or scared before he leaned down and started to kiss me.

OMG!! I KNOW!!

Okay, since I'm pretty well occupied and we have some time here, you know how every girl will never forget the song playing during her first kiss? You know, provided there's music in the first place. Well, my mom's first kiss happened while she was at a party in eighth grade. She was dancing with the kid whose house the party was at to Depeche Mode's quintessential song "Somebody." From what I gather, it was a very '80s moment. Anyway, guess what song I get. You have no idea? Alright, I'll tell you; the second Tristan's lips met mine, none other than "Learning to Fly" by Pink Floyd began playing. From the title of the song alone, you should be able to understand how ridiculously fitting this is for a first kiss.

Actually, I'm not sure how much time is allowed to elapse during a kiss for it still to be considered as *a* kiss before it must be constituted as making out. I think we might've broken whatever ground rules there are on that, though, because we didn't stop when the song ended...or the one after that...or the one after that. I'm guessing that's because neither of us seems to be interested in oxygen at the moment.

Although the music was just barely registering—and I wouldn't think this until later that night when I *could* actually think—I had to wonder if God was controlling the shuffle on Tristan's iPod. Honestly, the soundtrack to this most glorious of experiences was simply uncanny. Allow me to explain. The second song was Mazzy Star's "Fade Into You" and it seemed like that's exactly what was happening. As Tristan kissed me and I kissed him back, everything…our environment, sound, thought…simply everything faded away until it was just us. We were like one, living and breathing as one entity. Then with the third song, "Hanging by a Moment" by Lifehouse, well, if you take some of the lyrics that say, "...forgetting all I'm lacking, completely incomplete, I'll take your invitation, you take all of me"—which is basically what's happening here—and then these as well; "...and I don't know what I'm diving into, just hanging by a moment here with you"…well, hopefully you get my point. That is to say, it just really felt like I was living in lyrics.

Coincidentally, or maybe not so coincidentally, that last song also has a section of lyrics that goes like this: "...there's nothing else to lose, nothing else to find, there's nothing in the world that can change my mind." But as it would happen, I'd discover that's not quite so true.

Anyhow, we were just getting into the fourth song in God's playlist—Limp Bizkit's "Build A Bridge," which I'd unfortunately find to be just as appropriate—when we so very rudely interrupted by Tristan's cell phone jingling "The Chicken Dance" song. Tristan let it go to voicemail at least thrice times (that means three) before he broke the mind numbingly thorough kiss.

He collapsed with his face in my neck in defeat, whimpered for a second and then grumbled, "I swear to God, I'm gonna throw both of our cell phones in the ocean."

Now that I was becoming coherent again, I started giggling. I would've gladly kept kissing him, but the polka music streaming from his phone was damned funny and I couldn't help laughing.

"Is that Jeff?"

"Yeah, how'd you know?" He asked and while blindly reaching for his phone that was polka-ing again, he began to absentmindedly nibble on my neck.

It almost seemed like he thought, "Well, since I'm here, I may as well make myself at home." I welcomed him by lifting and tilting my chin a little so his lips could get more comfy along my jaw line.

"The Chicken Dance song? Who else could it be? Hey, put it on speaker, let me talk to him."

It's only fair; Tristan answered my phone when it was bugging him, now it's my turn. And as a side note: Holy cow! You should see the size of the goose bumps he's giving me!

"Tell him to go to hell," Tristan murmured, handing me his phone while he continued to nuzzle my neck.

As much as I wanted to do as he asked, I was thinking it was going to be difficult because I was having a *really* tough time concentrating, but, I gave it a go. Here's the transcript:

Me: "What's up, he who shalt not be the blithering ninny any longer, but henceforth shalt be dubbed, the vexing hindrance." (My "Ye Olde English" that I picked up mostly from *Monty Python and the Holy Grail* isn't as good as it could be but I'm being distracted—and very well at that.)

Jeff: "Uhhh. *Camie?*"

Me: "Yes, good for you. You finally got something right."

Jeff: (Pause) "I did dial Tristan, didn't I?"

Me: (Pause while I pull my mouth away from Tristan's and he moves a piece of hair away from my neck for better accessibility—I think.) "Uhhh, yes." (I'm chanting "focus, focus, focus" to myself.) "You have not been deceived, My Lord Irksomeness. I have a message, are you ready?"

Jeff: "Uh, I don't know. So far I haven't understood a damned thing you've said...but, go ahead I guess."

Me: "Thou wilt be condemned into everlasting perdition for this much grievous offense thou hast committed." (Tristan apparently loved that, because now he's laughing into my neck.)

Jeff: *"What?!"*

Tristan: "Do they speak English in What? It means go to hell, Jeff." (He starts kissing me again.) (Oh, and that first part was definitely a quote from *Pulp Fiction*.)

Jeff: "Oh, you're there...Hey! Am I on speaker phone?"

Tristan: "Yes. What do you want?" (He kisses me some more.)

Jeff: "Oh, right. Hey, we're here, come help us unload the wood."

Tristan: "Unload it your *damned* selves." (He goes back to inspecting my neck with his mouth. I'm thinking he might have some vampiric tendencies—which I'm totally cool with of course.)

Jeff: "What the hell is wrong with you guys?"

Tristan: "You and your girlfriend are a pain in the ass." (He rolls away from me to make a gesture telling the phone to f-off and then pulls me to him for more kissing.)

Jeff: "Whatever. Dude, come on...we need help and I know you're already down here 'cause I saw the bus, so if you don't want me to hunt you down, you'll get your ass over here."

Tristan: (He stops kissing me, sighs in defeat again and rolls his eyes in exasperation.) "You're a dick."

Tristan hung up on Mr. Chicken, tossed his phone aside and gave me a look that I think was him contemplating kissing me again, but I'm not really sure because it's kind of dark in here now. Then he sighed. "Come on, he'll just come over here and drag us out anyway."

When he opened the doors of the bus and I went to climb out, I shivered with the chilly beach air. I hadn't thought about this little issue when I agreed to stay down here with him all day. All I have to wear is what I've got on and I'm pretty sure I'm gonna freeze my butt off in shorts and a t-shirt even *if* the bonfire resembles Hell's little cousin. Plus, I think I might have a bit of a sunburn and that's just going to make it worse.

When Tristan saw me rubbing my arms he asked, "Are you cold?"

"Yeah. I'm not acclimated to the weather yet and I think I might have a sunburn."

"Yeah, your cheeks and nose look a little pink. Lemme see if I have something you can wear." He climbed back into his bus to search through storage compartments and then he turned back around, holding out a pair of lifeguard-red sweat pants that have a faded orange logo down one leg. "Here, these should work. We'll have to roll 'em up, but they'll be better than what you have now."

I gratefully took the sweat pants. "I don't care, anything will be better than wearing damp shorts right now."

As I was shimmying out of my shorts, I realized how much sand was still in my suit and I considered, for one brief moment of lunacy, going commando. I think that would just be too much for either of us to handle with dignity, though, especially since I'm still unsure about *his* underwear status. Better to be chafed by sand then have to think about knowing that he knows that I'm wearing his clothes without any underwear—again.

He turned to hand me his Letterman's jacket and said, "I *am* gonna want this back but you can wear it tonight."

"You got it. Since I don't play any of these sports and it doesn't fit, I don't think it'd be an appropriate addition to my wardrobe." After having pulled it on, though, I looked down at myself and groaned at my fashion statement.

"What?"

"I'm a fashion nightmare. I look like a seven year old playing dress up *and* I clash," I said, referring to the red sweat pants with the orange logo—of which the ankles are rolled *several* times over so they don't drag on the ground—my purple and white striped t-shirt, and his blue and gold jacket which I'm swimming in. Really, it's quite disturbing.

"I think you look cute," he said and kissed me once sweetly.

"Whatever. I think you're biased...they're *your* clothes after all," I pouted and took the blanket he handed me to carry.

"You see my point then." Ha! Kate was right! He's making me into a walking poster board that says "Back off, I'm with Tristan tonight." Pretty cool, huh? "Okay, you've got that, I have the cooler...I think that's it...let's go." Tristan locked the bus and then giving me another quick kiss, he took my hand and we left.

We made our way to where a lifted, extra-cab truck filled with firewood was backed into a cul-de-sac, and met up with Jeff, Mike, and my not-stalker, Pete. Really, there's been absolutely nothing to indicate that Pete's been spying on me for Tristan. I know that Kate said he's really dialed in and everything, but, I hardly ever see him around school and I practically never hear his name mentioned by anyone—I mean I don't even know what the guy's last name is for crying out loud! He seems like a genuinely nice guy, but he's almost always so quiet you don't even notice him, and although he appears to be a really close friend of Tristan's and Jeff's, my conclusion is that he's clueless in regards to Tristan and me and, that the three of us girls have just been paranoid in that respect.

As Tristan let go of my hand and jumped into the bed of the truck to start unloading wood, I deduced that the truck must be Pete's because Mike was locking up a BMW, and as we now know, Jeff drives an old Jeep CJ7.

Mike told me that Kristen was holding the fire-ring down on the beach, so I headed off to find her while the guys did the manual labor of unloading and carrying the wood to the beach. By the time the fire was getting started, Kate showed up, Melissa and Keith following soon after. Since it was still sort of early and everyone aside from Pete was coupled up, the environment was nice and mellow. Pete didn't appear bothered by the fact that he was odd man out, but instead it seemed like this is typical.

He did, however, along with pretty much everyone else, lift an interested eyebrow at how Tristan and I were sitting; making me think *this* sight isn't so typical. Forming the mirror image of Jeff and Kate, I was sitting in front of Tristan with my back against his chest; he had his chin on my shoulder and his arms were wrapped around my waist, like it was the most natural thing in the world. As atypical as it might be and being the object of undisguised interest as we were right then, I didn't care. I was totally *loving* it!

The intimacy didn't last very long though, as kids started trickling in to join us. With the appearance of others, our little group abandoned sitting on blankets to mingle with those who were standing, and what had began as a gathering, started to become a shindig. I'm hoping that with the entire beach surrounding us, I won't feel so claustrophobic if it progresses to be a hootenanny. Oh and the fire is more closely related to Hell than being a little cousin, so I ended up taking Tristan's jacket off too.

"Hey, you guys want a beer?" Jeff asked Tristan and me as he dug through a cooler.

"No, but grab a Gatorade out of my cooler," Tristan answered over his shoulder as he pulled his phone out to presumably read a text.

"You're not drinking?" Jeff asked, sounding somewhat surprised.

"No, I'm driving Camie home tonight." Aw, staying sober just for me.

"Oh, okay. What about you, Camie? Want a beer?" He asked and handed Tristan the fruit punch flavored sports drink.

"Uh-uh, nope, negatory, no way, no." I actually shivered at the thought.

"What was that little shaking thing about?" Jeff asked, having noticed my minor epileptic fit.

"She doesn't want anything, so drop it," Tristan snapped, sticking his cell phone back in his pocket and valiantly rescuing me from having to divulge my dirty little secret to anyone else. Then he cracked open the Gatorade and handed it to me before meandering away to talk to some other people.

"Jesus...you're being a moody son of bitch tonight," Jeff called out to Tristan's departing back.

In answer, without looking back and still walking away, Tristan raised his arm and flipped Jeff off.

About midway through the evening, I was chatting with a group of people a little ways from the fire when I started to get cold, so rubbing my arms again; I left them and headed over to the other side of the fire and Tristan's cooler where I'd left his jacket. Halfway there, I was waylaid by she who must not be named. However, instead of snickering behind my back, this time she opted to taunt me to my face.

"That's a stunning outfit. What did you do, get dressed in the dark?"

I rolled my eyes. Seriously, my six year old cousin could've come up with something much more original.

"Teresa, you know…I'd tell you to bite me but I don't want rabies or any of the other various strains of disease common in your species," I said, not quite politely. Although I did say it with a smile, so that has to count for something, right?

"Did you just call me a *dog*?" She asked, sounding as if she were unsure of my meaning.

"That's amazing. You lack the ability to use the English language to any degree aside from the most vulgar yet you understand it sufficiently well. I'll admit I find that to be quite the conundrum." I had to stifle a little giggle when I noticed Tristan standing behind her, fighting his own laughter.

Looking really confused, she made another attempt at degrading me. "Whatever. Really though, who in the hell dressed you? Helen Kel—"

"I did," Tristan said, cutting her off mid-sophomoric insult and stepping around her to my side to hand me his jacket.

Teresa was just standing there, her mouth hanging open, *finally* at a loss for words. Oh and did I mention that I'm picturing Tristan astride a magnificent white stallion while wearing chain mail right now? Well I am. Join me, won't you?

I put his jacket on then smacked his arm. "See? I told you I clash."

He chuckled and loud enough to be overheard he whispered, "Fight fair, Camie. You know she's unarmed without a dictionary."

"I know, but she started it."

"I bet. Now come on...you two should be separated," he pronounced in a very parental manner. Then he picked me up in a big, bear hug and turned to carry me away, my feet dangling well of the ground. "*You* need to learn how to avoid your enemies."

As Tristan bodily removed me from Teresa's presence, I stuck my tongue out at her over his shoulder. I was a little disappointed though; I don't think she actually saw me do it.

Tristan however, did see my childlike "last word" and he chuckled again. "Don't be a tease, put that away."

When I looked at his face in question, he flashed me one of my favorite lopsided, yet cocky grins and then gave me a lightning quick kiss. I didn't even get a chance to pucker for this one.

"Here, you like Kate. Now be a good girl and play nice." Tristan deposited me on the ground in front of Kate who'd witnessed the whole scene and was laughing, and then without another word, he walked off.

While Kate and I wandered up to the bathroom together, I quickly and quietly filled her in on the details of the day and evening. She teased me about my apparel, congratulated me on my upcoming date and finally getting to partake in the much desirous smooching. In turn, I thanked her for her perseverance in trying to reach me, because that was what really started the whole thing off in the first place. She got a kick out of how he asked me out too. I mean I couldn't have asked for a better way for him to do it, although I guess it's not something he usually does. From what Kate said, he's always just asked girls out the normal way. And yeah, having never been asked out before, I don't really know what the "normal way" is, but whatever.

The rest of the evening passed by in a blur as, excepting that first party, I'm finding this type of merriment is wont to do. And once again before I knew it, my alarm went off, announcing midnight had arrived and the time to leave lest Tristan's bus turn into a pumpkin and I end up in rags on the side of the road. However, not being able to locate Tristan in the rumpus the bonfire had become, I was thinking I'd have to extricate Kate from her blanket in front of the fire where she and Jeff were cuddled up together. So by now, I'm sure you can imagine how startled I was—yes, I think I even squeaked—when Tristan came up behind me, wrapping his arms around my waist and kissing my neck all too briefly before asking if I was ready to go. We gathered up his bonfire paraphernalia, said goodbye to those within hearing range, and then left. Actually, there wasn't that much stuff really, only the blanket and cooler…I just like the word "paraphernalia." It's fun to say and it sounds better than stuff or gear.

On the drive home, Tristan and I exchanged cell numbers so we could coordinate for Friday and since he was driving, I got to do all the programming. However in doing so, I inadvertently invaded Tristan's privacy. Well, sort of. See, here's what happened; Tristan had handed me his phone and when I hit the button to "wake" it up, part of a text conversation was on the screen.

G: just bring him back in the am.
Tristan: 4get it. if u want him back, u come get him.
G: ok but fyi…im sleepin in

See? It was a complete accident and I don't know if it really counts as an invasion of privacy because the whole thing was so ambiguous, I have no clue what it means. I mean the person doesn't even have a name! And it's not like I'm gonna ask, you know? So instead, I immediately closed the message screen so Tristan wouldn't see that I'd read it. Yeah, I know… I felt *totally* guilty. Plus, how embarrassing would it be for me to actually admit that even though I didn't mean to, I'd just done something that could be considered equal to reading a diary?! *Especially* knowing how much he likes to keep what he does outside of school private. I know, right? Also, I really don't want to screw up my chances with him and I think saying anything could be potentially problematic. I mean I'd probably do a lot of embarrassing stuttering…he'd probably get pissed at me…yada yada yada. Ugh, no thanks.

Erasing the text from my mind and pretending like I hadn't ever seen it, I found Tristan's address book and typed out my number on his phone with the name "WHTC PREZ." He's pretty quick so I'm sure he'll figure it out. Nevertheless, I did control my impulses by not assigning myself a specific ringtone. I was thinking it might not go over so well at this point if I made it the "Wedding March" like I was tempted to do. Although I think I'm gonna download Faith Hill's "This Kiss" or "The Way You Love Me" for his ringtone on my phone. I'll have to look up the lyrics and see which one fits best. I'd use the *JAWS* theme song, but that's my ringtone on Kate's phone.

The rest of the drive passed without incident but unlike the last time he took me home, the gentleman lurking under Tristan's surface walked me to my door and kissed me goodnight for several earth shaking minutes. Truthfully, I don't know if kissing is always like this, but my head was literally buzzing when we stopped. And actually, stopping seemed kind of hard to do. There wasn't anything specific that makes me say that, but I felt a definite reluctance to part come from both of us. We eventually did part, though, and looking back at each other over our shoulders once, we went our separate ways.

All in all, I've had what I'll think of fondly as my own version of *The Little Mermaid* fairytale today. It even had an evil witch from whom my prince rescued me. Oh, I should mention that I returned Tristan's jacket to him but I'm seriously considering holding his pants hostage until he gives me my shirt and bra back. And speaking of my bra and trophies, my perfect day was topped off when I went to climb in bed and found *the* best souvenir of my day waiting for me under the covers. Apparently Jillian hadn't been as innocent as she'd led me to believe.

I pulled back my blankets and saw a little homemade scrapbook decorated with sand and seashells; it was filled with pictures of Tristan and me playing in the ocean. She'd even captured the two of us just talking on the beach and the whole struggle of getting me in the water. See? When she uses her powers for good, it can have quite an impact. So becoming a little teary with sentiment and appreciation, I flipped through it several times before turning my light out and whispering a prayer of gratitude for all of the many gifts this day held.

And let me tell you, if I'd known what was coming, I might've appreciated those gifts even more…

12.

Why In God's Name Is There So Much Glitter In Here?

Sunday morning dawned fine and clear. So much so that from my bedroom window, I could see the quilting on the toilet paper that was hanging in the uppermost branches of the trees.

Hearing the frown in my voice, Kate asked, "What's wrong? I would've thought that after yesterday you'd be totally thrilled..."

"Oh, I'm filled with exuberance about all of that, it's just that my house was gift wrapped in Charmin some time during the night," I told her and shifted my phone to my other hand so I could pour some milk over my Grape Nuts cereal.

"Oh, that sucks. How'd your parents take it?"

"Not too bad...my dad is making Jill and me clean it up though. Jillian let her age kids take the wrap for it but we both think it was Teresa and the trampy twosome she leads around by the nose."

"Yeah, that fits, especially considering that little scene at the bonfire. Seeing it was funny enough but I wish I could've heard it too," she said and giggled at her memories of it.

"It *was* pretty comical. Hey, that reminds me...I wanted to ask you something about that."

"Shoot..."

"Well, when I stuck my tongue out at Teresa while Tristan was carrying me away, he said 'don't be a tease, put that away' and I'm a little embarrassed to admit it, but I'm not too sure what he meant. Plus, when I looked my question, all he did was give me that super fast kiss."

It's true, I've been noodling on that since I went to bed last night and I think I might know, but I'd rather hear Kate's interpretation. I still trust her more about these things than I do myself.

"Oh, don't be embarrassed, Camie. All this stuff is still really new to you. I mean it hasn't even been twenty-four hours since your first-ever kiss."

"Yeah, I know. I just really dislike not understanding things...it bugs the crap outta me."

I know that there are times I come off sounding somewhat confident and probably even like an intellectual snob, but I think it's mostly a defense mechanism. I *hate* looking and sounding stupid. Sadly, I seem to end up looking and/or sounding exactly that more often than not.

"I get that. So in answer to your question, I'd be willing to bet my dad's life savings that he was implying you were tempting him to either kiss you flat out in front of *everyone*, or, drag you back to his bus so he could kiss you as much and for however long as he wanted to. He could've done either I suppose, but being that it was still kinda early and the party hadn't quite gone into full swing yet, both probably would've raised some eyebrows so I'm thinking that's why you got the fast one. It was for him, not you. I'm guessing he was self-soothing, you know? Like he felt he couldn't do what he really wanted to so he pacified himself with a quick kiss instead of nothing," she expertly explained once again.

"Huh. I guess that makes sense, because he didn't actually kiss me at the bonfire except that one time and then briefly on the neck before we left. He also didn't hang around much," I told her, lining up what she said with everything that happened. Thinking back, we did actually kiss for real quite a lot, but it wasn't in front of a soul; we were always alone.

"Yeah, I saw that, but by that time there were so many people around, I doubt anyone would've taken much notice or really thought anything of it. It seems like he's still playing things pretty close to his chest, but you've come a long way in a really short time...I'm kinda surprised actually."

"What do you mean, why surprised?"

"Well, I think he's falling for you. And kinda hard, judging from what I've seen so far and all the atypical stuff he's been doing. But I also think he might be afraid of getting burned so I think he's holding back so as not to rush things, if that makes sense. He's been declaring himself little by little and now that he's let you in on his interest, you need to keep it. Remember what our original strategy was, be yourself but make him chase you. If you make it too easy by calling or texting him all the time or trying to get his attention at school, I think he'll jump ship faster than you can blink an eye."

I'm thinking this is her way of saying "keep your eyes on the prize and don't do anything to jeopardize your tremendous advances."

"Well that would totally suck. I definitely don't want him to do that."

"No, you really don't. Getting him back in the boat would be practically impossible...the stubborn ass," Kate predicted and then almost incoherently and around what sounded like a big yawn, she asked, "So, do you wanna go shopping later and maybe get some dinner or see a movie?"

My answer was probably just as incoherent as hers though, if not worse as my mouth was full of crunchy cereal goodness. "I'd love to but I really shouldn't...I have to get this toilet paper mess cleaned up and I have some homework that I don't wanna wait until the last minute to do. Plus, my dad said something about wanting to go out to dinner as a family tonight."

"Okey dokey," she said and then yawned again.

"You sound totally exhausted, Kate..." I opined as I chewed.

"Because I am…I don't get it. I mean I got like nine or more hours of sleep and I slept great, but I can't seem to keep my eyes open this morning."

"Huh. Maybe you need some coffee or something to perk you up."

"Nah…coffee's okay and everything but too much of it is murder on my stomach. Besides, I'd much rather get my caffeine in chocolate. And that being the case, the only coffee really worth drinking in my opinion is a Starbucks mocha and I don't feel like getting dressed."

"What about Jeff?" I asked, dumping my spoon and now empty cereal bowl in the sink before turning the faucet on.

"What about him?"

"Would he bring you Starbucks?"

"Oh, totally. Well, that is if he heard his phone and chances are, he won't. He's such a deep sleeper…I swear, sometimes it's like trying to wake the dead."

That reminded me of my fortuitous nap with Tristan so, starting to giggle; I told her how cute and little boy whiny I thought he was when we woke up. In hearing that, she informed me that the initial crankiness I thought I heard from him yesterday was not imagined nor is it uncommon. He loves his sleep and consequently, being woken from a nap really kind of pisses him off. So, it seems Tristan and I have yet one more thing in common.

I hung up with Kate after having made some plans to get together on Monday afternoon, and then Jill and I bent to the task of cleaning the trees and bushes. It was a giant pain and seemed like it took forever so although we didn't know for sure if she was responsible, neither of us felt too terrible for passing the time by picturing Teresa locked in an old fashioned stockade as the townsfolk threw rotten fruit and vegetables at her. When we finished that, I moved on to my homework and my sister moved on to…something I guess…I kind of lost track of her after that. But, by the time I was finished putting my laundry away, Jillian and I were reunited when my dad announced that it was time to leave for dinner.

The restaurant we went to was a new one that my mom had read a review for and wanted to try. I thought we'd stick close to home, but come to find out; the place was downtown; about thirty minutes away. It was larger and more upscale than what I was expecting too. It was the kind of place with intimately dim lighting, unobtrusive wait staff, and high booths and potted plants that screen the quiet patrons while they enjoy their Oysters Rockefeller. You know, the kind of place that isn't exactly known for its extensive children's menu. Not that it matters really, unless of course you find yourself asking the question, "Why would anyone bring an infant to a place like this?" Which was exactly what I was asking myself on my way back from the bathroom after we'd finished eating. Although I'd kept my question to myself, I ended up getting an answer. And to say that the answer was worrisome would be kind of a freaking understatement.

The whole roundtrip was a series of uncomfortable and disquieting scenes and it ended with me wearing someone's freaking Caesar salad. No, I'm not kidding. First, because I'd downed at least three sodas and a virgin piña colada during dinner, I had to pee like a racehorse. Sorry about the tired metaphor, but, it's true, so, there it is. That being the case, I of course got lost both going to and coming from the ladies' room. Second, I did find my way to the bathroom but only with help. What's more is that help actually had the nerve to be irritated with me for disturbing her during her oh-so important task of folding cloth napkins to make them look like fans. And even then, her directions were lacking and by the time I finally got to the restrooms, I was unable to appreciate the pristine cleanliness and pleasant flowery aroma the ladies' room provided. Honestly, I would've been happy with a port-a-potty or a freaking bush.

Thus I found urinary relief but when I left the bathroom, I must've turned the wrong way because as I was walking, I noticed that the kitchen was on the opposite side of me from where it should've been. Seriously frustrated, I turned back around and tried to find a drink station or some other point of reference so I could get back to where I came from. Truthfully, Hansel and Gretel probably had an easier time finding their way than I did in that place. Anyhow, I was walking along a path running parallel to a row of booths with a chest-high wall topped with plants that were keeping the diners and the foot traffic separate, when I heard the baby start fussing. Well, fussing doesn't quite cover it but whatever. That was the moment I asked myself the aforementioned question. However, the moment I stuttered to an utterly shocked halt and became entirely unable to keep myself from eavesdropping was when I heard the infant call "My Tristan" *his* "Da-Da."

How do I know it was "My Tristan" you ask? Well, because when the baby very clearly said "Da-Da," a woman I can only assume is Tristan's mother said, "Tristan dear, he wants you." And then Tristan, whose voice I've come to be able to hear in my head at will, replied, "I know…come here, buddy." I'd be lying if I said I didn't stand there rooted to the spot not only listening, but peeking through the plants to see as well. And don't you judge me either…you know you'd do the exact same thing.

Anyway, this was what my limited and rather shameful surveillance got me:

A man and a woman were sitting on opposite sides of the table, facing each other, and Tristan, sitting at sort of an angle to me in the curved booth, was hugging the baby to him and trying to quiet his crying. In hindsight, I was really touched by how Tristan cooed to the chunky little monkey he was holding, making kissy faces and soothing him by rubbing his back and stuff like that; it was quite precious.

Then the woman spoke up again. "Why is it they always say Da-Da first?"

"Well at least this one talks…I don't think he opened his mouth until he was almost two," the man, who I guess is Tristan's dad, said.

"He just wanted to get his words right, Stan…and he was *not* almost two," Tristan's mom said in lighthearted defense of her son.

"*He* can hear you, you know…hey Dad, see if you can find his elephant in the bag."

Digging through what I guess is a diaper bag and sounding dismayed, Tristan's dad said, "Why in God's name is there so much glitter in here?"

"Well Dad, you see, that's what happens when a guy has a baby with a prostitute...she gets hooker dust all over the f-u-c-k-i-n-g place," Tristan answered in what sounded like extreme displeasure, literally spelling out his swear word for, I assume, the baby's benefit.

"Tristan, I know you and Gina don't exactly get along anymore, but calling her a prostitute isn't right," Tristan's mom admonished gently.

"Well, she uses her body for money…pretty much the same thing in my opinion," Tristan retorted.

"That's what dancer's do, dear," Tristan's mom returned.

"Especially the ones on the pole…" Tristan's dad intoned.

"Oh Stan…"

"See? Dad gets it! I mean Jesus Christ, Mom; you make it sound like she's a ballerina or something and she's not, so just say it. Joey's mom is a stripper. A lying b-i-t-c-h stripper who still insists the condom broke."

"It was entrapment, Son, plain and simple…everyone who matters knows that."

"Yeah, well that doesn't exactly make it okay, now does it?" Tristan sighed. "You know what, never mind…can we get off this subject? He's a great kid and it's not his fault." He then started using the stuffed elephant to play peek-a-boo with the baby, now known as Joey.

"You're right dear, he's a wonderful little boy…and he's getting *so* big. Just look at those chubby little fingers and toes…you know, Tristan, you had the cutest rolls of baby fat when you were nine months," Tristan's mom mused.

"Oh good lord…" Although I couldn't see him do it, I could picture Tristan rolling his eyes.

"Well I can't help it…maybe if I could spend more time wi—"

The sound of what was clearly a diaper being soiled cut Tristan's mom off and laughing, Tristan said, "Well, it wasn't a bell but I'll take the save anyway…okay you guys, lemme out so I can go change him before our food gets here."

When it became obvious that Tristan was about to stand up, I came to my senses and skedaddled myself the hell out of there before I got caught spying. I was hurrying around a corner, trying to put as much distance between myself and Tristan's table, or the bathroom, or, both actually, and that's when I ran into a waiter carrying a tray of Caesar salads. Luckily, the dressing had very little anchovy in it, so I'm calling that a bonus.

Ugh.

I couldn't even begin to process the startling scene I'd just witnessed and since I was still picking Romaine off of my person when I finally got back to my table, I used that incident as a more than reasonable excuse for wanting to leave right away and not discussing what was, in truth, my more than a little guilty preoccupied silence. Even Jillian kept her distance and didn't once try to pick my brain for any other possible reasons as to why I was being so reserved. I took a shower immediately once we got home and then faking a series of yawns, I went to bed. The reality is though; I wouldn't sleep a wink.

I kept turning the information over repeatedly in my head, trying to decide how I feel about dating a guy who has a baby. I mean the age difference is one thing, and the experience he has is as well, but a baby?! Getting involved with someone who has a baby is pretty serious and I can only imagine how complicated and difficult it would be to do. And I'm only fifteen for crying out loud! I mean yes, technically I'm old enough to have a child myself, but that doesn't mean I'm ready to play any kind of remotely prominent role in the life of a baby.

But what about Tristan? Doesn't he deserve to have a life too? Or should he be branded an outcast, never to have a relationship in his young life because he's a teen father? No, I don't think that's fair at all. However, is this something *I* should get involved in at this stage in my life? Well…I just don't know. I mean I really like Tristan and we seem to have this connection that's becoming pretty amazing for one thing, but I'd also like to say I'm the kind of person who can keep an open mind and not judge someone based on a past mistake, you know? And this doesn't sound like a mistake even, but more like Tristan having been a victim. True, he could've not had sex with the girl in the first place, but who knows, maybe she tricked him into doing that too. It's possible I guess, and having that experience would kind of explain some things. Like why he detests when girls go after him they way they do and why he tries to keep his life as private as possible. I mean if I'd fathered a child with a stripper while I was still in high school, I sure as hell would be doing my damnedest to keep that from being public knowledge too!

No wonder Kate said he keeps things mostly minor! He's already paying majorly for not doing so previously. And, that could also be why Kate mentioned how he doesn't talk about his sex life and that he has skeletons—plural. Knowing him as well as she does, she would know about Joey and I mean the cheerleader is like a teeny-tiny thing to having a baby in my opinion, because this is one pretty freaking humongous skeleton, you know?!

All of that was still spinning in my head the following morning when I left the house early to go for a walk around the park. I still haven't come to a decision and I kind of want to figure out how I feel before bringing this whole thing up to my sister, Kate and Melissa, Tristan, or, anyone really. On the one hand, I'm sure my friends as well as Tristan will understand my position if I say this is too much for me. But on the other hand, they all might think of me as being piously self-righteous. After all, none of them have seen fit to mention this to me and maybe that's because this kind of thing has happened before with other girls who've found out about Tristan's son. Plus—and not that I did so intentionally—I still feel inordinately guilty for finding out the way I did.

Thinking about that last part, though, was actually what told me what to do. I have to tell him. Even though I don't know where I stand now on *dating* Tristan, I know I have no problem being his friend. The only problem is that I can't expect him to want to be my friend until I'm honest with him, which means I have to confess that I know about Joey, *and*, how I came to know about him. And yeah, I'm taking a risk here but maybe once I talk to him, I'll have a better idea of what I'm really looking at getting into. So, that's what I determined to do; only I didn't expect to have the opportunity to do it quite so soon.

When I made my way around the park and to the part where the playground is, my feet came to another stuttering halt and my lungs momentarily forgot what their primary function is. Nevertheless, sucking in a deep breath and fighting everything inside me that's screaming for me to run and hide, I slowly started forward again to approach where Tristan was just pulling Joey out of a toddler swing. It was still early, but there were a few other kids already playing on the jungle gym; their moms seated on benches here and there, chatting with each other. I really was planning on just walking up to him, but...I didn't. Right at the moment when I would've called attention to myself, Joey's mom showed up and immediately, she and Tristan started to get into what appeared to be a heated sort of argument.

I couldn't quite hear what they were saying, though; they were both keeping their voices down and Joey had started crying the moment Tristan removed him from the swing. However, I did catch little things like Tristan accusing her of being on drugs, and her flat out demanding her son as she forcibly took Joey from Tristan's arms. Then she bent down and grabbed the diaper bag.

My heart just about broke when, pleading, Tristan said, "Please, Gina...*please* don't do this. *Please*...I'm *begging* you."

"I'm not doing *anything*, Tristan...thanks for taking him on short notice," Gina said, quite insincerely. Then she turned around, got in her car and left.

Tristan thrust a hand into his hair and watched them drive away. Then he turned around. He still hadn't seen me, though, when he threw the stuffed elephant as far as he could in visible anger and frustration. I ducked as it sailed over my head and I watched it land a good distance behind me. Then looking back at Tristan, I saw the light of recognition dawn in his eyes as they found me standing there. His lips lifted into a small smile so I started towards him again.

Meeting me halfway he asked, "Hey...what are you doing here?"

"I've been out walking... Um, are you okay?"

"Huh? Oh... Yeah, I'm fine...that chick just *really* pisses me off. I mean she shows up obviously tweaking, and thinks I'm gonna be cool with letting her drive a baby?! Fuck! I mean *I* wouldn't even get in a car with her when she's like that, but, I have no fuckin' say so what am I gonna do, you know?" He vented as we walked over to retrieve Joey's toy.

Now, being that I'd just very recently come to the decision of telling him I know about him being a dad and all, I haven't had a single minute to prepare what I wanted to say. However, after seeing and hearing all that, I was kind of mad on his behalf so I opened my mouth to try my hand at compassionate sympathy. What I *actually* did was quite simply put my ignorant foot in my mouth. Well, not "quite simply." No, what I did was botch things up between Tristan and me so badly, God himself would have a hard time not calling me all the names synonymous with nincompoop that His thesaurus holds. And I imagine that's one enormous thesaurus, you know?

"I'm so sorry, Tristan...but, if she's an unfit mother then why don't you sue for custody? I mean fathers have a lot of rights now that they didn't used to have."

"Yeah I—wait. Did you just say *I* should sue for custody?"

"Well yeah, it's a lot easier for fathers to do now than it used to be."

This was when it all of sudden occurred to me that Tristan was wholly incredulous—and, *pissed*.

"You think *I'm* his dad?!" He asked in what could best be described as outrage.

"Well I—"

Tristan cut me off, being close to shouting now. "What? You see me with a baby and you automatically assume he's *mine*?! What the fuck?!"

I didn't get a chance to say anything in my defense, though, because he snatched the stuffed toy from the ground and then pointing it at me in accusation he said, "You know, I really thought you were different."

He stormed over to his car and started to get in; I was stunned. But, I was also desperate. I ran to catch up with him, not wanting anything—er, *everything* to end like this. "Tristan wait! Will you please let me explain?"

"There's nothing to explain here, Camie. And for your information, if he *was* my son, you can be goddamned sure I would've fought for custody and won a long fucking time ago. Oh and you can forget about our date." Then he slammed his car door shut and took off, tires screeching.

So yeah. That's what I get for not only invading someone's privacy on multiple occasions, but for also using the limited information gleaned from said invasion to assume probably the worst possible scenario. I think this would be the perfect place for an expletive but, I don't got one. I was also at a complete and utter loss as to what to say, what to do, or, how to fix it. Actually, fixing it is probably out. I mean even if I explain myself, I can't imagine Tristan will be likely to laugh off my narrow-minded ignorance. And just this once, I think I'd really like to have someone laugh about how stupid I can be, provided of course that the laughter isn't the much-evil sneering kind and that he's laughing *with* me and not *at* me.

Once the ramifications of what'd just happened actually hit me, the tears came. I sat on the swings for at least a half-hour and got it all out as best I could. Then, knowing I was probably wasting my time, I sent Tristan a text asking him to please text or call me back. He didn't respond. And even though I was tempted to send him another one explaining everything, I didn't. Besides, I really think this kind of thing would be better done face-to-face. So now that I was emotionally as well as physically drained, I walked back home. Then, saying a brief hi to my mom and telling her I was exhausted, I went to my room and went back to bed.

After not sleeping last night, I wasn't shocked that I didn't wake up until I heard the telltale sound that means a monster Great White is about to chomp on another unsuspecting swimmer. I went to answer Kate's call but just barely missed it so on a sigh, I called Tristan while I waited for the voicemail I was sure Kate would leave. Again, I wasn't surprised when he didn't answer. Sure he wouldn't pick up, though, I was prepared to leave a message. The voicemail I left him was one of sincere apology for hurting his feelings like I had and I asked him to please let me at least explain. I also told him he could still hate me afterwards. Honestly, it was entirely unintentional but I still wouldn't blame him if he thought I was a superficial bitch.

I got out of bed and while giving myself a good look in my bathroom mirror; I listened to Kate's voicemail. I was a little surprised to learn she hadn't heard about the incident already from Jeff, but again, who knows…maybe she just didn't want to chastise me in a message. She'd asked if we were still on for a movie so I called her back to accept, thinking I'd just explain everything to her when she picked me up. Needless to say, she heard something in my voice and I ended up crying into the phone instead as I told her what I dunce I am.

"Oh Camie…I wish you would've asked me about that. I mean I could've told you the deal with Joey," Kate said after I spilled my entire sordid tale.

Come to find out, Joey is actually the nephew of the guy who was down to his boxers at Mike's party; his name is Wayne. And because he and his parents are out of town, Tristan was the next person on the babysitter list. Apparently, Tristan has a soft spot for kids and it was obvious from what I saw, Joey adores him. Not only that but I guess Tristan's and Wayne's parents are kind of close friends; therefore Tristan is close to their children, making it not uncommon for any one of the three to be called in to babysit in a pinch. Also, from what Kate explained to me, the texts I read were most likely from Wayne's older brother and Joey's real father, Gary. She told me that Gary and his wife, Gina, only got married because Gina got pregnant. Additionally, their wedding took place only after Joey was born and a paternity test was done. Everyone who knows the family well thinks that Gina trapped Gary into marriage by getting pregnant on purpose. Regardless of whether that's true or not, they have some serious problems and Gary is apparently trying to make it work for the sake of his son and that relationship.

I mean I felt like a heel before but with knowing the back-story, I now feel like a freaking size thirteen and a half boot. Kate told me I should just talk to Tristan and explain why I thought what I had, and yeah, I totally agree but, that's kind of hard to do when Tristan won't give me the time of day now. So with that being what it is, Kate and I were back to talking strategy. Only this time, our strategy didn't have anything to do with getting Tristan to be my boyfriend. This time it's solely about trying to figure out a way to get him to listen to me. The plan we came up with however, did include doing a little stalking, or rather, a lot of driving around.

Because Kate and I had originally made plans together, Jeff had made his own. He'd told her he was doing something with Tristan, but she didn't know what they were doing or where they were hanging out. She didn't think it'd be the best idea to call him and ask, though, because if he forewarned Tristan that I might be coming and if Tristan really didn't want to talk to me, then he'd take off for sure. Instead, we drove around looking for them. It took close to two hours but we finally spotted Tristan's car at a pizza place that is, ironically, only about five minutes from my house.

"Are you ready?" Kate asked, pulling into a space in the mostly full parking lot and shutting the engine off.

"Not exactly…I mean what if he freaks out and screams at me again? I don't know, Kate…maybe this is a bad idea. I think if he wanted to hear anything I have to say he would've said so by now, you know?"

"No, I don't know that. I mean Camie, he likes you…really, *really* likes you. I can totally tell. Hell, anyone who saw you guys at the beginning of the bonfire could see that plain as day. If you can just explain it to him the way you explained it to me, I'm sure everything will be okay. I mean he still might not wanna go with you on Friday, but just tell him what happened and then give him some time to get over it…I bet he'll ask you out again once he does."

"You think so?" I asked, feeling the tiniest seedling of hope begin to bloom within me.

"Yeah, I do. Because honestly, this really isn't that big of a deal…it was a misunderstanding, nothing more. He just took a hit to his ego, that's all. And now that I think about it, I don't think that's ever happened to him before so that might be why he flipped out like you said he did."

"Okay, but what about reading the texts…that really doesn't qualify as a misunderstanding."

"Well, the way I look at it, he was the dumbass who left them up on the screen and then literally handed you his phone, so what does he expect? I guarantee if he'd been in your shoes he'd have read 'em too. And for all we know, he could've done that! I mean who knows what he was doing while you were sleeping. Plus, he actually *answered* your phone and you didn't flip out on him for doing that, you know?"

All true. I mean not the dumbass part really, because I didn't *have* to read what I did just because it was in front of my face, but the rest of it is true and I let it give me courage. So, with that little bit of bravery in me, Kate and I walked into the pizza place, resolute. Actually, resolute is stretching it. I was as nervous as Melissa was before her first kiss and I had to stop myself from making an unnecessary trip to the bathroom to hide. That inclination, though, was partly because the place was fairly well packed with guys, all wearing blue and gold letterman's jackets declaring them to be athletes from my school.

I looked at Kate with questioning eyes and she leaned in to whisper, "I don't know what this is about but they're his boys…from the water polo and swim teams. And it looks like a few guys from the baseball team are here too, and of course Conner, but, he works here..."

Looking around at all the guys milling about, laughing and guffawing with each other in the dining area, I couldn't help wondering if Tristan felt so injured that he had to circle the wagons himself for protection, or if they just instinctively flock to their wounded like freaking geese. I mean they were everywhere…going from table to table, talking and eating as they did. Some were playing pinball, others were playing air hockey, and still some were simply watching highlights of a baseball game on the TVs hanging in the corners of the room. All told there had to be at least two-dozen of them. However, not one of them was Tristan.

"Hey Katy, what're you doin' here? I thought you were goin' to a movie…" Jeff said, coming up behind us and wrapping his arms around Kate in an affectionate and rather tender greeting.

"Oh um, well, I'm hungry so we decided to get something to eat…" She turned and answered, hugging him back, while over Jeff's shoulder she gave me a look that said, "I don't get it…he doesn't know."

"Oh, well cool…are you guys gonna hang out or get it to go?" Jeff asked, holding Kate's hand and swinging it in a playfully sweet manner.

"Uh, I don't know…what's going on, why are the guys here?" Kate asked him, maintaining the secret of our real motive for being here.

"It's Coach Jackson's birthday so some of the guys decided to throw him a little party…you guys should stay," Jeff answered and then turning to me he said, "Tristan's in the back room throwin' darts."

"Oh, um…okay." What I really wanted to know, though, was if Jeff had meant that as a warning and that maybe I should think about taking evasive action. I'd really hate to give Tristan a live target, you know what I mean?

Silently asking for some backup, I widened my eyes at Kate. I ended up stifling a whimper though; help wasn't forthcoming. All she did was take a bite of the pizza Jeff presented her with while giving me a "go on, you can do it" look. So, go on I did, alone and not quite with my tail between my legs but close.

Passing Conner who'd just come through them, I pushed through the saloon-type, swinging doors that opened into the practically unoccupied room, trying to not think of this as a showdown like the Old West is infamous for as my eyes instantly landed on Tristan—just as he aimed a dart and let it fly. It hit the board squarely in the center but I think it'd probably been thrown too hard because instead of sticking, the dart bounced off the board and then clattered to the floor.

"Shut up," Tristan said, grabbing a handful of M&Ms out the big bag sitting of the table and shoving them in his mouth before he bent down to pick up the wayward dart.

At first I thought Tristan was talking to me because I hadn't seen Pete sitting there quietly in the shadows. But once I noticed him, it was clear he'd been about to comment on Tristan's sub-par performance. And from the way Tristan said it, it was apparent that wasn't the first time one of his darts had missed its mark tonight. Pete chuckled at him but rather than actually saying anything to rub it in, he just casually leaned back in his chair and without taking his eyes off Tristan, Pete let go off the dart he'd been holding. It sailed with frightful accuracy to hit the almost dead center of the dartboard.

Supremely confident, Pete didn't even bother to confirm his bull's-eye, he simply stood up and gave Tristan a conciliatory pat on the back.

"It's just not your game."

Tristan turned with his hands in the air, questioning, as Pete started to walk away. "Where're you goin'? I thought we were gonna work it out a little…"

"We just did…plus you got your own stuff to work out," Pete answered with a head nod in my direction. "So, I'm gonna give you some privacy while you do it."

"*You're* gonna give *me* privacy? Since when?!" Tristan asked with sarcastic disbelief, like Pete had made some kind of ridiculous joke.

"Since it's the off season, dude. Besides, you know I'll just watch the re-run on Borg TV come spring anyway, why see it twice?" Pete replied with a chuckle. Then as he walked past me, he dropped his voice and whispered, "He's *all* yours…good luck."

Not to get off topic or anything, but let me ask you something really quick…did he say *Borg*? Like from *Star Trek*? Or was it *bored*? I know…neither makes sense but I really think it sounded like Borg. Huh…that's just weird.

Oh, sorry…where was I?

Oh yeah…

I watched Pete leave the room and didn't have a clue what he meant about the off season or watching whatever on Borg(?) TV in the spring. I figured by how they'd said all that though, it was some kind of inside joke, but since it didn't have anything to do with me or this situation really, I just left it alone. I mean I'm not really in any position to be asking for more details about Tristan and his relationships with other people right now.

However, everything they said informed me that although Tristan might not have said anything to his best friend about what happened, he'd clearly said something to Pete. I found that interesting but ultimately disregarded it as irrelevant to my task. I just need to bite the bullet here, say what I came to say and then see where that leaves me. I just hope I don't end up being a blubbering mess by the time I know where that is.

I approached Tristan slowly, biting back a wayward giggle when I heard him mutter to himself, "*Asshole.* Little sneak thief stole my goddamned M&Ms..." As I moved closer to him however, I felt like flinching when the previously jocular attitude he'd had while he'd been bantering with Pete was suddenly replaced with frigid emptiness.

Ignoring me, or rather, not being willing to even look at me, he yanked Pete's dart from the board and preparing to leave the pizza place via the back door he said, "I have nothing to say to you."

And so I began…

"Fine, then you'll be free to listen," I said, catching up to him before he got all the way outside.

"You don't get it, do you? I'm over it. And I don't hate you either, Camie…that would require me to feel something for you and I don't. I just didn't return your messages because none of this is worth my time."

Tristan said it all like he very much meant every word. Then he finally tasted the fresh air as the door closed behind him.

Yeah. It hurt. I felt tears begin to sting the backs of my eyes but then something occurred to me… The other day Tristan told me that Zack and he take turns throwing punches and that, right now, it isn't his turn. Only it is. I'd hurt him this morning and he's fighting back. I'll be honest; it kind of pissed me off. I mean here he is, trying to hurt me on purpose and I could *maybe* understand that if I'd hurt him intentionally, but the big obstinate jerk won't even give me the chance to explain that the whole thing was just a ridiculous, yet *totally* believable series of misunderstandings and that I had freaking *grounds* to think what I did!

Okay, maybe being *kind of* pissed off isn't quite accurate.

I shoved through the door, hot on his trail, and as calmly as I could for being as morally peeved as I was I said, "I don't give a rat's ass if you're over it, Tristan! I'm not and I deserve the chance to be heard and if you don't give it to me, then *you're* not worth *my* time."

"Yeah see, that's the beauty of being me in this…I get to not care about any of that because of the two of us, I'm not the new kid trying to fit in."

It was a particularly snide thing to say and made me show my distaste in my face. And just so you have an idea what that looks like, my dad calls that expression the "I smell a fart face." It's not the most ladylike way to put it, but hey, it's spot on.

Now, I don't know what exactly made me say it but a reminder of what he'd said to me this morning came out of my mouth and changed the course of—well, everything I guess.

"This morning you said you thought I was different…well, just so you know, I thought you were too. And I can assure you, the disappointment is entirely mutual. Not to mention that from now on, watching my favorite TV show is only gonna remind me of a callous jerk and how completely wrong I was about him." Crestfallen and with tears pricking the backs of my eyes again, I turned to go inside.

He caught my arm to stop me, the jolt of his touch producing an almost irresistible desire—an unfathomable longing for the impossible. In that single moment, all I wanted was to press my body to his and have his lips on mine. I shoved the thought and inclination away with force and ignored them. And I tried to ignore him too; I couldn't. I just couldn't ignore his words and their subtle suggestion that we have something...and that it might be worth trying to find out what exactly that is.

"I wanted to hate you. I even tried, but...I can't do it. And it's not because I don't feel anything."

"So do you maybe think we're both still right?"

"About being different?" I sniffled back my tears and nodded. "I honestly don't know, but I do know that I don't like making you cry…I don't especially care for what being wrong would mean either."

"Um…I don't know what that means," I admitted and felt my face flush just slightly.

I'm hoping it means Tristan might be willing to get back in the boat of his own volition. It might seem like a lot to hope for at this point, but that tender compassion I'd heard from him at Mike's was very evident in his voice and expression again so, I'm gonna go ahead and hope. And at the very least, now I know he hadn't truly meant the cruel things he said before.

He looked at me for a thoughtful and unnervingly long minute before letting out a small *"Humph."* Then he said, "I guess it means that if you're game, we can give it another go."

I swallowed my inner whooping and jumping for joy and tried to just play it cool. "Yeah, I guess…my Friday just opened up so I think I can squeeze you in then."

Tristan grinned at my attempt at lightening the mood. "Sure, pencil me in for Friday. Just do me a favor, Camie, try not to have me father any other kids from now on. Oh wait, I take that back. As long as we're not successful, I'm up for trying if you are."

Yeah, I was stunned stupid *and* speechless. I just stood there, not knowing what to say about his blatant suggestion that we have sex.

Then I realized Tristan was trying to lighten the mood in his own way by teasing me and making a joke about my faux pas when he flashed me an impish look and innocently asked, "What? Too soon?"

In relief, I blew out the breath I wasn't aware I'd been holding and with my own puckishness I said, "Uh, ya think? I mean my cheeks aren't even dry yet, Tristan. Plus, we barely know each other. Not to mention that success is pretty important to me. I hate not accomplishing the things I set out to do…it makes me feel like I'm a failure."

Tristan started laughing about that and when he stopped; I explained why I'd thought what I did. Now that he'd allowed himself to cool off and was finally prepared to listen to me, he was pretty great about seeing the situation from my side. When I finished, I looked up and noticed he was staring at me in sort of an odd way, like he was debating something. I wasn't going to say anything but when he started drumming his fingers on his thigh, I just couldn't resist.

"What? Why are you looking at me like that?"

"Mmm…just out of curiosity, would it have mattered?" He asked in a way that made me think that wasn't what he'd actually been questioning.

"Would what have mattered?" I asked, not following at all.

"If I *had* been Joey's father would it have mattered to you?"

I wasn't prepared for that and I hadn't ever come to a decision about it so I just told him the truth. "Honestly, I don't know. I mean I spent the entire night awake asking myself that exact question and I never came up with an answer, but I do know that I would've had no problem being your friend. That I'm sure of."

"Humph," he uttered with a small nod.

I thought he'd asked what was on his mind but he was still looking at me in that undecided way, making me wonder if there was more to it or if my answer just wasn't as definitive as he was wanting it to be. "You're still staring at me…"

"Oh, well I kinda wanna kiss you right now," he told me in a rather contemplative, yet offhanded way, like he was just thinking out loud while he was trying to decide if he should or not.

"So why not just kiss me," I said, trying to help him out of his conundrum. I mean I certainly wouldn't be opposed to doing a little smooching after this narrowly avoided disaster, you know?

"Mmm, I *would,* but I kinda don't wanna just kiss you."

Of course I didn't really know what he meant by that. I mean, does he not want to kiss me or does he? This really isn't a hard question, you know what I mean? Well, that is unless you acknowledge the possibility that he could've been talking about having sex again. Regardless, I wanted to know what he meant and I was about to ask but right then, Kate, Jeff, and another guy found us outside and all three of them informed us that Tristan needed to come check Conner out; he'd either just sliced through his finger or burnt himself on the pizza oven, or I think maybe both. I don't know though...the guys were doing that excited talking over each other thing so it was hard to follow.

"Why Tristan?" I asked Kate, looking for an answer as to why he was needed in this scenario.

"Oh, he's a State Beach lifeguard and like the next best thing to a paramedic. Conner doesn't wanna go to the hospital and half the guys think he should and the other half doesn't, but they'll all shut up and listen to what Tristan says."

"Oh," I said and then realized she didn't look too good. "Um, are you okay?"

"No, I'm not. That was seriously gross. I mean he was bleeding all over a pepperoni and sausage pizza. In fact, if I don't stop picturing it I'll totally throw up," Kate answered with a nauseated grimace and then, nodding to Tristan with her chin as we followed him and the guys back into the main dining area, she asked, "Did you guys talk?"

"Yeah, we got it all straightened out and we're back on for our date."

"Thank God... Okay well, I'm guessing he's gonna be a while so do you mind if I take you home? I really don't feel good anymore," she told me, looking more than a little green around the gills.

"Yeah sure, no problem," I answered automatically.

I'd love to stay and hang out and watch Tristan do whatever it is he does, but if what Conner just did to himself is as disturbing as it sounds, then no thanks, I think I'll pass. I mean playing Tristan's nurse in the surgery of him getting dressed is one thing, but aiding him in actual bloody first aid is quite another.

Kate caught up to Jeff to tell him we were leaving and when Tristan overheard, he turned back to me and with twinkling eyes and an unmistakable playfulness, he confirmed our date by saying, "So don't forget to put me down for epic failure and a complete lack of success on Friday...say about six, okay?"

I couldn't help it; I rolled my eyes and just gave him a sarcastic thumbs up. Actually, the eye roll was more for me because although I'm sure if I'd agreed, he'd no doubt have gone through with his prior teasing proposal, and I now think that's exactly what it was. He'd been playing with me and I totally fell for it. And not that I really mind, but it seems we've set a precedent with this kind of teasing so I guess I should try to learn when to take him seriously and when to laugh him off.

I climbed in bed that night feeling overwhelming relief about having made it through what I thought was sure to be a disaster of epic proportions. I listened to the playlist I'd made of the songs Tristan and I kissed to on Saturday and instead of crying like this morning when I'd listened to it, I found myself unable to wipe the smile from my face, thinking about what our date on Friday would be like. When the last of the four songs started playing—the one by Limp Bizkit—I snuggled down even further into my pillow and with a sigh, I fell asleep, congratulating myself on having built a bridge with Tristan, even though the situation didn't quite fall apart and my heart wasn't broken like the song says.

Little did I know it though, I wasn't quite done living out the lyrics to that particular song, or, as it would turn out, several other songs as well…

13.

The Worst Sort Of Vengeance

My morning at school was weird. All the kids in my classes, including Michele, were giving me odd looks. After last week, I kept wondering if I had something in my hair again but each time I checked a mirror, my hair was fine. I mean, Teresa was her usual self—running her mouth behind her hand—but the only thing she has on me this time is my atrocious appearance on Saturday night. And honestly, I really don't care if she tells the entire world I was at a beach party in mismatched and ill fitting clothing.

English gave me a much-appreciated break from having my wardrobe critiqued, though, and as a bonus, Tristan and Jeff abandoned showing up early to class so, Tristan and I actually sat next to each other. Plus, instead of directing most of his conversation to Jeff, Tristan included Kate and me in it, which just adds to my relief of last night. Of course there was no real direct communication at lunch, but he didn't bolt when I walked up to talk to Kristen, which was where he was standing with Mike. That was also when I found out that Conner hadn't needed to go to the hospital.

I guess once Conner's wound got cleaned, it wasn't found to be deep enough to warrant stitches and the burn wasn't a big deal either. From the way it sounded, I'm guessing Kate over-reacted. Either that or she just gets queasy at the sight of a little blood, which I can understand. I mean I don't get sick watching horror movies or anything, but real-life blood and gore is different for some reason. Oh, during that conversation I also found out that Tristan had agreed to talk to Conner's ex for him. Apparently she's the girl I'd overheard breaking up with her boyfriend over the phone; her friends sound just as shallow now as did they did then. Get this, they think Conner is beneath them simply because he comes from a single parent household and has to work to help out with the family's finances, plus, he doesn't have his own car. I mean really, this is exactly the kind of stuff that makes you ashamed to be a member of the human race.

Anyhow, that pretty much sums up my Tuesday. I know, it's not much in the way of excitement but what do you expect, I'm in high school. Besides, it was a Tuesday for crying out loud. I mean, does anything noteworthy ever really happen on Tuesdays?

Wednesday however…well, Wednesday brought some drama, as they are wont to do at times. I got to school and once I'd taken my seat in geometry, I immediately knew something was up. No one said anything but it was totally obvious. And I knew I was at the center of whatever was going on when the looks I'd been getting yesterday became increasingly more plentiful, and, more odious as the morning wore on.

Fed up, I cornered Michele after our fourth period class and asked her point blank what was going on. "Okay, *what* is going on? You and everyone else are acting really weird."

"Don't pretend like you don't know, Camie," she snapped.

"Pretend like I don't know what?! If I knew what was going on, why would I need to ask? I mean, did I screw up the bell curve or something?" I asked, totally not getting why she's behaving like this.

"Fine, let me ask you something then…what happened at that party when you got that drink spilled all over you?" She asked stiffly.

I'm getting the really suspicious feeling that Michele is waiting to pass judgment on me about something, but I've no idea what for. I mean no one aside from a few toddlers and their moms, Tristan, Kate, and apparently Pete know about what happened yesterday. But even if everyone knew, that really doesn't explain these repellent attitudes towards me.

"Umm, I got a pitcher of red booze poured all over me, I learned to play Quarters, and that's pretty much it. Oh, Tristan Daniels gave me one of his shirts to wear because mine was totally drenched and later he drove me home because my ride had been drinking," I explained, giving as many details as I could remember that might have some bearing on this.

"And the party this past Friday?"

"Uh, let's see…I played Quarters for a little bit, got shoved in the pool…good thing I was already wearing my bathing suit, which the punch fiasco had inspired me to do, and umm…I sat in the hot tub with Kate and a bunch of other people." Jeez, this feels like the freaking Spanish Inquisition. Not that I was there to know what that felt like, but I'm just sayin'...I imagine it was rather uncomfortable for those being grilled.

"That's it? That's the truth? Nothing else happened?"

"Yeah, that's it. Oh, well I'll tell you but *please* don't tell anyone else, I'd be really embarrassed about it…I sorta threw up on someone's dog at the party Friday night," I admitted, thinking maybe that's what this is all about.

She laughed about that, apologized for acting so strange, and then explained why she and half the school had been staring at me for almost two days.

After hearing what Michele had to say, I was not only mortally offended and shocked, but I was fucking pissed off. I know, the swearing…but trust me; it's definitely a good time for an expletive. Additionally, I ended up being late to English. I was too mad to say anything when all three, Kate, Jeff, and Tristan looked at me as if to ask "what the hell is wrong with you?" and I was only able to stammer out a partial to Melissa and Kate after class when everyone had left the building for lunch.

"Okay, *what* is wrong with you? You look like you're ready to commit murder," Kate asked me with concern.

"I am. Teresa is a walking corpse! Are you ready for this? Apparently I'm a skanky whore!" I spit out venomously.

"Oh my God. Are you saying that rumor I heard this morning is being said about *you*?" Melissa asked aghast, obviously having only heard one rumor of this kind lately.

"Yeah, I am. And since you've already heard it, I'm sure the rest of the school has too," I said, fuming.

You see, since I didn't do anything embarrassing enough on my own, Teresa decided to fabricate the worst sort of vengeance. She's telling everyone that I not only slept with a random guy at Mike's party, but *three* of them, and then essentially the same thing occurred during Friday night's party at Pete's. Which she wasn't even at!

"Eh, maybe…but there wasn't a name attached to the girl I heard it about. And you know what? That's good. That means specifics are being lost in translation, like in the game Telephone. Also, we can take care of it really easily even if your name does get put with it…at least in our clique. Besides, everyone who was at those parties knows where you were and who you were with the whole time. No one in our circle will perpetuate the lie," Melissa stated with the confidence of a leader, cheer or otherwise.

"That's not entirely true you know. I was out of public sight when Tristan dragged me to the bathroom to get me cleaned up. Even though he wasn't one of the guys I supposedly slept with, everyone saw me with him while he was without a shirt and that was right after we were without the benefit of witnesses."

"No, people were there too…remember you told me about the group getting high in Mike's parents' room? Did Tristan close the bathroom door?" Kate asked.

"Uh, no, he didn't…it was wide open. Do you think it'll matter?"

I'm only semi-relieved that I have at least someone who can account for my whereabouts during every minute of every party, though. The reason behind the necessity of having those people *really* freaking pisses me off. So much so that this whole time, I've been fighting back angry tears.

"Honestly, I don't think much of it'll matter…we can nip this in the bud as far as the upper-classes go and ultimately, it'll trickle back down to sophomores and freshman," Melissa said reassuringly.

I hope she's right, because from what I understand; this sort of thing is near impossible to live down regardless of how farfetched and untrue it is.

"Besides, Camie, do you honestly think Tristan and Jeff are gonna let something like this go when they hear about it? I can guarantee you they'll squash this rumor like a big, fat bug…guys talk about loose girls more than we do and if need be, they'll have the entire boys' locker room willing to testify to your innocence in court by the end of the school day."

"And Keith will back 'em up, which conveniently puts the football program on your side. That includes the JV team too, so with that and the mixed grade locker room, there's our trickle down point," Melissa chimed in, offering her boyfriend's unwavering support.

"Do we have to tell them? Tristan and Jeff, I mean. This is bad enough without having to endure looks from Tristan too," I complained.

I may do a lot of unwarranted whining, but this is justified. I mean it's like freaking Karma. Even though we cleared everything up on Monday, I can practically hear Tristan laughing about how what goes around comes around. Not only that, but I'm afraid that after some of my possibly ill-advised teasing the other night combines with this whole thing, he might think I was being partly serious.

"Mmm…I really think it'd be a good idea. They're bound to hear it eventually if they haven't already and the sooner the guys know it's about you, the sooner they'll wanna stop it," Kate answered.

"I concur. We should get started during lunch so let's get a move on. I mean we can always text, but it's better to do this kind of damage control face-to-face in groups," Melissa determined.

So with that pronouncement, we left the English building to wage war against a lie. Well, Kate and Melissa did anyway; I decided to hide in the library. It was as uneventful a thirty minutes as I could've asked for. Although on my way to P.E., my phone started vibrating and I immediately started to panic thinking about my mom. When I pulled it out and checked the caller ID though, my stomach started to flop around for an entirely different reason; the name on the screen was Thumper. You know, because I'm twitter-pated like in *Bambi*. Yeah, I know. Not the best I could come up with, but I think it's cute. Besides, I really like how being twitter-pated describes young love…it's just *so* accurate for how teenagers act. Anyway, here's what the text said:

Tristan: avoiding enemies or hiding?

Ah, so he knows it was Teresa throwing another punch at me…that's good, isn't it? I was about to reply but then I thought about what Kate said the other day and decided to hold off for a bit. I don't want to appear overly anxious, right? I mean technically I'm not playing hard to get. Seriously, how can I? He's already got me. And if I'm being totally honest, he had me at "Hey Paul, you forgot this back there." But even so, I do need to curb my enthusiasm a little to keep him on the hook. At least that's what I'm assuming Kate was saying. I waited until P.E. was over and replied after I changed from my gym clothes into my dance clothes. Neither Kate nor Melissa had made it to the locker room yet so I was on my own. Since the other piece of advice Kate had given me was to be myself, I decided to go with the truth and said:

Me: hiding

Although after I sent it, I wondered if it would be like an admittance of guilt about what was being said. Crap. It's too late though. It's not like I can re-text and say something like, "Oh no, I'm not hiding, I'm umm, sparing Teresa's life…yeah, that's it." So with that concern in mind, I practically tackled Kate and Melissa when they got to the locker room in my anxiety over what they thought.

"You have to tell me I didn't just totally shoot myself in the foot!! Here, look at this!" I shoved my phone in their faces for them to read the messages. "Did I screw up?"

They laughed and told me not to worry. Even *if* someone would've taken it that way, it certainly wouldn't be Tristan. In fact, they said he'd been royally pissed when they told the large majority of people in our group of friends that the rumor about the slutty girl is meant to be about me. And apparently he wasn't the only one. Walking down to the dance room, I got two texts in a row. Here's what the first said:

MaryAnn: camie i just started going out w/your cuz derek. i want u 2 know im going 2 give mark a warning 2 relay 2 his bitch sister. this will b over soon!

Aw, that's so sweet! My cousin's new girlfriend is going to bat for me and we hardly even know each other. I should mention that this is a big bat too, because MaryAnn is the Senior Class President and happens to be the captain of Varsity Cheer. Anyhow, this is what the second text said:

Tristan: chicken

I giggled about that one and showed Kate and Melissa so they could laugh with me. I find it interesting that he replied relatively quickly after my response, don't you? I'm still going to wait until after class is over before I reply though. I think I'll opt out of standing around afterwards, too. I *of course* want to see him, but my mom always says absence makes the heart grow fonder, so, we'll see if she's right or just repeating an antiquated adage that isn't applicable to today's youth.

After dance, I scurried back into the locker room, changed, and then I thoughtfully typed out my reply.

Me: wont jeff b jealous about u using your pet name 4 him 4 someone else? o and make up your mind...am i a tease or a chicken? :-p

Ah, the joy of flirting from afar…

When Kate pulled up to a stop sign in front of school on our way to my house, she looked at me sitting in the passenger seat and asked rather suddenly, "Did you reply to Tristan when you were in the locker room?"

I was wondering by her tone if I should've waited for her to help me with it. "Yeah, why?"

"Because I saw him come out of the boys' locker room looking at his phone and laughing his ass off. What did you say?"

Obviously I did fine on my own. Yes I'm flattered, but please, hold your applause.

Just as I was pulling my phone back out to show her my reply, though, it went off again.

Tristan: both :-*

Oh my God!! My first text kiss! Heehee!

"Kate! I just got my first text kiss!" I squealed. Then bouncing up and down, I showed her the screen.

Kate glanced at the surrounding cars looking for any of Tristan's possible spies and finding none, she then got giddy with me. I probably should've thought about the possibility of being watched, but come on! No way was I going to be able to hold in my glee. I'm also really glad Tristan had bailed from school before he sent it or that could've been problematic. I don't need him seeing my goofy reactions to him. That's also probably why I got the text kiss when I did. He wasn't at school anymore and he probably figured I was out of the public eye as well. I don't think he really considers Kate as part of the public, not after last weekend anyway.

"Hey Kate? Do you think he knows I tell you all this stuff?"

"I'm sure he probably assumes you do. He knows I'm your best friend and naturally, that's what girls do. I don't think he cares though. Besides, he's the one responsible for the way you guys were sitting together when the bonfire started. Even though he eventually went on his merry way when other people started arriving, he still showed something of his intent to the rest of us sitting there. Plus, he answered your phone when I called…he totally knows that I know."

"Do you think he'll be more careful around you then? You know, like what if he suspects you're helping me." If so, that might be bad for me. Even though I did okay patching things up with him the other night, I feel like I still need Kate as an interpreter.

"Nah. He's still totally clueless that I ever put it together weeks ago and have been coaching you ever since then. Hell, he might even be hoping that I'll encourage you at this point. I don't know though, I've never really involved myself in his life like this. However, Jeff did mention to me how cranky Tristan was about having to help unload the wood and how weird you both were on the phone before that, plus he still doesn't know what happened on Monday so it seems that Tristan isn't telling *him* everything," Kate said thoughtfully as she turned onto my street.

"Huh. That's kinda odd actually…you'd think he'd be telling Jeff everything. *Unless* he likes you way more than he wants to admit right now… Jeff would totally pick up on it and point it out, not to be mean or anything, but to tease him. Hmm, I think this means Tristan might be trying to save himself from my jackass's jokes."

"Huh. That is interesting. Hey, how are things going with you guys anyway? It seems like all we talk about is Tristan and me," I said, thinking about how she hasn't really said much about Jeff. I mean, they look happy and I haven't wanted to be nosey, but she *is* my best friend. Plus, I don't want everything to always be about me, you know?

"Oh, things are really good. It's funny that I don't quite realize how terribly unhappy I am when I'm apart from him until we're together again. It's like I have nothing to look forward to without him and my life is just sorta blah when I'm not with him, you know? Like everything just lacks luster and seems kind of pointless.

"But, he brightens up my whole world and I feel like there's a purpose to life when I'm living it with him, so, I'm glad you gave me a reason to take him back. I just have to remember that he's gonna screw up and make dumb decisions, probably more often than not, and then I need to try to be forgiving when he does. I'm not perfect either and he does a really good job of overlooking the things I do that irritate him."

"What can you possibly do to irritate *Jeff*? He seems so kickback about everything, I can't picture him ever being upset." Really, aside from Pete who's practically invisible, Jeff is the most laidback guy I've ever met.

"Um, well...oh! He really doesn't like it when I lecture him. It doesn't matter what it's about, it just bugs the crap outta him and I tend to do that without even realizing I'm doing it. I know there has to be other stuff but I can't think of anything else off the top of my head. Maybe I'm more perfect than I thought...I'll get back to you on that." She started laughing.

"You crack me up...I'm glad you guys are doing so good though, I'd hate to think you were suffering through all of his love and affection for you on my behalf."

"Oh, yeah. It's torture! Please, Camie, tell me I can dump him so I can stop being treated like a queen," Kate said, feigning distress by throwing the back of her hand onto her forehead and fluttering her eyelashes.

"Nah, I think you deserve to do a little more time for your bad behavior. Oh! That reminds me, what should I do now? Should I kiss Tristan back?" I asked, getting out of the car.

"Oh, totally! I wouldn't instigate anything, but if he's gonna start it then there's no reason for you not to finish it... HA! How funny would it be if neither of you stopped? It could end up being like one long, text make-out session! That would be hysterical... See you tomorrow!" She called out her window and waved as she pulled away.

Grinning to myself about that idea, I walked into my house to tell Jillian everything that'd happened today and gave her the green light for anything she might want to do to Teresa. Then I waited another hour—which totally killed me to do—and replied to Tristan.

Me: back at ya :-*

14.

In Totally Uncharted Waters

I made it through Thursday with dignity and without hiding in the library like I had yesterday. I'll admit it had been my intention to do just that, but walking through the library door after fifth period, I received two texts that essentially forced me to face the music.

Jillian: you are better than this...out of library now! (You know you suck when your twelve-year-old sister knows what you're doing without being there and then proceeds to tell you that you're being childish.)

Tristan: c'mon champ. get in the ring. eye of the tiger baby, eye of the tiger :-* (Oh wow! This is the first text from Tristan today and apparently we're text kissing at *school* now too. I wonder what Kate will make of this...)

Two web links for song lyrics accompanied Tristan's text, the first being "Get In The Ring" by Guns N' Roses. I imagine he's trying to tell me that if I stand tall and "get in the ring," Teresa won't be willing to antagonize me openly because she's a coward. The second was for Survivor's "Eye Of The Tiger." That one was easy to figure out. If you've never seen *Rocky 3*, you might not get it but it's about having a fighting spirit.

Thus having been chastised in one text and encouraged in the other, I made my way to the stage for lunch. Hearing the *Rocky* theme song in my head, I even went one better than just showing my face; I made it a point to walk right through the lunch group the Trollop Triplets were a part of that day. Feeling empowered by the show of support I could see from my friends ahead and some of the lyrics, I then stopped, turned around to look Teresa in the face and said, "Hey Teresa, just so you'll know where to find me, I'm usually over by the stage during lunch. You know, on the off chance you suddenly grow a spine and decide to confront me face-to-face." And then without waiting for a response or looking back, I continued my way over to my ever-growing circle of friends.

By Friday morning when Kate picked me up for school, I was completely over Teresa's stab at ruining my reputation. The rumor mill had come to a grinding halt when it hit the well mortared brick wall of my friends…and their friends, and in turn, their friends, and so on. However, now that my anxiety over that piece of drama is gone, a new nervousness has taken up residence in me… My date with Tristan is *tonight.* I don't know why, but I'm kind of freaking out.

"So what are you guys doing tonight?" Kate asked as we headed to school.

"I have no idea." I shook my head to emphasize my words. Seriously, I don't have a clue. That could be why I'm nervous…

"You guys *are* still going out tonight, right? I mean you did make plans, didn't you?"

"Uh, yeah...sort of, but I have no details aside from what time he's picking me up. I was just so relieved our date was back on that I didn't think to ask and now I'm kinda wishing I would've," I explained and pulled out my cell phone. Maybe I'm nervous because this is my first date ever…

"Are you asking him?" Kate asked, watching my thumbs fly over the Qwerty keyboard of my phone as she turned the engine off.

"Yeah. I didn't care what we were gonna do before, but now I wanna know." … Or maybe it's because I don't feel like I have anything to wear…

"No way, are you guys *still* kissing?" She asked in astonishment after reading what I wrote and seeing my kiss.

"Yep, even at school now. I forgot to ask your opinion on that when it first happened yesterday. What do you make of it?" … Huh. Not knowing what to wear could definitely be the cause of my anxiety. I wonder if Tristan would let me rummage through his closet for something suitable, seeing as how I seem to end up in his clothes more often than not anyway. Who knows, it might be a nice change to just start out in them for once.

Kate was shaking her head in disbelief. "Camie, I gotta tell ya…I have no clue what to make of that. You're in totally uncharted waters here. I'll see you later, okay?"

With that, she left me by my geometry class and swiftly headed towards her own first period class as the warning bell rang. I swear, eventually Kate and I will have to figure out how to get to school early enough so that we're not rushing to make it to class on time.

I didn't hear back from Tristan until I was walking down the hall to fifth period. The little stinker was actually typing it out as he passed me too. This is what he said:

Tristan: 2 late. u should've asked days ago. :-*

He's a total brat, isn't he? Because of that I decided to break my rule of not replying right away, so after I got settled on the ground I typed:

Me: hint? :-*

I watched him read it and was kind of surprised to see that he was replying right next to me—well, across from me. The four of us are in a circle on our stomachs preparing to play hangman. It *is* Friday after all and unlike "Bland Tuesday" and "Topsy-Turvey Wednesday"; Friday is most commonly known for its frivolity.

Tristan: k. pay attn 2 game :-*

Huh. It's his turn to pick the word or phrase for us to guess, so I suppose whatever it is will be my hint. After three rounds of guessing this is what the phrase looked like:

nitt_ _ritt_ _irt _an_

I was studying it, trying to figure out what letter to guess next when Kate guessed 'y'. Filling in two more blanks, it read like this:

nitty _ritty _irt _an_

Having a hunch—if I'm right, he's cheating…you're not supposed to use proper nouns—I guessed 'd' and lo and behold it turned into this:

nitty _ritty dirt _and

I knew it, the big cheater. So, I decided to call him on it. I didn't actually call, though, that would just be silly. I sent him a text…

Me: cheater :-*

I can tell by the looks on both Kate's and Jeff's faces that neither of them know what it is yet, but I'm not sure if it's because they aren't thinking he'd break the rules—which isn't likely as they know him better than I do—or if they just aren't familiar with the Nitty Gritty Dirt Band. Still in my hand from sending the text, my phone vibrated with a new message from Tristan.

Tristan: sue me. have a guess? :-*

The only well known song I can think of by them that he might be referring to is called "Fishing In The Dark"—which I happen to think is a really great song—so I replied:

Me: fishing? :-* (I know. Not what you'd expect for a first date activity, but who knows? Maybe I'm totally wrong.)

I solved the puzzle on my turn and from then on, there really weren't too many pauses in between texts so I'll just transcribe the conversation for you:

Tristan: ya hopefully :-*
Me: y hopefully? :-*
Tristan: depends :-*
Me: on? :-*
Tristan: if dad sees mountain lion trax 2day :-*
Me: O. good reason. what should i wear? :-*

You'll understand why we spent the rest of class trying to one up each other with some pretty ruthless teasing when you see how he replied…

Tristan: clothes…or not. up 2 u but i vote not :-* (Yeah, not only did he go there, but he did it with a straight face too.)

I narrowed my eyes at his blank expression and replied.

Me: might b 2 chilly 4 nudity… should i bring a change of clothes? :-*
Tristan: not unless u want 2 sleep over. :-*

When I read that, I couldn't keep myself from looking at him in question again. The answer I got more than validated my need to figure out when he's joking; the reprobate actually had the nerve to raise his eyebrows as if he was challenging me to accept his—if I'm totally honest—highly intimidating, yet mighty tempting invitation.

Hoping I wasn't blushing and that I was right in thinking he's playing with me, I spent a moment trying to come up with a clever reply. All I could manage was:

Me: tempting, but not on date #1. lil help 4 the wardrobe challenged here. :-*

Tristan: idk something u can get dirty in :-*

Whew! I guessed right, he's joking. But, as I was mentally going through clothing items I'd consider getting dirty in, a scene from the movie *New in Town* with Renee Zellweger and Harry Connick Jr. popped into my head. And after Tristan's last couple of comments, I couldn't resist. With a straight face of my own I replied:

Me: r u saying i should wear a thong fishing? :-*

I knew I hit the mark because when he read it, he started cracking up. We'd been playing the game the whole time and even though Kate and Jeff hadn't said anything about the text war they knew was going on around them, they both looked up in question when he started laughing. He ignored them completely but responded with:

Tristan: not what i meant. but yes! by all means plz do. i promise i'll return it & your bra. :-p :-*

I think having finally gotten a reaction like that from him must've given me an adrenaline rush—or I just completely lost my mind—because this was when it could be said that I went a tad bit overboard…

Me: keep it. it's 2 small anyway. color preference? :-* (That first part is actually true, I've outgrown all my bras…I really should go shopping.)

He chuckled to himself when he read that and came right back with:

Tristan: not 2 picky but partial 2 black. u sure u dont wanna stay the nite? :-*
Me: ya. i'd hate 2 have another rumor start after getting my righteous rep back. :-*
Tristan: i wont tell a soul. :-*
Me: not gonna risk it. people would still talk :-*
Tristan: dont b a jeff. :-*
Me: r u calling me a chicken again? :-*
Tristan: if the beak fits… :-*
Me: ok fine :-*
Tristan: good. what do u want 4 breakfast? :-*

I'd intended to make that my acceptance of being called a chicken, but I guess I should've been clearer. He either misunderstood or he's just being a brat again. Regardless, I have to decide if I should keep the farce going or put a complete stop to it. Seeing as how I've already gone off the deep end, though, I may as well continue. There are only a couple of minutes left in class anyway and I'm sure school time texting will stop when the bell rings, so it can't hurt, right?

Me: if u fry up some wilbur and get jeff 2 lay some eggs, i'll b a happy camper. :-*

The bell rang to dismiss us for lunch but instead of responding to my text, Tristan looked over at Jeff while they were walking out the door and asked, "Hey, can you do me a favor this afternoon?"

As I thought, the texts did stop after that, but I was still in a quandary over how to dress for tonight and now there's the added underwear issue to consider as well. It's totally my own damned fault and I accept that, but I feel I need help in answering the question from my guidance counselors. So, after dance while we were walking to the parking lot, I showed Kate and Melissa the correspondence and waited for their response to the whole thing.

"I can't believe he had the nerve to tease you like this," Melissa giggled, re-reading the texts. When she got to the part about Jeff laying eggs again, she started laughing hysterically.

"Oh my God, Camie, that's the funniest damned thing I've ever read! You know he's gonna figure out a way to check," Kate told me, trying to control her laughter as well.

Melissa handed my phone back and at the same time, she gave me her two cents. "Oh, he *totally* will."

I forgot that Melissa might be speaking from experience… I'm not jealous at all, but I *am* wondering if I should ask her to give me a "dating Tristan history lesson." They didn't make it past two dates if I remember what Kate said correctly, and I'd really like to know why.

"That's what I was thinking too. So what should I do? Do you guys think I should go through with that part?" I'm thinking it'd be like having the last word if I do, but again, I'm not all that savvy about this stuff…and I don't even own a thong.

"YES!" Kate and Melissa said in emphatic unison.

"Alrighty then, you guys get to take me shopping," I informed my two mentors and got an identical pair of diabolical grins from them in return.

While we were shopping, my purse started singing "This Kiss." Oh yeah, I forgot to tell you I went with that one. I ended up choosing it for several reasons, but the clincher was the mention of Cinderella, Snow

White, and a white knight. I pulled my phone out and was relieved to see it was a text and not a live call. I mean come on, what would I say if he were to ask where I am? Stocking up on bras and panties just in case? Yeah, not likely. Anyway, here's what the text said:

Tristan: fishing's out. i'll pick u up @ the same time still. :-*

Aw, that sucks…I was sort of looking forward to that. It sounded fun—minus the mountain lions of course. Ugh, and I *still* don't know what to wear! I need to get some kind of idea here so I replied:

Me: any chance you'll tell me what we r doing or what i should wear now? :-* (I'm not holding my breath for a real answer though…)
Tristan: we've been over this but if u insist on clothes i recommend something comfy. :-*
Me: k. comfy i can do. c u l8r. :-*

Huh, go figure. He actually gave me a pretty decent—okay, maybe not *decent,* so let's say straightforward answer. I was about to toss my phone back in my purse when the incorrigible flirt responded with:

Tristan: nothin 2 comfy tho plz. also dont forget…i'd b happy w/black. :-p :-* (I think I might've created a monster, but at least he said please, right?)

Holding up and looking at the various options Kate and Melissa have given me to consider; I'm pretty damned sure neither of those requests will be difficult to comply with…

Kate dropped me off at home before heading to the football game with Melissa, and I started putting away all my purchases that ended up taking a nice sized chunk out of my car fund. I'm not expected to foot the bill on the basics, so my mom will at least reimburse me for the bras and panties, which is nice, as they're responsible for the larger portion of that chunk. Then as I was hanging it up, I giggled to myself over my Halloween costume.

After some debate, Kate, Melissa and I decided that it'd be hysterical if we convinced Pete—whom I've started mentally referring to as "Lonely Pete"—to dress as a sheik and then we would be his harem. Pete was easy to convince, but we're all being really hush-hush about it; it'll be even funnier if no one knows until we all show up together at Mike's costume party next Saturday. The costumes are super cute, but pretty revealing.

They're actually real belly dancing costumes and we're now debating on whether we should go so far as to even choreograph a dance to go with the theme. I'm really excited about the whole thing; it should be a hoot!

Anyway, my shopping excursion was without a doubt a success and much to my surprise, I found when I went to change for my date I wouldn't be able to comply with the not too comfy part of Tristan's demands after all, although I did honor the black part. While shopping, I'd treated myself to a new *Aeropostale* fleecy knit outfit in black and green, so with my black flip-flops, my hair pulled back in a basic ponytail, and the last gift from my great grandma being simple, but real, diamond studs in my ears, I thought I was looking quite the epitome of comfy.

After I was dressed, I wandered down to the kitchen for a quick snack. Again, I don't know if I should be eating or not, but I'm not about to go hungry later; I'm thinking an ounce of prevention at this point. It was about a half-hour before Tristan was supposed to pick me up when I walked into the family room and stopped abruptly, seeing my dad and sister sitting around the coffee table. I turned and stalked back upstairs, going straight into my parents' room to appeal to my mom.

"Mom, you have to do something! Dad's gone insane! He's gonna completely embarrass me, I just know it!! I won't even be able to blame Tristan for never asking me out again because it'll be Dad's fault! Please Mommy, help me?" I whined, bouncing on my hands and knees on their bed next to my mom.

She laughed softly at my hysteria. "Calm down, Camie. Are you really asking me to rob your father of his basic right to grill your first date?"

"*YES!!* I could handle it if he was just gonna play the tough dad, but Mom! He's pulled out *all* his guns and he's sitting down there "teaching" Jillian how to clean them and stuff!" I explained in utter distress.

Seriously! This is not okay on so many levels! *AND* Jillian already knows how to not only clean them, but also dismantle and load them too!

My mom finally grasped the gravity of my predicament. "Oh no, is he really?"

"Yes! Please stop him!" I begged.

"Hand me the phone, honey," my mom said with a determined look on her face, thank God.

I listened as she ordered Chinese food and then gave her a quick kiss on the cheek before I hid from site when she hollered for my dad to come up. From inside their closet, I could hear most of what they said and man; I owe my mom big time! I think Jill might get some of her deviousness from my mom too because here's what was said:

My Dad: "What's up, babe? Are you okay?"

My Mom: "Honey, I'm fine. Actually, I was getting hungry so I just ordered Chinese for our dinner and was hoping you wouldn't mind running over to pick it up."

My Dad: "Oh, of course. Did you order some orange chicken for me?"

My Mom: "Kevin, how long have we been married? Of course I ordered your favorite."

My Dad: "You want anything else while I'm out? A movie or some ice cream?"

My Mom: "Oh, that sounds fun but don't go to any trouble. If you're gonna do that though, you should leave now so the food doesn't sit there."

My Dad: "Ooh, that's right...okay, leaving right now. We don't want soggy Chinese."

Jeez, how much does my dad love my mom? He didn't balk even once at having to drop what he was doing to go pick up dinner that my mom ordered on a whim. I mean he even offered to rent a movie and get her some ice cream for goodness sake! When I grow up, I hope Tristan and I are in love like my parents are with each other. And hey, I'm just utilizing the power of positive thinking here, know what I mean?

15.

The Wall Of Infamy

With my dad out of the way I decided I could relax a little, so I was watching TV in bed with my mom when Tristan showed up a few minutes early. I swear I practically broke my neck flying down the stairs to get to the door first, but Jill had beaten me to it and had let him in. Crap! I was really hoping to make a clean get away…

Without even saying hi, I grabbed his arm and turned him around. I was pushing him back to the door when, sitting at the gun-laden coffee table again, Jillian spoke up. "Have fun you two, don't do anything I wouldn't do."

"Yep, you bet, bye!" I called; managing to finally shove Tristan outside and then I slammed the door shut.

I was trying to pull him down the porch steps with me, but he seemed stuck. I looked at him and saw he had an incredulous look on his—oh my God, he really is gorgeous—face.

"Come on, come on…we gotta get outta here," I said and tugged on his hand again.

Finally moving, he asked, "Camie, was your sister actually cleaning and assembling guns?"

"Yeah, let's go." I urged him forward at a faster pace towards his car, which was another relief. I was afraid he'd be driving the bus and that someone in my family would question the wisdom of letting me go with him in that. And probably for good reason too.

"That's not normal…" he said, disquieted, opening the passenger door for me.

"I keep trying to tell everyone and no one believes me!" I agreed, throwing my hands up in the air as if to say "At last! Someone sees my point!" Then I threw my purse in the car, emphasizing my frustration.

"What? No overnight bag?" Tristan, clearly recovered from his previous shock, asked with a very definite teasing twinkle in his eyes.

"Shut up. Seriously, can we get a move on? My dad could be back any minute."

He chuckled at my anxiety and then put his hand on my head to make me duck as he shoved me into his car.

"Okay, so where are we going?" I asked as he drove in the direction of school.

"First, we're gonna make a pit-stop at my house to swap vehicles."

Uh…

"Um, out of curiosity, why didn't you just drive the bus in the first place?" I really suspect this wasn't an oversight on Tristan's part.

"Camie, gimme a little credit. I'm not stupid enough to pick up a fifteen year old girl whose parents have never met me while driving a damned bedroom on wheels."

Nope, no oversight. Damn, when you hear the facts that way, you gotta wonder what the hell I'm doing with this guy… It's really very interesting, too, I get all jittery and nervous about this stuff in my head, but when it comes right down to it, I'm completely relaxed when I'm with him.

So that's what I was thinking about when I asked, "Okay, I appreciate your pains to deceive my parents, but why do we need to swap? Is fishing back on?"

"Unfortunately, no. My dad not only saw tracks out at our property, but the lion that made them, so no fishing in the dark for us tonight. I wanna swap because the bus is a lot more comfortable for the movies," he explained with a mischievous grin.

I was about to question why it mattered what we drove to the movies in when my phone rang. "Damn it, we were so close," I groaned.

"What, do you need to go back?" Tristan asked, becoming concerned. Aw, he's so sweet sometimes; don't you just wanna eat him up?

"No, keep driving…maybe even a little faster," I told him and answered my phone.

And I did that by saying, "Hi Daddy." But I was really thinking this: Aw shit.

Without having even greeted me, my dad requested I put him on speakerphone "so I can talk to the boy." I whispered a quick apology to Tristan who's finding this all very amusing. Then I turned the speakerphone on, held my phone up, and hung my head in misery.

Me: "Okay Daddy…go ahead." (I'm silently praying…)

My Dad: "Can you hear me, boy?"

Tristan: "Yes sir." (Thank God he has the common sense to use the proper amount of courtesy here and keep the amusement out of his voice…even if he did just wink at me.)

My Dad: "Good. Do you own a watch, son?"

Tristan: "Yes sir." (Now I get the "where is he going with this?" look.)

My Dad: "Do you know how to tell the fucking time on that watch?" (Oh crap! Did my dad just drop an f-bomb?!)

Me: "Dad!" (Tristan just slowed the car down and I think I'm going to have to kill my father.)

My Dad: "I want her home by midnight, not a second later."

Tristan: "Absolutely sir."

My Dad: "Alright then, have fun kids. Oh, and boy?"

Tristan: "Yes sir?"

My Dad: "My gun's got night scope."

Tristan: "I understand sir." (He's now making a U-turn.)

I ended the call and started giggling uncontrollably.

"What are you laughing at?" Tristan asked almost indignantly, but I think he's actually still sort of shaken by my dad's threat.

"I've been teetering on the brink of a mental breakdown since Monday and I think my dad just pushed me over the edge, because oh my God, I thought that was so damned funny!" I explained to him while wiping the tears off my cheeks. "Are you taking me home now? I totally wouldn't blame you."

"No! Jesus, you really have lost it," he answered and started laughing at me.

"Then why did you turn around?" I really was trying to get control of my giggles, but I think I've finally cracked under the stress.

"Oh, well maybe it's not the best idea to take a gunman's daughter to the drive-in movies in the aforementioned (Aforementioned? Oh, we are so totally made for each other.) bedroom on wheels..." He stopped at a red light and winked at me.

That just made me laugh even harder and when I could catch my breath I said, "And you think he's gonna somehow know about that?! Oh God, that's even funnier!"

Tristan then pulled over to the side of the road to read my face. "That sounded suspiciously like you just called me a chicken."

"If the beak fits..." I said through my laughter, remembering the taunt he'd used on me earlier today.

"Uh-huh, that's what I thought." He chuckled to himself and made another U-turn. "Just so you know, I'm not likely to forget this."

Uh-oh.

That sobered me up pretty quickly. Trading cars wasn't so bad when I didn't know where we're going, but now I do. Not only that, but it sounded ominously like Tristan just gave me a warning—or, a threat...

We exchanged vehicles without issue and we talked about random stuff as we drove to the theater then Tristan asked, "Did you eat?"

"I snacked a little so I'm not really hungry right now."

"Please tell me you're not one of those girls who refuse to eat in front of guys," he said and narrowed his eyes at me like he could decipher the truth by looking at me intently.

"I'm not, but why would you think that?" I asked and returned the narrow-eyed glance, which made him laugh.

"Because all I've ever seen you eat is a few bites of pizza and I had to practically shove it down your throat." Ah, memories…

"Oh yeah, I forgot about that. That was really good pizza too... And I promise I do enjoy the eating of food. I'm even well versed in protecting my plate with my fork if anyone so much as dares to think about sneaking something off it…I could even be on a competitive team or something.

"I'm honestly just not all that hungry for real food. I'll be good with popcorn and some licorice. I love licorice. Red not black, I hate black licorice…it tastes like jet fuel and turns everything it touches a sickly shade of bluish-gray," I rambled as he turned into the entrance for the drive-in.

Well isn't this mighty fine timing… Hello nervous speech, how I've missed you. It's fine when you ramble in your head, but when you actually have diarrhea of the mouth...? Well, that's usually embarrassing.

"Okay, you pick…which theater?" Tristan asked when we came up to the split in the road, not once calling attention to my outburst that I feel closely resembled verbal Turrets.

The decision was a no brainer for me though. I'm just hoping he isn't in the mood to watch the double feature with a drama and a slasher-type thriller, because I am so not. I pointed to the left. "The one that's playing *The Hangover*."

"You sure?"

"Yep. Unless you'd rather see something on the other side."

Hmm. I wouldn't peg him for being a horror movie kinda guy, but maybe the drama is supposed to be good. I haven't heard much about it so I don't know.

He grinned and pulled forward to the left. "Nope. I was hoping you'd pick that one. I didn't get to see it in the actual theater and I really wanted to…I just wanted to make sure."

"I didn't get to see it either, but it's supposedly hysterical."

Whew! At least the first one is a movie neither of us has seen and one we'll both probably want to pay attention to.

Tristan parked in the back so the bus didn't block any of the smaller cars, and before shutting the engine off, he tuned the radio to the correct channel for the movie. Then, holding hands—teehee—we walked to the snack bar for some munchies. We got in line behind a group of five other teenagers who were being loud and obnoxious like many teenagers are, but I ended up not paying any attention to their antics as that was when

Tristan turned me to face him and said, "Hi" then he gave me the first real kiss since last Saturday night. It'd also be the first of many to come tonight, and again I say teehee!

I was so wholly absorbed in my new favorite pastime, Tristan wound up proving his prowess in the art of multitasking. He had to; otherwise we would've never gotten our snacks. I'm also kind of thinking we'd have missed the first part of the movie. Before I understood what he was actually doing, he picked me up in a hug—without breaking the kiss...how's that for impressive? —and it wasn't until he set me back down that I realized he'd moved us forward in line. Not willing to stop kissing either, he did that a couple more times before it was our turn at the counter.

When we got back to the bus, Tristan raised the overhead compartment where we would be watching the movie and then we climbed up to, not idly by any means, wait for it to start. It was during this time that I came to accept the fact that when Tristan and I kiss we tend to become if not oblivious, then at least indifferent to what's going on around us. And I'm also now wondering if he'd already figured that out last Saturday and that's why he'd avoided kissing me at the bonfire and at the pizza place, because I have a feeling that's all we would've done for the several hours we were at the beach, and that Conner might've slowly bled to death from his minor cut. I know that for me personally, I probably wouldn't notice or care if someone put a tray of ice cubes down the back of my shirt or told me that aliens have invaded Earth and the movie *War of the Worlds* is becoming a reality...I'm that rapt.

When the film finally started rolling he mumbled, "I think the movie's starting."

"Mm-hm," I mumbled in reply. What are we supposed to be seeing again?

After a few minutes—I think. I really have no idea how long it was—he moved down to my neck and murmured, "Thank you for the ponytail."

I angled my neck a little more. "My pleasure."

No really, it is. He's not the only one who can plan ahead...I wore it up for this exact reason. Ahh, here come those utterly delightful goose bumps!

Sometime later and again through a kiss, he mumbled, "Did you wanna watch the movie?"

Uh, movie? Are we supposed to be seeing a movie? Honestly, all I'm thinking about is how his astounding lips are moving, leaving me breathless, but not...if that makes any sense whatsoever.

"I forgot what movie it is..." I told him truthfully as he nibbled his way down my jaw line.

I suppose I could've been embarrassed by admitting that he'd essentially kissed me into some kind of amnesia-like fog, but he started laughing and said, "Me too. Okay, we gotta stop or neither of us will hear either alarm."

Oh yeah, I forgot to mention that he'd set his phone alarm as a back-up to mine, which totally adds credence to my theory that he gets just as befuddled as I do, because we have like five hours before either of them are scheduled to go off.

Somewhat grudgingly, we peeled ourselves apart and readjusted our positions so we could at least try to be good and enjoy the movie. Which we did; it was probably the funniest movie I've seen in my life—the parts I saw anyway. However, and I'm not sure who started it, we ended up making out again for, give or take, the last fifteen minutes of the movie and part way into the intermission. I should also mention that for the most part, Tristan's been really good about keeping his hands to himself. I was kind of expecting him to take advantage of my delirium to check on the whole thong thing, but he either doesn't want to spook me or he's simply content with having his hands on the skin of my back or in my hair. Yeah, even as appreciated as it is, the ponytail has gotta be looking pretty pathetic by this point.

Let me see if I can come up with an adequate example of what it's been like for you… Oh, okay, here's a good one; kissing Tristan (or being kissed by Tristan, whichever…) is like an extreme sport. It's entirely exciting, it produces a monumental quantity of adrenaline, it's absolutely and altogether addictive, and it requires plenty of fluids. When we stopped kissing the first time, both of us ended up draining our sodas within ten minutes and I'm pretty sure our thirst and bladders were what halted us the second time. It's kind of ironic, isn't it? Alien life forms massacring the human race can be completely ignored but nature calling will get your attention every time.

I ran a brush through my hair, thus killing the small woodland creature that had decided to nest in it, and then we got out of the bus and wandered over to the bathrooms. That's when we found them.

"Oh! Poor kitties…oh, you're so itty-bitty," I cooed to the two kittens mewing and shivering in the corner by the snack bar.

Tristan bent down next to me and scooped one up. "Oh wow, they really are…I wonder where their mom is..."

"I don't know, maybe the guy in the snack bar has been feeding them though. They don't look like they're starving," I replied, cuddling the black and white one.

"Come on, we can go ask," he suggested and then he stood up holding the black one that I could hear purring its little heart out.

The snack bar attendant told us that a car had hit their mother two weeks ago and there used to be five of them, but he hadn't seen the other three in a week. He also said that the manager was planning on calling animal control to come get them if they didn't disappear this weekend like their mom and littermates had. Really, what a jerk. Not the attendant, he's cool, but the manager…

"I can't just bring them home…my dad will flip out, but maybe if I pick the right time to ask he'll let me keep one. I don't know about both though," I told Tristan and gave him a pleading look with big puppy dog eyes.

He chuckled. "Fine. My parents won't care, but I'll have to keep them separate from the dog."

"Oh you're the best!" I said with glee and gave him a gentle hug so I didn't squeeze the life out of the ball of fur he was holding against his chest. And speaking from experience, that spot happens to be prime real estate so the kitten should feel honored.

"No I'm not…you're just determined to make me a father in whatever way you can."

"Oh shut up…" I told him and nudged him with my shoulder.

He gave me a grin and a wink. Then he asked, "Do you care about seeing the second movie?"

"I don't even remember what it is, so no," I answered and nuzzled my own bundle of fluff that was purring just as loudly now.

"Okay good. I'm thinking we should probably go to the store for kitten supplies and then take them home."

"Do itty-bitty babies wanna go shopping? *Yeeesss.* Get some *toys*, and *fooood*, and more *toys*, and..." I trailed off from what I was saying when I heard Tristan clear his throat. Then I looked up and caught the crooked grin he gave me at my use of baby talk that I'd been speaking to the kittens with.

We took the kittens into the store with us and loaded up a cart with all the things any two kittens in the world would ever need or want. Judging from their size, we figured they were probably about six weeks old so we bought both wet and dry food for them just in case they couldn't chew the dry yet. Tristan got a little irritated with me when I insisted on splitting the bill down the middle, but laughed when I told him to quit being a caveman and get over it. Even though I know he was teasing me before, I'm thinking that playing house and going through an adoption together isn't typical behavior for two teenagers who are on their first date, but that's honestly what this feels like. What's even stranger is that neither of us thinks it's weird…as if we frequently decided to raise pets with our dates. Well, dates being plural for him, singular for me.

By the time we got back to Tristan's it was about ten o'clock and it occurred to me that even with the open relationship he has with his parents, they might not be so thrilled that he's bringing a girl home at this time.

"Um, won't your parents think it's a little late for visitors?" I asked, hesitantly following him to the front door.

"I doubt it, but they're not even home. Every Friday night is date night and they don't usually get home until around one," he answered, flipping house lights on in the entryway.

I followed him to the stairs. "Every Friday?"

"Yeah. When they got together in high school they made it a rule that no matter what, they would spend Friday nights together…and they have, even when they're working. It's kinda cool actually," Tristan explained and then pushed open the door to his room.

Oooh! The Inner Sanctum!

We walked in and after we set the bags down, Tristan turned to hand me the black kitten. "Here, you take this and I'll go get the rest of the stuff." Then he kissed me on the head and walked out, closing the door behind him.

The first thing that struck me about his bedroom was not the size, although it is pretty humongous. It was the large picture window presenting a view of the valley below that commanded my attention, and by default, his bed, which was pushed up against the window, as if the window was serving as a headboard. The room was also fairly tidy but I wouldn't go so far as to call it spic-and-span clean; leaving out the few stray candy bar wrappers on the floor that hadn't quite found their way into the trash can, I'd say Tristan's room was more of an organized mess. Additionally I noticed that he has a sliding glass door and a big deck with stairs leading to what I assume is the backyard.

It was when I turned around to look at the rest of his room, however, that my eyes probably could've used some help back into my skull. On the wall next to the door we'd entered through was a huge floor-to-ceiling bulletin/whiteboard combo and hanging from a thumbtack on the bulletin board amongst pictures and other various sorts of memorabilia was my bra. It'd been washed but it still had a good many blotches of pink on it. If that wasn't shocking enough, the dialogue written over the last two weeks on the whiteboard pertaining to said bra certainly was. I'll include the copy just so you can truly appreciate what I'm dealing with here.

Tristan's Mom: What's this?

Tristan: A size 34B lace covered slingshot.

Jeff: Nice!

Tristan's Mom: Do I want to know?

Tristan: I don't know, do you?

Tristan's Mom: Not really. Are you planning on returning it or did you win some kind of prize?

Tristan: I plead the fifth.

Tristan's Dad: Well done son.

Jeff: Ditto!

Tristan's Mom: Don't encourage him.

Tristan: Gee, thanks mom.

Tristan's Dad: Can't a father be proud of his only child?

Tristan's Mom: He doesn't need your help…obviously.

Tristan's Dad: That's because he takes after me.

Tristan: Was there anything else I can do for you two?

Tristan's Mom: Tell her I tried to get the stains out, but I'm afraid they set in before I got to it.

Tristan: I'm sure she'll appreciate your effort, but if I'm any judge (and I'd like to think I am) its size has caused it to become obsolete and she needs to trade up.

Jeff: I'm so proud.

Tristan: Thanks man.

Tristan's Mom: A name would be nice you know.

Tristan: Camie.

Tristan's Mom: Do we get to meet her?

Tristan: Sure. I'll have my people call your people and set it up.

Tristan's Mom: I don't know why I bother. Do you want anything from the store?

Tristan: Yeah, Camie's sleeping over tonight and I promised her bacon and eggs for breakfast. Jeff's got the eggs covered but could you pick up some bacon for us and maybe a box of Twinkies for the bus? Thanks, you're the best.

Jeff: I have the eggs covered?
Tristan's Dad: He gets his sense of humor from you.
Tristan's Mom: Flattery will get you everywhere. How would you like your eggs prepared dear?

Okay, so how the hell am I supposed to respond to this? This has been a running conversation for two freaking weeks! *And* no one seems to think there's anything odd about the fact that some random girl's bra is hanging on the wall! Oh! Not to mention "Dear Jeff's" involvement… I'm at a loss. Honestly, I think it's time for me to just throw in the towel and join the Dark Side because it's glaringly obvious I don't stand a chance. I feel like I'm being assimilated by The Borg in *Star Trek*. And no, I never did figure out what Pete said but after having it in my head, I couldn't help watching an episode of *Star Trek: The Next Generation* on Netflix…

Anyhow, shifting the kittens and holding them in one hand, I added my own message to the outrageously politically incorrect whiteboard that said:

Me: If it wouldn't be too much trouble, I prefer mine sunny-side up. Thanks Mrs. D., you're the best. (I know his mom was being sarcastic about the whole thing, but I just couldn't resist.)

A little ways away from that somewhat disturbing to my equanimity dialogue is another, except this one has nothing to do with me or my underwear. I think it's funny, though, so I'll share… Hanging on another thumbtack is a Ziploc bag with what I can only assume is marijuana inside and here's what has been said regarding it:

Tristan's Mom: What's this?
Tristan: Oregano.
Tristan's Mom: Clearly.
Tristan: I swear, I'm only holding it for a friend.
Tristan's Dad: I didn't know that Jeff is Italian.
Jeff: I bake too.
Tristan's Dad: In the immortal words of Bill Clinton, "I never inhaled."
Jeff: Nice!

Tristan: Hey mom, can you pick up some brownie mix with the bacon and Twinkies? Thanks, you're the best.
Tristan's Mom: Just clean up your mess in the kitchen and don't drive.

I know he said he doesn't have many rules, but Tristan's parents put my parents' cool factor to shame, don't you think?

After reading and making my contribution to what I'm going to call "The Wall of Infamy," I wandered over and plopped down on the foot of the bed, setting the kittens next to me. Tristan came back in with all the rest of the supplies and then we got down to the business of setting up their stuff. The first thing was to introduce them to the litter box, which Tristan had wisely put in his bathroom. Then we fed them. Seeing as how the kittens were frantic over the food, I'm thinking that maybe they were closer to starving than I'd thought before. Either that or they're closely related to voracious Compy dinosaurs.

"So what do you wanna name 'em?" Tristan asked while he put together a small climbing apparatus.

"Well, I've been giving that some serious thought and I think the black and white one (It has four white paws, a small white patch on its chest and white whiskers…other than that, it's all black.) should be Phineas an—"

"Lemme guess, the black one would be Nigellus," he interrupted, referring to a character from *Harry Potter* who had the last name of Black.

I ripped open a package of little catnip filled mice. "Um, no, but that's pretty good too. I was thinking Ferb."

"From the cartoon?" He asked with a sarcastic smile. Even though Phineas and Ferb is a kid show, I think it's pretty witty and fun. Plus it has a really catchy theme song that always gets stuck in my head if I'm not careful.

"Yeah, I like it. Do you wanna tease me about that now or wait until later?" I'm pretty positive that if he doesn't tease me now, it'll go in his arsenal for a later time.

"No, I'll wait. But um, Camie…I think these are girl kittens." No wonder they purr so much around him.

"So? I don't think they'll mind too much. After all, this is something I have a little experience with you know," I said, scratching behind the kittens' ears as they plowed through their food and getting a good laugh out of Tristan.

"Okay, kitty condo is built. Did you get their toys unwrapped?"

"Yep, all done." I waved a wand with a feather and a bell attached to it as proof that I hadn't been slacking on my assigned parental duty.

After they ate their fill, we played with them on the floor until one by one, they passed out. Tristan glanced at the alarm clock by his bed and said,

"Okay, we've got a little over an hour before you have to be home…unless of course you wanna change your mind about sleeping over."

I looked at the teasing yet hopeful grin on his face. "Oh, why not…seeing as how I already put my order in for room service."

"What?" He asked, not having noticed my addition to the board.

I stood up, walked over to it and pointed. "Tristan, this whole thing is about as normal as my twelve year old sister knowing how to disassemble and reassemble weaponry."

He got up and came over to read what I wrote and then started cracking up. When he finished laughing, he instigated tonight's third heat of the new Olympic game that's sweeping the nation—"Teenage Pairs Smooching." In this round of the event however, a small costume adjustment resulted in a new technical element being introduced to our routine. I don't know how I managed to stay standing for as long as I did, but maybe Tristan was supporting my weight or something because this kiss totally put the extreme in my analogy of kissing him being an extreme sport. It also made my legs feel like they were made of Jell-O. I think he might've realized that too because he moved backwards towards the bed, taking me with him. Although, it was completely my fault that we both ended up without shirts before he pulled me down on top of him on the bed.

I honestly don't know what's wrong with me, but I'm going to blame the over-active and under-used hormones that are running rampant right now because it almost seems like I'm trying to make up for lost time or something. Oh and Tristan is no longer concerned with spooking me nor is he content with keeping his hands occupied with my back and hair. I found that out immediately and in a variety of ways, but that's also when he discovered that I'd held up my end of the "Black Thong Bargain"—that kind of sounds like a *60 Minutes* exposé, doesn't it?

I didn't even give it a second thought when his hands slipped under the soft waistband of my pants, but I certainly noticed when he hooked his thumbs and index fingers under each side of the satin encased elastic of my surprisingly comfy undergarment, raised it, and then let it snap sharply back into place.

"Ow!" I yelped and looked at him in consternation. It mostly took me by surprise but it honestly did sting a bit too.

He lifted his eyebrows once quickly and had *the* most wicked grin on his face when he asked, "Black?"

"What do you think?" I retorted and noticed his eyes.

They were such a beautiful, deep-dark blue that I could honestly drown in them and not care one bit that I'd died. Seriously, I'm glad it's customary to kiss with your eyes closed because if I had to see his face during all of this, I'm pretty positive I wouldn't have stopped at just getting rid of our shirts.

This is what's going through my mind when Tristan asked, "Can I see it?"

O. M. G.

Immediately, a little angel and a little devil popped into my head and started arguing, but the angel won and so chuckling to myself I said, "No."

"Why not?" He's now playing with the elastic like he's about to snap it again.

"For starters because I only said I'd wear it, not that you'd get to see it. Secondly, you didn't say please. And lastly, I swear if you snap the freaking elastic one more time, I'm outta here…so don't push your luck, just be happy with what you've got."

Instantly, I felt him gently lower the bands and then pat them in place. His hands are still under my pants and on my bare butt though…

"Okey dokey, I can do that," he said with another sinful smile.

Then Tristan flipped me onto my back, reached over me to set his alarm clock and then proceeded to be thoroughly happy—or maybe a better word would be ecstatic—with what he had.

At one point however, I had to remind him of his boundaries when his hands made their way to the clasp of my bra. It's new, it matches the thong, and I'd kind of like to wear it more than once before it ends up hanging on a thumbtack. It was a lot easier to do than I thought it'd be too…all I had to do was mumble a very distracted "mm-mm." He relented but growled at me a little in the process. I don't know why it mattered so much though…seriously; it's not like a thin layer of satin serves as an effective barrier.

Honestly, where does the time go? I have to wonder about that because about thirty minutes later, Tristan's alarm clock started blaring. He blindly reached for it and hit the snooze button—which I'm now re-naming the "you may continue button"—giving us approximately nine more minutes to engage in what has come to remind me of as a full-body contact sport. When the alarm went off the second time, though, it was accompanied by both his phone alarm and mine, which means the party's over for realsies this time. He rolled onto his back, covered his head with a pillow and muttered his frustrated complaints into it. I think he said something about f-ing daylight savings time and that all curfews should be banned among other things.

With the absence of his body heat to keep me warm, I shivered when the air hit my damp skin. I say damp because it got a little warm and I was perspiring. Okay fine, that's a lie. If you must know, his mouth has been doing laps over almost every inch of my bare skin like a member of NASCAR. Anyhow, that's when I realized it would be a good time to locate my shirt and put it back on. The only problem was...I couldn't find it.

"Are you freaking kidding me with this?" I grumbled, scanning the floor. I mean really, am I destined to have some kind of clothing mishap every time I'm around him?

I was hanging over the side of the bed thinking that maybe my shirt had found its way underneath when all of a sudden; I felt Tristan's warm breath on the small of my back, just seconds before he softly kissed the base of my spine right above where a strip of black satin was peeking out from the waist of my pants. The goose bumps I already had turned into hills as a tingling shot of heat went streaking through me.

"I like it, it matches. Oh, that reminds me..."

I felt him fiddle with my bra and looked up over my shoulder to see him refastening one of the hooks. Damn, the dexterity and nimbleness of this guy's fingers is frightening. I didn't even realize he'd been that close to undoing the thing in the first place.

"Well you know how I feel about clashing," I told he who's now kissing my back thereby sending waves of heat through my body with much force as my blood started to rush to my head from hanging upside down. The combination of which, I must say, is an odd sensation.

"What are you doing down there?" He asked, stretching out halfway over me like he was getting in a comfy position so he could maintain lip to back contact.

"Looking for my damned shirt! It's disappeared...totally vanished! How can that even be possible? I mean, does the cosmos have it in for my clothes or something? Seriously Tristan, why does almost every night I'm around you end with me being in want of some form of apparel?" I asked out of pure frustration.

He was laughing against my back but he managed a reply just the same. "Maybe the cosmos agrees with my theory that you wear too many clothes."

"Ugh, you're impossible. Come on, the witching hour is at hand and I don't think you'd care to be shot tonight." I grabbed the shirt he'd been wearing earlier and pulled it over my head. "And I certainly won't be happy if I get grounded."

While Tristan wandered into his closet for another shirt, I used his bathroom and tidied up my hair again. When I was done, I found my flip-flops and hurriedly took one last look around his bed to see if the cosmos had had second thoughts about my shirt, all the while wondering how I was going to explain why I was coming home in a boy's clothes. Again. I guess I'll just go with the same excuse as I had the night of Mike's party, which was basically the truth; I got a drink spilled all over me and Tristan was gentleman enough to surrender his shirt because mine was no longer appropriate for me to be seen in. You know, I figure telling my parents I spilled soda on myself at the movies will go over umpteen times better than saying "Oh, well Tristan and I were making out in his bedroom, see, and I decided I just *had* to be able to run my hands all over the taught skin of his marvelous torso and I figured if he was going to be shirtless, then it was only fair that I was too, but it's the damnedest thing...I couldn't find my shirt in the mess we'd made of his bed, so, you know..."

Tristan drove me home and on the way, we made tentative plans to meet up tomorrow night. They had to be tentative because neither of us knew where the good party was going to be yet. Actually, the first thing he asked was if I wanted to go back to the beach with him and Jeff tomorrow afternoon. I had to decline though; I'm going to a family bar-b-q at Derek's house. I'm thinking that because he wants to see me again so soon, that tonight was a success on both sides. I mean it was for me obviously, but that doesn't automatically mean he feels the same way.

Because we lagged leaving his place, he actually had to drive pretty fast to make it to my house on time and he got me to my door with just two minutes to spare. Since I was technically home, I made a judgment call and pulled Tristan over to sit on our porch swing with me. Okay, so I'm being kind of a rebellious brat, but it's such a pretty night and I'm trying to keep the magic going any way I can. He and I just sat there, swinging together, looking at the stars and talking for about thirty minutes before a light in the house came on. We gave each other one last kiss then I scurried inside and he drove away.

I met my dad at the top of the stairs and said defiantly, "I was home at 11:58."

"I know you were. Anyone with half a brain would recognize the sound of the small block that boy's got in there, although I'm glad to see he didn't take you out in that VW of his," my dad said with a knowingly raised eyebrow.

Well, so much for keeping that a secret—he must've seen Tristan drop me off last weekend. "And I'm not here to argue semantics with you either but do me a favor sweetie, lemme at least meet the boy before you spend half the night on the porch swing with him," he finished, looking at me fondly.

"Okay. I'm sorry Daddy," I replied heavy with guilt and hugged him.

I was all keyed up for an argument but my dad wasn't upset at all. And he has a point; he really should get to meet the guy who wants to date his teenage daughter. At some point I'm going to have to tell him about the age thing too. He deserves to know the truth.

"Honey, I think I have a pretty good idea of what you're goin' through. After all, that's the same porch swing your mom and I spent many a night in high school swingin' on and fallin' in love with each other…it's also the same one she was sittin' on when she told me she'd marry me. Your Grandma and Grandpa Cameron gave it to us as a wedding present," my dad told me with a dreamy look on his face before we said goodnight and he went back to his room and my mom.

Did you notice that he didn't even *try* to tell me I'm too young to fall in love? Wow. I guess my dad's a total romantic, huh? You know, my parents might not be as lenient as Tristan's but I'd bet Kate's dad's life savings that they love each other as much as his if not more.

I started moving towards my room when my dad suddenly stopped at the other end of the hallway and turned back around. "You wearin' the boy's shirt again?"

Nope. Definitely not as lenient. "Oh. Yeah...I'm a klutz...I tripped going down the stairs after the movie and spilled soda all over myself. Tristan had an extra shirt in the trunk."

"He's quite the boy scout, ain't he?"

I smiled a little and shrugged. Then something occurred to me. "Oh crap, I just realized I left my shirt in his car again..."

Yeah I know. I'm a liar and a horrible daughter.

16.

A Piece Of Red Licorice

I woke up Saturday morning to the melodic sound of Faith Hill's voice. It automatically made my blood sizzle and all the nerve endings in my body tingle at the memories it evoked in me. I scrambled out of bed trying to grab my phone before it stopped ringing on the off chance I might get to hear the sound of Tristan's voice on the other end. He's never actually called to talk to me but I can hope, right? Looking at the screen, I discovered I'll have to continue to hope but I'm not too disappointed because instead of a text, it's a picture message. I smiled and caught myself speaking baby talk at the picture of Phineas and Ferb sleeping sprawled on top of each other.

Oh! They're just so stinking cute! I looked at it closer and realized what they were sleeping on, or rather, in—my missing shirt. I'm guessing that the itty-bitty kitties must've at some point when Tristan and I were oblivious to everything including nuclear war, stolen it and made a bed for themselves out of it. It's kinda funny actually, we bought them a kitty bed but rather than using *it*, they dragged my shirt right next to it and crashed there instead.

Looking at the pictorial evidence and thinking about the success of date number one, I of course started thinking about what date number two might hold in store for me. It hasn't even been planned yet, but this is where I'm doing the positive thinking thing again.

And okay, now I know it might sound like a bad idea to do at this point, but I'm going to call Melissa. I don't want any details (Um, can you say uber-awkward?), but I'm hoping that if I have some "speaking from experience" wisdom to keep in the back of my mind, I can capitalize on the progress I've already achieved with the human father of my feline children. I waited until after breakfast and when I thought would be a respectable hour to call, and was gratified when Melissa answered on the first ring.

Melissa: "Hey Camie, what's up?"

Me: "Well, I kinda wanted to ask you something. I hope I'm not out of line and you can totally tell me it's none of my freaking business if I am, but would you be willing to tell me why things with you and Tristan didn't work out?"

Melissa: "Oh, sure. I don't know why I never thought to tell you before, but it's really not that big of a deal. I think our personalities just didn't mesh all that well. I mean, we get along great and everything but I think I might've been too high maintenance for him."

Me: "Oh. What makes you think that? I mean did he say something that would make you think that, or is it just a guess?"

Melissa: "Mmm, a little of both. I don't think we would've ever really been good together and he knew it before I did, but we still probably would've gone out more than three times. And honestly, I think the reason we didn't was mostly my fault." (Huh. I thought it was only twice…)

Me: "Your fault?"

Melissa: "Well, yeah, kinda…I mean, technically, there really wasn't anything that happened for blame to be placed, but Tristan and I went out a couple times over a period of a few weeks or maybe it was like a month…I don't remember, but anyway, the weekend after our second date I saw him totally making out with this older and really sexy looking girl I'd never seen before. Actually, I never saw her again after that either…but, whatever, I didn't handle it well. I mean he and I were *not* an item by *any* stretch of the imagination so my reaction wasn't really justified, you know?"

Me: (No, I don't really know, but whatever.) "Um, yeah, I guess…what was your reaction?"

Melissa: "Well, I didn't freak out or anything that night but when we went out the third time I was *really* clingy. I think I thought that if I could just somehow capture and keep his attention we'd be good, you know? But he was *so* not having any of that…he wasn't a jerk or anything about it, but he did say something like he felt too much pressure to meet demands.

"I forget how he put it, but I took it to mean that I was putting pressure on him to act in a way that he was uncomfortable with. You know, like he couldn't be himself around me. And you know what, he was right. Neither of us would've been happy if he hadn't recognized what was going on and put a stop to it. I'm sorry, I know that's not much, but there honestly wasn't all that much between us and it was a long time ago."

Me: "Oh, no…don't apologize. This is what I asked to know. I just wanted to talk to someone who'd been there before, you know? I really appreciate you telling me all that."

Melissa: "Oh no problem, I hope it helps. And while I have you on the phone, I wanna say something else...he's pretty much the same now as he was back then, and well…Camie, I've never seen him act the way he does around you with any other girl, and I don't know why or what it is about you, but there's most definitely *something* there. I mean, he hasn't even so much as *checked out* another girl since he met you and honestly, for a guy who pretty much can and frequently does take his pick of any single girl during any given time to essentially play with however he wants, that's really saying something."

Me: "You know, I kinda don't know what to say…I mean, the way you and Kate make me sound sometimes…I don't get it, Melissa, I'm really not that special. I'm just me, you know?"

Melissa: "Yeah, I know what you mean, but *he* apparently thinks you are and maybe it's *because* you don't put on an act for him or anyone else. You know, Camie, there's something to be said for just being yourself. I mean think about it…he didn't wanna date me anymore because he couldn't be himself around me and I *wasn't* being myself around him…maybe you guys hit the jackpot with being able to just be yourselves with each other and it works without effort. I know this whole thing started out being kinda contrived, but there really hasn't been any actual acting going on. You guys have been behaving like you normally would and you just naturally clicked."

Me: "You really think so? Honestly, I keep thinking the same thing, but I just don't wanna read into something that's not there. But seriously Melissa…we found kittens last night and adopted them and I swear it felt like playing house. In fact, he already sent me a picture of them sleeping this morning and the title was "the kids"…I'm right in thinking that's not normal teenage behavior, aren't I?"

Melissa: "Uh, I'm gonna go with no. It's damned cute, but no, not normal."

Melissa and I chatted for a little longer and by the time we hung up, it was time for me to head out for one of our freakishly large family gatherings. They would definitely fall under the hootenanny category but they're usually so much fun, I can honestly call it that with love. I really do have an amazing extended family and it might be cheesy to admit it, but I like hanging out with them.

While we were there, everyone participated—adults too—in a jack-o-lantern carving contest. In addition to that, my aunt, Karen, made a ridiculously fun obstacle course for the kids, and of course we went on a scavenger hunt in their neighborhood once it got dark. All in all, it was chocked full of hoot and a little bit of nanny but it was a rip-roaring great time just the same.

We didn't leave until almost 9:30 and I'd been kind of stressing about not getting a ride to whatever party Tristan was at. Shortly before we got home however, Kate sent me text telling me to meet her at the party conveniently taking place just around the block from my house.

After changing, running a brush through my hair and putting on some lip-gloss—my parents are cool with lip-gloss—I padded back downstairs and said to my family at large, "Okay, I'm gonna walk over to that party for a while…I'll be home by midnight."

"Honey, are you sure you still want to go out? I'd think you'd be tired after today," my mom said on her way upstairs.

"Yeah I know, but Tristan and I told each other we'd meet up somewhere tonight and Kate's waiting for me there."

My mom shrugged and nodded in that "okay, do what you want" kind of way, and I kissed her on the cheek. I said another quick goodbye before leaving the house and then I practically sprinted down the street. I was walking up the driveway of my destination when I got a text from Kate who was just then walking out the front door.

"Oh, *there* you are…I just sent you a text. I'm leaving, do you wanna come with me or not?" From her tone and expression, it was beyond evident that Kate's irritation was *massive.*

"Oh, I'm sorry for making you wait for so long, we just got home…um, are the guys here?" I asked, thinking that I really want to spend some time with Tristan tonight but I don't want to be at a party without my wingman either, even if she seems to be in a horrifically bad mood.

"Sorry Camie, I just realized how bitchy that sounded. I'm not upset with you and yeah, the guys are definitely here, but that's why I'm leaving." She pointed to Tristan's bus parked across the street as proof of their attendance.

I was having the growing realization that Kate and Jeff may be experiencing trouble in paradise again so I put my best friend hat on. "Okay Kate, tell me what happened."

She sighed deeply in frustration and then Kate *raged.* "Not a goddamned thing actually happened but remember when I told you I need to try to be forgiving of Jeff's bullshit?! Yeah, well this is me removing myself from a fucked up situation that would make doing that really fucking tough for me…I mean shit, Camie, they're both *totally fucking obliterated*…I mean *completely* baked out of their *fucking* minds!! At least *your* jackass is more or less passed out so he's not being a *fucking asshole* like mine is!!"

Eesh! I've never seen Kate *this* angry before.

"I'm so sorry, Kate, I don't know what to say…" I don't either.

I don't think I've ever seen Tristan actually drunk before, let alone high, so I can't pretend to understand how she's feeling and man, she's *really* pissed.

"Don't be and I'm sorry Camie, I know you probably really wanna see him, but I've had kind of a bad day and I just don't wanna deal with this shit tonight," Kate said with real understanding but quite a bit of impatience to be gone from here as well.

"No, I understand…I mean, I don't know how you feel, but you know what I mean. Um, I'm gonna go with you but I told him I'd see him tonight…can you give me like maybe ten minutes just so I can at least say hi? I promise, I'll just run in, say hi, and then we can go do whatever you want…"

I'm totally gonna back my best friend here even though my baby daddy (baby, kitten…whatever) is in the house and I really, really want to see him—stoned or not—but seriously, what kind of friend would I be if I let Kate go off all by herself? By the looks of her, I think she could really use some girl time, you know?

"Yeah, I can do that. I'm just gonna wait in the car though, okay? I don't wanna give that *asshole* any opportunities to trap me here," she spit out venomously in the direction of the house. "But Camie, be prepared…he might not even be conscious anymore."

"He's that bad?"

I started feeling my nerves and anxiety kick into gear. I just can't picture Tristan passed out and for some unknown reason, trying to do so is kind of freaking me out.

"Well, when I was just in there he'd pretty much commandeered the whole couch in the family room and was semi-awake, but he's got his earbuds in and his iPod on and he was keeping his eyes shut, so I'm guessing it's only a matter of time before he's totally out for the count," Kate explained and then walked to her car, leaving me standing in the driveway—alone.

Taking a deep breath, I headed into the house, thinking that Kate's big issue is how Jeff acts when he's not sober, and her irritation probably comes from him being her boyfriend and being such a clown in the first place. Tristan isn't like Jeff in either regard, therefore, maybe Tristan's intoxicated state isn't something I really need to worry about. I mean, how bad could it honestly be? After all, if he passes out, he'll be the one to deal with a Sharpie mustache, not me.

I couldn't have *been* more grotesquely wrong.

I made my way through the sea of bodies and into the family room where Kate said Tristan would be. Even though the room was more or less packed, my eyes found him immediately. Looking just as drop-dead gorgeous as ever, he was sprawled on the couch with his hands behind his head and his eyes were closed exactly like Kate had said. I could tell he wasn't comatose, though, because there was a piece of red licorice in his mouth and it was getting smaller as he chewed on it. Before I could get anywhere near him however, I watched in absolute horror as some girl I vaguely recognize from school crawled across the arm of the couch to essentially cover him completely with her body, boldly take the licorice from his lips with her own, and then start kissing him.

Seriously, it was like witnessing a car vs. motorcycle accident that's about to happen that you can't tear your eyes from even though you know it's going to be ghastly and brutal. I honestly thought I was going to throw up. Especially when the philandering prick actually brought one of his hands to the back of her head and slipped the other under her shirt and started kissing her back.

Yeah, *way* ghastly and brutal...I'm beyond devastated.

Holy fucking hell...I really think I'm gonna be sick...

Even though it all happened in a flash and not much more than thirty seconds could've passed, I knew I had to get the hell out of there and fast. I'm starting to shake and sweat, the tears are gonna come any minute, and I know I'm suffocating because my throat is burning and closed so tight that it's making breathing impossible. I turned on my heel to flee the gut wrenching scene I wish I would've never witnessed in the first place and ran right into the last person in the world I wanted to see; she was teetering on her feet and holding a wine cooler of Canadian Spiced Whisky...

"You din't ashlly (Ashlly? Was that supposed to be actually?) tink he liked *you*? Tris-*hiccup*-tan sfar outta your lea—" Teresa drunkenly slurred before I cut her off. She's totally hammered; you have no idea.

"Teresa, get outta my face...I don't want your fleas and frankly...you reek," I told her and tried to push past her.

Honestly, the air in the house is so stale and there's a sickly alcoholic stench wafting around her that my queasy stomach can't handle, and if she doesn't back the hell off, she's gonna end up with my aunt's pumpkin stew all over her, which I'm pretty sure won't taste or smell nearly as fabulous after being in my digestive system for a few hours.

Barely keeping the tears at bay, I'd just managed to edge around her but before I could even make the hallway and beyond that, freedom, I ran headlong into a brick wall of another person. I looked up in nauseated shock and anger at Zack smiling down at me. Even as distraught as I was, I got the distinct impression that he'd impeded my progress on purpose.

Jesus, this is a fucking nightmare. All I want to do is get the hell out of here so I can fall apart in private, is that too much to ask?

"Hey Camie, where you headed off to so fast? Come on, stick around...we've never really had a chance to get to know each other, which *I* think is a damned shame," Zack said with what appeared to be good natured intent and a smile.

"Uh, sorry I can't...Kate's waiting for me," I choked out and shouldered my way by him, finally escaping into the cool and merciful evening air.

Once outside I took a brief second to collect myself. However, a sudden fear of being followed or discovered had me abandoning the porch and hurrying on wobbly legs down the street to Kate's car. I wrenched open the passenger door and then threw myself in the seat.

"Okay, please get me the fuck outta here…in fact, just take me home."

Kate took one look at my face, cranked the ignition and peeled out in her haste to get us away. "He wasn't passed out, was he?"

I covered my face with my hands and through the onslaught of tears that finally slipped their leash I said, "No. I just caught the live show of him being self-destructive and I'll never eat licorice again."

I'll have to try to remember to thank her for promptly turning the stereo off; I still caught part of "Cryin'" by Aerosmith before she did though. I really like the song, but it's just not what I should be listening to right now if you get my meaning.

Kate pulled up to my house, turned the car off and looked over at me. "Why don't I stay the night? I think we could both use a big, fat tub of ice cream and I *know* I don't wanna be alone."

I nodded my agreement, wiping the tears from my face. Then taking a deep, calming breath, she and I got out of the car. Unlike my mind, the house was silent and utterly still. I quietly entered my parents' room to whisper to my dad I was home and that Kate was sleeping over. He grunted his acknowledgment and was out like a light again before I exited the room and closed the door behind me.

Walking into my bedroom, I flipped on my bedroom light, put my keys and phone on my dresser, and then I fell into Kate's open arms, bawling again.

"What happened?" Jillian asked after opening my door uninvited and then closing it again behind her.

I couldn't even appreciate the comedy of the t-shirt she was wearing. It had a picture of a guy in a suit that had no sleeves, revealing the man to have hairy, bear arms; a caption under all of it read, "The Second Amendment."

"It wasn't a good night all around," Kate told her while rubbing my back.

Jill placed herself down on the edge of my bed. The look on her face, of the utmost concern and compassion, was one I haven't seen her wear in a very long time. "Was it Teresa again?"

"Oh God, that's right…she saw the whole thing and just couldn't resist adding insult to injury…" Sighing and wiping at my cheeks again, I told them everything about my misadventure with Tristan, the bitch, and Zack.

"Do you want me to make an example out of him? I will if you want me to…just give me the word and I'll teach him *and* everyone else what happens when they mess with *my* family," Jillian declared, resolute—her eyes on fire and an eagerness for justice pervading from within her, proving her to be my stalwart champion in times of distress.

They'd met briefly before, but this being her first *real* introduction to my sister, Kate looked nervously back and forth between Jillian and me, finally witnessing and therefore *believing* all I'd shared about the genius standing righteously justified before her.

On a painfully tight sigh, I shook my head and firmly said, "No Jilly. Even though I feel like there's a huge gash in my chest from where he ripped my heart out, I can't accept your offer, but thank you."

"What about the waste of lip-gloss?" She asked hopefully.

"Dispose of her as you will," I replied.

Please understand something, I know Jillian isn't about to physically hurt Teresa or anyone else. She might take some of her cues from the movie *Heathers* and Teresa might wish she'd never been born, but Jill's not psychotic on *any* level.

"Alright, now we're talkin'!" She enthused as her eyes lit with excitement before she looked at me with concern again, her exhilaration fading to a simmer. "And how are you gonna handle ah…things?"

"Honestly, I don't have a freaking clue. I'm really hurt but the more I think about what just happened, the more mad I get and then I start thinking about all the really great stuff that's happened between us which just reminds me why this hurts so much…it's like a never ending cycle and it's making me nauseous. I know there's no possible way for me to face him for awhile though, so I think I'm gonna act sick to get outta school…" I started sniffling again as Jillian stood up and gave me an uncomfortably intent look that I couldn't decipher.

"Uh-huh… Okay, well I'm gonna get packed and get outta here…where's the party?" She asked while still giving me the incomprehensible look.

Truthfully, I have no idea what's going through her head right now, but it's giving me the creeps. It's almost like she's peering into my soul and doesn't like what she sees.

"Um, do you want me to come with you?" Kate offered. So maybe Kate didn't *quite* grasp what kind of person my sister is. True, a twelve-year-old girl sneaking out of the house late at night by herself isn't the safest thing, and maybe Kate hasn't noticed Jill's shirt or she just doesn't know what the second amendment of the Constitution is, but truth be told, I'd be more fearful for anyone who might come across my sister than the other way around.

"Oh, that's nice of you to offer, but I prefer to work alone," Jillian replied with a wink and then left us to wallow in self-pity.

Deciding that we didn't want to talk about the events of tonight any longer, our pity-party commenced. We raided the freezer of all the ice cream it held, grabbed the new package of Double Stuff Oreos and watched a couple of chick flicks. We fell asleep in the middle of the second one and never heard Jillian return home. I didn't think I'd be able to sleep soundly with everything playing through my head like a broken record, but I must've because when Kate and I woke up Sunday morning, there was post-it note stuck to my forehead that read:

For Your Listening Pleasure,
Please Push Play on Your Stereo.

Knowing this was Jillian's way of trying to communicate something to me, I climbed out of bed, walked over to my stereo and pushed the play button as per requested and immediately heard her voice; it was followed by a *slew* of songs...

Jillian: "Camie, I'm not even gonna pretend I know what you're feeling right now because...well, I'm twelve and I still think boys are stupid. And I know you didn't ask for my opinion or advice either, but before you go running to Mom claiming to have a heartbreak induced stomach flu, please hear me out... You're stronger than that and you have options. The following selections are meant to be inspirational and motivational, so pay attention, and, enjoy."

As Kate and I listened to Jillian's encouragement and suggestions made by way of music and lyrics, I was thinking how truly amazing my sister is. I also believe my parents have done a damned good job of indoctrinating her in music appreciation as well. The music she chose made it clear that some of the options she'd mentioned are things like; making him miss me, getting even, making him jealous, confronting him, being strong and persevering, and showing him what he has in me. I also thought you might like to know how she communicated that, so here are just *some* of the tracks she included:

"Man, I Feel Like a Woman" – Shania Twain
"Jealous Again" – The Black Crowes
"All I Have" – Jennifer Lopez feat. LL Cool J
"Maybe He'll Notice Her Now" – Mindy McCready
"Don't Tread On Me" - Metallica (This also happens to be Jill's self-proclaimed theme song and her ringtone on my phone.)
"Look At Me I'm Sandra Dee (reprise)" – Olivia Newton John (Grease Soundtrack)
"The Climb" – Myley Cyrus

"Bring On the Rain" – Jo Dee Messina feat. Tim McGraw

When I thought we'd heard the last song, Jillian's voice came back and was, ultimately, what really finally got to me:

Jillian: "I saw and heard some things tonight that gave me some insight into what happened and I don't think you're operating with all the facts, but regardless, no matter what you choose to do, I'll back you all the way. But here's the thing, Camie, you have to do *something* because this is one thing you *cannot* hide from. So come on…I dare you."

She then drove her point home with the force of a three hundred pound linebacker with one last song: *"I Dare You to Move" – Switchfoot.*

Overwhelmed, moved, and crying, Kate and I looked at each other.

"Wow. She's right you know, Camie, you have to deal with this because it's not gonna go away. Tristan really likes you but this isn't surprising behavior for him…I mean this kind of thing happening was always the main drawback to the mission, you know? And I guess we've reached the crux of the situation…you need to decide how much you want him and how much you're willing to go through to have him."

"*Ugh*, I can't believe my little sister just totally called me out like that…and yeah, I know she's right (she's always right, damn it). I just don't know what to do. I like him *so* much Kate, but I don't know if I wanna go through another night like last night. I mean, I'm not gonna do what Melissa did and push myself on him...I know I need to be myself, but I don't know how to go about doing that right now. What do you think Jill meant about not having all the facts?" I asked and cuddled my pillow.

And just so you know, I'm leaning towards just putting what happened behind me and doing the "keep on keepin' on" thing, but man, that's gonna be rough. However, it might be the least of the evils at this point; my stomach already clenches horribly at the thought of never again experiencing the euphoria of what happens when he touches me or kisses me...

"I have no idea, but your sister scares me," Kate admitted with a shaky laugh.

Hoping for some clarification on that, we got up and knocked on Jillian's door. We didn't get an answer. When I tried to open it, I found it to be locked which suggests to me that my sister has headphones on and is a *very* busy beaver. I have a feeling that Teresa is screwed...

Oh, later that afternoon while Kate and I were shopping, which is always good for a pick me up, I got a text from Tristan:

Tristan: where were u last nite? :-*

Rather than being elated like usual, my first thought was, *Aw shit.* Now I really have to make up my mind…

17.

The Difference Between Manslaughter And First Degree Murder

Monday morning I was still vacillating on what I wanted but I'd replied to Tristan last night after quite a few hours of thinking. I went with a partial truth by telling him that Kate was mad at Jeff and she'd come over to my house for a sleepover. I also went ahead and text kissed him back even though his felt like a lie. I guess I'm hoping I can get over what he did and stick to the original plan. After all, Kate was right. I was warned in the beginning that this was likely to happen; I just didn't realize how hard it'd be when it did. Or, maybe I was in denial about it even happening at all.

For the very first time, Kate and I actually made it to school with plenty of time before our first class. When we arrived she and I were astonished by the flurry of excited talk thrumming throughout the student body. Everywhere on campus kids were huddled together and when we stopped by our lockers, we found out why. Stuffed inside each and every locker was a full page flyer with four insanely clear and detailed pictures of Teresa puking her guts out in front of the house where I left my battered heart Saturday night with a caption that read:

PUBLIC HEALTH ANNOUNCEMENT
How to recognize the early warning signs of liver cirrhosis brought on by teen alcoholism.

We'd like to thank SOPHOMORE TERESA AUSTEN for providing us with this most-excellent visual aid, and coincidentally in doing so, she has also helped us to illustrate that pizza mixed with vast quantities of liquor is not only totally gross when it comes back up, but it's also inevitable that it will. So, make sure you give her a big round of applause when you see her this week and don't forget to check out Teresa's live show at the following YouTube address.

Damn. I shudder to think what she could've done to Tristan but regardless of the possibilities, I'm sure it would've been a far cry worse than a Sharpie mustache and being thrown in a pool because she was pretty ticked at him when she left Saturday night. I wonder if I should at some point mention to Tristan that he owes me huge for keeping him out of Jillian's line of fire.

I spent the entire day with a brittle smile on my face; feeling like it could crack at any moment. I also semi-seriously considered kicking Teresa out of whatever dank hole she'd found to spend the break in so I could hide for the duration of my English class. Having finally finished the book, Mrs. Henderson held a debate on what we think the underlying meanings in *Pride & Prejudice* are. However, Kate didn't allow the fact that she still isn't talking to him stop Jeff and she from using the topic to wage a war against each other, letting me see first hand that Jeff really can get worked up just as much as anybody. Additionally, I witnessed the fact that he knows how to verbally fight back fairly well too. Unfortunately, it also made the rest of us in class tense and uncomfortable. That is, everyone aside from Mrs. Henderson. She was totally pleased with them for clearly grasping the concepts and backing up their arguments with fervor, even if it was hostile. And of course, Tristan, he just thought the whole thing was funny. Seriously, he was acting like nothing had happened at all, like everything was right and just in the world, and that it hadn't stopped turning the second his lips met some other girl's, and by the time lunch rolled around, I felt too sick to eat.

The only positives to my day are that Teresa has apparently moved into the aforementioned dank hole for the foreseeable future, and that Kate wanted to hightail it out of school the second the bell rang dismissing us from our last class. We didn't even change back into our regular clothes. Also, when Tristan sent me a text shortly after school, I knew exactly how to answer and could be completely honest, however I *did* wait to respond until right before I went to bed around 10:00.

Tristan: want 2 go out fri? :-*
Me: cant. plans w/kate. :-*

Kate and I decided to forego any festivities Friday night after the game and go to the movies by ourselves instead; it would give both of us some time to think. She told me she'll eventually forgive Jeff but she wants him to really work for it and prove to her that he can be a grownup.

Tuesday morning Kate pulled up not quite as early as yesterday and when I got in the car she had some unexpected news for me—along with puffy eyes. It looked as though she'd been doing a *lot* of crying. I wanted to ask but she waved me off and then dove right into her news.

"I think I know what your sister might've meant by not having all the facts. Jeff called me last night *again* and I didn't answer *again*, but instead of leaving me another voicemail, he hung up…except, he didn't. I don't know what you're gonna do with this information, Camie, but you should hear what was recorded without them knowing about it."

She dialed her voicemail and handed me the phone so I could hear the conversation; one that progressively became a heated argument between Tristan and "Dear Jeff." You'll see why I'm back to calling him that in a minute. After listening to it, I figured Jillian must've heard a little something of what they were discussing while she was staking out the party, but she either didn't know what to say about it or thought it didn't make too much of a difference. I'm gonna go with the second one though, only because Jill typically gives her opinion if she thinks it's pertinent. Anyway, here's what the voicemail said:

Jeff: "Fuck! Fuck! Fuck!"

Tristan: "Voicemail again?"

Jeff: "Yep. She's gonna make me grovel on my fuckin' hands and knees this time, I just know it."

Tristan: "How?"

Jeff: "I watched her change her ringtone for me at lunch today to 'Head Like A Hole'—Ouch, you little fucker!"

Tristan: "Ooh, that's harsh."

Jeff: "Yeah dude, tell me about it. Which one is this again?"

Tristan: "Uh, Ferb… You know she'll get over it eventually." (I hear part of the song "Gotta Be Somebody" by Nickelback start playing) "God, finally…"

Jeff: "At least Camie's still talking to you."

Tristan: "Yeah, barely. I asked her out like five hours ago thou—aw goddamn it! You and your girlfriend are seriously getting on my fuckin' nerves! Your fighting is spilling over into *my* life now, so could you please hurry up and bow down…*before* I start going through withdrawals?"

Jeff: Yeah, I'll get right on that, thanks for the support, dickhead. Quit climbing my leg, you little shit! You told her what happened, didn't you? Aaahh! That *hurts*!"

Tristan: "Hell no! Why in God's name would I do that? Here, just give her to me…"

Jeff: "Because you really care about her and if she doesn't already know, chances are she's gonna find out anyway. It'll be better if she hears it from you first, trust me."

Tristan: "I really doubt she'll find out...everyone's talkin' about Teresa puk—"

Jeff: "Dude! You're makin' a mista—"

Tristan: "*Am I?!* Tell me what Kate would say if you told her *you* were the one so baked out of your mind that you started makin' out with some chick at a party thinkin' it was her!"

Jeff: "Oh that's easy…Katy would totally string me up by my balls and eviscerate me on the goddamned stage in front of the entire school during a fuckin' pep rally if I cheated on her like that."

Tristan: "So you see my point."

Jeff: "No dude, you're missing mine…I'd still tell her."

Tristan: "Why go through that when there's a good chance she'd never even fuckin' know?!"

Jeff: "Because I respect her! Give Camie some credit...if you tell her the truth I bet she'll surprise you. Besides, do you really wanna risk hurting her even worse or *completely* losing her trust if she finds out from someone else? Because I'm tellin' ya, that's *exactly* what'll happen. And I swear to God, dude, if you don't take this seriously it'll be like the fuckin' Titanic going down on—"

Tristan: "Don't I wish…is she the boat or am I? I'd be happy either wa—" (Oh, for the love of God, please tell me he did not just go there…he's making oral sex jokes *now*?)

Jeff: "You're fuckin' *unbelievable!* Dude, you can kiss all hope of *anything* like that *ever* happening if you don't come clean…you'll be lucky if she takes you back let alo—"

Tristan: "You just want me to rat myself out so I end up groveling next to you…that's fucked up, man."

Jeff: "*Listen to me, you dick!* You're gonna end up on your hands and knees anyway and I'm tellin' ya, you're makin' a *huge fuckin' mistake here!*"

Tristan: *"Oh and you're the expert?!"*

Jeff: "In this? Yeah, I am! Dude, you know your way around chicks better than anyone I know and I couldn't be more proud, bu—"

Tristan: "Thanks man."

Jeff: "Let me fuckin' finish, would ya?! You don't know jack shit about girlfrie—"

Tristan: "Camie's not my *goddamned girlfriend!*"

Jeff: "*Oh yeah?!* Nice fuckin' ringtone!"

Tristan: *"It's just a fuckin' song!"*

Jeff: "*The hell it is!* You're only foolin' *yourself* with this bullshit, because I swear dude, you're *theme* song should be that Enrique Iglesias song 'Addicted'! Take a good look at this picture and tell me I'm wrong! And did you even bother to look up what this scripture says? I mean Christ! Even her little sister can see the writing on the wa—" (Okay, now I'm lost…a picture, Jillian, and a scripture? Like from the actual Bible? Wow, what the hell happened the other night?)

Tristan: "Her sister is fuckin' *criminally insane!*"

Jeff: "*I don't give a fuck! She's not blind!* When are you gonna just sack up and *admi—*"

The voicemail cut off and I never got to hear what Jeff was saying Tristan needed to admit, but the rest of it simply floored me. Seriously, I'm speechless. Oh and what did you think of "Dear Jeff's" side of the argument? I know, huh? I guess he deserves more credit than what's been previously given to him. Because of course, he's absolutely right. I've been battling with how to feel about this for days and now not only am I hurt, I'm so pissed I can't see straight. Tristan doesn't even want to give me the chance to hear what really happened, like he doesn't trust me to handle the truth or something. He's completely okay with keeping me in the dark about something he obviously feels guilty for doing, and he doesn't seem to give a shit about the consequences of not being forthright with me.

Before hearing all this, I thought he was just being himself and it was a "par for the dating Tristan course" kind of thing and I could maybe just accept it and still go out with him, but now I don't know if I even want to. What makes it even worse is that we've essentially been here before! I already came to him and admitted my screw-up even though I knew there was the possibility he wouldn't forgive me and now that the shoe's on the other foot, he's not giving me the same respect or courtesy!

I looked at Kate as she parked in the back lot of school and sighed. "Shit, Kate. What the fuck do I do know?" I know, apparently I've completely kissed my aversion to swearing goodbye…I'm a wreck.

"I don't know, Camie. That was pretty intense though, wasn't it? They were both *highly* irritated with each other…I mean I've *never* heard them argue with each other like that before. And I had no idea Jeff's been thinking of you as Tristan's girlfriend either, that was a huge shock. And trust me, from everything he said that is *definitely* what he believes you are whether Tristan admits it or not."

"But I'm not. And as much as I really wanted to be, I don't know if I even *can* be now. Jeff was right, Kate. God, this is such a mess…why can't he just tell me the damned truth? I mean that would make it so much easier," I said, rubbing my temples in an effort to assuage the pain from the massive headache that's brewing. I swear, I haven't felt like physical crap for so many days in a row since I had Scarlet Fever when I was nine.

"Would it really? I mean before now you thought he was being typical Tristan…hell, I even told you he does this shit all the time, but after hearing all that…? For all intents and purposes, Camie, he cheated on you and that changes things. You get that, right? Even if you guys don't have a spoken understanding, both Jeff *and* Tristan are looking at what happened as *exactly* that.

"Do you see what I'm getting at? In some kind of warped, undeclared way, Tristan sees himself as your boyfriend, and he cheated on you. This isn't about trying to *land* him anymore, Camie, it's about whether or not you're gonna forgive him and take him *back*. And Camie, from how he sounded to me, he's utterly and completely guilt ridden over the whole thing," Kate told me bluntly while searching my face for signs that she was getting through to me.

"Okay, even if you wanna call it cheating and everything that implies, if he came to me and told me the truth about what happened I'd at least know he respects me in some manner of speaking, and I'd have the *opportunity* to forgive him. But you heard him, he's not going to and as long as he continues to rob me of that, I *can't* forgive him. I'm not saying I know I could completely get over it for sure, but I'd like to think I could find it in me to extend *some* grace, you know? I mean speaking from experience here, people make mistakes all the time, but what he's doing *now* is premeditated…it's like the difference between manslaughter and first degree murder."

Really, I'd still be crushed about him kissing someone even if it was an accident, but come on, now he's gonna lie by omission about it? What the hell does he take me for? A complete fool?

"I see your point… Oh shit! Come on, we're gonna be late again," Kate said, noticing the time.

The rest of Tuesday sucked almost as much as Monday, but at least I didn't have to sit next to Tristan in English. Kate took one for the team by letting me sit on the end and taking the cushion next to me, so of course Jeff, whose hands and arms are covered in scratches, grabbed the opportunity to sit next to her during class. All day he's been throwing Kate these looks that appear to be concern, apprehension, love, and joy all rolled into one. Of course I could be wrong, especially because it seems like such an odd mix, but that's what it looks like to me.

Oh and one other thing happened on Tuesday… When Melissa, Kate, and I were walking back to the locker room after dance, Zack waylaid me. I caught site of Tristan walking to the boys' locker room and when his eyes hit us, his body's forward motion almost propelled him to the pavement when his feet stopped moving.

I should also mention that when I tried to ask Jill about what she heard Saturday night, she was very cagey with her answers but I have no idea why. She flat out refused to tell me how she heard any of what she did. The whole thing was very frustrating but knowing I wouldn't get anywhere with her if she didn't want to tell me, I just gave up. What she *did* tell me, though, was that she overheard Tristan tell Jeff exactly what happened when he was getting dry clothes from the bus, but she didn't how he'd gotten wet in the first place. I'm guessing it was probably the latter part of the punishment for passing out at a party and he was thrown in the pool.

I think it could be said that lunch on Wednesday was a turning point… I'd been pretty much ignoring Tristan all day and I'd been hearing "Are You Happy Now?" by Michele Branch in my head since yesterday, but the tension really became charged when Zack tried his best to dominate my attention the entire thirty minutes of lunch; and he did it right in front of Tristan who was standing *directly* behind me. I could tell from the waves of anger rolling off him that Tristan was becoming livid, but he didn't say a single word.

Kate and Melissa verified my appraisal of his reaction after school when we were alone in Kate's car. They both think that Zack is now not only interested in me again, but that he's also deliberately screwing with Tristan because he knows we had something going on. They're also assuming he must've witnessed me witnessing Tristan's transgression and that he thinks it's either over or that he just doesn't care if it's not. And at this point, I don't care what Zack's reasons are. In addition to all of that, Tristan himself seems to have caught on that everything might not be as right and just in the world as he thought. That or his guilt is eating away at him because I got these texts Wednesday after school:

Tristan: u mad @ me or something? :-*

Me: should i be? :-*

Tristan: no. :-*

Me: then im not. :-* (This is the first time I've actually lied to him. I'll be honest; it was hard and it hurt.)

Tristan: would u tell me if u were? :-*

Me: of course. :-* (And that was painful lie number two; it was unfortunately followed by my eyes leaking.)

Thursday saw our little area of English feeling like Antarctica…being that we were all rather frigid with each other. Here's the order of how we sat; it went Kate, Me, Jeff, Tristan, and there was practically zero communication between any of us, as if the silent treatment reigned supreme. I also strongly suspect there might be more going on with Jeff and Kate than she's saying right now, but I'm not going to push her for details. I know that when she's ready, she'll talk to me.

Like yesterday, Zack cornered me at lunch and again after dance, and you know what? He's really not all that bad like I'd originally thought. I mean aside from him playing basketball, as it's really one of my very least favorite sports. I still think he's mostly using me to piss Tristan off though, and believe me it's working, but neither Tristan nor I are willing to swallow our pride and fess up to anything that's going on. I'm still holding out because I'm hoping he'll just come to me and tell the truth. I really want him to anyway.

Can you tell that I'm not the most emotionally stable person? I keep waffling between being mad, hurt, wanting revenge, and wanting him to just kiss me and make it all better…talk about the proverbial emotional roller coaster.

On Friday however, I thought Tristan was gonna totally lose it…

I sat with Zack and some other people during the pep rally instead of the usual gang that consists of friends like Mike and Pete, both of whom have caught on that something is afoot. They haven't asked or said anything, but they're paying attention. And then I received a "pumpkin-gram" from Zack. They're mini pumpkins that the ASB is selling to raise funds for something or another and students buy them and then have them sent to other students throughout the school day. However, Zack just "happened" to choose the one class I have with Tristan to have mine delivered in.

When the student courier handed it to me, both Jeff and Tristan stared at me. I interpreted Jeff's pleading expression to say something like "Aw, Camie… you're gonna kill him if you let this continue," but Tristan's look was beyond pissed off and condemning, like everything was *my* fault.

Seeing Tristan's expression, I met his eyes defiantly and said, "What? I didn't ask for it you know."

He made a disgusted sound and rolled his eyes, then meeting mine again he said, "Whatever." Then he spent the rest of the class and school day fiercely ignoring me.

That night during the football game, I again sat with Zack and some of his friends who I'm finding are more than a little obnoxious. So feeling like I wanted some space, I went to the snack bar on my own, and you could say I was lucky not to have peed myself in surprise when Jeff came out of nowhere, covered my mouth with his hand, and physically dragged me out of line to privately grill me about what was going on.

"Oh my God, Jeff! You scared the shi—"

"Shhh! Sorry, I didn't mean to scare you, but I only have a few minutes because he doesn't know I'm talking to you and he'll kick my ass if he finds out, so what the hell is going on with you and Zack?" He questioned in a low voice so that no one would overhear him and notice us standing under the bleachers.

"Nothing," I answered very simply…and more or less honestly.

I'm not really attracted to Zack in the least, but he's been really nice and I don't see why we can't be friends, especially since Tristan appears to be done with me. And just so you know, the knowledge of that very real probability is making my heart cry and bleed because I still want to be with him more than I can stand.

The look he bent on me was one of being wholly unconvinced and pretty damned disappointed at the same time. "That sounds like a load of bullshit…I expected more from you, Camie." His words echoed his expression and I can't help thinking that Jeff will make an excellent father at some point…he's got the guilt trip voice *down pat.*

"Jeff, honestly, there's really nothing going on with me and Zack. He might like me but I'm not interested in him…besides, I don't see what the big deal is anyway." I was again, one hundred percent truthful.

"You and I both understand what's happening here and don't pretend you don't know how much is really at stake either. You can still fix this if you want to you know," he told me except it sounded a lot more like he was asking me to.

"What's there to fix?"

I know perfectly well what Jeff's talking about and I'd be willing to lay some heavy odds that Jeff has figured out that I know about what happened on Saturday, but it sounds like maybe Tristan hasn't and it doesn't look like Jeff is going to enlighten him either.

"Oh my God…you're just as stubborn as he is. I swear to God you guys are gonna fuckin' implode and it's gonna be really goddamned ugly because he's reached boiling point with Zack in the mix. I'm beggin' you, Camie, please do something… Fuck, go off on him or make him beg if you have to…it'll be better than how you're punishing him right now," Jeff said, confirming my guess about him knowing that I know.

I tried but couldn't stop it from happening. So while tears filled my eyes and relentlessly spilled down my cheeks, I let Jeff in on my pain and why it's as bad as it is. "Why should he be let off the hook, Jeff? Huh? Tell me, I really wanna know why because *you* know what he did…Christ, what he's *still* doing! But you wanna know something else? I'm still crying at night and being lied to about what I *fucking SAW at that goddamned party Saturday night!* So tell me why *I* should be the one to fix anything when *I'm* the one who's *still* being hurt?!"

"Son of a bitch…*I knew it.* I told him this was gonna happen and now he won't listen to a fuckin' thing I say. Hell, we're barely even talking... God, Camie, I know how much this must be killing you, too, but he's in denial and totally blind right now, it *has* to be you. He's crazy scared but he l—Oh shit, here he comes…I gotta run. Camie please, *please* don't give up on him yet, please!" Jeff pleaded with me over his shoulder as he took off under the bleachers, leaving me alone with the utmost sincerity and compassion he'd ever spoken to me with still ringing in my ears.

Great. I was finally coming to accept, painfully as it was, that everything with Tristan was over and now Jeff has to go ahead and plead to my conscience, which of course is steered by my heart and that organ hasn't been functioning properly for almost a week now. I don't know folks; the jury's still out on this one...

Oh and one other thing, when I got back in line at the snack bar, I had to cope with the intrinsically uncomfortable sensation of Tristan staring at me. I swear if eyes could actually drill into stuff, I'd be riddled through and through with holes. He didn't approach me or say anything, but he was certainly communicating some things; he's angry, hurt, jealous, and on the whole, miserable…definitely *not* happy now. And I say, join the fuckin' club, pal.

After the game Zack tried to convince me to go to a party with him and when I declined by saying that Kate and I were going to the movies, he tried to insert himself into our plans by suggesting that he and one of his friends come with us. Patiently, I explained that it's strictly a girl's night while thinking that not only do I not want to lead him on, but if Tristan were to see me actually leave with Zack, there would be hell to pay and I just don't think I have the emotional funds to cover that particular check right now.

Our drama aside, I must say that going to the movies with Kate was quite a snack extravaganza. She bought so much freaking junk food, I'm afraid our costumes for tomorrow night won't fit. I stayed completely away from the licorice and contented myself with Milk Duds, but of course I still dipped into her vast array of crap and by the end of the movie, I felt pretty sick. Kate however appeared to feel fine.

During the course of our evening, I put my jacked-up love life on the backburner so I could avail myself to being a friend and a listening ear. Even so, Kate wasn't up to talking a whole lot about her relationship woes. Although she did say that she and Jeff had talked a couple of times. The first time being after she'd heard that voicemail which told me I was right about her puffy eyes being from crying. She also told me that although he wasn't out of the dog house yet, Jeff promised her that he's perfectly willing and ready to jump through whatever hoops she holds out for him. I was glad to hear it because that seemed to really make her happy.

And I gotta tell ya, after hearing Jeff go to bat in English, in that voicemail, and then tonight, I'm beginning to see part of why Kate loves him so much. The guy is a definite clown like she said, but his dedication to her does him immense credit. Not only that, but he's got a pretty good grasp on how to express love and he's not afraid to let anyone see that he does it with unparalleled passion.

18.

Just Beggin' For Trouble

Now I have to admit something here, if all the previous untruths haven't been enough, I also lied to my parents about where I'd be sleeping Saturday night...

Mike's Halloween party was going to be *LEGEND*, and since his parents were in Cancún, he'd extended an invitation to select people to crash at his house. Kate, Melissa, and I were a few of those chosen. When we found out about our invite two weeks ago, we all thought we should take him up on the offer because chances were, we'd all want to be drinking at least a little. I mean I figure I can handle a beer or two if I stay hydrated and away from all forms of bubble baths, you know? It was also rumored to be a *really* fun night and none of us would be ready to leave by the time my curfew rolled around. I'm guessing it won't be your typical kegger if what I've heard is true; Mike apparently goes all out for this event every year.

We got ready at Kate's house and then we picked up Pete so we could make a grand entrance. We purposefully showed up about an hour after the start time, ensuring enough people would be present to witness the ridiculous spectacle we made of ourselves by hanging all over "Lonely Pete." Little did I know it at the time, but the events that would unfold during the evening would lead to the longest and most emotionally exhausting night of my life thus far.

It would also probably go down as the most photographed. Mike, dressed as Hugh Heffner, and Kristen who was his Playboy Bunny, had requested people remember their cameras. He also supplied an ungodly amount of disposable cameras like people do for wedding receptions, except I swear, it seemed like every person at the party had one. Once full, the cameras were to be left in big buckets stationed around his house, although what he plans to do with the pictures, I haven't a clue.

Our entrance went off without a hitch and from what I could tell; Pete loved every minute of it. Throughout the first part of the night we took turns fanning him with a big palm branch, bringing him drinks and even feeding him the grapes we brought with us. It was a total riot. It was also a really good idea that we'd decided to stay the night; Mike was serving the very yummy Pirate Punch again except this time, it's in one of those tiered fountain things and there's dry ice in the bottom bowl, making it bubble and look like blood. Lime green Jell-O shots that I discovered are pretty damned tasty and hard to pass up, were also plentiful.

Now, I'm not sure who suggested it—actually, I wanna say it was someone dressed as Darth Vader, because in hindsight, I seem to remember hearing the suggestion come from the dry rasping that's indicative of Darth's mechanical voice, however I can't recall actually seeing a Darth Vader at the party, but anyway—being just a tad bit tipsy and probably taking the joke too far, Melissa and I both allowed Pete to do body shots off of us amid much hoopla, cheering, and flash bulbs. Keith was cool with it because he knew it was part of the gag, but Tristan was *so* less than thrilled with having to watch some other guy suck liquor out of my bellybutton. As soon as he realized what was about to happen, he turned pale and violently stalked out of the room. After what I'd witnessed last weekend had done to me, I felt my causing that reaction was only fair. He also literally shoved a couple of people out of his way when they were slow to respond to his facial expression and I was told later by Kate, he practically bit their heads off when he growled "Get the fuck outta my way, now!" at them. Oh and just so you know, we were doing this while being draped across the counter of the wet bar in a room of the house that's meant for formal entertaining. With that, the strobe lights and the music playing, it was probably a really steamy scene, but honestly, it wasn't meant to be.

A short time later I overheard a partial conversation between Tristan and Pete and it sounded like Pete was apologizing…or, pleading for his life.

"—was just all in good fun, you *know* that, right dude?" Pete asked with concern very evident in his voice. He was also having a hard time looking Tristan in the eyes. I'm not sure if he's worried about his health or what, but he *is* worried.

"Yeah, sure…no blood, no foul," Tristan said with *much* hostility and a heavy dose of animosity.

By the way, Tristan isn't wearing a costume so much as a damned funny shirt. It's a picture of French fries with a single onion ring in the middle of them and across the top it reads: "One Ring to Rule Them All" which is totally meant to be a play on the *Lord of the Rings*.

"I promise I won't so much as *touch* her ever again."

Tristan looked like he was about to go through the roof at the mere suggestion of it happening again, but he only turned around and left Pete staring at his fiercely rigid back.

Now really, what the hell? I do *not* belong to him, so where does he get off with this proprietary attitude towards me? For Christ's sake, he's not even talking to me anymore, so I don't see how he can justify this behavior in the least! I went to find Kate to complain and found her sampling some of the tasty treats laid out in the formal dining room. I don't know if Mike had this thing catered or what, but you should see the spread here... There's all kinds of food; from a honey-glazed baked ham all the way down to pumpkin shaped and colored rice crispy treats with chocolate drizzled over them, and there probably isn't any kind of booze not present and there's definitely no short supply of it either. All out indeed!

"Can you believe the nerve of him?" I asked Kate with massive indignation after describing what I'd just heard and seen.

Kate was licking chocolate off of her fingers, having just eaten her third chocolate covered marshmallow spider. They have licorice—blechk—legs and M&Ms for eyes...they're really cute and I'd have a couple if it wasn't for the licorice.

"You know, Camie, it sounds like he's coming apart at the seams...Jeff (who's dressed as a bathroom wall complete with graffiti, paper seat covers, and toilet paper...freaking hilarious!) thinks a massive meltdown of some kind isn't far off. He also thinks you should give Tristan a break, but totally understands why you're not."

"Yeah, well this whole thing is his own damned fault. What's your opinion? I mean, what do *you* think I should do?" I asked and watched her survey the sixteen-seat table laden with real food.

She shrugged and started building a sandwich. "Honestly, I think this is something you have to figure out on your own...I mean you have to do what *you* feel comfortable with, you know?"

"I get that, Kate, I do. I'm just looking for some direction...or feedback, *something* that'll help me figure out where I'm at and where I should go."

"Okay, well, Melissa believes that deep-down, you still really wanna be with him, but the question is still can you put this behind you and forgive him, and also, you need to consider how long he'll wait for you to figure it out. He still wants you, that's obvious, but if this goes on much longer, Melissa and I *both* think there's a very real possibility that he'll decide to just say fuck it and move on. However, Jeff's opinion is that Tristan's fighting a losing battle by not admitting how he really feels about you and he's not handling the guilt well at all. I personally think that if you guys can just hash this whole thing out, things might be okay but, I'm not you, if that makes sense," Kate told me through a mouthful of her ham sandwich.

Sighing, I looked into my empty cup and then stuck it under a spout for more O Positive. "I just don't know, Kate, I mean...I feel like there's this amazing connection between us and I do desperately wanna be with him but, I feel betrayed and so much more. I can't get a handle on any of my emotions so maybe he *should* just move on because I don't know if I'm ever gonna be able to confront him. And it's obvious that I'll have to be the one to do it but even if I did, I don't know what I want so it seems kinda pointless for me to do right now."

Despite hearing those honest thoughts on the matter, I left Kate in the dining room without having gotten any further in knowing what I should do. Our conversation informed me though, that Kate and Jeff are now really talking again and apparently, Jeff's being completely upfront about what's going on with Tristan and me. So, it seems, the only people who *aren't* talking openly about us, is us...

With everything else going on, I'm sure you can probably imagine how the tension climbed several notches when dressed as an unimaginative pirate, Zack showed up with a good handful of his friends. In the beginning he was simply friendly and we hung out in a group in the living room for a while. It really wasn't a big deal; at least I didn't think it was. However, when Mike asked me to help him bring out some more Jell-O shots from the second fridge in the pantry, I was surprised to find his intentions for asking me were something entirely different from needing another pair of hands.

The second he shut the door and we were alone, Mike turned serious and got straight to business. "Look, I don't know what's goin' on with you guys and quite frankly, I don't need or even wanna know, but I like you Camie, so I just hope you know what you're doin' by spending time with Zack."

"Mike, I appreciate the concern but really, I'm not interested in Zack and I don't get why talking to him is such a big deal. Things between Tristan and me are really messed up right now and we're not even talking. Besides, it's not like he has any rights to me anyway, so it's ridiculous for me to have to pick and choose who I'm friends with based on him."

I'll be honest, I'm feeling slightly annoyed. I really do like Mike, but I'm getting tired of being told how much Tristan hates Zack...it's like everyone telling Jillian how much I hate Teresa. I mean come on, I'm more than aware of that fact. Not only has he personally told me, but I see it in Tristan's face and I can even feel it, but he's the one who refuses to actually say anything about what's going on now *or* how feels about me and it's pissing me off!

"Alright, if you say so, but I just wanna warn you...even if you don't like Zack, that feeling is *not* mutual and when, not *if*, but *when* Zack does something to prove that fact and Tristan sees it, because I goddamned guarantee you that Zack will pick the worst possible moment to rub it in his face, things are gonna get bloody. And I'd stake my life on it happenin' tonight. You might believe Tristan doesn't have rights to you, but Camie, I promise you, *he* thinks he does and most every guy here acknowledges that. And another thing, your costume is just beggin' for trouble. I already know he's *really* unhappy just with the looks you're gettin' from other guys...fuck, he almost tore Pete apart after those body shots and they're really fuckin' good friends. Seriously, I think the only thing that saved Pete from a trip to the ER was that Tristan didn't watch him actually do any of 'em...

"What I'm getting at here, Camie, is that I don't think there's anyone else in attendance tonight with a fuckin' death wish who'll put his rights to you to the test *aside* from Zack who's actually lookin' for an opportunity to do it. So when the shit goes down, I hope you're ready...that's all I'm sayin'." Mike then opened the door for us to re-enter the party without having brought out any Jell-O shots whatsoever.

So yeah, Mike pretty much says what's on his mind alright and now thanks to his little version of an intervention, my nerves are wound tighter than a watch spring. Mike also gets to keep his life because he was right about tonight and, well...everything.

Feeling the weight and strain from what "Heff" had seen fit to confide in me, I did a couple Jell-O shots—I don't know, maybe it was more like five...I'm in no condition to do math of any kind. I refilled my cup and then, to get away from the strobe lights inside, I went outside for some fresh air.

All the trees and bushes were decorated with dimly lit ghosts and bats with purple lights strewn throughout, while with the aid of realistic looking headstones and cobwebbing, strategically placed buckets of dry ice and multiple fog machines, the rest of grounds were done up to look like an ancient graveyard. The effect wasn't so much creepy as it was mysterious. At least it would've been if the party music hadn't been piped outside through a surround sound system with speakers that looked like rocks. That and add the myriad people milling about the backyard snapping pictures; the mystery factor was toned down quite a bit.

I decided not to tempt fate by deliberately socializing with Zack and his friends, who by the way were all being rather rowdy. Instead, I returned to hanging out with my regular group. Tristan, however, was nowhere to be seen.

Some time later I was trying to not think about my predicament by dancing the night away, but because of Tristan's unknown whereabouts, I didn't try to find a way to skirt Zack when he came up to stand next to me. Jeff was throwing daggers at him with his eyes, but he did a really good job of keeping his cool for Kate whom he was periodically holding out a bowl of shrimp cocktail for her to munch on whilst she boogied. Mike was merely watchful and most everyone else pretended like it wasn't an issue, although everyone knew it was. Melissa joined the largish group of us dancing while Keith came up and stood next to Zack with his arms folded across his chest. His stance gave me the distinct impression that although Keith and Zack are friends, Keith wasn't too happy with Zack at the moment.

And then, in the blink of an eye—which is pretty damned quick—the shit Mike had warned me about finally came down. It all happened so fast and in a blur that a lot of details are next to impossible to give, but it all started when Zack simultaneously leaned down to say something to me, which totally looked like he was about to kiss me. And now that I think about it, I think maybe he was because he also put his hand smack-dab on my ass to pull me towards him. As I glared at him and made to swat his hand away, I heard a variety of voices saying different things, but all spoken essentially at the same time…

Pete: *And* here come the fireworks, right on schedule...
Mike: Oh fuck, this is gonna hurt…
Jeff: *Shit!* Katy, get outta here! *Now!*
Kate: Wait! What's going o—Oh my God!
Keith: Zack, you fuckin' idiot!
Melissa: Camie! Watch out!
Tristan: *Oh that's it!! You're a FUCKIN' DEAD MAN…*

Before I even had a chance to process the fact that Tristan had materialized some unknown distance behind me and seen what Mike had said he would, Pete grabbed my arm and yanked me out of the way, then he threw me into Melissa who dragged me back even further.

All I can say that I saw with any clarity was Tristan in a blind rage take one swing at Zack, which I'm pretty sure would be considered a TKO in boxing. He would've gone down but Tristan held onto to him, apparently not satisfied with it only taking once. At the same time Tristan's fist made first contact with Zack's face, what looked like a massive brawl erupted. Really, it reminds me of a scene out of *West Side Story*, except instead of it being the Jets vs. the Sharks, it was Us vs. Them. Them being Zack's buddies and you should know who Us is by now, although I might've not mentioned *everyone* who would be considered an "Us." There was *a lot* of yelling, swearing, shoving, and a good many punches being thrown.

Now absurd as this is, I'm thinking God must be playing D.J. again because the moment the fight started, none other than Pink's "So What" began playing…The Big Man certainly has a sense of humor, doesn't He?

Almost immediately after the fight broke out, Jeff wisely and expertly disengaged Tristan. He had the front of Zack's costume in one hand and was about to put the fist of the other one in Zack's face again, but with amazing strength and skill, Jeff held Tristan back from doing any more damage. After an all too short moment and still being more than fuming—I think it's safe to say he's still raging—Tristan literally threw Jeff off him but instead of rushing back into the fray, he came straight at me.

I had no time to react—I honestly don't know what I could've done anyway…run maybe?—before he seized me from Melissa who I'm now realizing had actually been holding *me* back from trying to get to Tristan while he was fighting. Then without a single word, he threw me over his shoulder. He must've looked terrifying and I must've looked petrified because just as Tristan turned to cart me away, I saw and heard Keith swear and make like he was going to try to stop Tristan from abducting me. I felt like saying, "Yeah, good luck, Keith. Did you not see what he just did to Zack? Since I'm a goner, you may as well save yourself. I appreciate the thought though, buddy."

"*No!!* Let 'em go…this needs to happen," Pete said, running up and catching Keith by the arm.

"Fuck, that was an explosion alright…" Mike commented.

"No shit. I've never seen him so pissed…you don't think he'll hurt her, do you?" Keith asked, wiping blood off his lip.

"Hopefully not more than he already has anyway…" Jeff responded grimly, having come up next to them.

"Jesus, he better not…" Pete said with what sounded to me like some concern. And to this day, I'm still not sure who the concern was for; me or Tristan.

Although the guys were following Tristan and me, they were keeping a safe distance and their voices were fading. However, I heard Mike shout at Tristan before he reached the sliding glass doors of the house with me…

"Don't break anything and STAY OUT of my parents' room!!"

Oh and just so you know, I have a great view of Tristan's really nice butt from up here, although what he needs is a good, swift kick in it instead of having it admired. And yeah, I'm thinking that none of the guys' last remarks bode all that well for me or for what's about to take place, but as Tristan crossed the threshold of the house, God's next track was in stark contrast to that opinion. "I Gotta Feeling" by The Black Eyed Peas could be heard through all the speakers both outside and in, making me wonder if God is just as confused as I am…

19.

I'll Need Some Gum

Now mind you that because I'm still folded over Tristan's shoulder and for the most part staring at his ass, I can't see people's faces—Shoes, I see a lot of shoes. Therefore, it's impossible for me to know how everyone in the house is reacting to the epic biblical picture we must be presenting. I say biblical because the way the bodies are filling in the empty space behind us as he carries me through the house; it makes me think it must look an awful lot like Moses parting the Red Sea. I'm not even bothering to struggle either because A) I know it won't do any good. And B) Pete is right; this needs to happen. I don't know how much will actually be solved, though, because I'm so up in the air—no pun intended—and I really have no idea what's going through his mind either, but we still need to get some things said.

I'd also like to call attention to the fact that I'm extremely impressed by Tristan's endurance and this amazing feat of strength he's displaying...I mean I only weigh about 105 pounds, maybe closer to 108 after the movies last night. Seriously, we ate a ton of food... But just picture it if you will, he's now taking the *Gone With the Wind* stairs two at a time! I mean come on! Impressive, right?

Once reaching the hall upstairs, Tristan didn't turn the same way as when he'd taken me to Mike's parents' room the night of the infamous punch fiasco, but instead he took a path to the right, through a game room with a pool table and down another hallway. I'm assuming that's what it is but there are quite a lot of people up here so I could be wrong. He didn't even stop to knock or anything when he reached the closed door of his choice, but rather, he aggressively grabbed the handle and threw the door open, causing it to ricochet off the wall and the startled couple in the room to shout their protests.

"Get out." From the dangerous menace of his tone, I'm guessing Tristan's still very angry.

"*What the fuck?!* Tristan, get the hell outta here!" The guy yelled.

The voice is sort of familiar but I don't know who it is and regardless, I felt embarrassed for all of us...

Again, I remind you that I can't see what's going on because I'm still hanging upside down and yeah, the blood has totally rushed to my head, but from what Tristan then said, I'm deducing that he's *completely* interrupted a sexual interlude. I mean at this stage of the game, awkward doesn't even begin to cover it.

"You have ten seconds to cum and get the fuck outta here or you're gonna have an audience." And let me impress upon you; that was no mere warning in Tristan's dark voice.

The couple was *not* happy with him, but they did vacate the room rather quickly after recognizing what he'd said wasn't just a threat. I'm assuming they threw on *some* clothes, but I don't think they took the time to actually get dressed. So, from my vantage point when I saw two pairs of bare legs and feet exit the room, I congratulated myself on being right, and then when Tristan slammed the door shut behind them so hard that the window actually rattled in its frame, I wished I could've gone with them.

Yeah, at this point I'm pretty much regretting not having been rescued by Keith or struggling to save myself and I'm also praying that Jeff and Pete wouldn't allow me to be alone with him if I might be in actual physical danger.

I'm beginning to learn that God does answer all prayers, but there's a caveat; you have to be *really* specific with what you pray for…

With my blood marching in time through my head to the sound of its own thumping cadence and "Paralyzer" by Finger Eleven vaguely recognizable to my ears, Tristan slowly lowered me to my feet, so close to him that I swear you wouldn't have been able to slide a single sheet of paper between us. One look at his face and I knew he was still irrationally emotional but some time in between beating the shit out of Zack and slamming the door, the pendulum had swung in the complete and total opposite direction from the all consuming fury it'd been at. And with that one look, I was right there with him.

And let me tell you something, this was no tender meeting of lips by any means. It was wildly passionate and, I'll be very honest here, rather violent. He broke the kiss for only the split second it took him to hastily pull his shirt over his head when my fervent attempts to remove it myself failed. No longer impeded, his mouth crashed down on mine again and through this one kiss, we proceeded to vent every single emotion we'd ever had for one another since the day we met.

I have to admit as inappropriate as it might sound for this particular moment, I have a scene from *Star Wars* running through my head—the one where the Red Leader is telling Luke to "stay on target" when he's about to blow up the Death Star. It's there because I'm still *really* pissed at him, but I can't seem to muster the will to keep us from where this is obviously going—and fast, and you and I both know damned well Tristan's not going to stop. Seriously, I'm so caught up in sharing Tristan's burning desire and zealous urgency, the sensation of my costume being torn from my body barely registered.

Now would be an excellent time to describe for you what my costume actually looks like. It's two pieces; the skirt is long and reaches my ankles, but it's made of see-through, filmy strips of fabric rather than being all one piece, which means that when I walk, it separates showing both of my legs entirely. The waist rides very low on my hips and it has little gold coins on it that make a tinkling sound when I move. The top piece is similar to what a strapless bra looks like except it has a wider band that sits just above my ribcage, and again, little gold coins adorn it as well. Oh and since I'd bought it the same day as the thong and was trying to plan in advance, my costume is of course, black.

Having entirely divested me of my skirt, Tristan had a hold of the back of my thigh, thereby keeping my leg around his waist, and he was about to lift my other leg around him with the intent of carrying me, willingly, to the bed. My delirium was so great; a hurricane ripping through the room wouldn't have snapped rational thought back to me. The slight feeling of my phone slipping to the ground as my top began falling away did, though. I unwrapped the leg I had around his waist and managed to grab hold of my top with one hand, clutching it to me to keep from having my breasts *completely* exposed, while with my other hand, I shoved him away.

Honestly, adrenaline is some freaking powerful stuff because Tristan is no lightweight by any stretch and he didn't exactly let go of me willingly…and, he was most *certainly* unhappy about having to do so.

"Goddamn it Camie!" He bellowed at me.

"*What the hell, Tristan*?! Where do *you* get off yelling at *me*?!" I shouted back.

"I think I'm pretty fuckin' justified after you laid yourself out like a goddamned *buffet* for Pete and then let Zack paw at you all night!" He accused with disgust.

"OH! You think *that* was bad? You're such a *fuckin' hypocrite* Tristan! So lemme get this straight, you have the right to throw a goddamned *violent* temper tantrum when anyone barely even *touches* me, but I'm supposed to just accept it when you decide to full-on *make out* with someone else?! Is that it?!" I yelled while gesturing emphatically with my one, free hand.

"Ah *FUCK! Who* the fuck told you about *that?!*" He asked angrily.

I almost got the impression that he's mad at me for knowing, but I'm not sure. And I guess Jeff wasn't kidding about Tristan being blind. I mean how could he not know that I knew about that after this week?

"Does it honestly fucking matter? *You* should've been the one to tell me, you ignorant son of a bitch!" I hollered and shoved him in the chest again.

"Oh, I'm gonna fuckin' kill him," he ground out between clenched teeth, his eyes flashing violence once more.

After the argument they had, you know he's thinking that Jeff told me, right? But no way am I letting Jeff take the blame for being the voice of reason that was *completely* ignored.

"Okay, you wanna know who to blame for that, Tristan? Well, just look in a fucking mirror!" I shouted.

"What the fuck does that mean?" He asked, his expression and body language declaring his earnest confusion.

Unbelievable. He honestly doesn't know.

"I was *there*, Tristan. I *saw* the whole goddamned thing…" I informed him, the anguish of my memory practically choking me.

He was stunned. There's absolutely no other way to describe his comprehension.

"No. You did *not* see that," he said, barely shaking his head back and forth, as if the movement would somehow make his words come true.

Jeff obviously wasn't kidding about Tristan being in denial either…

"Yeah, I did. And you know what? I really have to thank you for making one of my favorite treats nauseating to me now," I shot at him, the added information about the role the licorice had played proving I really had been there.

Without looking at me, Tristan resignedly raked a hand through his hair and said, "Oh my God."

He sat down on the edge of the bed and buried his head in his hands for several moments before finally, yet briefly looking up at me again. Then he closed his eyes and sighed in abject defeat. When he opened his eyes again this time, he seemed to become aware for the first time that I was holding my top to my chest. He bent down to pick up his shirt and then held it out for me. "Put it on."

I just stared at the shirt without making a move to accept it. "You know, I think I'd really rather get my own clothes and wear them for once."

"Uh-uh. No fucking way are you leaving this room. We're gonna talk about this," he told me firmly, sure in the knowledge that I'd bolt if I had the chance.

I yanked the shirt from Tristan's hand in frustration and just when I was about to tell him to close his eyes or something he said, "Seriously Camie, you've gotta be fuckin' kidding me..."

Then he stood up in irritation, grabbed the shirt back, and pulled my top from my hand—yeah, I know—then he tossed it on the bed and pulled his shirt over my head. It was a particularly uncomfortable and oddly exciting moment, for me at least, but neither of us acted on the sexual energy that was zapping at us. I think that's mainly because I'm still pretty mad and he not only knows that, but I also think he's feeling some form of remorse for his actions, although he still hasn't uttered an apology of any kind.

Then he sighed. "I didn't know. I mean I thought...Christ, I was so fuckin' blazed…"

"That's your excuse?" I asked somewhat incredulous. I mean I can understand that in small part, *maybe*, but I'm more bent about the fact that he never told me in the first place.

"I didn't say it was a good one…but honestly, Camie, I was *so* fuckin' stoned that I actually thought she was you. Maybe if I'd been sober enough to think of looking at her when she first crawled onto me I would've known but...I was laying on the couch listening to my iPod and thinking about that day at the beach...so, when she kissed me, I guess I just went with it because I wanted it to be you. Then when I realized she wasn't, I pushed her off me and then I went straight outside and threw myself in the goddamned pool to sober up," he told me dismally and in a pleading way, he tugged at the hem of my shirt (his shirt, whatever). "I swear to God it was an accident, Camie. It didn't mean *anything*, it didn't," he insisted softly, pulling me to him.

I allowed him to draw me into a genuine hug. I couldn't help myself and it felt so incredibly good just to have his arms wrapped around me that I almost forgot I was still mad. And I am actually still very angry with him so when he bent and lowered his head to kiss me, I turned my face away.

"Why?" He asked, hurt that I'd shunned him.

"Because I'm still really mad at you, Tristan, and when we kiss, everything else completely disappears. Do you know what I mean?" I asked him seriously.

I know how I get when his lips are on me and even though it might not be the same for him, I'm not ready to get swept away right now. I haven't forgiven him.

"Oh hell yes. Everything fades away until nothing matters anymore, not even breathing. Everything around us, the entire world and every little thing in it vanishes and absolutely nothing matters except *you* and *me*," he answered, giving his own startlingly accurate description of what happens when we kiss. Then he sat down on the bed again, but pulled me with him so I was cradled in his lap.

"Why *is* that?" I've been wondering about this since the very first kiss and I'm thinking "he who knows his way around chicks better than anyone else "Dear Jeff" knows" will certainly have an answer to this simple quandary. I mean come on, he has to have kissed a bunch of girls and felt that before with at least some of them.

He sighed, resting his forehead against mine. "I don't know."

Jesus...my track record for being wrong is becoming disturbing.

"Why not? Haven't you ever experienced that before?" I asked as he gently brushed my hair from my face and gazed longingly into my eyes; the rawness of emotion swimming in his just about undid me.

Also, in case you haven't picked up on it, this is a very tender and open moment for us…it's pretty freaking great. I mean it doesn't change anything, but it's wonderful nonetheless.

Tristan seemed to find my query rather amusing however, and he started chuckling. "Fuck no. Camie, I've done a lot of stuff and I've done it all with *a lot* of girls and that's definitely one thing that's at the top of my Only Camie list. In fact, that's what made me realize I wasn't with you…"

For some reason, I didn't care for how blasé he'd said all that and I began to feel rigid again. The problem, though, was that Tristan didn't notice my adverse reaction to his words.

"I mean there were other things that were off too…she didn't smell like you, she was built differently, she certainly didn't taste like you, and when she unzipped my pants and wrapped her hand around me, I remember thinking it was a totally unexpected surprise coming from you...not that I was gonna complain or anything (Something inside me just snapped and now I'm irate.), but when I went to roll to my side with her, my earbuds got pulled out… I mean it was instant. All of a sudden I could actually *hear everything* around me and I knew right away she wasn't you… Jesus, if that hadn't happened, it would've been *so* much worse," he finished, shaking his head in disbelief and not realizing his re-cap of what was very clearly a near miss in a sexual misadventure had smoke coming out of my ears.

Now I'm fucking livid.

"Huh. So, I'm curious…why did you stop?" I'm totally fuming fire and brimstone.

"What?" Tristan asked like he'd misunderstood the question.

"Well, I know it's been probably what? Eight weeks or so since you fucked that cheerleader from Valhalla and you sure as hell weren't getting anything from *me*, so why didn't you just end your dry spell last Saturday? Unless of course there've been *other* girls I don't know about, and let's face it, you wouldn't tell me even if there was," I spewed venomously. I'm really so very out of my mind with anger right now that I *want* to hurt him.

"*What?!* How the fuck do you know about *her*?" He asked, totally shocked and even a little angry now himself.

I pushed myself off of his lap and glared hatefully at him. "Not from you, that's for damned sure. And I'm guessing because you didn't deny there having been others in the last two months, and much to your dismay, you *know* I wasn't doing it for you, that's why you didn't feel the need to finish what that skank started last week. You know actually, you're just as despicable as she is. Really, you guys should go out, you're the perfect slutty couple. I mean that's all you're interested in anyhow...you proved that on our 'date'," I said, my voice dripping in scornfully noxious sarcasm.

He stood up to face me and yelled, "Where the *fuck is this* coming from, Camie? I don't know what the fuck you're getting at here, but so we're clear...I haven't so much as *looked* at another goddamned person since I met you, I've never *once* pressured you, and that is *NOT all I want from you!*"

I snatched my torn top from the bed, held it up and shouted, *"NO?!"*

"Oh my God, Camie, you fucking *know* what that was about!" He shouted back at me.

"Oh really?! You're such a fuckin' liar Tristan! Tell me what you *really* want from me...tell me what you *wish I would do*," I said malevolently. I'm moving towards a dark place here and I know it, but I really don't care right now.

"What I wish? I wish you'd fuckin' get over this and believe me! *I am not only looking for sex!*" He hollered.

He sounds very angry again and I think even hurt, but I'm so not rational right now. On the contrary, I'm about to step into the deep and ugly rabbit hole of vulgarity...

"Uh-huh...tell me Tristan, who's the boat? Because if it's me, I'll need some gum," I said with a callous sneer.

That got his attention and not in a good way either. He narrowed his eyes at me and clenched his teeth, and I knew, without a single doubt, this was gonna be vicious...

Tristan reached into the pocket of his jeans to retrieve a pack of gum, then he tossed at me and off kicked his shoes. Then, he started unbuttoning his pants. He stopped abruptly with the zipper more than halfway down and almost like it was an afterthought and he was just trying to be considerate, he said, "Oh, did you wanna be the one to do this?"

I threw the gum back at him and I swear you could've choked on the vile and rancorous atmosphere swirling around us.

He caught the gum in one hand, threw it aside and then said vindictively, "Okay, I can be the boat...I'm *more* than good with that, but *I* won't need the gum."

I was standing there, already shaking with rage, when he went one step further... The surround system is wired for the entire house so music's been playing the entire time and when he recognized the song coming in through the speakers, he cocked his head to the side slightly, listening to it or considering it in some way, and then cruelly he said, "Hey, you hear that? They're playing your song."

At the exact same time Tristan said it, Mike opened the door with his hands over his eyes so he wouldn't see something he shouldn't and said, "Don't mind me, I just gotta get something..."

Understanding that Tristan had just called me a bitch, because the song that's playing is "Bitch" by Meredith Brooks, I spit out contemptuously, my voice full of acid, *"Go to hell."*

Then, just as I turned and started for the door, Tristan infused his chivalrous words with icy coldness and said, "Ladies first."

Mike was just standing there in stunned silence looking back and forth between us when I left the room. I didn't run in my escape, but...maybe I should've. I would've at least gotten farther than the game room before I heard the thunder of Tristan's roar. Without looking back to see if he was coming after me, I picked up the pace but he caught up to me so fast that I didn't even get three feet into the game room that still was crowded with people.

All of a sudden his arms were around my waist and I was in a vice-like grip, my arms trapped to my sides as he lifted me from the floor. This time, I did try to struggle. It was a valiant effort on my part but it really didn't do any good. The power of my substantial fury was no match for Tristan's even more considerable physical strength. Plus, out of the corner of my eye, I saw that our host had caught up to us.

So, while I writhed and thrashed about, Mike abetted my captor by saying, "Move along folks, nothing to see here..." and with a large box of condoms in one hand, he began waving back all the people who were staring, gawking and snapping pictures; ultimately obliging Tristan with a clear path as he manhandled me back towards the room.

"Let go of me!" I demanded furiously.

"No, goddamn it! We're gonna fuckin' talk about this if it takes us all goddamned night!" He growled.

With that declaration and remembering what Mike was waving about, I'm thinking I have just as long a night ahead of me as Kristen must...

20.

Single Or Double Digits?

Once back in the room, Tristan slammed the door shut and I started to rail at him again.

"You are a *fucking ASSHOLE*!" I screamed at him.

I should mention that he's completely blocking the door too or I would've tried to fly again. He's also surprisingly calm.

"Yeah, and you were being a fuckin' bitch, Camie," he told me in a normal tone of voice. Honestly, it's like he's done a complete one-eighty from where he was just minutes ago.

Instead of using words to attack him this time, I went the physical route and started hitting him. Not in the face, though. I tried, but he caught my wrist before I could make contact. Other than that, he's letting me wale on him without trying to defend himself in the slightest.

"You can beat the shit outta me for hours, Camie, verbally or otherwise, but I'm not gonna hit back again...that was way over the top. You just came at me really fuckin' hard and it was gut instinct, but I won't go there again even if you do. I don't know how you heard what I said and I know Jeff's not stupid enough to tell you or anyone else, but you need to understand it had absolutely *nothing* to do with you," he told me very rationally, patiently taking the beating I'm giving him. I'm fighting tears now too, though.

"Do you actually exp—"

"Shut up and hear me out please," he said quietly.

"Why should I?" I took a step back, not only losing the boxing match with him, but the fight with my tears as well.

"Aw Camie..."

The deep-hearted compassion he imbedded in those two simple words when he saw the waterworks pouring forth from my eyes was too much for me. I allowed him to draw me back into him, enveloping me in his arms again, but instead of being vice-like, they were wonderfully comforting.

So while I cried into his naked chest, he began what I've come to think of not as round two exactly, but more like where we should've started in the first place rather than the knock-down-drag-out fight we've been having, which, I'm afraid, has left some scars.

"Camie, I'm not gonna lie, I do want you far more than I've ever wanted anyone before and if I thought you were willing, I'd have you stripped naked and in this bed in less than a heartbeat, but that is *so not all* I want from you. I made that boat comment to Jeff because I didn't wanna hear what he was saying... I didn't wanna acknowledge that he was right and I didn't wanna admit that what I did would hurt you. It was a self-defense mechanism, just like what I said to you however many minutes ago was. Camie, look at me." He took my chin and forced me to meet his imploring eyes. "It has been *killing* me all week long knowing regardless of whether you ever found out, that what I did would cause you pain. I don't even know how to *begin* to make up for that. But, I can't go back and erase that any more than I can the other things I did before I met you...can we just please move past all of that and start over?"

"What...like a do-over, Tristan? I don't think I can do that," I told him quite honestly. I mean really, if only...

"Why not?" He asked, disappointment very evident in both his tone and expression.

"Okay look. Kate's voicemail recorded almost all of that argument you had with Jeff and even though *I* thought we weren't being exclusive, well...honestly Tristan, I was having a problem with what you did even *before* I found out you weren't planning on telling me. And I thought I could maybe get over it because I wanted to be with you in the most desperate way, and afterwards I kept praying you'd just come and tell me the truth, but you *never did*." I stopped and sighed with tears streaming down my face. "And now, I just don't know if I can or if I even *want* to be with you."

Tristan looked like I'd just slapped him in the face but he didn't lose it in anyway. Instead, he was set on convincing me that I could still be with him, and he tried demonstrating time and again that I want to be as well. His endeavor even included what you might call light groveling. For instance, there was the time when I tried digging into his graveyard...

"How am I supposed to prove to you I'm not only interested in sex, huh?" Tristan asked me in frustration when I'd thrown that out again.

"Well, I don't know...but from everything I've heard a—"

"For the love of Christ, you're basing all this off of gossip, Camie...I mean come on."

"No, not all of it...you yourself said you've done a lot of stuff with a lot of girls...so what am I supposed to think?" He was quiet then and refused to meet my eyes so I went on. "I mean just tell me, Tristan...what stuff and how many girls?"

"Camie, I don't talk about this shit for a reason, okay? It's no one's busin—"

"Uh, it kinda matters to me, so I think it *is* my business…I was a fucking *witness* to a hook-up with a random girl you would've had *sex* with if your stupid earbuds hadn't fallen out! And you were in a room *full* of people for Christ's sake, Tristan! I mean how the hell do you even pull that off without people noticing?! And if you can do *that*, it begs the question of what else have you done?!"

"What do you want me to say, Camie?! Use your imagination! I've fucking done it all! Okay?! *Fuck!!* But that doesn't mean that's who I am as a person and you *know* that!"

"I wanna know that but…you were so casual about admitting she didn't mean anything to you…I mean it just makes me wonder how often this happens and how many girls there've been and I don't understand why you won't tell me…especially when you're asking me to trust you. Plus, I think I have a right to know if I'm dating the school slut or not!" Well, that is if I can get over his lying to me first.

"I *can't* tell you because I don't know! Alright?! Damn it, Camie, jus—"

"Oh come on…you have to kno—"

"You want me to make up a number for you?! 42! There! It's the answer to everything!"

"Oh my God…this isn't *Hitchhiker's Guide to the Galaxy*, Tristan." I rolled my eyes at him and the number I automatically knew he got from a Douglas Adams book.

I mean really…it's funny and all but come on.

"Well I don't know what else to tell you, Camie, I don't fucking keep track!"

"Well-uh…single or double digits?"

Taking a calming breath, Tristan looked at the ceiling and clenched his jaw. I know he isn't thrilled with this line of questioning but I'm not going to back down. I mean like I said quite some time ago, I do *not* want to be a number or a statistic. And yeah, I do appreciate on some small level that he's not the kind of guy who actually keeps score, but still. I want to know what I'm really looking at getting involved with before I make any decisions.

I didn't think he was going to answer me but on another resigned sigh, Tristan closed his eyes for a moment and when he opened them again he looked me straight in the face and said, "Double. Easily. But that's as much as I'm willing to say…I'm not gonna sit down and make a list just so I can give you a more accurate number because the fact is, they're girls, Camie, not numbers and also, the amount of girls I've hooked up with *or* slept with doesn't define me. What does is that I've always treated them with respect before, during, and after, regardless of whether the act means anything to me or not and I don't go running my mouth about anything I've done with any one of them as sign of that respect.

"So please, can you just accept that so we can move on? I want you to believe me, Camie, I'm not in it for sex…if that's all I was interested in, I could walk out that door right now and find someone willing in less than three minutes, but I won't, because although I enjoy it a whole, whole lot, sex isn't *that* important to me. Not like this is..."

So yeah, light groveling was done and Tristan parted with some personal information I'm sure he would've much rather kept to himself. And I appreciated it, I really did, but because we're both so stubborn and this whole ordeal has really messed with my emotional stability and I still really haven't made up my mind about what I want, we went round and round and talked in circles for *hours*. One minute I'd think, yes I can do this, and then a little voice would whisper everything that's happened back to me, playing on all my fears and hurts. And then of course, anger would start bubbling in me again, so we were back to what looked surprisingly like square one. And it went on like that over and over and over again. It was exhausting. It was also like a roller coaster, with lots of ups and downs and quite a few sudden changes in velocity.

"*What* are you doing?" I asked, totally perplexed.

I mean we're right in the middle of a pretty intense "debate" where he'd asked what I'm having the biggest issue with; that he cheated, that he didn't tell me, or that he has a rather colorful past. Of course it pissed me off to be told that I have to choose, so we were arguing again when at one point, Tristan pulled out his phone and started typing a text.

"I'm listening, but I'm fuckin' starving…are you hungry?" He asked, his thumbs poised over the keypad in a holding pattern, waiting for my reply.

"I could eat." Huh. I'm actually pretty hungry, and thirsty…

"Anything you want in particular?"

"Uh-uh. Surprise me, but I'm seriously thirsty."

Honesty, this whole evening has been the definition of surreal to begin with and now we're literally ordering room service. I mean I really feel like by going to public school, I must've entered some kind of time portal to an alternate reality, because outside of the movies, none of this stuff ever happens. Seriously, when was the last time you heard about someone you go to school with being the cause of a big ol' brawl before she's carted up a huge staircase to then engage in a screaming fight with a guy at a party, and then the two of them taking a break from yelling to call down for fuel so they can continue to holler at each other on full tummies? Yeah, that's what I thought.

Anyhow, the reason we're getting phantasmagorical food is because Tristan's been adamant that we come to some kind of agreement *tonight*; therefore we're not leaving the room. I have a feeling he's not gonna get the answer he's looking for in the time frame we have, though, because when I say "agreement," I mean that rather loosely. Tristan wants *his* way, which is me telling him that we're good, everything will be great, that I can forget everything bad that's happened, and we can go back to the way things were before, which of course is simply not possible. Nevertheless, he does throw out some compelling arguments for his case, which I gotta give him credit for.

Also, after going through what I did on Saturday, the idea of going back to the way things were before is really unappealing to me. Leaving out the drugs, which I've come to find, I do have an issue with, I honestly don't think I can do the uncommitted relationship thing with him or anyone; it just doesn't work for me and I *think* he's having a small problem accepting that. He didn't actually say anything when I told him that, in fact he kind of changed the subject, but there was definitely something uneasy in his expression and body language. I'm not sure if it's a matter of him wanting his cake and being able to eat it too, or if he's just freaked by the idea of not having the freedom he's accustomed to having, or, if it's just not in him. At this point I can't help remembering what Melissa told me about why he didn't want to go out with her anymore.

Anyhow, some time later Jeff and Pete showed up with food and drinks. I'm thinking Pete must be dying to make sure I'm okay because when Tristan answered the door, barely allowing enough room for the food to be passed into the room, Pete did his darndest to look past him to find me but, Tristan wouldn't budge. I'm getting the feeling that he's being kind of protective, almost like he's a dragon who's trapped a princess in a tower and everyone poses a threat to his intention of keeping her there.

"Okay, here you go…no licorice as per your request," Jeff said, handing two large plates of food to Tristan. Then he turned to take a two-liter of soda and a six-pack of beer from Pete so he could hand those over as well.

"Jesus Pete, she's fine but I swear to God if you don't back off, we're gonna have a problem. I'm still not happy with you, so watch yourself," Tristan snapped.

To me it sounded as though jealousy was the instigator of what was a very definite warning for Pete as he was still trying to peer into the room to confirm my wellbeing.

I walked over to the door and whacked Tristan upside the back of his head. "Quit it, you ass. Pete, I'm okay…I'm being held here against my will but other than that, I'm fine," I said and took the plates back over to the bed.

Tristan shut the door in their faces, Jeff's teasing comment coming from the other side. "What, no tip?"

Our conversation went on hiatus while we ate and it was almost like we haven't been having the fight of the century, being quarantined until we work things out. For crying out loud, we had a freaking picnic in the middle of the bed and we even laughed. We were lying side by side, propped up on the pillows, when I looked at him stretched out and couldn't help myself by asking his stats.

"Hey, how tall are you and how much do you weigh?" I've been highly curious about this almost from day one, but mostly from the first time I saw him without a shirt.

He gave me an odd look but answered anyway. "Just over six-four and shy of two-thirty. Why, how much do you weigh?"

Damn. He's a lot bigger than I'd estimated—I guess muscle really does weigh more than fat because he has tons of the former and not an ounce of the latter.

"I'm not gonna tell you how much I weigh!" I'm not one of those girls who obsess about their weight; I've just had my female relatives pound it into me since I was little that you should never divulge your weight; your age either, once you reach a certain age that is.

He laughed at my indignant response and then looked at me for a moment of consideration. "You're about a buck-five."

"How the hell do you know that?!" Truly shocking!

"Educated guess."

That was all the answer I got. Tristan took a drink of the beer we're sharing—sharing it seemed fitting, what with the picnic and all—and when he was finished, he handed the bottle back to me and said, "Nice, there goes Mix Master J.C. and the Apostles again…"

"*What* are you talking about?" I asked dumbfounded. Honestly, it came out of nowhere and I've no clue what he means.

"The song, Camie. Haven't you ever thought the music that happens to be playing when we're together is ludicrously appropriate? Like Jesus is playing DJ or something…seriously, I picture Him wearing a white robe, sandals, and headphones and he's standing there gettin' His groove on in front of an old-style turntable," he admitted and took the bottle back.

I choked and almost spit out the beer that was in my mouth. Oh my God…don't you just *love* the mental image he painted?! I mean really, bravo! I hadn't even been paying all that much attention to what was playing, but when I stopped and listened to it, I'd agree, as the song is "Breakfast In Bed" by UB40. I almost feel like I should try to remember to give kudos to Mike or whoever is responsible for tonight's unexpectedly varied music selection. I mean I even heard Lynyrd Skynyrd earlier in the evening!

"Oh my God, that's so funny…I was thinking the *exact* same thing earlier tonight when you decided to assault Z—well, when the fight broke out and 'So What' was playing. I also thought God was controlling the shuffle on your iPod at the beach that night," I told him and having made sure I'd swallowed completely, I started giggling.

Tristan on the other hand wasn't able to keep the fluid in his mouth from escaping on hearing what I said. He started cracking up, causing delighted warmth to spread through me as I smiled at the sound. I just love hearing him laugh; it's better than snickerdoodles.

"I know, right? I have a *ton* of Pink Floyd on that thing, not to mention all the other shit, and I still can't believe out of all the songs that could've started the second our lips meet for the first time, it just so happened to be four minutes and fifty-three seconds of perfect, especially when you take into account that everything totally fades away and it really does feel like flying when we kiss." Okay, he actually knows the song length…that *has* to mean something, right? "He didn't do so bad with the follow-up songs either, except fuckin' Jeff had to ruin that moment for us… Oh and thanks for not saying his name." Just so you know, he's talking about Zack, not Jeff. "I don't think I could take hearing it come out of your mouth," he said, staring at my mouth as I smiled and took another drink from the bottle.

And then of course, the mood, along with the color of his eyes, morphed—*again*.

It is very safe to say that Tristan and I have issues. First, we both have tempers and we both push each other's buttons. Second, we're both very stubborn. Third, neither of us has a whole lot of patience and we're impulsive, which is important to keep in mind when you take into account that fourth, we're *beyond* attracted to each other and have a mighty hard time keeping our hands off one another.

This time when we came together, it wasn't nearly as carnally primal as when he ripped my costume from me, but the plates of food did get carelessly swept from the bed onto the floor. Oh and remember when I said a while back that a thin layer of satin really isn't an effective barrier? *WRONG*. It makes all the difference in the world. Therefore, I have a feeling that the *only* reason I was able to speak the word is because I completely and totally mentally freaked when he took my hand and brought it down for me to feel his rock-hard penis. I mean we're not naked, but we're pretty damned close and I can deal with feeling his erection riding against me here and there while we're making out, but grabbing hold of it intentionally? Nu-uh. And I don't care if my hand was only gonna touch him over the well-fitted cotton of his Calvin Klein's either—*I'm not ready!!*

When I jerked my hand from his, he lifted his mouth from where it'd been lavishing attention on my left breast and slowly raised his head to meet my eyes.

"Stop."

"Oh God, Camie, *why? What* is it *now?*" He asked with unadulterated frustration ringing in his voice.

"I can't do this, Tristan, it doesn't feel right." I'm still pretty much a basket case so what we've been doing feels great physically, but emotionally? Not so much.

"It feels pretty fuckin' right to me so I do *not* understand how you can say that, Camie…really, I don't! You have to *know* that we work! I mean why can't you just fucking get over whatever it is that's keeping you from me?" He snarled a mite bitterly.

"Don't. Don't start that."

"I can't help it! You're fucking killing me with this, Camie," he told me and rolled onto his back in irritated resignation.

I'm rapidly becoming upset again. I get that he's frustrated because I'm so all over the board and won't make a decision either way—I mean *I'm* frustrated by me, but Jesus…putting pressure on me isn't gonna help his cause here.

Great. Now I've got "Under Pressure" by Queen and David Bowie stuck in my head…

"Well I'm sorry, Tristan, but Jesus, why don't you try understanding what it feels like to have been lied to, emotionally battered, and then physically pressured and tell me if you'd trust the person who's doing all that to you!" I said heatedly. I didn't yell, but I'm definitely emotional.

It has to be at least three in the morning and I'm freaking exhausted in addition to everything else that's been going on. Oh, and yeah, I'm crying again.

"*Fuck!*" He growled, leaving the bed and me to pull his pants back on, and then he paced the floor.

He left his jeans partially unzipped and unbuttoned, revealing his marvelously chiseled abs and his hips in their entirety, which is one of *the* sexiest things I think I've ever seen in my life.

Surprisingly, I was able to locate our shirt. Yeah, I'm just gonna refer to it as ours because it's easier… I shrugged back into it and we argued, again, for a while longer.

"Camie, tell me what you want me to do?" He asked wearily after we'd been over everything another time or two.

"Tristan, I'm not sure you can *do* or *say anything*, but I'm so tired...can we *please* just not talk about this anymore right now, I need a break..." I begged for respite by pleading fatigue through my tears.

He really wanted to continue and he's highly upset with me, but I swear we're beating one seriously dead horse here. Nevertheless, I'm guessing about a half-hour or forty-five minutes of silence passed where neither of us said anything. He was stretched out in a chair while I was curled up in the bed facing away from him with my eyes closed when I heard the door creak open and the following whispered conversation:

Jeff: "Hey, you asleep?"

Tristan: "She is. What do you want?"

Jeff: "I brought her bag up..."

Tristan: "Just put it down right there."

Jeff: "Well, you didn't kill each other, that's a plus. I mean, at least you're both still living..."

Tristan: "This is living?"

Jeff: "Yeah dude, it is. I take it things aren't going well..."

Tristan: "Fuck man, how do you *do* this? I mean Jesus, you and Kate are constantly fighting...don't you ever think to yourself, fuck it, I'm done?" (FYI, this is just one of my fears...)

Jeff: "Nope, never. Dude, I've loved Katy since before second grade, you know that...you were there."

Tristan: "Yeah, I know. But is it worth it? All of this bullshit?"

Jeff: "Trist, it's different for me...I don't think of Katy as just a girlfriend...she's more like my wife, you know? I mean, she's gonna be the mother of my children some day...at least I hope she will be...so yeah...it's worth it. Christ, you know my ringtone for her is that song 'I'll Do Anything for Love', right?

Tristan: Yeah, gotta love Meatloaf.

Jeff: Right, but I chose it because I *would* do anything for her and I'll fight for her *until the day I die* because I wanna spend my *entire life* with her." (Okay, *wow*. I mean this guy really wears his heart on his sleeve and I'm actually tearing up at hearing the deep devotion and intensity in his voice. I also couldn't help looking at him while he said all that, but I closed my eyes again because I don't want them to know I'm listening.) "But you have to ask yourself what *you* want, you know?"

Tristan: "I know I don't want it to be over..."

Jeff: "Does she?"

Tristan: "Hell if I know…she's so goddamned confused right now and I can't seem to get through to her. Jeff, she heard us arguing…Kate's voicemail caught most of it from what I gather…"

Jeff: "Ooh, ouch. That had to be fuckin' *rough*."

Tristan: "You have *no* fuckin' idea. It was grisly, man. Shit, she heard all of it, including the Titanic thing…we were so goddamned ferocious with each other over that and I fought really dirty…just a fuckin' nightmare. She was at the party and actually saw what I did too. You were right about everything. I hurt her, I lied to her by omission, and when she came at me tonight I hit back really fuckin' hard and now she doesn't trust me…it's killing me Jeff and I just don't know if I can do this for much longer…" (I heard Tristan get up and walk somewhere close by...I think he might be standing behind me next to the bed, but I'm *so* not moving right now to check.)

Jeff: "If you love her, you won't give up." (Wait, *what?!* Did I just hear him right? This is when my eyes popped open again and I saw Jeff leaning on the wall directly opposite me with his hands raised in a pacifying manner.) "Okay, okay…dude, don't get your shorts in a bunch…so you're not quite there yet, but Trist, *I know you* and I'm tellin' ya, you're not far from it…" (Oh "Dear Jeff," what would I do without you? He just winked at me and gave me a slight nod as if to say, "Trust me, I'm right about this." So, I closed my eyes again and just listened.) "Lemme give you some advice, dude, and seeing as how you ignored my most-excellent wisdom before and it got you here, you might wanna listen this time."

Tristan: "Bro, I'm almost at the point of being willing to do just about anything to fix this fuckin' mess so whatever you got, lay it on me."

Jeff: Good, 'cause if you want this to work—no, if you want *her*, you'll get down on your hands and knees and fight for her like a real man. You're gonna have to find a way to prove to her that you mean business or she'll never take you seriously and you'll lose her."

Tristan: "And what if I can't? What if it's too late and she can't get past all this?"

Jeff: "Well my friend, in that case you'll be left with just *remembering* what Phil said. But I have *faith* in you, Trist, you'll think of something…" (Um, who's Phil?)

Tristan: "Thanks man, now get out." (He's getting in bed now…)

Jeff left and Tristan quietly lay down, molding himself to me, and with barely a feather's touch, he kissed my shoulder. I fell asleep for real this time with his arms wrapped around me while thinking about what the two of them said to each other and asking myself the same thing Tristan asked Jeff… What if it's too late and I can't get past all this?

I've no idea how long I was out and I've no clue what time it was, but I was roused from a deep slumber by the sensation of Tristan slowly and gently running his hands over me. Now, let me explain a couple of things here… I'm still *more* than halfway asleep and I'm not planning on waking up either. Also, what he's doing isn't so much sexual as it feels scholastic. I know, odd way to put it, but it almost seems like he's learning through touch. It kind of reminds me of a blind person reading Braille or something.

"What are you doing?" I mumbled. Like I said, I'm totally out of it and I'm not going to actually wake up, but I'm curious to know what he's up to.

"Memorizing…just in case. Do you mind?" He whispered back.

See? I told you—there's no intent to take advantage of me while I'm zonked out.

"Uh-uh, just no new landmarks," I answered sleepily. I mean really, it's not as if he hasn't already been over *almost* every inch of me before. And the other thing is, he's not kissing me…it's just his hands, so I feel safe in not being tempted to go somewhere I'm nowhere near ready for.

"I promise, no new landmarks," he said quietly. Then he gently drew our shirt off me and went back to his reverent studies in a way that almost felt like devout worship.

I went back to sleep.

21.

There Was Voting?

When I woke up again the sun was streaming in through the window and I could feel Tristan's steady sleeping breath on the back of my neck. Sometime during the wee morning hours we must've swapped sides, though, because I'm not facing the door anymore. We're in a super-glued spoon position that feels particularly protective and actually, if I'm picturing what we must look like correctly, his half-naked body is acting like a shield to mine. It makes me wonder if we had any other guests while I was sleeping. Or maybe he'd just been concerned that we would and he didn't want anyone seeing me without a shirt, for which I'm most grateful.

His arm was wrapped almost loosely around my waist but the second I moved to slip out of bed; it tightened, holding me to him. So apparently he isn't as asleep as I thought, either that or it's a reflex.

"Don't go," he whispered in quiet desperation.

Nope. Not a reflex.

"I have to," I told him softly, knowing full well that I'll never be able to get my head on straight and figure things out being around him. A point he proved when he started to sweetly kiss my shoulders and the back of my neck. "Tristan, you need to let me go. I need some time to work things out in my head and I'll never be able to do that if I'm around you," I said, feeling the truth of my words as I fought back the intense desire to roll over into him, thereby allowing him to sweep me away into insanity once more.

"How much time?" He asked in between soft, yet maddening kisses.

"Honestly, I just don't know. I haven't been myself all week and I feel so lost right now…it could be a long time, Tristan," I told him and held my breath, expecting him to give me an ultimatum that I'll never be able to meet.

All I can think about is what Kate told me about the possibility that he won't wait, and what he told Jeff about not knowing if it was worth it and not being able to wait. But, I refuse to make a decision under duress, so if he can't wait for me then that's that. And while thinking about time and waiting, I was once again reminded of that damned Limp Bizkit song. Jeez, will I ever be done living out those freaking lyrics?

It took him a minute or so and several more kisses that are rapidly causing my hormones to become frantic before, albeit reluctantly and with a sigh, he loosened his hold on me and said, "Alright, but when you find you, come back to me."

"Did you just quote David Cook?" I asked with amusement and some relief while I started to sit up to look at him.

If he did, I'm taking it to mean that he'll wait for an answer regardless of how long it takes me to give him one, which makes getting to one so much easier for me. Don't ask me why, it just does. It also makes me happy.

He chuckled a little. "Yeah, if the song fits, use—" Tristan's words suddenly broke off, being immediately replaced by a hiss as he sucked his breath in sharply.

I turned completely to look at him and saw he had his eyes closed tightly and an almost pained look on his face. "What's wrong?"

"Oh Jesus, Camie, you gotta put the shirt on," he gasped and I swear he started holding his breath.

Yeah, I forgot about the being topless thing. How you might ask? Well, apparently I lost my exhibitionist inhibitions at some point last night. I'm guessing that had a lot to do with him for one, but also the alcohol. I really had quite a bit to drink last night but was never drunk enough to lose complete control...just a little control.

"Well where is it? Tristan! I'm like repellent for shirts! Find it!" I'm almost frantic.

Seriously, he's doing a really good job of controlling himself *right now*, but I can tell from how his hands are flexing in fists as he grips the blankets that he's not gonna make it much longer and then…well, let's just say I'll most likely end up losing more than my reluctance to be half-naked in front of him and I'm really not prepared for that.

"Camie, I can't. If I open my eyes to look for it, I promise you won't need the shirt anymore and you sure as hell won't be leaving this room any time soon," he said through almost clenched teeth before he rolled onto his stomach and buried his face in the pillows as an added precaution.

I was just standing there, picturing the long list of don'ts the animals at the zoo have on their cages, afraid to hunt around in the blankets for the shirt because I didn't want to pester, harass, harangue, tease, or provoke him when all of sudden, I remembered that Jeff had brought my bag up.

Tristan must've remembered it at the same time because he waved an arm in my bag's general direction and said into the pillow, "Forget the shirt, your stuff's over there somewhere."

I dug into my bag with the proper amount of haste a situation like this calls for, and grabbing the first piece of upper-body apparel I laid my hands on, I yanked the hoodie on, zipped it up as far it'd go and then said, "Okay, the coast is clear…you can stop suffocating yourself now."

I heard a muffled groan come from him but he didn't move so I reiterated, thinking he hadn't heard me. "Tristan, I've got a shirt on…it's safe now, you can look."

He kind of laughed in a way that sounded distinctly self-deprecating and then said, "Actually Camie, it's not. I did a really phenomenal job at memorizing and it won't make a difference if you have clothes on anymore… As much as I'd love to see you right now or even better, kiss you goodbye, if you wanna make it outta here, you just better go now because if you come anywhere near me right now, I honestly don't think I'll be able to stop myself."

You gotta appreciate his honesty—in this area at least.

Not wanting to make matters worse or more difficult, I quickly collected my stuff and left the room without another word. Turning to walk down the hall, I almost tripped over Pete who'd crashed sitting up with his back on the wall. I thought about waking him up to tell him I'm okay, but then I thought better of it. My rationale is that I should just get out of here while Tristan is letting me and I still have the determination to go. It was really hard to leave him just now, but until I am away from him, I won't know if the reason behind that is because I actually want to be with him or if it's just a sheer physical thing and me being impulsive.

I tiptoed around Pete and pulled my phone out to text Kate and Melissa to see if they're awake yet. I looked at my phone and thought, oh crap… I have two missed texts, one from each of them. The bright side though, is at least I didn't miss anything from home. One of Tristan's things last night while we were sequestered was that our phones be on vibrate so we wouldn't be interrupted. In fact, he turned his clear off except when he sent texts asking for food or reinforcements.

Tristan had chosen a room—why, I've no idea—that didn't have a bathroom in it, but there was one right across the hall. Anytime I had to go he'd stand guard over the bathroom door in case I tried to sneak away, and then when he had to go, he'd actually have Jeff or Mike provide backup to make sure I stayed in the room. It was either that or being taken into the bathroom with him, or, both of us staying put and me having to watch him pee out the bedroom window. He did give me the choice though.

Anyhow, I looked at the time stamps of the missed texts and saw that Melissa's was first and Kate's was only about ten minutes ago, so, the vibrating from both of them might've been what woke me up. I continued downstairs and found them and some other girls sitting outside around the still smoldering fire pit, talking.

"Hey, sorry I didn't answer you…I was asleep," I told them, leaving out all details because of the others present.

I have no idea who knows how much about anything that happened last night, but I really don't want to be subjected to another volley of rumors that I have no way of disproving. However, now that I think about it, dozens of people saw Tristan drag me back to the room last night so maybe it's too late. I don't think our screaming at each other at any point in the night will make much of difference either, even if everyone heard it.

"No problem. We were just talking about getting something to eat, wanna go?" Melissa asked cheerfully.

"Yeah, that sounds good." I'm hoping that it'll just be the three of us though; I need to talk...

"Okay, well go get dressed and then we'll get outta here," she said, calling attention to my lack of adequate attire. All I have on is a pink hoodie and a pair of black dance shorts that barely conceal the tops of my thighs...not exactly appropriate even if it is just Denny's.

"Um...I'm kinda hung-over and I really should eat before I take anything for my headache...I'm afraid it'll be a bad one too, so can we just go now? I'll throw my pants on in the car," I said, meeting Kate's eyes. I'm really hoping that saying I'm hung-over will make my desire to escape as quickly as humanly possible look less suspect to these girls who are kind of eyeing me strangely.

"Yep! Let's get goin' then," Kate said, getting my meaning at once. She knows full well I could care less about having food before aspirin and even more telling in my statement was, if I was actually hung-over; I wouldn't want to have anything to do with food.

We left the house quietly, not wanting to wake up any of the other partygoers passed out in assorted places throughout Mike's house, and once we were safely driving down the street, both Kate and Melissa threw a barrage of questions at me. The first of Kate's being more of a statement.

"You were running," she said and looked at me in her rearview mirror.

"Yeah, my window of opportunity to leave was closing. Actually, I almost slammed it shut myself but, that would've just made everything else so much harder to figure out so, I had to make a quick getaway...thanks for picking up on that," I told them honestly and thanking Kate once more for her awesome powers of divination.

While she drove, I covertly finished getting dressed in the back seat, simultaneously filling them in on various parts of my night. While rummaging in my bag for my bra though, I came across something I hadn't packed so holding up the condom I asked, "What the hell is this and how did it get in my bag?"

"Oh, it's a party favor. Turn it over and read the other side," Melissa told me and giggled.

Reading it, I can understand why she thinks it's funny. First, the condom is day-glow orange and written on the wrapper is the phrase: "I slept with Mike Foster." Also included is the date of the party with a pumpkin next to it. Then I noticed it has a keychain through one corner of it.

"Everyone who stayed the night got one and were also included in the judging panel…pretty funny, huh?" Melissa said.

"OH! That's what the box of condoms was about…when I saw Mike waving it around last night I was thinking Kristen and I were gonna have a really long night but for totally different reasons. That's really funny! Who put it in my bag though? And what judging panel?" I asked while laughing about what I can now clearly see is a novelty condom keychain.

"I think Mike did right before Jeff brought it up to you. He wanted to make sure you got one, especially after you and Tristan won this year's most memorable party moment hands down... The awards ceremony will be at lunch on Monday. The people who slept over were the judges unless they happened to be nominated in whatever category was being voted on. Oh, and the four of us won first place for best costume…we think Pete should keep the trophy," Kate chattered.

"There was voting? So, not only did I get held prisoner all night and cried through the majority of it, but I missed voting and winning awards too…that totally sucks."

"Yeah, but you wouldn't have been happy during the voting process…there was a lot of 'well what about when' kinds of things being thrown out because no one could choose which part was the most memorable and all the choices were you guys in some way or another, so, you probably would've felt kinda uncomfortable hearing like three or four dozen people relive their memories of the night. Mike actually halted the debate and called it a draw.

"I was sorta leaning towards when you let Pete do the body shots and Tristan's reaction to that, Jeff and Pete were pushing for when Tristan threw you over his shoulder and stormed away with you...they were really pleased with Tristan for that by the way, and I think Mike was liking when Tristan lost it and beat the shit outta Zack (That figures…it was his prediction and all.) who might have a broken nose...oh, there's a bet going on about that now too…I think there were a few others… Melissa, do you remember any other moments that were nominated?" Kate asked while trying to remember the public highlights of my night.

Okay, so there will be no preventing of rumors. I mean come on, there was freaking voting. Ugh.

"Um, there was the call for room service that everyone thought was hysterical and someone said something about when you tried to leave and he dragged you back kicking and screaming, but not that many people who stayed the night saw that. Mike did say it was pretty funny though. The bathroom breaks were kind of popular…"

Huh. I'm sort of surprised about that one. Although, it was kind of funny that no one in line seemed to mind that we would cut right to the front of it, almost like they knew what was going on and were just happy to be helpful. Oh hell. Yeah, everyone knew what was going on, there's just no way I can delude myself any longer.

"Oh, Kristen and a few girls mentioned how once you guys were inside how he carried you up the stairs…they said seeing it was pretty spectacular and totally romantic," Melissa added and turned around to look at me for confirmation.

Yeah, I think they all had the night pretty well covered…that's just freaking great.

"Okay, Mike's an asshole, he did absolutely nothing to help me but that last one I'll agree with. Personally, I was thinking it must've looked pretty similar to Moses parting the Red Sea, but then he took those stairs two at a time which was probably very romantic looking…" I said and then gave them a few details of what transpired directly after Tristan got me to the room. I wouldn't have necessarily called it romantic at the time, but yeah, Kristen and the other girls were right; it was.

We got to the restaurant and while we ate, we talked about the whole evening with me giving them a pretty comprehensive play by play but without giving up too many intimate details. I mean I did give them some, like the memorizing thing and what'd happened this morning, but overall, I left the specifics of what Tristan and I did pretty much out. And I wasn't the only one who did some censoring in their re-cap of the night...

Without getting into specifics either, Melissa told Kate and I how after they'd retired for the night, Keith had been a bit more amorous than usual and that's why she was relieved when he eventually started puking from all the drinking he'd done earlier. Apparently the puking was followed by Keith passing out and Melissa getting a pressure free and peaceful night's sleep...

"You know on top of everything, I'm pretty irritated that he never actually apologized…I mean he didn't once say he was sorry for any of it," I told them as we were finishing up our post-party nourishment. Actually, Melissa was the only one who ate a real meal. I'd ordered fruit and I also picked at the French fries Kate had ordered but wasn't really eating much of.

Kate looked at me thoughtfully for a minute or two and I could tell she was onto something, but was reluctant to say what she was thinking. I'm not sure why she'd be hesitant, but I gave her the go ahead to spit it out anyway. I'm more than aware that I need some help in sorting through my feelings on this so whatever she's thinking, I need to hear it.

"Okay well, I'm wondering, do you really need him to say the words? I mean I never thought about it before but, Tristan is so not like Jeff or Mike in the way that he practically never says what's on his mind."

She stopped and sighed when I just sat there giving her an "I don't get what that has to do with anything" look.

"Alright, lemme see if I can explain this...uh...Oh! It's kinda like a book my parents have...I picked it up once when I was pissed at Jeff a long time ago and it's all about something called love languages and how people give and receive love...not just romantic love, but you know what I mean...anyway, I found out that my love language is something called acts of service and Jeff's is actually a combination of two of them, quality time and words of affirmation, and that's why when I lecture him it bothers him so much, because when I talk at him like that, it's like I'm taking one of the main ways he interprets love and use it to punish him without really meaning to.

"I mean, I've been thinking back over everything, Camie, not just last night, and it's obvious to me now that Tristan is not only pretty complicated, but he's a very physical person (uh-huh...duh) and from what I'm hearing, it sounds like he spent the entire night trying to show you that he's sorry. I'd be willing to bet anything that Tristan's primary love language is physical touch with a big acts of service kicker and if that's true, I don't know how much you're ever gonna actually hear come from his mouth on the stuff that's important. If you decide to take him back, you might need to learn how to interpret the things he does instead of hearing the words, because he might never say them, you know what I mean?"

"That actually makes a lot of sense, Camie. I already told you I've never seen him behave the way he does when he's around you and I think Kate's right. Little by little he's been showing you how he feels for weeks and then last night was like a giant exclamation point.

"I mean he wouldn't even let you out of the room until he made sure you heard what he was trying to say. That in itself is pretty telling in my opinion...because he let you go this morning even though he knew he could've stopped you. If you think about it, he even told you in a round about way that he was fighting his gut instinct to give you what you said you need from him, which is time and space...and it was obviously really difficult for him to do because he knew you hadn't heard him," Melissa elucidated for me as we headed back to Kate's car.

"Huh. I guess I never thought of it like that. I mean I know he's physical, sometimes in a scary way too, but I never realized it was his primary mode of communication. Now that you point it out though, I can totally see where you're probably right. And actually, that could explain why he hates it when girls throw themselves at him or hang on him...

"If touch is how Tristan expresses love, then girls doing it in such a shallow way would be to him how Jeff feels punished when you lecture him. So if that's really the case then, I guess it kinda says a lot that he let me hit him in anger last night too. I think he felt really bad about the boat stuff and calling me a bitch, which I was totally being, but he let me punish him because he felt like he deserved it, especially after everything else he'd done.

"OH! Wait, he actually said something like that...oh crap what did he say...? Oh damn, it was something about how what he did last weekend was hurting him because he knew it'd cause me pain or something like that and that's when he said he didn't know how to make up for it and he couldn't take back anything he'd already done and asked me if we could just start over...so I guess maybe that was the acts of service part of him trying to apologize...he just didn't know what he could actually do though."

He kept asking what he could do or how he could prove himself so this acts of service thing lines up with why he actually gave me an answer on some of the sex stuff too...it was very clear he didn't want to but he did it all the same.

We left the restaurant and all the way to my house and into my room, we talked about every instance we could think of and how this new theory about how he works could explain the things he's done. We'd decided during breakfast (or brunch, whatever...) that we'd come back here to hang out and just recoup. Kate and Melissa were positive that both Jeff and Keith would be sleeping most of the day anyway—not that Melissa was all that keen to see Keith today, but regardless... And I'd be surprised if Tristan hadn't passed out shortly after I left because I don't think he slept at all last night. I only got a couple hours myself, maybe, and since I'm like death warmed over I'm thinking if he's not asleep by now, he's gotta be like the walking dead.

We filled a remotely interested Jillian in on our new theory and most of what happened, and the four of us were watching a movie—well, I was half asleep—when out of the blue, I remembered another point of contention I have.

"What about the fact that Tristan totally side-stepped, or rather completely ignored what I said about me not being able to do the casual uncommitted relationship thing? Because that's really kind of a big deal for me. Assuming I can get around everything else, I can't go back to the way things were...not now, not after everything that's happened. I kinda feel like he's expecting me to be the one who does all the compromising here and that's just not right."

"Mmm, I don't really have an answer on that one. I totally get where you're coming from though and if it was me, again, assuming I could get over everything else, I'd stick to my guns on that. But really, if what you heard when he was talking to Jeff is true, you know when Jeff told him that he's gonna have to think of a way to prove he's serious and if Jeff really does believe he's that close to being in love with you…then I honestly think it's a non-issue. If he decides to go for it, you just might have to do some interpreting of his actions like I said before for you to know what he means by whatever he comes up with doing," Kate said with a contagious yawn.

I was almost asleep again when Jillian's phone startled me awake. I looked over at her and saw that she was sending a text, but I didn't question it until the reply came back seconds later. She replied with another one and then stood up to leave.

"What was that all about?" I asked out of pure curiosity.

As a rule, Jillian doesn't text like the rest of us do. Basically because she's just not that into it yet, but mostly because she feels like if it's important enough to say, you should just pick up the phone and say it…unless you simply can't like the time she chastised me at school for hiding in the library.

She shrugged. "Oh, just this stupid boy who needs help with something."

"A boy? This sounds promising…is he cute?" I asked, teasing her a little. On second thought, I wonder if I should warn her away from all involvement with boys—cute or not. The cute ones are even more troublesome.

But then again, maybe I should be warning the boy...

Looking bored as usual, she blandly replied, "Oh, he's totally hot but he's head over heels for someone else. Besides, I'm not helping him because I like him in that way."

"Oh, why are you gonna make the effort then?" I'm really curious now. Jill is usually kind of stingy with her time unless there's something in it for her.

"Well, he's sorta calling in a favor, but mostly I'm helping him out so I won't have to buy him the box of Twinkies I kinda owe him. Anyway, I'm gonna ride my bike over to the park and meet him there so I'll see you all later," she said simply and then left.

Not having to buy a box of Twinkies for someone is totally good motivation for her to do something she wouldn't necessarily do. Jill is even stingier with her money and junk food than she is with her time.

Kate and Melissa both looked at me in question but it was Melissa, who I think is becoming dangerously fond of Jillian, who asked, "Is she telling the truth or is she up to no good? Because if she's off to be stealthy, I wanna follow her!"

"Totally telling the truth...she loves her money and junk food more than she loves me," I said quite honestly.

Okay, I might be stretching it a little, but I really don't think she'd be the one to ask for a Ding Dong if you were starving or even worse, P.M.S.-ing because all you'd get is an uncompassionate look of "it's not my problem."

"That sucks," Melissa said, disappointed. "I can't believe you guys didn't follow her last weekend...I so would've trailed her just to see how she does it."

"Melissa, you would've never gotten past the front door...she'd smell a stalker a mile away," I told her and laughed with Kate at the wounded look on Melissa's face.

The three of us talked some more and at one point we all napped, but I gotta say, having friends like Kate and Melissa has been really invaluable. Not just in my dilemma, but overall. I really do feel blessed to have them in my life. You might think that your best friends would just bash the guy who did you wrong as a means of supporting you, but they really helped me to see both sides of the coin in what's been going on with me and Tristan, which I think proves what good people they are.

I'm still not one hundred percent sure about what to do, though, because a lot of things hinge on him. I'm totally over the need to hear Tristan "say" he's sorry, but like Jeff and Kate said, he needs to prove he's serious and I'm not going to give him pointers on that. Also, I want a spoken—hell, I'd prefer written—commitment. I'm thinking if he can show me, then he can tell me too, and this is one thing I'm not going to budge on. And then there's another thing I'm thinking I'm going to meet some pretty serious resistance on, but I'll deal with that if and when I get past the other two things.

So, I guess you could say I'm in a kind of holding pattern until he decides to prove himself to me. I'm not expecting much this next week, though, because, well...we'll be at school. And since that's not really a venue any of us thinks he'll choose to lay his cards on the table at, I'm guessing it won't be until next weekend at least before he really gives me anything to go on.

I'll admit I think it'd be nice if Tristan were a little more like Jeff so I don't have to decipher his actions like a code. I told Kate what Jeff had said about her during my incarceration and it wasn't news to her at all. Apparently he's already said much the same thing to her. And repeatedly from what I gather. Kate actually agrees with him and told me that, yes she'll most likely end up having his children and marrying him someday and that's basically why it's not the end of the world for either of them when they fight or break up. They both acknowledge and accept the fact that they'll always get back together, and she also agrees with him about their relationship being more like a marriage than that of a boyfriend-girlfriend thing; even though they're not actually married right now, they both know it'll happen one day.

Oh and since I was dying of curiosity, I also asked her if it was true about Jeff loving her since the second grade and I gotta say, Jeff may not be a romantic per se, but you will never-ever doubt the sincerity or dedication of his intentions. Here's the story of how they came to be a couple:

The three of them have known each other since birth, but when Kate was in first grade and the guys were in second, the extremely close-knit friendship started to change. Jeff would tease Kate relentlessly and then turn around and be colder than ice, but he also took Tristan away from her, which, from what she said, really hurt. It wasn't until after the guys had to repeat a grade two years later and they were all in third grade together that Jeff finally worked up the nerve to walk up to her with Tristan in tow during their lunch recess and told her in no uncertain terms how he felt. Kate told me she remembers it like yesterday and she said this is what Jeff did: He confidently strode right up to her while she was sitting with a couple of girlfriends, pulled her to her feet, kissed her on the lips once and then said, "I love you, Katy, you belong to me and I'm gonna marry you someday, just so you know," and then he turned around and walked away. Kate, even then having her super powers of being able to read people with frightful accuracy, of course had already figured out what his problem was a year or so before that, but she wanted him to be the one to admit it and so she'd patiently waited. They've been together ever since.

Kind of amazing, isn't it? I mean it's not your typical storybook romance, but I think it's almost better. Now, it's my turn to wait patiently—Ugh—to see if I get the happy ending I'm looking for or not…

22.

A Definite First

Mondays suck.

And you know what? *This* one can kiss my almost sixteen-year-old ass…

I'm not even going to pretend that I don't swear anymore because that would just be a bold-faced lie and Kate warned me this would happen. I've been totally corrupted, thanks in large part to Tristan and his goddamned lips.

Sigh.

Have I mentioned how much I freaking hate my alarm clock? Well I do. I detest—no, I absolutely loathe it. Especially today. You'd think I would've slept the sleep of the dead after having been awake almost all night on Saturday, but *nooo*. I hardly slept at all. I kept turning things over in my head trying to make sure I'd come to the right decision when, or more aptly, *if* Tristan decides to prove himself and I gotta say, I think this next week is gonna be pretty freaking brutal. If it's anything like last week, I'm gonna be in for a world of hurt because that was just miserable. Maybe because we're not mad at each other anymore it won't be *as* bad, but I still think things will be uncomfortable and awkward, especially considering we're getting an award at lunch today, which I'm *so* not looking forward to.

I know I can probably speed the process up a *little bit* by telling him the ball's in his court now, but that sort of defeats the purpose of him proving himself, which he really needs to do so that I can be sure of him. There's no doubt in my mind that he wants to be with me in "some" way and I'm sure I want to be with him now too. The question is how much is he willing to do in order to be with me though; because there's only one way I'll do it. Plus, I need to see that he can be the person I need, if that makes any sense at all. I hate to put it this way, but there are some strings attached to what I'm willing to do. It all kind of comes back to what happened with him and Melissa. If he feels like I'm asking him to be someone he's not, then it won't work for either of us, the possibility of which scares the crap out of me.

So, here I go… I'm dragging my utterly emotionally and physically exhausted butt out of bed to embark on a new day and I'm doing it filled with firm resolve…*and* a hefty dose of nauseating fear.

I opted to skip breakfast due to the fact that my tummy is a jittery mess as I really don't know what my day is going to be like or how the rest of the week will play out, but as I was brushing my teeth, I was given the nerve-wracking information that I'll be finding out way earlier than I expected.

"Camie, your ride's here," Jillian told me as I rinsed.

I looked at the bathroom clock and began choking on the water in my mouth. "Holy crap! Kate's *way* early! I know we've been trying really hard to get to school on time, but jeez... Just tell her to come in and I'll be down in a minute..."

I dashed into my room to pull my shoes on and was shocked even further when some rather loud music floated in through my window from outside. I recognized the song almost immediately. It's "Whatever It Takes" by Lifehouse. I walked over to my window to see what the hell was going on and what I saw instantly filled my eyes with the biggest crocodile tears *EVER*... As I stood there captivated and crying, my entire family wandered in to join in witnessing a moment that I'll be sure to remember long after eternity is over.

"Well, it's not Peter Gabriel, but you really do have to give him credit," my mom said tenderly and with a little sniffle of her own.

"I'll say this for him, the boy definitely has style...and sweetie, I don't know what he did, but anyone willin' to pull a *Say Anything* like this guy is doin', certainly means business," my dad told me, thereby confirming my thoughts exactly.

If you haven't figured it out, Tristan, my absolute, no question about it, *soul mate and love of my life*, is quite literally standing in front of his car in our driveway wearing a tan trench coat, holding an ancient and decrepit looking boom box straight up over his head and asking me for a second chance through the use of an epically romantic '80s movie moment and *one heck* of a perfect song.

I turned away from the window, grabbed my purse and just as I was about to fly down the stairs still weeping for joy, I heard Jillian talking to herself as she crossed the hall to go into her bedroom.

"I'm so proud...our little boy is all growed up," she muttered, shaking her head and closing the door behind her.

Not caring to take the time out of my perfect moment to ponder what that was about, I shook her musings off, bolted down the stairs, out the front door and flew straight into Tristan's arms. He just barely had time to put the boom box down before he caught me with a kiss as he swung me around once.

"I know you asked for time but I just couldn't bear the thought of another day let alo—"

"Oh my God, you just totally proved that I don't need any more time," I interrupted. Then as the song played out, I slowed down the ecstatic Snoopy happy dancing I've been doing in my head and started praying he wouldn't balk yet. "But Tristan, I have some conditions…"

"Alright. Let's go talk," he replied without a moment's hesitation.

Then he kissed me on the cheek and opened the passenger door for me, bringing the tempo of my mental dancing back up to where it'd been. Once we were on our way though, and I recognized we were heading to school, I figured I should let Kate know I wouldn't need a ride.

When Tristan noticed I had pulled out my phone he asked, "What are you doing?"

"Letting Kate know she doesn't need to pick me up."

"Uh, I kinda already took care of that," he answered, a devilish grin playing on his lips. Then he decided to explain when I just stared at him. "Well, I didn't wanna assume my impersonation of Lloyd Dobler would allow me to drive my girlfriend to school this morning, so, I sorta hedged my bets and had Jeff prevent Kate from picking you up…"

Wait. Go back… Girlfriend? Did he call me his girlfriend?

"Wow, that's pretty devious, Tristan. But I wanna go back to something else you said," I told him, completely distracted from any irritation I might've felt at his intended form of hi-jacking me by his usage of the word girlfriend.

He pulled into the deserted back lot at school, shut the engine off and then turned to face me. "You've got my undivided attention, go."

"Well, you said 'girlfriend' so, does that mean you're willing to be committed to me and only me or were you using it as a more generic term? Because when I mentioned it Saturday night you completely avoided the subject," I said and waited for the other shoe to drop because really, this just seems too easy.

He grimaced a little and as I was about to throw down condition number two, he stopped me. "Okay, I know what you're thinking but let me say some things before you get all worked up about this. I'm gonna be honest here, Camie… Yes. I did avoid the subject because frankly, it freaks me out. It'd be a definite first for me and something I haven't ever felt capable of doing, and plus, we just honestly don't know each other very well yet...*but* that doesn't mean I'm not willing. However, before I agree, I need you to accept some things first."

Huh. He has terms too. Well who'd a thunk? I'm honestly kind of unprepared for this, but I hesitantly asked what there are anyway. "Ookaay, what are they?"

"Okay well, the first thing I need you to understand is that I get hit on. A lot. Like all the fuckin' time."

I shifted uncomfortably in my seat, feeling my temper begin to flare. I don't know where he's going with this and scenes from that party are beginning to flash through my head so I'm getting irked in thinking he's about to try justifying what he'd done. Seeing my rising irritation though, Tristan hurried on.

"Camie, it's not something I'm proud of, believe me...I mean people don't understand what it's like. Most of 'em think having chicks continually throwing themselves at me makes me a beast or makes me feel special or important or something, but the fact of the matter is, most of the time I find it almost degrading. It's just that uh...until very recently, I haven't really ever done anything to make my feelings known or done anything to discourage girls from making an um...effort. So, I just need you to be aware of all that because even though I cut myself off a while ago, people still aren't used to the idea of me not being down for casual hook-ups anymore and until they are, chances are excellent that girls are gonna try to hit me up.

"Although, if you decide you can handle all my baggage and shit, I promise you I'll do my damndest to not fuck shit up for us again like I did at that party. Which leads me to the second thing and that is, truthfully Camie, I can fly through water but I *can't* walk on it so contrary to popular opinion, I'm not perfect. I know that might come as a shock to many people and I'm even surprised by it myself from time-to-time so I need you to accept that I'm gonna make mistakes, and chances are, you're going to as well.

"Also, I am *not* Jeff. I don't know how he and Kate do it, but *I do not* wanna go through anything even resembling last week or Saturday night ever again. I mean I understand there's a good chance we're gonna have an occasional argument because we're both way too similar in temperament not to, but seriously Camie, that was just way too much for me. So, can we agree that when we screw up, we don't carry it around like poison until it kills us?"

"Deal. But just so we're clear…I'll be it, right? No other girls?" I need to make absolutely certain that we're on the same page here.

And I think this condition is more than fair, wouldn't you agree? In fact, I think it's an excellent one because I don't want to relive anything like that either.

"Yep. Just you. And actually if I'm being honest, Camie…it's *always* been you," he told me with that lopsided grin of his that I've missed so very much.

YAY!! Oh, but umm, always?

"Um, what do you mean always?" I asked, knowing he meant something other than what I'm understanding.

"Camie, I've wanted to be with you and only you since before I ever met you...from the very first time I laid eyes on you...over *four months ago...*" he confessed and waited for my reaction.

Which was essentially stunned silence...

"Uh, I don't understand," I said because really, I don't...four *months*? How is that even possible?

Oh wait, I got it...he must've meant four weeks...duh. I know I'm a little slow on the uptake sometimes and it's really early, on a Monday no less, but I eventually get it together.

"I wouldn't expect you to. Kate's good, but she's not omnipotent and Jeff doesn't tell her everything when it has nothing to do with her," he informed me and waited for me to put those pieces of information together.

Oh shit! I wonder exactly how much he knows about what we've been up to...it sounds like he's known for quite a wh—wait, what the hell?

"Okay, you're not telling me something...spill."

"Call me, Camie," he said simply, like that was an answer or something.

"*What?*" I'm totally not seeing what he's getting at.

"Call. Me. Do it...right now," he told me, being very mysterious in my personal opinion.

Okey dokey... I pulled my phone out again, dialed him and then heard the chorus and part of Nickelback's "How You Remind Me" as he handed me his phone.

"You changed your ringtone," I said with some disappointment. Not that I have grounds to be disappointed here, seeing as how I changed his on my phone to "Should've Said No" by Taylor Swift.

"Yeah, I got obliterated Friday night after the game and it seemed fitting at the time, I'll change it later," he returned and watched my face as I took in what he was trying to tell me.

The first thing I noticed is that my name is no longer "WHTC PREZ," but is now "My Somebody" and then I saw what he really wanted me to see and...Oh my God. I'm looking at a picture of me sitting on the beach with my arms wrapped around my legs and my cheek resting on my knees almost like I'd been posing for it...and it's *not* one that Jillian took. I know that because she's given me all the ones she had *and* I was wearing a different bathing suit. A bathing suit that's probably taking up space in a landfill right about now as I got rid of it in August. I'd gone swimming one day at my aunt and uncle's and afterwards I put it over a chair to dry, but my cousin's puppy got a hold of it and chewed it to pieces.

"Where did you get this?" I gasped, pretty much stunned silent again.

Well, I guess this answers the question about what picture Jeff was talking about…it's actually a *very* good picture of me and I'm kind of at a loss.

"I took it the fourth time I saw you," he answered softly.

"The *fourth* time?!" His phone slipped from my grasp in my shock.

"Mm-hm. I actually saw you a grand total of five times over the summer…mostly at the beach, but the second time was at the Del Mar Fair when you were there with Derek. I didn't know what you two were all about, but when I saw you again and again at the beach I decided to take the picture. Actually, Jeff had made a joke about the way I was staring at you and that's what gave me the idea to take it… I swear to God, Camie, trying to see you was like being on crack. I went surfing every fuckin' day hoping you'd be there, but, after I took the picture I only got one more day... Then you vanished," he explained, essentially admitting that *he'd* been stalking *me*. Oh the irony…

"You never said anything…then or later...why?" I asked, still trying to wrap my head around all this.

He sighed, looking like he was taking the time to weigh his words. "Well first off, it never seemed like the right time and you were never alone. Plus, I was essentially laboring under the false impression that you and Derek were going out and I didn't feel right about trying to break you guys up…and fuckin' Jeff...he was riding me pretty relentlessly about my little obsession with you over the summer and that's wh—well then you showed up out of the blue at school and I decided I didn't give a shit if you had a boyfriend or not.

"But then I opened a big fuckin' can of worms for myself with Kate… I knew she could've been an even bigger pain in the ass than Jeff if she ever found out about any of that, so I convinced him not to say anything even though I knew she had a pretty good idea of what I was up to. And then I didn't say anything to you because by the time I found out for certain that Derek and you are actually cousins, I was already in pretty deep and again, it freaked me out."

WOW. Did you see *any* of this coming? I sure as hell didn't… But something about how he said all that gave me the feeling he almost said something he didn't mean to.

So, knowing there *was* something he'd left unsaid, I asked, "What did you leave out?"

He just narrowed his eyes at me and shook his head infinitesimally as if to say "Nuh-uh, absolutely not" which of course not only confirmed my suspicion, but it also makes me want to know that much more.

"Tristan, I'm done playing games...if you can't tell me the complete truth after everything that's happened, especially when I know you're keeping something from me, then I won't be able to trust you...period."

I'm totally getting the feeling that I'm not gonna like it, but shit, not knowing whatever it is feels like a slap in the face, *especially* after all the crap we've finally just dealt with.

He closed his eyes and mimed hitting his head on the steering wheel while growling at me or himself, or, both of us...I'm not sure.

"Camie, please don't ask me to tell you this...it's a really fuckin' bad idea and it's not important," he told me, shaking his downcast head.

When I didn't say anything, he looked at me. Then he rolled his eyes and sighed in what seemed to me to be disgusted irritation. "Aw *shit*...this is gonna come back and bite me in the ass, I just know it. This is blackmail you know, so for the record I'm only telling you this under duress because you asked for complete honesty and I can't have you holdin' something over my head that doesn't fuckin' matter one way or another...and I still don't know how you know about her, but I left out that goddamned cheerleader."

Oh shit, yet another thing I didn't see coming and like another bad car accident, I can't make myself stop listening.

"Jeff was being such a *fucking* pain in the ass about you and I couldn't stop thinking about you as it was and it was making me insane! I mean I swear to God, you two were pulling me right the fuck apart and I knew I had to do something before I snapped, and since Jeff sure as hell wasn't goin' anywhere and I didn't even *know* you, I thought maybe goin' back to my old ways for a night would get Jeff off my goddamned back for a while and get you outta my head once and for all so, I fucked the cheerleader. There, are you happy now?!"

My reaction was instantaneous so I really couldn't help it when I bitterly snapped, "And how'd *that* work out for you?" But as soon as it was out, I felt calmer. He was right too, I didn't need to know, but it goes to proving how seriously he's taking what I ask of him, which is great.

"Obviously not all that goddamned well, thanks. *Fuck!* You see?! It's been less than ten goddamned minutes and you're already mad about something I did before I even *met* you...Camie, I can't fuckin' turn back time, okay?!" He railed, but more at himself than at me.

"Tristan, I'm not mad! I mean yeah, I was at first, but you're right...I did force y—"

"Camie, I swear to God this is why I shouldn't talk, we'd get along *so* much better if I just stick to what I'm best at doing...you know what, I'll prove it." He switched gears so fast it made my head spin. Or maybe it was the intensity I felt in his lips that did that...

As per usual when we kiss, we became utterly possessed. Actually, it seems like we only get this carried away if we've been arguing beforehand, which is interesting and something that possibly warrants further looking into. At another time, of course, because as I just mentioned, we're wholly absorbed in the occupation of trying to crawl into each other's skin via our mouths. Thus it wasn't until the horn blew—I think my ass accidentally hit it—that it dawned on me that I was in the driver's seat straddling Tristan's lap. With great effort, I forced my lips from his and started to say something, but he beat me to the punch so to speak.

As soon as I pulled away and took a breath to speak, Tristan smooshed my lips together with his fingers and in a kind of childlike, pleading way he said, "No no, no talking..." Then he replaced his fingers with his lips.

When I just sat there not kissing him back, which took an astonishing amount of willpower on my part, he mumbled against my unmoving mouth, "Okay, this isn't bad but it works so much better when you move your lips too...did you forget how? 'Cause I can show you...see, it's like this..."

I pulled my mouth away again and hid from my expression my amusement at his whimpering reaction. He's totally pouting like a little boy; it's really cute and damned funny.

"Tristan, this is another thing I wanted to talk about..."

He gave up on getting me to kiss him back and chose the next best thing available to him at the moment, which is my neck. Fighting the shivers he's giving me, I tried again, albeit not quite as resolved as before.

"Please don't make this harder for m—"

"Not possible," he murmured and shifted suggestively underneath me, thereby calling my attention to the massive Freudian slip I'd made.

Yeah, I can't blame him for this one though...I totally walked into it.

"Okay, see? That right there...that's my other condition..." I finally spit out.

Jeez, you'd think I don't know how to converse or something. I also finally got his attention, but the look on his face was more like amused consideration. Okay, so maybe it didn't come out *quite* like I thought it did in my head.

"*Ugh*, that didn't come out right..."

"Would you be surprised if I beg to differ on that point?" He asked, chuckling at me with a hint of cocky smugness.

"Not one little bit, and that's the point I'm *trying* to make...I wanna go back a base or two," I told him, being more or less straightforward.

I mean I know that's not the only thing he wants, but I'd be lying if I said it didn't scare the bejesus out of me. Because honestly, I have a really difficult time making sound decisions when we're doing anything aside from holding freaking hands.

My request didn't have the effect on him that I thought it would though…

23.

A Beautiful Morning For Baseball

Tristan started laughing like I'd just told the funniest joke he'd ever heard, but when I just sat there staring at him, he sobered up and his eyes got wide with understanding.

"Oh God, you're *serious*..."

"Dead."

"Bu—wh—*why?*" He stammered, totally disconcerted by my request.

"Honestly, because your ah...*proclivities* worry m—"

"Oh, I don't think I like where this is going...I fuckin' *knew* telling you about all that would bite me in the ass. Camie, we've been over this, I can't go back in time and I can't change what I—" he said before I took the conversational reigns back.

"I know that, and I'm totally not asking or expecting you to either...but Tristan, look where I'm at and where your hands are," I said for added emphasis to prove my point.

He's got one hand under my pants on my butt and the other has been more than busy above my waist. I mean we're at *school* for goodness sake!

"But it's not their fault! They can't help it if they've been given the good fortune to travel!" He defended himself by way of blaming himself.

He really does have a great sense of humor, it just might not always seem like it because of his intensity.

"Besides, you have a really great ass, Camie, that can't be ignored...I mean ignoring the perfection of your ass would be like an affront to God."

"Thank you. But it's not even your hands that concern me so much as my reaction to when you've got your lips on me and frankly, it scares the shit outta me, Tristan. I mean it's just too much too fast. I need us to go slower and go back a bit until we can learn to pace ourselves better. Oh and would you mind re-hooking my bra for me, please?"

Yeah, I told you before, uber-dexterous and lightning fast fingers on this guy. Seriously, Tristan's talent with bras reminds me of Joey from the T.V. show *Friends* who could just look at one and it'd pop open.

While he refastened the clasp quickly and deftly, he kind of narrowed his eyes at me but not in any negative way; it was more petulant than anything else. He then took it upon himself to make sure my bra was in the proper place, which of course made me shiver and gave me goose bumps.

That is to say, goose bumps I couldn't hide, which in turn delighted him to no end so he continued his effort in producing them, *however*, we were still able to carry on a somewhat coherent conversation. Totally wrong, I know…

"So exactly what base are we talking about here? Because there's really quite a bit more than the three and home plate," he asked, doing a pretty decent job of using his hands to distract me.

"Uh…well, this will have to stop…" Of course I didn't have the willpower to tell him to stop. Actually, I'm starting to wonder what my reasoning behind not allowing this was in the first place.

"Why does this have to go? I'm even more fond of them than I am of your ass, which is *really* sayin' something…*besides,* you like it." He sounded serious as he reasoned but his eyes are twinkling so I know he's kinda playing with me.

Oh yeah, I don't think I've mentioned that I finally figured out that his eyes shift in intensity and color according to his mood, which I find both helpful and at times, a little unnerving.

"Uh-huh…I really do, but, uh…that's not the, um…the point here…" I muttered incoherently.

Tristan's reply came in the form of a wickedly cocky grin and an immediate deepening in his remarkable blue eyes before he pulled me down to him so he could kiss me.

"Stop! Hands where I can see them!" I mumbled into his neck the second I realized that my bra had become free again.

"Okay, okay…I'll fight fair," he conceded with a small chuckle. His eyes are still pretty dark, but they're twinkling again too, so I feel I can believe him.

"Thank you. I'm not asking you to live like a monk you know."

He kind of grunted about that while he re-re-fastened my bra for me. "Seriously Camie, if you want me to behave I'm gonna need an idea of boundaries, so, gimme an example of where you wanna stop."

So far, he's been dealing with this far better than I'd thought he would. However, I have a feeling that what I'm about to say will cause some fireworks. But, despite the fact that we're in a very enclosed space, I gave him an example anyway and then cringed, waiting for the explosion.

"Um, I'm kinda thinking during the movies."

"Oh please no…Camie, that's just—" he started to beg.

"That's just what? Unreasonable? Impossible?"

I couldn't help teasing him a little. I knew this was where I'd meet the most resistance if we got to this point and I don't really blame him at all. And although his eyes aren't twinkling anymore, he hadn't exploded, so at least I know he's making an effort to give me what I'm asking of him—even if his hands *are* still under my shirt.

"Well I was gonna say extremely fuckin' difficult, but I like your words better so let's use them," he replied with an uncomfortable laugh.

"No...when we were at the movies *and* at the beach, you had no trouble keeping your hands to yoursel—" I started to say before he cut me off with laughable disbelief.

"*No trouble?* Camie, you have no idea how goddamned painful that was for me! Not the beach so much because I was still pretty much shell shocked by what kissing you is like in the first place and that's why I tried to avoid it the rest of the night, but let's not forget who we're talkin' about here, so trust me when I say the movies took a *hell of a lot* of effort!

"I mean I'm not gonna say it's impossible, but I *really, really* don't wanna have to pick up the bat and swing again after you already pitched me a base hit, you know? I mean come on, that would be considered what...? A foul ball? And honestly, I don't how well I'd handle a bad hit like that, so, what about just tagging up at first a little? Not quite like Saturday night, but *something* along those lines. Still totally in the ballpark but not a foul ball either," he offered as a compromise.

Holy shit! *That's* what he's thinking of as first base?! Good grief Charlie Brown, he's so far out of my league that I don't think I'm even playing the same sport!

Taking a deep breath and trying not to reveal my sudden feeling of inadequacy, I was about to come back with a counter offer when a knock on the window startled me and I did what I always do...I squeaked, which Tristan thought was pretty hilarious. And for whatever reason, *that* embarrassed me. *Nooo,* not telling a guy I'd need gum in order to give him a blowjob, or being more than half-naked with a guy and almost having sex for the time, nor sitting on said guy's lap while he has an obvious erection...no, none of *that* embarrasses me. Nope, squeaking like a timid mouse in front of him...*that's* what turns my face bright red. I'm tellin' ya, I have issues. So because of that, I hid my face in his chest while he laughed and rolled the window down to see what the hell "Fuckin' Jeff" wanted.

Yeah, I'm kind of blaming Jeff for the cheerleader right now. I know it really wasn't his fault, but whatever.

"Jesus, Jeff, you scared the shit outta us," Tristan said, still laughing and hugging me to him.

Now keep in mind I'm still straddling Tristan's lap and one of his hands is still on my back under my shirt. Oh, and the fingers of that one hand are absentmindedly playing with the damned clasp of my bra again. I swear! It's like he just can't help himself!

"Whatchya guys doin'?" Jeff asked playfully, looking to be in an extraordinarily great mood.

"Talking sports and finalizing the terms of our contract…shit, I'm sorry. (I just swatted his hand away, but I'm pretty sure he got one hook undone already.) Oh there, ya see? I didn't even know I was doing that…what do you want?" Tristan informed Jeff, apologized to me, and then questioned Jeff all in one breath.

"Ah. It is indeed a beautiful morning for baseball...I thought you *might* be swimming. Want me to come back for you before school starts, Mr. October?" Jeff asked with a whimsical expression on his face.

He's obviously and totally picked up on what Tristan had implied, and I get his Mr. October comment referring to someone who plays professional baseball and hits a lot of homeruns during the race for the Pennant, but I don't get the swimming part of what he said.

Tristan looked at the clock and then at me for a thoughtful moment. "Yeah, why don't you come back."

"Swimming? How many damned sport euphemisms *are* there for what we're discussing?" I asked once he rolled the window back up and Jeff walked away.

He laughed again and shook his head. "No, he meant swimming literally…it's kinda my habit to get here really early and swim before school. I'm guessing he wasn't sure how things would go this morning either and was checking up on me…*orrr*, nope…he was checking up on you for Kate. See?" He pointed to Jeff talking on his phone.

"Whatever," I said a little testily.

So, apparently all three of them have super human powers of some kind or another in which to read people. I feel so left out.

"Oh Camie, don't be grumpy…where were we? Oh yeah, you were gonna agree to giving me the hit," he said and gave me another slightly cocky grin.

"Uh, no. I think we need to establish that there's a discrepancy in the version of baseball we're talking about playing…you're stuck on fast pitch and I'm still thinking of T-Ball."

"Aw come on, give yourself some credit! You're more than qualified to play in the big leagues. And I hate to be the one to tell you this, o' girlfriend of mine, but *you* are an *excellent* pitcher," he said in compliment with another teasing grin and a little eyebrow waggling. All of which went past cheering me up and took me right to giddiness.

He's really very irresistible when he teases like this and if I remember correctly, this is exactly the kind of teasing that led us to the "Black Thong Bargain" of a week ago, which gave me an idea.

"Okay, I may be qualified but I'd prefer not to leave the minors just yet, so, here's my final offer… *After* the movies at your house, *but,* we keep our clothes on. That way, we can just say you've been walked so the foul is eliminated and there's no need for you to be at bat anymore either."

He drummed his fingers on my butt while he contemplated my scenario. "I can do that but if memory serves, you pitched a fast ball that night and that's how we both lost our shirts…so, what happens in the event that you feel like throwing?"

"Huh. That's a good question…" I took a moment to noodle on that one. "I think I'm much more concerned with you running the bases and me not being able to field well enough to wanna stop you, but I guess if you're not actively *trying* to steal a base and *I* throw you a fast one...? Well, in that case, swing away Merrill, swing away…" I said, giving him the green light with a quote from the movie *Signs.*

I mean if it's me pushing ahead then that's one thing…he was totally able to stop himself that night when all I barely uttered was a sound telling him no. I'm just afraid of not being able to say no if he tries to steal second, third, or God forbid at this point, home.

"Nice! Good movie… Okay, so lemme just sum this up so we both know what the score is… I can hover somewhere around first, provided our clothes stay on and no stealing, but if you gimme the go ahead, I'm free and clear to swing at whatever you pitch, right?" He asked as his eyes flashed.

I think the flashing in this case is excitement…almost like he's excited to actually play baseball. I'm also thinking all this talk about sports may have gone to his head. I know it's gone to mine because I've had the song "Supermassive Black Hole" by Muse playing in my head this *whole freaking time*—it's the song that was playing during the baseball scene in the movie *Twilight.*

"Uh, I think so…Oh! What if I balk?" I asked, wondering about what happens in the event that I *think* I want to do something but at the last minute decide I don't.

"One word and we'll call the game on account of rain," he answered seriously and without any hesitation whatsoever.

"Can you be sure you'll be able to do that? I mean yesterday morning was close…you were *not* in control," I reminded him, remembering my necessary flight.

He grimaced at the reminder but confidently said, "Yeah, but the entire week and everything that went down Saturday night led up to that… Honestly, I'm really not that rabid, Camie. I think we'll be fine if we're not venting a week's worth of frustration and hostility out on each other like we were which is also why it's so important to me that we don't bottle shit up."

Well that's interesting. He's picked up on how carried away we get after or during a fight too. Now I definitely want to make a mental note to ask him his thoughts on that.

"I was pretty damned specific when I chose that song for this morning, so if whatever it takes means that I get nothin' when we're pissed at each other, then so be it. I mean I might not be happy about it, but whatever, I'll just deal. I absolutely do not want you doing anything you're uncomfortable with." Aw, there's my lurking gentleman.

"Okay, but only if you're sure."

"Whatever it takes, Camie," he reiterated with meaning, decisively nodding his head as memories of this morning soared through me.

"Hey that reminds me, I wanted to ask how you came up with *Say Anything*...seriously, how did you know that would get through to me?"

I mean, I don't think he could've picked a better way to make his point. It was very reminiscent of asking me out with Buffy which worked *very* well, but really, how did he know I'd get what he was doing? We really haven't talked a whole lot about my deep and abiding fondness for all things '80s before aside from maybe music, but even that encompassed a lot more than just '80s music.

"Oh, I wasn't sure it'd work because of you wanting time and everything, but I knew you'd get what I meant because you told me to do it," he answered like "duh, don't you remember?"

"*I* told you? When did I tell you?" I don't remember telling him any such thing ever.

"Yeah, Saturday night when I asked what you wanted me to do...you said you weren't sure if I could *do* or *say anything*, and then you said *please* can we just not talk...but the way you said it helped me take your words out of context and kinda read between the lines. So, once I had that, it was just a matter of finding the right song because while 'In Your Eyes' is an okay song, it just wasn't quite what I was goin' for and I knew who'd totally get what I was saying with the other one."

Okay yeah, he so gets me...I love him.

"You're kinda brilliant, you know that?" I gazed at him and watched his changeable eyes begin doing their thing again. "Okay, before we have a violation of our contract, let me call your attention to the fact that people are starting to show up for school and while I'm pretty comfy on your lap at the moment, I don't really wanna invite any other rumors to start circulating...it's gonna be bad enough after Mike's."

"I fuckin' *dare* anyone to say a goddamned *thing* about that," he said with more than a hint of adrenaline. Very physical indeed.

"Okay well, be that as it may, perhaps I should just go back over to the passenger sea—" He interrupted me with a not-so quick kiss and opened his door. "Or, we could just get out and go to school..."

"Oh hell no...school doesn't start for like what? Almost twenty minutes?" I told you, he picked me up *really* freaking early. "I was thinking of doing some batting practice," he informed me mischievously as he followed me out of the car.

"Um, batting practice? Here?"

You should be able to understand my confusion on this point. After all, the most physical contact we've ever had in front of kids we go to school with was at Mike's Saturday night, and that was more like a hostage situation without a gun or a blindfold.

"Mm-hmm." He lifted me up and then set me on the trunk of his car.

"Uh, what about your aversion to PDA?"

Before he brought his lips to mine—with people watching!—I think he might've mumbled an answer to the effect of "shut up and kiss me," but I'm really not sure.

Seeing as how I was indifferent once again, I've no idea what reaction the kids in the parking lot had to our public make-out session in which Tristan did a stellar job of prohibiting his hands from wandering by keeping them firmly planted on either side of me on the trunk. Although he and I were less than thrilled with the interruption and news that it was time to begin matriculating, I bet anyone who saw how Jeff got our attention probably got a good giggle out of it.

We both mumbled a mid-kiss "fuck off" when Jeff tapped us on the shoulders but instead of saying anything to us in response, he physically turned Tristan who only picked me up as I wrapped my legs around his waist so he could take me with him. Then Jeff guided us out of the parking lot and because Tristan can multitask so well, that was how we made our way onto campus and down to our lockers...never once having had our lips separated.

I honestly don't know how he can walk and kiss at the same time, but I'm really coming to appreciate that particular talent of his.

Tristan, quite literally, dropped me off at my locker and then Jeff, quite literally, dragged him off to their first period class they have with Kate, who I have yet to see this morning. I opened my locker to get my math book and thought for a moment I had the wrong one because there was a picture inside the door that hadn't been there before. When I stopped to look at it though, I recognized it's actually a photo of Phineas and Ferb. It looked like they'd been posed sitting next to each other and were staring up at the camera with big kitty eyes, and there's a message in a cartoon bubble written over their heads like they're speaking that says, "We miss you. Please come home." So, obviously Tristan had managed to get in my locker, but I've no idea when or how. I was about to text him and ask but he beat me to the punch again…

Tristan: wanna make out? :-p :-*

Of course my reply was "of course" and all thought of what I was going to ask him evaporated. We spent most of first period covertly text kissing back and forth until I got a text towards the end of class that I read as him being frustrated, which I found pretty funny.

Tristan: fuck this. meet me @ stage after class :-*

Me: what 4? :-*

Tristan: signing bonus! :-p :-*

I have no idea what he has in mind because we only have like seven minutes in between classes, but hey, I'm game! I honestly would've been quite content to sit in the parking lot all day kissing him so if he wants to smooch a little in between class, then I'm all for that! This is *so* the best morning ever! I really think I should take back what I previously said about Mondays because this one? Yeah, pretty freaking phenomenal!

The last ten minutes of class sucked, though. I'd completely forgotten to be concerned with rumors about Saturday night, but when our make-out session ended, all of a sudden I felt exposed. It was like I'd been in a protective bubble that shielded me somehow and now that I'm alone again I can't help but feel like everyone is staring at me. They aren't, but that doesn't seem to make any difference and the damned hands on the clock refuse to move forward. I swear it's taunting me. Add to that my giddy anticipation about seeing Tristan in eight-ish minutes and my stomach is a mess again. When the bell *finally* rang, I nearly bolted for the door. Or at least I tried to.

"Oh! I'm sorry, I didn't mean to run into you like that," I told the girl I'd just practically barreled into, causing her to drop her purse and a binder. I think her name is Brenna, but again, not sure…

"Don't worry about it," she said, but just as I was edging around her, she grabbed my arm.

I felt like screaming, "Oh for the love of God, I only have seven minutes, Brenna(?)!!! Let me go!" I just looked at her instead.

"Hey, I just wanted to tell you that I think you guys are gonna be really good together."

"Huh?"

"You and Tristan. I've been pullin' for you guys. I missed what happened at Mike's after Tristan kicked me and Conner out of the room, but I saw you guys in the parking lot so I'm guessing you two are finally really together now."

Oh.

OH...

"Uh, yeah, we are. Um, I'm really sorry about that whole thing..."

I wish I were still sunburned so no one could see my face heating up. I mean jeez, what do you say in a situation like this? *Yeah, sorry for my boyfriend being "rude" and threatening to watch you and your boyfriend have sex if you didn't leave in ten seconds?* Probably not...

"Oh, it's okay, really. Just um...if you could just not say anything about that I'd appreciate it. My friends really don't like him and they're gonna throw a fit the second they find out we got back together so we're kinda trying to keep things quiet for a while."

"I won't. Honestly, I didn't even know who was in that room...all I could see was carpet." I felt like saying "good luck with that" but refrained because I got the feeling Brenna(?) is in the middle of her own tug of war battle except she's the rope, which I imagine sucks royally when your friends and your boyfriend are the ones pulling you in opposite directions.

"Thanks. You know, you're really lucky you have Kate...Melissa too. It sucks having to sneak around behind your friends' backs so you can be with the guy you really like."

"Yeah, they're the best. Hey Brenna? I'm sorry, I really do gotta run but it kinda sounds like maybe you could use a friend who won't judge you, so if you ever wanna talk or hang out, lemme know."

"Thanks Camie. I'll see you later."

Whew! She didn't correct me on her name, so I must've guessed right. That deserves a little celebratory happy dance, don't you think?

I dashed out of the classroom with only four minutes left; thinking about all the complexities of a teenager's life that up until a month ago, I'd no idea even existed. However, all those deep thoughts flew from my mind on first sight of Tristan sitting on the stage talking to Jeff. He was twirling his car keys around one finger but as soon as he saw me, a slow grin spread across his face and he tossed his keys to Jeff who then turned around and began walking my way.

I think I heard Tristan say something like "If you beat us there, this'll be the first and last time you ever drive it."

"He might try, but don't let him talk you into skipping fourth. He's got a test in trig that he shouldn't miss."

That was it. Nothing else. No "hi" or anything. He didn't even stop or make eye contact when he said it which gave me the impression he didn't want Tristan to know, so, rather than staring at Jeff's departing back with my mouth agape as I felt like doing, I continued over to Tristan, more than a little curious to know what he has up his sleeve.

Turns out, I needn't have worried about the whole seven minute thing...

I glanced at my watch and inwardly groaned. I have three minutes to get to class which leaves practically no time for anything other than waving hi and goodbye. Tristan stood up and I opened my mouth to apologize for not getting there earlier, but he kissed me and before I knew it, he was multitasking again.

The sound of the bell ringing for class to start had me opening my eyes and bemoaning the thought of another tardy on my record. I didn't stop kissing him, though. Well, not until he put me down.

"What was that sound for?"

"I'm late for class...*again*."

"You can't be late if you don't go."

This is true...

24.

God Has A Wicked Sense Of Humor

So come to find out, Tristan's signing bonus entailed ditching both second and third periods. Having never even considered ditching school, well, needless to say, I'm a little apprehensive. He assured me it'd be a piece of cake, what with him having auto-shop second period where the students essentially have a free pass off campus whenever they want to "presumably" run to the auto parts store or test their work. And then with Jeff having office aid for third period, that would get us back on campus with legitimate passes and gives him the ability to doctor our attendance records to make them show we were in class when we weren't. I'm just gonna have to trust him on this stuff, though, because if I think about all the ways this could—to use one of Tristan's phrases—come back to bite me in the ass, I'll totally chicken out.

Jeff delivered Tristan's car to where we were waiting in auto-shop, then we got in it without being questioned by anyone and left school as the shop teacher, Mr. Caswell, looked on and waved. Tristan made one stop at the 7-11 by school for some snacks and a couple of Sharpie markers, and then from there we headed up to the top of Mt. Helix, which has an enormous cross perched on the top of it and the same view of the valley below that Tristan's bedroom window does, only better. Knowing that our destination is infamous for being a kind of "Inspiration Point" like in the old TV show *Happy Days* where people go to make out, I gotta admit, I was conflicted by the expectation of having our new contract put to the test. Surprisingly though, it really wasn't. We did do *some* smooching here and there, but mostly we just talked and I discovered that Tristan was being kind of literal about signing a contract. Only, it wasn't on paper.

He'd been doing some doodling during first period apparently, and liked what he came up with so much; he decided that we should tattoo our commitment to each other with Sharpie to effectively seal the deal in writing. He really wanted to put mine on my ass—Yeah I know, of course he did—but I reminded him that would be a violation of said contract, so he settled for my upper arm, which is where his is going as well.

So, sitting together on the brick wall overlooking the back half of La Mesa and Spring Valley while refining his rough draft, drawing on each other and eating powdered donuts, we took full advantage of the time we had alone. Not fighting or arguing or teasing or making out, we simply talked about pretty much everything under the sun. At one point during our conversation however, some of the happenings of Saturday night came up again and we ventured into the subject of how strongly and physically we react to each other when we fight.

"I was actually thinking the same thing about what happens when we fight, do you know why that is? I mean, is it normal?" He's kind of the expert here, but he didn't have an answer the other night for why we become indifferent to everything around us when we kiss, so maybe he won't for this either.

"Eh, I'm not totally sure what that's about, because like the kissing thing, I've never experienced it before but, I have a theory...wanna hear it?"

My mouth is currently filled with donut so all could get out was, "Mm-hm."

"Okay, well I think we're so right together that when we argue we're really fighting a losing battle against innate attraction, kinda like magnets. You know how magnets repel each other when they're on the wrong side but the second they're flipped, they come crashing together and it takes a hell of a lot to peel 'em apart ag—"

"Wait, did you get this magnet theory from reading the *Twilight Saga*?" I *have* to know.

"Uh, no. I'll admit to being a fan of Buffy, but that's as far as I go with the vampire shit...actually, I think I got the magnet thing from watching *The Cutting Edge* a couple weeks ago, but anyway..."

Tristan stuck the sharpie in his mouth, scrutinizing the artwork on my arm for a moment and then he went back to his drawing and theorizing. I have a feeling my tattoo is going to look a lot better than his...I can't draw to save my life. In fact, here...I'll just show you.

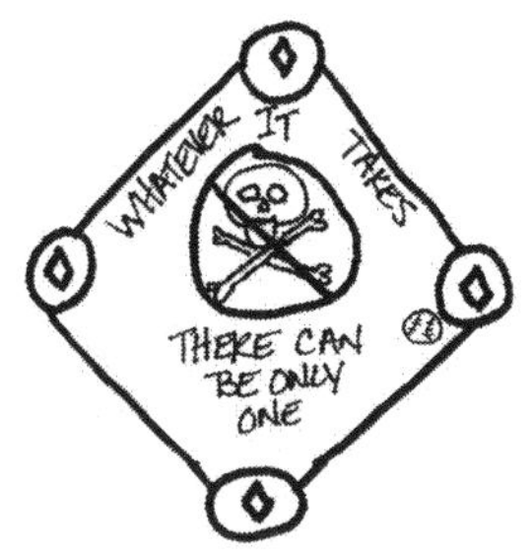

I added the part "There Can Be Only One," it's a tagline from the movie or TV show *Highlander*, which doesn't actually have anything to do with Tristan or me, I just like the phrasing. It sounds way better than something like "Don't forget you're in a committed relationship now and can't go off and screw random girls anymore." The tattoo Tristan is doing on me is *way* better and more detailed…I think he might be adding flames and stuff to it right now. Anyway, just thought I'd share my hideous artistic ability with you.

"Um, where was I? Oh yeah… Plus, there isn't anything about us being together that isn't extremely intense in some way, you know? Regardless of what's goin' on, there's always been electricity between us…like static electricity, we're just drawn to each other. It was even like that for me over the summer and I didn't know a damned thing about you... Honestly Camie, I think if you'd ever seen me one of those times, we'd have gotten together on the spot."

"Really? Because you pretty much ignored me my first week and I definitely saw you that first morning. And you know, it's kinda funny you used electricity to describe it because that's exactly what I remember feeling the first time I saw you…I remember feeling like I'd been jolted by lightning and then in the ocean too, but that was even more profound…I was thinking we would've made Ben Franklin jealous."

You know, he's always made me distinctly nervous in so many ways, but when it comes right down to it, I've also always been very comfortable with him. It's a total conundrum that I just can't explain, but I think that's why I've always been able to talk to him and not sound like a blithering idiot.

He stopped drawing on me to laugh. "Yeah, I got zapped pretty fuckin' hard when I grabbed your arm to keep you from falling that morning, but don't forget, I had a good head start and once you showed up for real, I was well on my way to being totally freaked out by you, so that's primarily why I went slow and ignored you in the beginning. Also, I wasn't sure what you were actually like as a person so I didn't wanna dive in headfirst and then find out you were a shallow bitch, because that would've sucked.

"And yeah, I almost came unglued that time in the ocean…and then when I kissed you and everything just sorta melted away, I didn't know what the fuck to think. I'm honestly surprised I even heard my phone ring. Really Camie, there's weird chemistry between us."

And now I have Oingo Boingo's song "Weird Science" as well as scenes from the movie playing in my head…talk about being weird.

"You really have no idea the amount of self control and restraint I've maintained over the last month…"

"What do you mean?"

"Well, let's see…I've wanted to kill Zack from the very first day, then I made myself leave the football game you went to with Derek for similar reasons, and then all I wanted to do at that first party was drag you off somewhere away from the mass of people. Then at Mike's I was pretty irritated with Wayne and those guys for being where no one should've been, but I did semi-seriously consider talking you into joining that strip poker game (I *knew* it!), which I'm still kinda regretting not doing (of course he is…), and all of that was only the first week.

"The next week was worse because I had a better idea of what you were like and that episode by Pete's pool was such a great opportunity, I couldn't resist, but then you started taking your clothes off...I had such mixed feelings about where I wanted to go with that...and *then* you actually asked me to take your fuckin' pants off! You nearly killed me with that you know."

I love that he's being honest and everything, but I'd be lying if I said that he's instilling the belief that he's not all about sex at this point…which I *know* he's not, I just can't seem to get past my concern that he'll bail if I don't give in relatively soon.

"Okay, you just got really quiet, what's wrong?"

I sighed in response.

"Come on, Camie, we're talking so just spit it out…I know something's buggin' you."

"Well, I don't want you to feel like you can't be open with me about stuff, but…" I couldn't finish. I totally want us to be able to talk about everything, but I really don't want to sound so prudish…it's kind of embarrassing. I mean, here he is with *so* much more experience, and well, I guess I'm just afraid to sound stupid or that he'll think I'm being immature.

"Alright, I think I know what this is about. Camie, look…I'm not an idiot, I know there's a part of you that gets a little nervous about…how did you put it earlier? Oh yeah, my proclivities. I don't know why that is and I really don't think you need to be, and I *know* I don't want you to be, but here's the thing, we need to be able to talk to each other without it being weird."

He has a point.

"Okay, you're right. I just don't wanna come off sounding, I don't know…like a total prude I guess, but I do get a little freaked out about your level of experience compared to mine…I mean for the love of God, you were the first person I've ever even kissed! So I guess I'm just afraid you have expectations I'm not prepared to meet right now and probably won't be for quite some time." *Whew!* I said it.

Wow, that was really hard… I watched Tristan's face as that somewhat embarrassing, but pertinent, information I'd divulged sank in, and for some reason, I was sort of taken aback when one side of his mouth lifted slowly into a "cat who just ate the canary" type of grin while his eyes both sparkled and deepened almost imperceptibly. I don't know what reaction I was expecting, but it wasn't that.

"Um, you're kinda just staring at me...and since you wanna talk without it being weird, it's your turn to tell me what's going through your mind." God, I really hope I didn't make a mistake in telling him that.

"Ahh, several things actually." He stopped to clear his throat and then continued. "First, I certainly wouldn't call you a prude...that would be just as ridiculous as it is completely untrue. And as far as my expectations go...well, you've already exceeded them so you can quit stressing. I've been waiting for somebody like you for a really long time and I'll be damned if I let myself screw this up by wanting more than what I've already been given."

I'm kind of stunned. I mean really, that was very touching and I'm finding myself actually holding back some tears... I did however take note of the fact that he hadn't mentioned anything about my candidacy for having a white wedding. And yes, now Billy Idol's voice has replaced Danny Elfman's. You know, my head is like a freaking disco sometimes. Maybe I should think about hanging a sparkly ball in there.

Anyhow, Tristan had said several things were going through his mind but he only told me two. And well, since we're talking...

"You're editing again, what didn't you tell me?"

He chuckled.

My face started to heat up.

"I think God has a wicked sense of humor, Camie."

"How so?"

"Well, don't you find it just a little bit twisted that He made a ah...promiscuous reprobate and a chaste ingénue rather perfect for each other, threw them together without warning and then for kicks, He tossed in an inordinate amount of sexual attraction and tension into the mix? It's like He's created His own warped version of Thunderdome. I'll bet He's even got Himself a bag of popcorn."

I couldn't help laughing at the truth of Tristan's description and in case you didn't grasp what he just did there, I'll explain. He's using his more than decent vocabulary and movie knowledge to be polite. Allow me to translate: Chaste = Virginal. Ingénue = Innocent or inexperienced girl. Promiscuous reprobate = Um, well...pretty much the opposite. Thunderdome = A Mel Gibson movie entitled *Mad Max Beyond Thunderdome* in which two men enter a giant cage and fight until one of them is dead.

"I can *totally* see that...but um...does my lack of experience bother you?" I'm kind of hesitant to know the answer to this but he's right, there's too much potential for awkwardness between us so we need to get this stuff out of the way.

He chuckled again and his eyes grew one more shade darker.

My palms started to tingle.

"Honestly Camie, it *really* does, just not in the way you're thinking."

"Explain please." Damn. I knew it would bother him, but what I don't understand is how it could bother him in any other way than what I'm thinking.

"Alright, well first of all I'm sure you're thinking I was irritated or disappointed or something to that effect by what you told me." Right again...*ugh.* "But here's the thing...I wouldn't have had a clue I was the first guy to ever kiss you let alone all the rest of it if you hadn't enlightened me. So was I surprised by what you told me? Definitely. Irritated? Hell no. Disappointed? Not in the least. Totally turned on? *More than ever.*

"What I mean, Camie, is I don't think you can truly appreciate how hot I find the fact that no one else has ever touched you...really, it makes me want you just that much more. And *that's* why I know God must be laughing His ass off right now. Hell, He just watched me sign a damned contract that essentially guarantees I'll be spending the foreseeable future being *completely* sexually frustrated and learning patience of all things."

Oddly enough, I don't feel embarrassed or vulnerable anymore. I think what Tristan just gave me wasn't just a verbal reassurance. He gave me power. Over him. And judging from his expression, he not only knows it, but he did it on purpose. He just willingly, albeit not in these exact words, told me that he's completely at my mercy. And, he's okay with it.

I started giggling. A lot.

Tristan turned the underside of his wrist over and checked the time on his watch. Then he hauled me to my feet and gave me a warning before shoving me into the passenger seat of his car.

"Be careful, Camie... Lemme just remind you that I'm not without my own power over you. I remember perfectly well why *you* want the first base part of our contract and if you don't play fair, I might be tempted to use your weakness to my advantage. Even though I'm gonna make a concerted effort to adhere to your guidelines, it's not always the best idea to tease someone who knows the rules better...I'm just sayin'."

Well maybe he's not quite as okay with it as I first thought, but still...

"You wouldn't..."

"Try me."

"Tristan, I'm *so* not gonna dare you to seduce me." I'd lose. In a big way, *and* in a hurry.

"Ah well, see that's a whole other game...wanna play?"

I started laughing again because his eyes are back to normal and totally sparkling so I know I'm out of the woods. "Only if you're cool with me choosing truth every time."

"Actually, I'm good either way…there's something I'm dying to know, but I don't want you freaking out, so…truth or dare?"

Shit.

So I'm either dared to do something I'm not ready for, but will probably enjoy, or I'll have to tell him something that he thinks I'll freak out about. What to do, what do to...

"You're a total pain in the ass…okay, truth." Hopefully it won't be that bad. I would've chosen dare, only to mess with him, but we'll be back at school any minute.

"So says the pot of the kettle."

"Just ask your damned question." He actually just called me a pain in the ass as well, the big loveable jerk.

"Alright, no freaking out… How did you know about the cheerleader?"

Ah. Well I've totally moved past that so I'm in no danger of freaking out, but I think I'll have a little fun with him. "I'll tell you, but you have to tell me something first."

He started laughing and then gave me a grin that warmed the cockles of my heart. That's right, I said cockles. "That's my girl, already breaking the rules of the game…not that I'm gonna necessarily play along, but what do I have to tell you first?"

"Well, I kinda feel bad calling her 'the cheerleader' so, I'll tell you how I know about her if you can tell me what her name is."

"Easy."

"Tristan!"

He started cracking up. "That's not what I meant! It's true, but totally not what I meant… Are you sure you wanna know?"

"You're the one who wanted to play…"

"True. Alright, her name is Samantha. Now, how'd you know? Was it Jeff or Kate?"

"What do you plan on doing to whoever it was?"

"Umm. Nothing?"

"Tristan…"

"Okay, I won't inflict any bodily damage, but can I at least shout at them?"

"Fine by me. In fact, you'll need to in order to be heard…"

"Huh?"

"Well, you don't really know the person who told me."

"Explain."

"It was Derek's friend, Brandon."

"Are you fuckin' kidding me?"

"Nope. I didn't know you guys kinda know each other so I brought Derek to that game to torment y—"

"Nice. It actually worked better that I did know him, especially after seeing you with him over the summer."

"Thanks."

I'm not ready to throw my cousin under the bus for having aided and abetted me in my scheme so that's why I'm not telling Tristan that Derek had actually been *in* on the torment, and why I simply accepted his compliment without further explanation.

"Anyway, he brought Brandon along and when I mentioned your name, he told both Derek and me about your um...grand slam…you're Brandon's hero by the way."

"Beautiful. How did he find out? Because if memory serves, she didn't want her boyfriend finding out…"

"She's a girl, Tristan. Girls talk to their best friends."

"Brandon's her best friend?" For being as smart as he is, this just goes to show how dense guys can be sometimes…hilarious.

"No, you dork. Sara is and—you know what, here… I'll show you."

I pulled my phone out and brought up the infamous email that Brandon copied himself on, which he then forwarded to Derek, who in turn forwarded it to me without having been asked. Then I handed Tristan my phone after he pulled into the parking lot of school. Originally, I'd been too afraid to read it when Derek sent it to me, then there was that whole thing with invading Tristan's privacy, and after that…well, I kind of forgot about it until now so all I still know is what Brandon blabbed.

I watched Tristan's face as he read what I'm assuming is a rather personal and detailed account of what happened and I had to seriously force myself to not laugh as his expression went from mild curiosity to astonished disbelief, and then, to being utterly horrified. Then, and without any warning, he started typing out something on my phone. I lunged to try to grab it back. I failed. Most of the time I love that he's big and strong, but not when he's being a snot.

"Give it back!"

"Uh-uh…not until I'm done."

"What are you doing?!"

"Forwarding it to myself so I have the contacts, *aaanndd* there. I'm done."

He tossed my phone back and gave me a look I couldn't quite decipher. But then when I looked through the email history, the message was gone.

"Wait, I think you deleted it…"

"Hell yeah I deleted it! Do you seriously think I want you re-reading *that*?"

"I never read it in the first place, you ass!"

He started laughing again while typing out a message on his own phone. "Thank God for small favors…"

"At least tell me how you convinced her to get back together with her boyfriend." I really was curious about that part.

"Oh look, a butterfly…"

I rolled my eyes at his attempt to distract me. "I wanna know!"

"I'm sure you do."

"Come on, Tristan, *please?*" Begging can't hurt. I can't stand being told no; it totally grates and just makes me want to know that much more.

"Maybe the next time we play." He's totally teasing me now, the brat.

"Fine. I'll just have Derek send it to me again." Ha! Two can play at that game.

"He won't." I don't know how he can be so confident about that, but he sounds pretty damned sure.

"Why the hell not? He sent it to me in the first place and I didn't even ask!"

"Guy code…I just sent him a text reminding him."

"So? He's my cousin, I think that trumps your stupid code or whatever."

"Not when I can play the MaryAnn card, which I'm more than prepared to do and told him so." That sneaky son of a bitch...he just blackmailed my cousin. And, he's typing again.

"Who are you texting now?"

"Not texting, I'm emailing the person responsible for that serious infringement of privacy, not to mention the partial cause of that huge fuckin' fight we had…I'll let her take care of Sara and Brandon."

Ah. I think I get it now…he's totally pissed, but knows he doesn't really have the right to be. It's kind of funny. And yeah, if I were Samantha, I'd be ready to murder both of them, so I'm sure she'll respond exactly the way he expects her to.

We were walking up to the office for our passes when he got a text—which he actually had the nerve to show me with an extremely smug and distinctly amused look on his face.

Derek: done deal. but i gotta say…bravo man.

"Whatever."

Apparently my irritation amused him further because he started laughing again.

"What's so funny?" Jeff asked from the office window.

"Camie's learning to play hard ball and she's not thrilled about it."

"You suck." I grabbed my pass and went to leave before Tristan caught me by the elbow, still chuckling at me.

"Okay, I'll make you a deal…I'm kinda bent about that whole thing and I don't wanna talk about it right now but maybe another time, so if you want to, you can ask me something else and we can be even."

Hmmm. I'm thinking I might only get one more question out of him and I'm picturing the scene in the movie *Indiana Jones and the Last Crusade*. You know the one…when Harrison Ford is trying to pick which goblet is the Holy Grail and the knight tells him to "choose wisely."

Ah-ha! I've got one… "Okay, who's Phil?"

"*Phil?* I don't know a Phil…"

"Umm, if I may interject something here?" We both turned to stare in question at Jeff who was grinning at us. "Dude, use your verbal photographic memory and think back to our conversation late Saturday night…"

Tristan studied Jeff's face for a brief moment and then rolled his eyes. "Oh shit."

In complete confusion, I looked back and forth between Jeff, who's laughing now, and Tristan, who's shaking his head.

Tristan took his pass from Jeff, grabbed my hand and towed me away towards the lower quad. "So how much of *that* did you hear?"

"Are you gonna tell me who Phil is?"

"What, not who, and no, I'm gonna show you…"

"All of it."

"Why doesn't that surprise me?" He stopped in front of his locker and gave me an unreadable look before he started to spin the dial, inputting his combination. "Tell your sister not to MacGyver the lock on the bus again…there's a key hidden behind the spare tire on the back. Oh, you can also let her know she doesn't owe me the box of Twinkies anymore either."

What the hell?! He's the stupid boy she went to help? My sister is a goddamned traitor!! I mean, I love her for it, but, *so* not the point! I should've tailed her like Melissa wanted to! Oh and see what I meant about the little, blonde sneak's true talent being counter-intelligence?!

"*You* were the stupid boy calling in a favor?" I had to throw the stupid part in there…

He laughed and pulled open his locker revealing a picture on the inside of the door…of the two of us at the beach…one that's been blown up so you can really see our faces…one that was taken right at that profound electrical moment when he almost came unglued. It's a *very* telling picture.

"That's a good one…you should see the others," I commented, staring at the stark emotion captured in our faces.

"After being the recipient of this 'message,' I figured there were more, but anyway, here's your answer." He pulled the picture down, flipped it over and handed it to me.

On the back written in what looks like my sister's handwriting is the following title she'd chosen for the picture, a short message and her cell phone number:

A Water Warrior Saved

Phil. 1:3

Just in case...

"OH! The picture and scripture from your argument with Jeff! I thought the picture he was talking about was the one on your phone, but I totally forgot about the scripture! What does it say?" My knowledge of Bible scripture really isn't what it should be. (Again, sorry God.)

"In light of what would've happened if you'd decided that you couldn't forgive me, I'd say 'I thank my God upon every remembrance of you' was rather appropriate, don't you think?"

"Uh, yeah. She never fails to amaze me... You know, before she left that night she offered to make an example out of you."

"I don't even wanna think about how she'd do that, Camie..."

"Well, I think she was actually hunting for another kind of answer by asking that. I mean she would've totally done some major damage if I'd told her to go for it, but when I firmly told her no, I think she took it upon herself to drop little hints that would keep us together instead. Because I'm tellin' ya, she would've never given you her number if she didn't think you'd need it or that *I* wouldn't *want* her to help you.

"And I mean, look at this picture Tristan...anyone looking at it would know immediately how we felt, and I think it was her way of proving that we weren't fooling anyone with the game we were playing except maybe ourselves. Oh, remind me to show you the message *I* got the following morning...although I gotta say, the stationary she used for yours is way better than what she used for mine."

"Huh... I didn't think of it like that. I thought she was trying to tell me to be grateful for every moment with you. I think that's what Jeff thought too and why he reminded me about the verse Saturday night when you were *supposed* to be sleeping."

"Oohh...is that what the memorizing was all about?"

"Exactly."

"Hold on, I'm confused about something now...she gave this to you a week ago, right?"

"Well, she didn't give it to me directly, she left it and an I.O.U. in the empty box of Twinkies ...she ate the whole damned box, Camie...but yeah, she left it sometime during that ill-fated party. Jeff found it the next morning when we were packing up the bus to go surfing."

"Then what did she do to help you yesterday?"

"Oh. She told me an exceptionally annotated version of what you and your co-conspirators talked about when you got home. Although I could tell she really didn't wanna tell me even that much...I swear it was like pulling teeth to get what I did out of her."

"Yeah, she can be uber-infuriating like that. Even though I love her, it's not always easy having her as my sibling..."

It's true too. Having a little sister who's so incredibly intelligent and whose brain functions on a wholly different plane than yours does makes living with her difficult at times.

"Yeah well, she singlehandedly made me feel grateful to be an only child...well, not really but anyway... I got an idea of where you were at and then she helped me come up with my plan for this morning, but I wanted to keep her on the hook for the Twinkies in case it didn't work and I needed more help."

Well at least she didn't give him step-by-step instructions because that would've pissed me off. Oh wait...did she?

"Well whose plan was it? Because I thought you said you came up with that whole thing because of what I said..." I'm so confused...

"I did. She asked what strengths I had to work with and when I told her about my *phenomenal* memory, she told me to go over everything I knew about you and suggested I replay every conversation we've ever had. She seemed to think that should've been enough to gimme what I needed to get started...and she was right, it was," he explained and closed his locker. "Oh, she also told me I could always resort to guilt warfare."

"*She what?!*" Oh, that's so not cool.

He started laughing at me...*again*. "Relax. She just suggested I might wanna use Phineas and Ferb to play on your parental emotions."

"I was gonna ask you about that...so who picked the lock, you or my evil sister?"

"Neither of us. I got in the same way I had your locker re-painted after Teresa vandalized it...I'm buddies with Henry, the school custodian."

Holy crap...you'd think I'd stop being surprised by now, but come on...

"Seriously Tristan, are there any other skeletons I should know about that you've been hiding from me over the last month?"

"How the hell am I supposed to know?! You keep surprising the shit outta me with what you already know!"

"Okay, how about the Pirate Pun—er, Jungle Juice thing…accident or planned?"

"Oooh, as much as I'd love to take credit for that, I can't. Total accident, but really awesome timing."

"Umm, keeping my bra?"

"Both. Originally I'd intended to return it, but when my mom posted it, I decided to see what you'd say when I didn't. I have one…Derek's text at Pete's party?"

"Oooh, that was fun but completely spur of the moment. I was hoping he'd be cryptic enough to get a reaction from you. Oh, earlier you said something about Kate being good…how long have you known?"

"From jump. I had my suspicions early on that first day because she was watching me like a hawk, so when she caught my reaction to Zack, I knew she knew. Oh, holy shit, I just realized something…she lied to Zack, didn't she?"

"Oh, about me breaking up with my boyfriend? Yeah, totally."

I told you he was quick. In doing the mental math he immediately realized I never had a boyfriend because if I had had one, he wouldn't have been my first kiss.

"Before or after that travesty of a phone call with Jeff?"

"Before."

"Her idea or yours?"

"All her."

"Huh."

"I have another one…what about Pete?"

"What about Pete?"

"Well, Kate was thinking he was spying on me for you…"

"Mmm, no." Tristan answered. Then his eyes dropped to the ground briefly before he somewhat hesitantly said, "He's ah…sorta *known* everything but, I never asked him to spy on you."

"Yeah, Melissa and I didn't really think so but I had to ask, especially when he was so willing to be part of our costume thing."

"Yeah, don't remind me. I'm trying really fuckin' hard to forget about certain disquieting events from that party because if I don't, I'm liable to knock some people the fuck out... Oh, speaking of that, this one's a big deal…what was really goin' on with you and Zack last week?"

"Oh look, a butterfly…" I said and looked around, giving Tristan a dose of his own medicine.

"That's not funny."

"It's pretty funny."

"*Shit.*"

"Sucks, doesn't it?"

He narrowed his eyes at me, growled a little and then said, "We'll talk about this later. Right now we gotta get to class before the bell rings or these passes won't be any good. Want a ride?"

Duh. Why even ask?

When I nodded, yes, I'd very much like a ride, he picked me up and I wrapped my legs around his waist like I had when we first came to school. But instead of kissing and walking, we just talked until he reached the closed door of my class.

"Are you gonna pout the rest of the day?" It's very apparent that he really doesn't like the taste of his own tactical medicine.

"Probably."

"If you're gonna withhold information, then it's only fair if I do too."

"Nu-uh! I'm pretty damned pleased with knowing I was the first guy to kiss you and I wanna know if I'm still the only one! *Especially* if it was him! Besides, you don't have to worry about a visual reminder…I have to see him five fucking days a week."

"Not true grasshopper…I have licorice-girl to worry about running into and that's a far more disturbing visual reminder than yours." Huh. That sucks…now I'm cranky too.

That got me a "*Humph,*" and an "I gotta go, I'll see you in about nine minutes," and then a very distracting kiss before Tristan put me down. I say distracting because I all but forgot I was irritated moments before and I barely noticed Teresa spitting hatred at me with her eyes when I went into my class with a stupid grin on my face.

The stupid grin was knocked clean off my face about ten minutes later…

I left third period still a little giddy from that goodbye kiss and quickly made my way back down to the lower quad for our eight minute "recess." When I first saw them standing together, all I could think about was trying to breathe. Or maybe a more pressing bodily function for me to focus on would be trying to not throw up. It didn't help that Teresa was heckling me behind my back again either. However, when my vision cleared and I began to walk towards them, I noticed Tristan was looking somewhat panicked and—oh my God…this is the funniest thing I've ever seen—he actually has his fingers together in the form of a cross in front of him, like he's warding off the much-evil licorice-girl from coming any closer, which seems to be her intent. I don't know if she thinks he's trying to be funny or what, but her expression changed from being flirtatious to confused when she went to hand him a folded piece of paper.

He freaked out.

The second she extended her hand with the note in it, his eyes got as big as saucers, and all at once he started shaking his head in denial, he raised both his hands like he was being held up, and like she was holding a ticking time bomb, Tristan began backing up in an attempt to put as much space between him and the offending piece of paper as possible as he said, "Take *that* and get the *fuck away from me!*"

The skank still stuck the note down the front of his jeans…

Now I'm pissed.

How many times has he rescued me from Teresa? Yeah, it's totally my turn to come charging in on the white horse. So, purposefully, I walked up in between them and with Tristan's expression upon seeing me being a hysterical mix of wild fear and complete relief, I removed the note from his jeans, noticing that he's holding his breath too. I'm not sure if that's because I just had my hand in his pants or if he's afraid I'd misunderstood what'd just happened, but regardless, I then turned to face my disturbing visual reminder.

"*Really?* What part of 'take that and get the fuck away from me' didn't you understand? Oh and let me be perfectly clear about something else…the next time you put your hand in my boyfriend's pants, whether he's drunk, stoned, or sober, it'll most likely be the last thing you do."

She looked legitimately embarrassed and tried to apologize. "I—I didn't know you two were toge—"

I wasn't having it. "Yeah, I don't wanna hear it. Now run along…" I turned back to Tristan, who's still holding his hands up and shaking his head, but his expression had transitioned into being somewhere between irritated and contemplative. "What?"

"Come on, get up here. I want my human shield." I looked at him in question as I put my hands on his shoulders and jumped a little as he lifted me up again. "I told you this shit happens all the time...and apparently, word about us hasn't gotten out yet…"

"Ya think? What was that you said about visual reminders?"

I have to admit, I'm still a touch pissed off, which he obviously picked up on because he spent the rest of the break proving I don't have anything to worry about with a wholly convincing kiss of fidelity.

After fourth period, in which I endured some looks that make me think word might've gotten out now, I was approaching the steps of the English building when Pete spun me around to face him, causing my sunglasses to fly off my face.

"What the hell?"

"You took off Sunday morn—"

"You're touching her, Pete."

The instant Pete heard the deep rumble of Tristan's voice; he removed his hands from my shoulders and backed up. I turned to see Tristan and Jeff standing a couple of feet away. Tristan was twirling an arm of my sunglasses with his fingers, glaring at Pete. Jeff on the other hand was doing a poor job of controlling his laughter.

"Oh come on! It's not like he put his *hand* down my *pants* or anything!"

"He's visual reminder number two," Tristan told me and started forward stiffly.

"You can't seriously still be upset about those body shots, Tristan...it was nothing! It was just for fun! I mean I don't even remember exactly how many we did, maybe like th—"

"Aaahh! Rain! Rain!"

I don't know what Tristan is shouting about because it totally isn't raining. Actually, the sky is blue, the sun is shining, and it's pretty warm so I decided to ignore what he's going on about and tried to finish my defense of Pete. "—three or four, honestly Tristan, it wasn't like his tongue—"

"Look, a *butterfly*!"

"—set up camp in my navel—"

"For the love of God, Camie! BUTTERFLY!!"

"What the hell are you hollering about?"

I looked around me to see Pete had disappeared—which was probably a good idea on his part—Jeff holding onto the rail of the stairs doubled over in laughter, and Tristan almost towering over me, looking particularly exasperated and slightly pained.

"Oh my God, Camie, I need to teach you about safewords..."

I just looked at him, not understanding.

"Alright, for our purposes let's just say a safeword is meant to be used to keep someone from ah…going where you don't want them to go. After talking this morning, I was thinking we might need one eventually. Well, hopefully eventually, but not until you gimme the all clear to round another base or two. I mean you will, right? Eventually? Maybe? Please?" I think he's really rattled because he's totally rambling…it's super cute.

"We'll see… So, you were trying to get me to shut up?"

"Yeah!"

Huh. I think I have a new weapon to add to my arsenal. Yay me!

I'm also thinking that after my run in with licorice-girl, I'm entitled to have some fun here, so as "innocently" as I could, I asked, "Because you didn't wanna hear about Pete's tongue—"

"Camieee…" I had to bite my tongue so as to not give myself away because what he said was totally meant to sound like a warning, but it came out like begging.

"—being in my belly button?"

I started laughing at his aghast expression.

"You totally suck."

And then since he walked into it, I went for the killing stroke. "Not without gum."

Jeff fell on the ground, laughing hysterically. Tristan froze. Then his eyes flashed and settled into a teasing flicker.

"Any preference to flavor? 'Cause personally, I'd really prefer it if you steered clear of anything in the range of cinnamon."

Jeff uttered a strangled "Ouch" in between gales of hilarity. I'm pretty sure that it was in reference to the idea of a blowjob being done with cinnamon gum but, he *is* laughing really hard so it could've been because he's in pain.

"You know, beggars can't be choosers, Tristan, but as long as it's not grape, I don't care."

"Promise?"

"You bet, but only if you can produce non-grape flavored gum before the bell."

I'm like 99.9% sure I'm safe here because I watched him take an empty pack of gum out of his pocket and throw it away this morning when we came back from ditching and he hadn't bought anymore at the 7-11. He purchased a surprising amount of Lifesavers candy, yes, but no gum.

He checked his pockets and narrowed his eyes at me when he came up empty handed. I started laughing at him and went to walk up the steps, being careful to avoid stepping on Jeff still gasping for air. Then I had to hop out of the way when Tristan attacked his best friend in a desperate search for gum, which of course only made Jeff and me laugh even harder.

"Do Tic-Tacs count?" He held up and shook the little plastic container of orange mints.

"Sorry, no."

Leaving Jeff on the stairs, Tristan grabbed my hand and dragged me to class. The moment my eyes hit Kate, it was my turn to freeze. Kate always has gum.

And he knows it.

"Kate! You owe me!"

"I do?" She looked back and forth between us.

Or at least I think that's what she did but Tristan suddenly shoved me behind him so I can't really see her or make eye contact with her.

"Well no, not really, but can I have a piece of gum anyway?"

I'm trying to signal "no" to her but he's furthered his imprisonment of me by clamping his arms around my body, pinning mine to my sides, and he has one hand over my mouth and the other over my eyes. I give up. My only shot is that the bell will hurry up and ring before she unknowingly sells me out.

"You're actually asking?" Kate asked, more than a little surprised.

"Yeah! I need a piece of gum! Hurry!"

"Uh…actually, I just tossed my last piece."

"You're a liar."

"I am not! I left the new pack in my car. Here, check my purse if you don't believe me…" He let go of me to catch her purse when she chucked it at him from the floor. "What is his deal? And why is Jeff so out of breath?!"

I looked around to the door to see Jeff stagger in, holding his side and breathing heavy.

"What'd I miss?" Jeff gasped.

Having actually gone through Kate's purse and discovering she'd told the truth (thank God), Tristan tossed her purse back to her and dropped to his knees in the middle of the room. Then he threw his arms wide and shouted to the room at large, "For the *love* of all that is *holy*, does *anyone* have a piece of gum?!"

The bell rang.

"Damn it!"

Hallelujah!

Still on his knees, Tristan grumbled and shuffled his way over to his cushion and pulled me down to sit on his lap which totally surprised just about everyone in the class including me. Then he whispered in my ear, "So exactly how freaked were you when you saw Kate?"

I smacked him on the shoulder and moved off his lap to the cushion next to him while he chuckled at me.

"I'm so glad the two of you finally worked things out, I was hoping you would… Oh, Tristan dear, did you need some gum?" Huh. She's not as oblivious as one would think.

Tristan's eyes lit up when Mrs. Henderson handed him a stick of Wrigley's before going back to her desk and her crossword.

I was about to protest a violation of the rules with him having not come up with it in time, but Jeff snatched it out of his hand and hissed, "Dude, that's teacher gum…you'd totally be picturing her face the whole fuckin' time, so you're welcome."

I beamed a smile at "Dear Jeff," but then thought about what he meant. *EW.*

Tristan echoed my mental sentiments by making a gagging sound which prompted me to pat his back like I was trying to aid him in dislodging whatever was blocking his windpipe, and in the voice I reserve for Phineas and Ferb I asked, "What's wrong, baby? You got a furball you need to get up?"

Kate and Jeff started cracking up at Tristan's resulting petulant expression. Oh God, it just gets funnier and funnier.

"Haha. Okay you guys, here's fair warning…the gloves are comin' off. That includes you over there across the room too," he warned while indicating Melissa, who'd been paying attention from her pillow on the other side of the classroom.

Melissa stuck her tongue out at him and started reading her book, Kate and Jeff kept laughing at him, and I began thinking I should probably be very careful about what I say and do around him from now on because, that's warning number two for me...

25.

I'd Like To Thank The Academy

When the bell rang dismissing us from class, I was honestly expecting to partake in the much-desirous event of walking to lunch with Tristan, but he bowed out by saying he'd meet me at the stage in a few minutes. So, with a quick kiss, he left me with my three good buddies. I know it's highly unreasonable to expect him to stay glued to my side, but after this morning and everything, I feel sort of lost when he's not.

And as I would discover, being lost in his absence makes it easier for me to be found by others…

Standing by the corner of the stage talking to Brenna and Conner, I knew something was coming. They were doing a poor job of maintaining their secret by holding hands and it wasn't the sudden looks of disbelief evident in their faces that alerted me; it was the foreboding sensation I felt in the pit of my stomach. Having thus been warned, I stiffened, immediately knowing it wasn't Tristan's arm that landed on my shoulder.

"I'm really sorry, Camie, I would've kept that asshole away from you but he got me with that sucker punch…forgive me?"

He's gotta be kidding. First of all, if you had been there you'd totally understand that it was *so* not a sucker punch, but he also had a verbal warning it was coming. Second, you, me, and basically everyone on the planet now knows I never wanted Tristan to be kept away—obviously. I mean, DUH.

I turned to face Zack and saw that, nope, he's totally not joking. I went to get out from under his arm so he grabbed my elbow to stop me from leaving. He honestly does have a death wish because if Tristan doesn't kill him, I might. I hate being manhandled. Well, by everyone aside from Tristan. For some reason it doesn't bother me one iota when he does it. Go figure.

"What asshole would that be, Zack?" I asked, realizing that Conner and Brenna have abandoned me, leaving me alone with Zack in the shadows of the trees to the side of the stage.

"Tristan the pool boy." Again with the lack of creativity...

"Zack, I swear to God, you need to take your hand off me *right* now...he's gonna have a massive conniption fit and end up hit—"

"Oh God, he didn't hit you, too, did he?"

Oh my God…he can't be freaking serious! Zack let my arm go, but only so he could remove my sunglasses, and then he dropped them in the grass at our feet. *Man*, they're having a rough day today! And really, how stupid *is* he?

I'm gonna go with severely because he then began to check my face for bruises.

"NO! But my *boyfriend* happens to have this odd aversion to other guys touching me, which I'm totally okay with in some circumstances, this being one of them. And if you'll remember correctly, your nose and his fist aren't the best of friends. Besides, from the look of it, a stiff breeze will make that thing bleed again and I really don't want blood on my clothes…that's a bitch of a stain to get out."

It's like he's not even listening because in his search for bruises, he's gotten a hold of my arm again and found my Sharpie tattoo under my shirtsleeve and he's absorbed in trying to figure out what it means.

"This is pretty cool lookin'…what's it all mean?"

I'm starting to not only get kind of panicked, but also, pretty irate. "Seriously Zack, I'm gonna hit you myself if you don't let go of me… Rain Man had more sense than you and he was a re*tard*!" I snapped, my wording and inflection being inspired from a line used in *The Hangover*.

As soon as the word re*tard* was out of my mouth, though, I heard Tristan's unmistakable laughter come from behind me. I had to turn my head around practically like an owl to see him leaning against the trunk of a tree, laughing his ass off, which honestly almost made me as mad as the idiot who's now staring at me like he's trying to decide if my attempts to pull away from him are some form of masochistic flirting.

"Oh God, Camie, please hit him…I'd so love that," Tristan said as he wiped tears from his eyes.

Zack's upper lip curled into an angry sneer and then he dismissively spat out, "Fuck you, Daniels."

"Come on, Camie, hit him…for me?"

This is bad. Tristan thinks this whole thing is pretty funny, but Zack is still clueless and he's getting pissed, and *I'm* caught in the middle. I was considering my options when Zack opened his big fat mouth again. No lie, his upper lip is cut and still a little swollen. Oh, and I think we're starting to draw attention from people who are in hearing range. I'm not sure, though, because Mike's fiddling with a sound system of some kind and there's a lot of feedback coming from the stage where he's setting up. *Ugh*, the awards ceremony that I didn't get to vote in. I'm still irked about that...

"What makes you fuckin' think she'd do anything *you* ask her to?! You made out with Lindsey Gilmore at that party while Camie *watched*, you totally treated her like fuckin' shit last week, and then from what I was told about the rest of Mike's party, you raged at her the whole night…I was just checking her for bruises. So really, shouldn't *she* be hitting *you*? Or are you too much of a pussy to let her get even? Go on, Camie, hit him…he's a dick and he fuckin' deserves it."

What the hell is happening here? Although I haven't heard *any* gossiping buzz about us which is weird, I find it so ludicrous that Zack has yet to figure out that Tristan and I are totally together even though I told him with my own mouth, and now he's actually trying to get me to punch my boyfriend in semi-plain view of the school lunch crowd! I mean really, *WTF?!*

Seeing my angry expression, Tristan's underwent some major changes to look about as mad as I am. In fact, he looks pretty freaking pissed—*at me.*

His eyes shifted color again; he lifted an eyebrow, unclenched his teeth and with an extremely callous and arrogant air that's very reminiscent of when he called me a bitch the other night, he said, "You wanna take a swing at me? Come on baby, gimme your best shot."

I think my life has turned into a damned soap opera…

Seeing Tristan so mad at me over Zack's reminder of *his* behavior last week, like it was all entirely my fault, had me seeing red. I yanked my arm from Zack—well, it was more like he consented to let me go, the jackass—I tossed my hair over my shoulder and then like I was gonna deck him—because by then, I wanted to—I marched up to Tristan who, seeing my angry approach, then dropped the cell phone he'd been holding to the ground and pushed off of the tree he'd been leaning on. I'm pretty sure Tristan knew what he'd done by deliberately provoking my temper like that because the second I got within contact range, I took one look at his face as I raised my hand and then instead of hitting him, I grabbed the back of his head and it was almost exactly like we were back in that room at Mike's house, venting all of our anger on each other through one rather fierce kiss.

I must say; it was a smart, but risky move on his part.

I wonder if sap is as hard to get out of clothes as blood is. Confused about how I go from being immersed in kissing to contemplating domestic endeavors such as laundry? Well, I just realized Tristan had turned us around and now has me pinned against the damned tree. And when he did that, I haven't the foggiest clue so don't ask.

He wrenched his mouth from mine and with a bit of effort he said, "So I can't even leave you alone for like five minutes."

"It's not my fault…no one seems to know yet. But um…about that safeword…I think we might need it sooner rather than later."

Not that I'd be coherent enough to use it. He's totally got one hand under my shirt with a decent amount of my right breast in his palm—I never even felt my bra come unhooked—and the other is once again, holding the back of my thigh, thereby keeping my leg wrapped around his waist. And I really hate to admit where *my* hands are. But, I *will* admit I couldn't resist making the elastic snap back into place when I removed them from his—*Good Lord!*—heaven sent derrière. Also, I don't know where the heck they came from, but *thank You, Jesus* for Jeff, Pete, and of all people, Conner! They're keeping us from being seen by pretty much everyone by standing almost shoulder-to-shoulder in a semi-circle with their backs to us.

"Ya think?" Tristan said, resting his forehead against mine, continuing to catch his breath.

"Where'd you go anyway?"

"Mm. I got you something." He kissed me again, but this time when he pulled his mouth away after having left me a parting gift, he waggled his eyebrows at me and then said, "You know I'll never not have gum again, right?"

I blew a bubble in response.

He groaned in frustration.

"What contest in hell did I win to end up with you?"

"Thunderdome, baby. Like you said, God's got a wicked sense of humor…"

He started cracking up again when I winked at him and blew another bubble.

"Are you two finished making some kind of pornographic point to Zack? Your bodyguard would like to go sit down before the awards ceremony is over."

"Hey, where'd he go anyway?" I just realized that Zack is totally gone…I never even heard a response from him, but I'm sure he must've had *something* to say about that whole thing.

"Oh, well, when you orally accosted my best friend it looked like he was about to say or maybe do something about it, but then Trist felt you up with one hand and flipped him off with the other so he kinda stormed off. The look on his face was priceless though...I hope the picture I took with my phone comes out clear enough."

Great. Can't wait to see *that* plastered all over freaking Facebook.

I looked at Tristan's overly smug expression and when he saw me glaring at him, he shrugged his shoulders. "You can't say I broke the contract because technically, you started it. Besides, your clothes are still on."

"You baited me."

The big jerk totally did all that on purpose. There's no doubt in my mind that he was angry as hell, but he was never angry with me.

"I told you the gloves were off."

He also warned me he knows the rules better and it might be dangerous to tease him. I hope I've learned my lesson, but knowing me, I kind of doubt it.

"You're an ass, but, better safe than sorry…up please." I lifted my arms so he could pick me up again. Which he did without question and at the same time, he re-hooked my poor, confused bra. Honestly, it mustn't have any idea why it keeps getting almost taken off only to be re-hooked shortly thereafter. It's kinda sad. And yeah, I suppose we could just hold hands to get the message out, but this seems to have sort of become our thing, and well… Oh who am I kidding? It rocks!

Kate and Melissa had saved some space on the grass in front of the stage and I was so happy to discover we'd only missed two minor awards. The whole event was a riot. Mike was wearing an actual tuxedo and to be heard, he was using a microphone. He'd also actually picked songs to go with the awards that were in sealed envelopes. And in a beautiful, floor-length gown, Kristen was handing the envelopes out to last year's award recipient after Mike introduced them. That is, if the award had been given out before and if the previous winner(s) were present. The previous winner would then announce the new winner and hand over the award. Most of the actual awards themselves are black metal picture frames with the name of the award, the recipient's name, the date of the party, and a jack-o-lantern all engraved on them in metallic orange. They also have a picture of the winner or winners already in place as well.

Melissa told me that during the opening ceremonies, Mike made a couple of inside jokes only party attendees would get; one was about the body shots, which probably would've pissed Tristan off so I'm glad we missed it. Then he thanked the voting panel and the paparazzi that'd "graciously" taken all the photos. Before the awards got under way, I guess Mike also let everyone know that DVD copies of all the party pictures are available for purchase with proceeds to benefit a group of missionaries in Africa or something like that. I'm dying to see some of them but I'm also kind of scared. It seemed like those cameras were going off *constantly*.

So anyway, as the previous winners and the category were announced, there was subsequently much excited chitchatting and anxious speculation going on about who would be the winners this year. As and far as the awards themselves go, there were several, but here are some of the best:

~ *Can't Hold Their Liquor* ~
Song: "Alcohol" by Barenaked Ladies

(That went to the first person to pass out who was this guy, Jason Kendall. He also still has the Sharpie mustache.)

~ *Funniest Costume* ~
Song: "Plexiglas Toilet" by Styx
(Obviously that went to Jeff. By the end of the night/morning there was so much graffiti and "potty poetry" on him, people had resorted to writing on his arms, neck, and pants. Oh and the song is so damned funny…really, you should look up the lyrics.)

~ *An Awkward Morning Is Better Than A Boring Night* ~
Song: "I Don't Even Know Your Name" by Alan Jackson
(I was a little concerned I was going to get irritated again when Tristan had to get up and hand this award out, which are t-shirts similar to his, but I had to laugh when Jeff stood up to go with him. Apparently there's a story there… Anyway, this was awarded to Stephanie Miller and Lance Paulson. They woke up in bed with each other but didn't know how they got there. Or, what they did together. —Yikes. Now I *really* want to know the story!)

~ *Best Original Costume* ~
Song: "Arabian Nights" from the Aladdin Soundtrack
(You already know that Pete, Melissa, Kate, and I won this one, but the picture was taken when we were fawning over him with the grapes and palm frond…it's pretty cute. Pete accepted the award on behalf of the four of us.)

~ *Yeah Sure, We Won't Tell Anyone* ~
Song: "Our Lips Are Sealed" by The Go-Go's
(Ah. This is why Brenna and Conner were holding hands; the picture is of them right after Tristan had extradited them from the bedroom. In fact, you can see his back and my hair just inside the door at the edge of the picture. During their acceptance speech, Brenna told her friends she was done sneaking around so they could just get over it. I whistled and clapped.)

~ *Best Place To Land A Fist* ~
Song: "Thunderstruck" by AC/DC
(Hilarious! Now contrary to who you may think this award went to, it wasn't Zack. Well, not exactly…it went to his nose. His *nose* actually won the award! The award itself isn't a frame or anything like that either; it's a basketball with a picture of Zack's bloody nose blown up and glued on it with an actual piece of medical tape over it on the picture, and there're

drawn on eyes and a mouth. And it's wearing a wig. I was sitting on Tristan's lap and had to duck when Mike presented Tristan with the award by tossing it to him. Then Mike made a short announcement about the "broken or not broken" bet winnings being paid out after school.)

The last award to be handed out was the one I was a tad bit nervous about because I didn't know what to expect from everyone watching…

~ *Most Memorable Moment* ~
~ Boy vs. Girl in the World Series of Love ~
Song: "U Got The Look" by Prince
(Traditionally, the memorable moment is engraved on the award but since Mike had called it a draw, he decided to combine all of the nominated episodes and gave it the above title that is actually a line from the song.)

I climbed aboard Tristan and he carried me up to the stage to get our award amid much clapping and whistling. Actually, a bunch of people even got to their feet to cheer. Since I was totally blushing—Yeah yeah, I know. I'm not disturbed by probably having tree bark in my hair but being on stage to accept an award I totally earned embarrasses me…whatever.—I was really hoping not to have to make an acceptance speech like everyone else had, so I pretty much kept my face buried in Tristan's neck. He, on the other hand, had no problem talking into the microphone. It wasn't so much of an "I'd like to thank the Academy" kind of speech though, as it was addressed to all the gossips in the lunch crowd.

"Alright, do we have any gossipmongers out there? Come on, don't be shy…lemme see you raise your hands…"

I started cracking up because I looked over my shoulder and saw several of my friends and acquaintances holding their hands in the air, looking a little confused and slightly guilty.

"Ah, there you are. I gotta say, I'm a little disappointed in you guys, so listen up… As much as I'd love to wear my girlfriend like a shirt 24/7, it's a little impractical and I'm sure the school administration will eventually call it a dress code violation, not that I give a shit about what they say, but the point is, you have my express permission to spread the word about Camie and me…so go on, talk amongst yourselves. Oh yeah, glad we could make your guys' night. And Kristen, I'm sorry for threatening to rip the film outta that camera…it's an awesome picture."

I was confused about that last part, but when Tristan handed me the award so he could take something else Kristen was handing him, I saw the picture in our frame is one of me sleeping and using his bare chest as a pillow. He's on his back kind of propped up on the pillows with his eyes closed and his arms are wrapped snugly around me. Apparently she snuck in to get the shot and that prompted our changing of sides in bed, but with the angle from which it was taken, the blanket, and the position of his arms, you'd have to look *really* closely to tell I'm topless as well.

I totally agree with him too, it's an awesome picture. It's also the center picture in a large-ish collage-type picture frame that has photos of every one of our nominated public displays, including a shot of me trying to tear out of Melissa's arms during the fight and a great one of Tristan hitting Zack. Kristen told us they weren't totally sure what the situation would be with us today, but she and Mike really wanted to give each of us something and they had all these fantastic photos, so she put the collage together.

The bell rang ending the festivities and, being that it is Halloween, the extended lunch period which was lengthened due to an optional, school-wide costume contest that had taken place in the "old gym" where we have assemblies and stuff. The ceremony attendees disbanded and Tristan walked me part way to the "new gym" where we actually do P.E. and sports. Then he gave me a sweet kiss goodbye and told me he'd see me after seventh period.

I was watching him walk away, admiring his aforementioned heaven sent derrière, and when I turned around, I practically collided with the Trollop Triplets and Michele. I was still high from everything that happened over lunch though. I mean for crying out loud, I not only have a tattooed commitment from Tristan with his signature on it, but he used a freaking microphone to announce that I'm his girlfriend! It just don't get no better!

So when Teresa opened her mouth to admonish me in some abusive way, I popped off with, "Hey there, Teresa! How's the liver?"

"You're such a fuckin' skanky bitch." She's calling *me* a skank? She who flaunts her thongs in front of everyone with eyes? Hysterical! "So who are ya gonna get to stop the rumors for you now? There's no way anyone will deny all of *that*! You're *never* gonna live down what happened at that party."

Huh. She must've missed the awards. Well, I guess I should enlighten her then.

"Why would I wanna deny anything that happened? Actually, I was hoping to run into you, just not quite literally…don't wanna get your fleas and all…but if you could do me a favor when you spread your rumors this time, could you please be sure to mention that I got an award? See?" Since Tristan has the collage with him, I held up the engraved picture frame for her to gape at. "I mean come on, there was voting and even a song! Oh! And you can call me a bitch all you want, but again, please don't forget to mention that I'm a bitch with one smokin' hot boyfriend. We even have matching tattoos, except of course, that's Tristan's signature…I signed him." This time I pulled my shirtsleeve up to bare my arm to the shoulder so she could get a good look at Tristan's signed artwork. "Anyway, it'd be super if you could make sure to work all that in there, he and I would really appreciate it, thanks! See you guys later!"

I gotta admit, that felt good. So good in fact that I almost want to turn back around and rub it in a little more. But, no. That would be overkill, don't you think? Maybe I can talk Tristan into doing a little gratuitous smooching in front of her sometime though. That could be fun.

I'm starting to think that Tristan's little lunch speech had effectively greased the wheels of the rumor mill. Well, it's not really a rumor going around, but you know what I mean. A bunch of the kids in my P.E. class were talking about what they heard about Mike's party and because there were *very* few underclassmen there, they were asking me what was true and what wasn't. It was a little weird. I wasn't embarrassed or anything, but some of the awed looks I got from people, both girls and boys, who obviously think of Tristan as a god or as their idol, made me sort of uncomfortable. Even though, I'll be honest here, I still fall in that category myself. The god one, not the idol one... So anyway, I was grateful for both Kate and Melissa in dance when they fielded the majority of questions worth giving an answer to with experience and expertise.

I guess this is what it feels like to be able to write your own ticket socially. It's popularity. And it's the good kind, but it's odd. I can now totally understand and appreciate why Tristan prefers to keep what he does private—even if it doesn't always work.

I also found out Tristan was completely aware of our bodyguard waiting in the wings during lunch. During dance, Kate told me that Conner had told Jeff what was happening and he in turn grabbed Pete. The three of them were just kind of observing but when Zack started running his mouth and they realized how Tristan wanted to handle it, Jeff sent Tristan a text letting him know they had us covered. And you might think I'd feel a little weird about Jeff knowing so much about how Tristan and I are together, but I don't. Jeff is good people just like Kate and I've kind of come to love him like a brother.

Anyhow, when the bell rang and school was officially over, Tristan, Jeff, and Keith, who's pretty much cut ties with Zack for the time being, joined Melissa, Kate, and me in between locker rooms for some frivolous flirting. Well, the other four did; Tristan and I don't really flirt. We tease, and we tease well, but it's not the same. And actually, a lot of times we were asked what we were talking about or what was funny because we were communicating in inside jokes that we haven't yet seen fit to share. Tristan never quite gave a direct answer to those questions either. During one of those instances, Tristan had taken his shirt off and was about to pull it over my head like he had during Mike's party when I was holding my torn top to my chest, when Melissa stopped him.

"Oh, you have one too… Camie, I hate to say it but, you can't draw."

"Yeah I know."

"So um…what is this exactly?" She asked, examining his arm and then mine in comparison.

"Our contract," he said it so simply but the look he threw me when he did gave me goose bumps. "Oh, that reminds me…be right back."

I shrugged my shoulders when he left us to go into the boys' locker room. Thankfully, "Dear Jeff" distracted Melissa from scrutinizing my tattoo further, and then she and Keith departed to the appropriate locker rooms to change as well. And it's not that I don't trust her or Keith or anything like that at all, but some things need to stay between Tristan and me. Kate might know what the symbolism means and she might not, but she hasn't asked and I doubt she will. And since I can't help it if one of Jeff's super powers just happens to be that he can pick up on almost any inside joke, whether he was inside or outside, I don't really care that he knows what it all means. Besides, he rarely says anything that Tristan or I would consider an invasion of privacy. He might tease us, but no one really gets what he's teasing us about, so it's okay. It's like he speaks in code.

OH! I can speak in code! I have a power! YAY me!

Having changed into his regular clothes, Tristan came back out and tossed something at me.

I caught the pouch of Big League Chew bubble gum and raised my ear to him as he bent to whisper, "For when we bring you up from the minors."

Then he pulled the cap off a fine tip Sharpie and added the letters NWOG on my arm in between second and third base where the short stop would play.

Yeah, he can keep dreaming, but I've discovered I like messing with him so I opened the pouch and pulled out a decent amount of the stringy gum, stuck it in my mouth and gave him a "look."

"Keep it up Camie…"

"I thought I was." I couldn't help it.

His eyes flashed at me and I worried for a second that I should've maybe just kept my mouth shut but he recovered fairly quickly. "Okay, enough of that, you're gonna get yourself in trouble. I'm gonna go collect my winnings from Mike, you go get changed and then we can get the hell outta here."

"Oh yeah, I almost forgot about that…wait for me." Jeff said over his shoulder as he ran into the locker room to change.

"You bet?" I asked. I don't know why I'm surprised though.

"Yeah, before I left Mike's on Sunday."

"Broken or not broken?"

"Totally broken."

"How did you know?" He just gave me a look like he was wondering how I could've had any doubts. "Well, it did look pretty ugly today but you didn't even see him after the fight so, I'm just wondering why you're so sure." I mean *I* certainly wouldn't have put money on it or anything.

"Trust me, I'm the one who did it…it's broken."

"I heard a doctor say it's actually kinda hard to break a nose," Kate commented.

"Nah, it really just depends on the angle and placement of where you hit 'em. It only took me one hit…I felt it go the second it did."

"You say that like you're disappointed or something." Actually, it sounded like he wasn't satisfied with having "only" broken a bone in Zack's face.

He gave me another look but I couldn't figure this one out. "Hurry up, go get changed and I'll meet you at the car."

"What car?" This time I was able read his expression. It was one of questioning how I'd had the time to get a lobotomy while he'd been changing. "Well how am I supposed to know?! I don't know what you do after school! I mean you have water polo um...stuff, homework, and umm, whatever else it is that you do and I don't like to just assume, you know?"

"Okay, well, let's put it this way," Tristan said to me and then turned to face Kate who was giggling at me. "Kate, you are hereby relieved of your chauffeuring duties indefinitely. And Camie, you might wanna call home and tell your mom you're gonna be late. I wasn't bullshitting with that picture I stuck in your locker...the girls miss you." Then he kissed me on the forehead and wandered away to find Mike.

Kate and I walked back into the locker room together and while we were swapping our dance clothes for regular attire, I asked her what she thought about that look of his that I couldn't decipher.

"He won't say it, but I really think Zack got off easy. Tristan's very much aware of his temper and that's essentially why he avoids people and situations that have the potential to get the better of him through it. Now throw in his massive jealousy over you and it's a wonder Zack even walked away from that fight. That's also why Jeff's been laughing his ass off about how Tristan's been treating Pete. He thinks Tristan's jealousy is hysterical and honestly, I think it's a little funny too."

I kinda do too...

26

Do You Wanna Tell 'Em Or Should I?

On the way to Tristan's, I asked him about the whole jealousy thing. Really, it's funny and all but I'm wondering if it'll ever ease up.

"So um, I wanna ask you something and I kinda need a straightforward answer."

"From the sound of that, I don't think I'll like being straightforward but ask away."

"Well, is the whole jealousy thing ever gonna wear off? I don't think I'll mind too much if it doesn't, but if that's the case then I need to have this information before I unknowingly cause another brawl by simply being friendly with another guy."

He gave me a quick glance that looked to me like just the *thought* of me being friendly with another guy isn't something he wants to consider. "I don't know, but I kinda doubt it."

"Okay, well how about giving me some guidelines…like with Pete, I don't wanna come between you guys."

"Pete and I are good..." I just waited because he totally said it like there was more. His eyes flicked to me again and he finished with a grin. "…*As* long as he doesn't touch you."

"At all?"

"At all."

"You can't be serious about that." I mean really, it's not like he has anything to worry about with me and another guy, especially Pete.

"I can and I am. It's not just him though… Really, Camie, I don't want a single other person of the male persuasion laying a finger on you."

Well I guess that answers my question then.

"Not even high-fives? Oh, and what about family? Because we're huggers and I'm prone to holding Derek's hand."

I'm kind of teasing him now. I really don't mind that he's jealous. In fact, I kind of like it. I'm thinking of it as one of the ways he has to show me how he feels about me without saying it.

"Holding hands with Derek is debatable...I remember how you used him to torment me all too clearly. High-fives I can probably handle. Hugging immediate family's okay too, but anything past hugging and I'll have some of the same issues God would have. Also, I can't guarantee hugging anyone past a first cousin will go over well."

He's got a really cute grin on his face now so I know he's playing along and able to find the humor in an otherwise sober situation, which I find to be sort of a relief. I mean sometimes, you just gotta be able to laugh at yourself, you know?

"Maybe I should just wear a hazmat suit." I'm totally joking, but I do think his earnest jealousy makes me hazardous to other guys' health.

"Hey, there's an idea!" He said and started to laugh.

"It might help you out with keeping to our contract too…I'm sure it'd slow you down at least a little bit at getting my bra undone."

"Nah. Zippers, snaps, hooks…pretty much all the same."

"I could look into padlocks…"

"I'd say be my guest, but I think I'd take it as a challenge and I'm sorta competitive. Besides, you're enough of a challenge on your own and I have a feeling you're not gonna make it easy for me to keep my end of the bargain as it is."

"Warning or threat?"

"Neither. I think I'm screwed."

"Well *that'd* clearly be a contract violation."

Tristan gave me another quick look and said, "You see my point."

He pulled down into the long driveway of his house and parked next to a Land Rover that I haven't seen before. I'm guessing it belongs to one of his parents, but I wasn't expecting to meet either of them today so all of a sudden, I'm finding myself approaching something like a panic attack. All I can think about is the conversation about my bra written in his bedroom. I'm assuming the damned thing is still hanging on the bulletin board too.

Ugh. This is gonna be uber-uncomfortable, I just know it.

"Relax. It'd have to happen eventually. If it helps, they'll be more afraid of you than you are of them," he said, chuckling at his little joke that was meant to induce confidence.

"I find that extremely hard to believe, Tristan."

"No, it's true! Watch, they won't know what the hell to do."

"Why not?"

"Hi, remember me? The recently reformed promiscuous reprobate? Yeah, I've never brought a girl home except Kate, and well, she doesn't count. Plus, the only time she's ever been here without Jeff was when my parents babysat her and even then, he was almost always here too."

Crap. That makes it even worse.

I started whimpering and dragging my feet.

"Want me to distract you before we go in?" He waggled his brows at me and gave me a teasing grin.

"NO! Are you kidding? I'm so not gonna meet either of your parents right after you kiss me! I'll look like I'm on drugs!"

He laughed at me. "Not either. Both."

"What?!"

"They're both home. Come on, let's get it over with…I promise you'll be fine but, how much do ya wanna bet one or both of them starts drinking before we leave?"

Oh God, please help me not make a complete moronic fool out of myself.

He led me to the door and gave me a really quick kiss, which actually did calm my nerves. Well, not exactly calm them, but I *was* more relaxed when he took me into the house and into the sunk-in family room where sitting in separate, but really comfy looking chairs were his parents. Tristan's dad was reading a newspaper and his mom was reading a book. I zeroed in on the title and saw that it was Homer's *The Odyssey*. Okay, nothing to freak out about…it's just a little light reading. NOT. I mean I've read it and I enjoyed it too, but it's not exactly what normal people read to pass the time, you know?! Anyway, his parents both welcomed him home but neither of them looked up as he led me by the hand to the sofa and plopped down on it, pulling me with him as he put his arm around me.

"So, how was your day?" His dad asked and I noticed he wasn't exactly "reading" the paper. He was doing the *New York Times'* crossword…in freaking *ink*.

Well, that's not intimidating at all either! And again I say *ugh*.

"Eventful," Tristan answered with nonchalance.

"How so?" This came from his mom. It's kind of funny, they have *no* idea I'm sitting here.

"Do you wanna tell 'em or should I?" Tristan asked me as he stretched his legs out on the table in front of us, looking particularly amused—and smug.

"Why don't you..." The sound of my voice totally got their attention though, and I have to give him credit here, Tristan did a splendid job of keeping his laughter at their shocked expressions from coming forth.

"So be it."

Uh-oh. That doesn't bode well… From how he said it, I immediately remembered that that's a line from Jillian's theme song "Don't Tread On Me" and now I'm wondering if he's finally going to get even for the teasing I've been doing today. I'll kill him if he does…

"Well, first I made a spectacle of myself this morning, however I had an excellent reason and it paid off, so I ditched two classes and got a tattoo, and then two girls put their hand down my pants, separately of course…the first chick pissed me off, but the second one is welcome to visit any time."

He's not getting even, but I still think I would've been better off telling them. And he said all that like it could've been an everyday occurrence! Once again, ugh.

"Let's see, what happened next? Oh yeah, I aced the test I took in trig, I missed an opportunity because I didn't have gum so I bought some, then I asked to be hit, I presented one award and accepted a couple others for my behavior Saturday night, and then I invited the gossips to talk about why I'd been violating the school's dress code all day. And finally, I won two hundred bucks. I think that's it.

"Oh, I almost forgot…this is Camie. Actually, her name is Cameron but I tried it out once and it didn't feel right, so, I prefer to use the cute nickname. And you guys probably won't believe this, but it just so happens that the events of her day sorta acted as a catalyst to mine. Well, aside from the trig test that is."

I couldn't help it. I clapped.

Tristan said, "Thanks baby," and then he beamed a not-so innocent smile at his parents who are still wide-eyed.

"Eventful indeed," his mom said, having finally recovered from her shock of either having me in their house or his version of our day, I'm not sure which.

And now that I can see them without leaves obstructing my sight, I can totally see where Tristan gets his god-like build from and if Tristan's body looks this good at his dad's age and we're still together, then I gotta say, WooHoo for me! He gets his drop-dead gorgeous good looks from his mom though. She's *beautiful.* And he totally has her eyes.

"He gets his sense of humor and good taste from you my love," his dad said and winked at his mom whose eyes are doing that sparkling thing that Tristan's do.

"Ah, I'm so sorry. In my shock I've lost my manners…it's such a pleasure to actually meet you, Camie."

"You too, Mrs. Daniels."

Tristan started laughing at his dad's awkward expression and then with a rather mild Texan twang, his dad explained. "Darlin', you gotta forgive us, his friends have been callin' us Mom and Dad for so long that when we hear Mr. or Mrs. Daniels come outta a young person's mouth, we automatically think of my parents. I'm Stan, that's Trinity, but you call us whatever your pretty little heart desires."

Aw, how sweet is that? My pretty little heart… I think I'm blushing.

"Really dear, we're just glad he brought you home."

"*He's* sitting right here you know," Tristan said blandly, but when I looked at him, his expression was still amused.

"Then *he* won't mind tellin' us 'bout the two hundred bucks. How'd that happen?" His dad asked enthusiastically.

"Oh, there was a bet on whether this guy's nose was broken in a fight at Mike's party. Most people went with the safe odds but I knew for a fact it was."

"How'd you know that?" His mom asked, fairly interested in the same way I was when I'd asked the same question earlier.

"I'm the one who broke it."

"I just hope ya had a good reason," his dad responded without any condemnation in his tone.

"I had excellent provocation plus, I won an award for doing it!"

"Tristan, what in the world did he do to make you want to hit him hard enough to break his nose?"

All of a sudden I became aware of the tension in Tristan's body next to me and I could tell he wasn't happy thinking about the answer to his mom's question, so I thought I'd help him out.

"He put his hand on my butt and tried to kiss me."

"Yep, that'll do it," his dad said, nodding his head in obvious approval.

"I would say so," his mom said in understanding.

"Yeah, that made him really very unhappy," I agreed with them.

"Okay, so on that note…if you two don't mind, I'll catch you up on everything else later. Camie hasn't seen Phineas and Ferb in over a week and they miss her."

With that abrupt statement, Tristan pulled me to my feet, tossed the basketball to me, grabbed the collage and then led me up to his room.

When he opened his door he called out, "Mom's home!"

Upon hearing his voice, our two little bundles of fur materialized from under his bed and came running. Grinning, I dropped to ground and cuddled them both as they climbed on me and began to purr. I almost forgot how completely adorable they are.

"My parents said I can keep them, so we can pack them up and I can bring them home with me when you take me."

"Well, I was thinking about that, Camie…I'm pretty attached to the little buggers."

"Oh." I wasn't expecting that. I guess he can keep them…it's not like they wouldn't be cared for here or anything; it's just that they've grown so much over the last week and I missed it.

Tristan was watching me play with them and I think he could tell I was disappointed with the idea of not getting to see them all the time. "I might have a solution though if you're game…wanna hear it?"

"Tristan, we can't split 'em up." I'm thinking that would really be the only way for him and me both to have them and that's just not gonna happen. No way am I going to separate them after all they've been through. I'd rather he just keep them.

"Oh God, I wouldn't dream of splitting 'em up! I was thinking of shared custody."

"Shared custody?" Huh. I never even thought about that.

We talked about that option for all of thirty seconds; decided it could work and then we came up with a rotation schedule while Tristan affixed a piece of paper over the picture in the collage of Pete in mid-slurp on which he'd written:

By Penalty of Death,
Do Not Remove.
EVER.

Then he hung the collage on the wall next to his bed. The schedule we agreed on says that I'll have the kitties one week, he'll have them the next and so on. That way they won't get used to being at one house for too long and since they've already been here for a week, it's my turn to have them. We also decided that in the future, we'll do the swapping on Saturdays or Sundays.

From what Tristan says, Phineas and Ferb eat like they're starving all the time so it wasn't just that first night, but after having played with them long enough for them to get hungry and actually watching them scarf their food again, I'm starting to wonder how much these cutie-critters are gonna eat out of my car fund. Really, I don't have a clue where they put it all. When they were done eating though, we packed up about half of their stuff and went to my house.

Oh and he was right by the way. I had to keep myself from giggling when we said goodbye to his parents because on our way out, Tristan jerked his chin in their direction, indicating that I take note of the fact that his dad was drinking a beer and his mom was holding a glass of what looked like champagne. All in all, the awkwardness I'd expected never really made an appearance and I feel like his mom and dad actually really like me, so I'm calling it a huge victory. After my unexpected meeting of his parents though, I was thinking Tristan might be a little concerned about having to meet mine. After all, my dad has already threatened Tristan's life, you know? I waited until he pulled up to my house and then I warned him.

"Okay, fair's fair...you have to meet my parents."

"I'm not worried. Parents love me." He gave me a cocky grin and turned the car off.

"And I'm gonna have to tell 'em about the age difference." I stifled my own amusement at his obvious discomfort about that.

"Maybe you can tell 'em about that when I'm not here..."

"I could, but that wouldn't be nearly as much fun. Come on, you big chicken…"

"Easy for you to say…my parents weren't cleaning hand guns."

I laughed about that but was thinking to myself that *his* parents were engaged in some intellectually intimidating activities instead. Apparently the rule about brains and/or good looks skipping a generation doesn't apply to Tristan's family.

We walked in the house to find Jillian sprawled on the couch with her back to us watching *John Tucker Must Die.*

Noticing what she was watching, Tristan said, "Hey Jillian. I see you're brushing up on vengeance plots." At least he gets it.

Without turning her head to look at him or give him a single word of hello, she raised her hand backwards to give Tristan a high-five.

"Where're Mom and Dad?"

"Dad went in late so he's not home yet, Mom's in the kitchen, and our new phones came in today...yours is on the kitchen table."

Hmm, I wasn't thinking I'd have to go through the introduction twice, not to mention informing them of the age discrepancy twice. That bites. I don't think they'll *really* freak out, like not allow me to see him or anything, but they might shorten my leash quite a bit, which would fairly well stink, in my humble opinion.

"Okay well, we're gonna get Phineas and Ferb settled in my room and then I guess go into the first wave of battle." I probably should've phrased it better because Tristan shot me a look like I'd robbed him of the chance to have worn armor.

"You gonna tell 'em?" Jill still hasn't taken her eyes from the TV but I know exactly what she's asking.

"Yeah. It's time to git-r-done."

She finally consented to tip her head back, but she was looking at Tristan when she said, "Chill-ax. Legally all they can get you on is contributing to the delinquency of a minor and there's no jail time with that."

Fabulous. Thanks Sis...

I looked at Tristan's face. He was slowly nodding in agreement and looking somewhat contemplative when he said, "True. I get to worry about that in February."

"What are you two going on about?" I thought she was just giving him a hard time but they're both being more or less serious.

"California State Law regarding age of consent," my sister answered matter-of-factly, having gone back to watching the movie she's seen like seventeen times.

"How do you know this?"

I was asking Jillian primarily so I was hard pressed not to laugh when she and Tristan answered in unison.

"I looked it up."

"When?!" This time I was mostly interested in hearing from Tristan.

"The night of your first day of school after I found out you were fifteen."

"Same here."

Her admission doesn't surprise me...she did tell me she'd have my back regardless, but his kind of did. Then again, it probably shouldn't have. I have a feeling Tristan is the kind of person who does his homework.

I rolled my eyes at them and said, "Whatever. I just kinda wanted to tell them together. I don't really relish the idea of going through it twice."

Sighing in resignation, I headed up to my room with a kitten supply laden Tristan following close behind me as if I were a shield.

"Do you think I can pass for sixteen?"

I laughed. "I doubt you passed for sixteen when you *were* sixteen."

"Humph."

We were getting the kittens settled—and fed again—when Jillian came in—uninvited—and after dropping my new phone on my bed, she then proceeded to wave my baby scrapbook in front of me. Oh and the new phone is simply because my dad's company—which pays for all the employee's and their families' cell phones—changed service providers so we all had to get new phones...

"What am I supposed to do with that?"

"Really Camie, do I have to do *all* the problem solving here? I can't believe you don't remember..."

I went to take it from her but she held it out of reach and said, "Not so fast." Then she turned to Tristan, handed him a piece of paper and a pen and said, "Sign it."

I honestly can't fathom what kind of contract she would've drawn up for Tristan to sign, but apparently he had no problem with it because he laughed and signed his name without question or hesitation. When he handed it back to her, she in turn handed *my* baby book—with all the embarrassing naked bath pictures, etc...ad nauseum—not to me, but to *him*! She really, *really* infuriates me sometimes.

"Hey!" I went to grab it, but she swatted my hand out of the way.

"Nuh-uh. This is your punishment for having forgotten and making me save you guys. *Again*. Page two, Bus Boy." Bus Boy?

"Lemme see that..."

I swiped the contract out of my irritating sister's hand while my first-ever boyfriend opened the infantile tool of mortification. Yeah, it's no longer a baby book; it's an implement to be used to send me scurrying under the darkest rock I can find.

I can see why he thought the "contract" was funny though. Jillian was practicing CYA and covering her perky backside with a signed statement that essentially absolves her of owing Tristan Twinkies or any snack food whatsoever, as well as stating that he will not now or in the future press charges against her for breaking into his bus that night. In fact, it states that he is to never bring it up to her or anyone else for the duration of both their lives.

"Ah. We're good," Tristan said to himself. Then, still studying my damned book, he said, "Uh Camie, in light of the situation we find ourselves in, I think we should thank your sister for remembering something that you really should've."

"Okay, thanks Jill. Now what the hell is it with page two of my baby boo—" Oh shit. I feel like such a moron.

"Took you long enough. Oh and if you want my advice…"

"Yes please, Master Yoda," I replied to my sister the savior.

"Tell Mom now."

"Good day?"

"Great day. Dad went in almost two hours late," Jill told me with raised brows. Ah. Quality time with Dad *without* the kids. "Besides, he's already got an in with Dad."

"Oh yeah, I didn't really think about that."

"Are you two gonna share?" Tristan asked, slightly irritated that he's having a hard time following our "sister speak."

"Cars. He loves 'em. In fact, he drives a '66 Nova."

"Oh shit, why didn't you say that before? This is gonna be easy."

And it was.

My mom was humming to herself and making dinner when Tristan and I walked into the kitchen holding hands. She took one look at us, studied Tristan for a somewhat disconcerting moment, and then with a quirk of her lips she asked, "How much?"

"Not much more than between you and Dad."

Page two of my baby book has photocopies of my parents' hospital pictures and all their birth trivia including their birth dates. You see, my parents *were* high school sweethearts and they *did* graduate together, but I'd totally forgotten my mom skipped two grades, one in elementary school and then one in high school. My mom is wicked-smart like Jillian is and she and my dad wanted to graduate together and get married that summer. I wasn't born until like five years after that, so no, it wasn't a shotgun wedding; they just really loved each other. My mom's parents were all for it, having been raised by parents who came from the Midwest during a time when people got married really young and had a butt-load of kids to help work on the farms and stuff. It's interesting how some family trends and lifestyles are passed down through the generations, isn't it?

"Damn it. That doesn't make me very happy, Camie (oh crap)…I owe your father twenty dollars."

"Excuse me?" I'm really thinking, *"What the hell?"*

Seriously, they placed a bet? What is it with everyone around me gambling lately?

"Your father's guess is that he's about two years older, I went with about a year and a half."

Just so you know, my dad is around a year and nine months older than my mom, so when I said there wasn't much more of an age difference between her and my dad, my mom knew she'd lost the bet.

"Tristan, is it?"

"Yes ma'am." Tristan's doing a stellar job hiding his amusement and maintaining a respectful attitude but I can tell by his eyes and his tone that he's dying to laugh.

"Alright, first of all, call me ma'am once more and you won't step foot in this house again. I refuse to be that old. That being said, would you like to stay for dinner? I'm making stroganoff."

Tristan lost control of his laughter at that point.

And that was it for the age problem. We didn't even have to say anything about it to my dad when he came home about fifteen minutes later.

Doing my homework in the kitchen with Tristan helping me with math and trying not to laugh at me over my hatred of it, we heard the garage door leading into the house slam shut and then my dad's deep voice say, "Where's the boy?"

We looked at my mom. Ignoring us, she stopped stirring the pan on the stove, greeted my dad with a kiss as he walked into the kitchen and then she playfully shoved a twenty-dollar bill in his face. It made him laugh so hard, his pretense of trying to be intimidating all but evaporated.

"Let's talk," my dad said to Tristan with a "come on, follow me" gesture of his hand.

Tristan winked at me and got up from the table to follow my dad out of the kitchen and as they headed towards the garage, I heard the beginnings of automotive male bonding and what I hope will turn into a beautiful friendship between my father and the almost adult guy who's dating his almost sixteen-year-old daughter.

"You can drive mine if I can drive yours."

"The Nova a coupe or hard top?"

"Coupe."

"Nice. Okay, you got a deal. Three on the tree?"

"Yep, kept it stock. Yours?"

"It came with a factory automatic but I wanted a four on the floor."

"Muncie or Saginaw?"

"Muncie."

"From the sound of it, you got a small block in there…"

"Yeah, a 327…it's built."

"Thought so…"

Again, dinner was a much louder affair at my house than it normally is. My dad was playing music as is typical, but the addition of my boyfriend's conversation and antics at the table added a new dimension to our meal. I was thinking Tristan seems to have fit in with surprising quickness and ease as he and Jillian had been doing some verbal battling of wits, which then escalated into the three of us throwing dinner rolls at each other. Then at one point when Jillian returned from answering the door for trick-or-treaters, she pulled my baby book from behind her back and presented it to Tristan again. I protested loudly and went to grab it back, but he held it out of reach with one hand and held me away with the other. Laughing, but with my head being shoved to the side, I caught my dad looking at my mom and followed his gaze to notice that she looked happier than I've seen her in a long time. She had the brightest smile on her face as she watched Jillian make faces at me from the other side of the table and Tristan flip through pages of my baby book, gathering ammunition by which to tease me with I'm sure.

It wasn't quite 6:30 when we adjourned to the family room for some TV.

"Mandy, it looks like none of our shows are on tonight what with Halloween, so let's take a vote on what to watch."

My dad raised his hands in apology for having even considered the foolishness of needing to vote when all four of us shouted *"Buffy!"* at him like "Duh! What else would we want to watch?" My mom shot a dazzling smile at Tristan when she heard his voice mixed in with in hers, Jillian's, and mine. Having been totally out numbered, my dad located a DVD from my mom's and my personal favorite season which is season three, and then the five of us settled in to watch some classic vampire slayer comedy.

Now I'm not sure why she opted out of trick-or-treating this year, but Jillian went to her room after we finished watching the first episode and I didn't make it through much of the second before I fell asleep on the couch with my head on a pillow in Tristan's lap. He had one arm wrapped around me with the fingers of his hand entwined with mine, the other was dangling off the arm of the couch and he had his legs stretched out on the ottoman in front of him with his ankles crossed. I'm assuming he'd crashed too because the sound of our front door screen being clicked closed woke me enough to hear my parents talking quietly through the open window. I'm guessing they're on their porch swing because I can hear it squeaking a little as it slowly glides back and forth.

"They both out?" My dad asked.

"Mm-hmm. I think so."

"Shouldn't we wake 'em up?"

"I'm surprised all the trick-or-treating noise hasn't already, but it's still early…let's let them sleep for a while. I think they had a long weekend," my mom answered.

"You enjoyed dinner quite a bit, didn't you?"

"I really did. You?"

"I think I can stand having the boy around."

"How'd your test go?"

"As far as I can tell, the boy's got a good head on his shoulders. He takes that car of his damned seriously…a person could get into a whole mess of trouble with the speed that thing is capable of. First time he let anyone else drive it was today. From what he said, his buddy drove it from the back lot over to shop for him…he timed the kid to make sure he didn't speed gettin' there. I gotta tell ya Mandy, I like him, I trust him, and I think he's more responsible than I was at his age."

"Good to know."

"Mm-hmm. It sure is, honey."

With my parents' positive verdict mixed in with the sultry scent of gardenias from the flowerpot on the porch floating over me with the breeze, I thought about the new ringtones that Tristan and I chose in English today. He abandoned Nickelback for the time being and went with a Collective Soul song called "Heaven's Already Here," and I went back to Faith Hill, but replaced "This Kiss" with "Breathe." Hearing the lyrics drift through my mind, I started thinking my choice couldn't get any more perfect as I nestled a little further back so I was tucked right up against him, safe and snug. And serenely smiling to myself and feeling more at peace than I knew was possible, I drifted back to sleep hearing the lullaby-like rhythmic sound of Tristan's heart beating in time with the deeply contended steadiness of his breath.

Sigh.

Epilogue

(Well not really, because now that my life is a soap opera, I'm sure there'll be more.)

My alarm clock and I have made our peace with each other. It has agreed to wake me up at an ungodly hour so Tristan can drive me to school and still maintain his habit of getting there early to swim the lanes while I watch and doze from time to time. I in turn, have agreed to not throw it out the window when it does.

So that's what I was thinking about as it went off at 5:00 on this dawning November day a couple weeks or so after Tristan and I made things official. I scooped Phineas and Ferb off of my chest and tucked them into their own bed, which Tristan has stuffed inside my missing shirt so they'll sleep there. And while I continue with my new morning routine of getting ready for another day in paradise, I'd like to take the time to update you on Tristan's Wall of Infamy conversations, simply because they're kind of funny and I'd forgotten to share them with you on that "eventful" Monday.

This first one pertains to my bra, which by the way, is *still* hanging up there for all the world to see. Oh and I'm including the last couple of sentences of dialogue just to help you remember where we left off the night of my first date.

Tristan's Mom: Flattery will get you everywhere. How would you like your eggs prepared dear?

Me: If it wouldn't be too much trouble, I prefer mine sunny-side up. Thanks Mrs. D., you're the best.

Tristan's Dad: Oh, I think I really like her.

Jeff: Yeah, she's cool but I hear her sister is scary.

Tristan's Mom: I like her too, not that it matters. He'll never bring her home.

Jeff: Especially if he doesn't tell her...just saying.

Tristan: Don't fucking start with me.

Jeff: Dude, you're going to need kneepads for the insane amount of groveling you're going to have to do.

Tristan: Can I borrow yours or are you still kneeling and being whipped?

Jeff: Take them. You'll need them more than I do.

Tristan: I'm not talking to you anymore.

Jeff: Whatever, but I'm going to crash here Sunday morning after the party...just letting you know.

Tristan: Want to stay here and get drunk with me tonight after the game?

Jeff: How about if I live vicariously through you and just watch you get drunk?

Tristan's Dad: "Fat, drunk, and stupid is no way to go through life, son."

Jeff: Nice! I love Animal House!

Tristan: Whatever. You're a dick.

Tristan's Mom: Not sure how any of that applies, but I'm going to the store tomorrow, did you want anything?

Tristan: You'll need to restock the liquor cabinet after tonight so lots of booze, but other than that, nothing I can think of. Thanks, you're the best.

Tristan's Dad: Should I pencil you in for a face-to-face?

Tristan: Nope. Self-medicating should do the trick.

Tristan's Dad: Let me know if you want to talk.

Tristan: Will do, but I wouldn't clear your calendar if I were you.

Jeff: I've never seen someone abuse alcohol like you did last night. Dude.

Tristan: Well, you know how seriously I take my ringtones.

Jeff: Indeed.

Tristan: I think I'm still drunk. Let's go surfing.

Jeff: I'm driving.

Tristan: Well now I'm sober. This sucks. By the way, I'm not going tonight.

Jeff: You'll go.

Tristan: I want to murder him and I can't face her.

Jeff: I won't let you and you can.

Tristan: It's not a good idea, man.

Jeff: Told you you'd go. Ah...I see we have a new conversation started over there...I must go put in my .02 ₵

This next one is new and from the way it reads, I think it was written mostly on Sunday morning after Mike's party, but it kind of goes along with the bag of pot which is no longer there; probably because Tristan and Jeff baked it into brownies the afternoon before the licorice incident. However, a picture of a marijuana leaf with the words "Just Say No" written under it is thumbtacked in place of where the baggy was.

Tristan's Mom: What's this?

Tristan: The Gateway to Hell, where I've spent the last 7-ish days.

Jeff: I tried to tell you dude...

Tristan: I Know. Next time beat the shit out of me until I hear you. Never mind. There won't be a next time.

Tristan's Dad: You inhaled, didn't you son?

Tristan: Worse. I accidentally shared a piece of licorice and lied about it.

Tristan's Mom: As long as you didn't drive.

Jeff: Nope. We passed out in the bus like good teenage delinquents.

Tristan's Dad: I'm so proud.

Tristan: You shouldn't be on this one.

Jeff: Being a bathroom, a prison guard and a room service guy is exhausting...I'm beat. Hey Joey, want to take a nap? (Seeing as how Joey the baby can't read and Tristan is the one who responded, I think this might have something to do with an episode of *Friends*, but who knows with these guys.)

Tristan: Love to. Can't. Going to the park to fraternize with the criminally insane.

Jeff: Nice! Bring mace so you have a shot at dodging bullets in case she's packing.

Tristan: Wouldn't surprise me if she were.
Tristan's Mom: I'm heading to the store soon, did you change your mind about wanting anything?
Tristan: YES! An assload of D batteries. Thanks, you're the best.
Tristan's Mom: What on earth for? Oh wait, I don't think I want to know.
Tristan's Dad: I do...
Jeff: Me too.
Tristan: Serious business that requires that aged ghetto blaster you two have kept in the garage. Thanks for that by the way, you're the best.
Tristan's Dad: I think I got a pair of your uncle's penny loafers out there too if you want them.
Jeff: That's wrong. So how'd your play date at the park go?
Tristan: I made a deal with the devil. How was your nap?
Jeff: It's never the same without you.
Tristan: Oh, that reminds me, can you work some magic and keep Kate away from Camie tomorrow morning?
Jeff: I got your back dude. Good luck.
Tristan: Thanks man.

This is the last one I have for you and I think it's pretty stinkin' cute:

Tristan's Mom: What are these?
Tristan: Your granddaughters.
Tristan's Dad: Don't worry honey, you don't look old enough to be a mother let alone a grandmother.
Tristan's Mom: Again with the flattery, thank you dear. Where did they come from?
Tristan: Camie gave birth last night.
Jeff: I didn't know she was pregnant.
Tristan: She wasn't. It was a miracle.
Tristan's Mom: Do they have names?
Tristan: Phineas and Ferb.

Jeff: From the cartoon?

Tristan's Dad: That figures, he named the dog Scooby.

Tristan's Mom: They sound like boy names.

Tristan: Mom! Shhh, you'll give them a complex.

Jeff: If that Ferb one climbs my legs again I'm drop kicking it.

Tristan: That's child abuse and I'll press charges. Besides, they just miss their mom.

Jeff: I'm calling CPS (cat protective services)...

Tristan: What for?

Jeff: Because you're making your kids live in a broken home unnecessarily.

Tristan: I'm not talking to you anymore.

Jeff: Fine, as long as you to talk to her.

Tristan: Back off.

Jeff: Nope, not gonna do it.

Tristan: I'm warning you man.

Jeff: You miss her too.

Tristan: Yeah, so?

Jeff: So do something about it.

Tristan: Happy? Last night was miserable and I think it's too late.

Jeff: You still have a 12 year old ace in the hole.

Tristan: Saving it as a last resort.

Tristan's Dad: Honey, do you have a clue as to what they're talking about?

Tristan's Mom: No and I don't want one.

Jeff: I'm just helping my nieces get their parents back together. Dude, it's time. Make the call.

Tristan: Alright, I did it. But I get the feeling I'm about to do business with the mob. I hope I don't wake up with the head of my horse in bed with me tonight.

Jeff: Well, a good father will do anything he can to protect his family, even if that means he runs the risk of sleeping with the fishes.

Tristan: Okay girls, your aunt helped Daddy come up with a plan and if it works you should get to see Mommy today. Cross your paws, or claws, or whatever...just cross something for luck.

Pretty funny stuff, huh? Well not all of it, but a lot of it. At least Phineas and Ferb weren't thumbtacked by their ears to the bulletin board like everything else. And yeah, I know you're probably thinking that this bulletin/white board thing can't possibly hold all this communication but I'm not kidding, it does. The thing is huge. It's floor to ceiling and literally takes up the whole damned wall.

Well, Tristan just pulled up so I have to get going, but before I do, I'll give you a quick re-cap of everything...

In the end, both Derek and Brandon won their bet. I saw some action within a week, but it took exactly four weeks from the first time I saw him before Tristan and I entered into the first committed relationship of both our lives. And actually, even though neither of us is prepared to admit it at this point, I'm really thinking it all started with both of us experiencing the much-fabled love at first sight, although we experienced it over four months apart from each other. And I'll admit it, I did spend some time in the beginning thinking it'd be nice if Tristan were like some other people because I thought they had desirable personality traits that he lacks and I've since realized I wouldn't love him if he was anything other than who he is.

I've also learned Tristan *is* the kind of guy who's capable of making grand gestures and speeches fraught with emotion, even though they're not exactly the most eloquent—if they're even spoken at all. And although it takes some effort to understand what he's saying sometimes, I think I prefer the way he communicates with me. I mean when it comes right down to it, he and I speak the same language...we just have different accents. Ultimately, we get each other and that's worth more to me than fancy words and having everything spelled out.

And just so you know, Tristan was right; I finally feel like I'm one of them and I fit in. And hey, it only took a few weeks filled with a lot of mistakes and humiliation. I mean it could've been worse, right? I might not have even made a single good friend by this point let alone the several I have now. So, I think it was worth putting myself out there and risking looking stupid every now and then, don't you? Because after all, everyone makes mistakes and no one's graveyard stays empty forever.

Through it all I've learned a lot of things about not only myself and other people, but God too; like it pays to be nice and just be you, but sometimes people do or say some not nice things because they're scared or insecure, and when that happens, it would behoove you to remember that you're not perfect either. God has excellent taste in music and has a sense of humor as well, which is kind of a relief and goes to proving my newly adopted theory that He won't cast me into Hell for swearing. And yes, cancer still sucks but I'm starting to truly believe that God really can turn bad things around for good and I wholeheartedly agree with Tristan's ringtone for me. I really do feel like heaven is already here because I just don't see how life can get any better than it is right now.

Who knows though, maybe I'm wrong again and this is really only an uber-phenomenal beginning…

COMING SOON

The Other Fish in the Sea

Book 2 in the Grab Your Pole Series

Turn the page for a sneak peek

1.

Kool-Aid and Honey

It was almost instantaneous. When Tristan and I got together my house turned into the "Kool-Aid house." You know, the house where all the kids conjoiner at when there isn't anything else to do. I think that happened mainly because Tristan is there all the time, which means Jeff is there all the time, which, in turn, means Kate—Jeff's girlfriend and my best friend—is there all the time, and so on... My mom absolutely loves it. Again, in case you've forgotten, her name is Mandy and she has breast cancer, which is thankfully in a kind of remission. And because my mom loves having all my friends hanging around constantly, my dad, Kevin, loves it too. I think my mom would've loved to have more kids so she makes all my friends feel as welcome as family. I swear you can practically hear Sister Sledge chanting "We Are Family" from my house on any given week night. So, that's why it was no big deal when Kate threw my front door open one Sunday evening before dinner without having knocked and informed us of the following:

"Well, they're arguing again so I hope there's room for one more!"

Kate is a cheerleader and normally she's spunky, but she's been a *little* moody lately. I think it's probably because her parents have been arguing kind of regularly.

"Will it just be you tonight or wi—" my mom started to ask but another voice answered her question before she even got it out.

"Hey Mrs. R, what's on the menu tonight?" Jeff asked, walking in and kissing Kate on the top of her head.

Completely unfazed by Jeff's unannounced entrance, my mom answered, "Kevin and Tristan have been in the kitchen for almost two hours trying to follow an old family recipe I found for meatloaf, so we might be having pizza."

I had to work hard to stifle a laugh because as soon as my mom finished her sentence, both my dad and Tristan came out of the kitchen looking disgruntled with either each other or the state of dinner. I'm guessing they're worried about the food, though, because it seems like they're wearing a good portion of the ingredients. At least they're wearing aprons as well, although that just makes it even funnier.

In order to appreciate the comedy of errors this whole thing is, you should know that neither my dad nor Tristan can really cook but they both think they can. Not to mention that my six-foot four and about two hundred-thirty pounds of solid muscle boyfriend is wearing a pink gingham apron and if that isn't hysterical enough, it's also trimmed in lace. Jeff didn't work at all to stifle his laughter one bit...he just started cracking up.

"It just *has* to be a mistake," my dad said to Tristan who was wiping his hands on the pink gingham like he has motor oil on his hands and the apron is a garage rag.

Just so you know, Tristan and my dad have totally bonded over the last couple weeks by spending both quality and quantity time in our garage. They're both really into classic cars, muscle cars, hot-rods—essentially, anything with wheels. I'm completely pleased with that of course, but sometimes I wonder if my dad thinks I brought Tristan home for *him* to play with. I didn't. I brought him home because *I* like to play with him, but whatever. I'm not going to complain because when we're alone, Tristan does a really good job of reminding me that he prefers toying with me over tinkering on cars with my dad.

"I don't think it was. I mean why would it be there right in the middle of the recipe?" Tristan asked, completely ignoring Jeff's hilarity.

"Boy, (My dad calls Tristan "The Boy.") I hope you're right. 'Cause I wouldn't have added it...oatmeal just doesn't go with meatloaf, it just ain't right."

Oh good lord. They put oatmeal in the meatloaf...

"I know! It's just crazy, but *that's* what the recipe said to do."

"I'd like Canadian bacon and pineapple on my pizza please," I teased and had to hop out of the way as the dishtowel my father was holding almost made contact with my butt.

"Young lady, you could at least show some respect like your sister. She's been in there the whole time reading and hasn't once said anything negative," my dad told me with a twinkle in his eyes, demonstrating that he isn't upset with my lack of confidence in his culinary skills. He talks a big game but really, he's a softie.

But can we go back to my "respectful" sibling for a moment? I mean seriously, uh-oh.

"Um, Dad? Tristan? Did either of you happen to think *why* she might've chosen to read in the kitchen while the two of you were so diligently preparing what I'm sure will be a delicious meal?"

My dad *might* have blinders on when it comes to Jillian, however, Tristan really should know better.

"Dude! You're toast!"

Jeff started laughing at Tristan again as my dad looked back at the closed door of the kitchen, contemplating what the big deal was. Only this time, Tristan didn't ignore Jeff. His facial expression as the catastrophic possibilities dawned on him was to-die-for funny.

"Hi everyone! Who's toast?" "Lonely Pete" asked upon entering our family room, having just let himself in as well.

I call him that because even though he's a really close friend of Tristan's and Jeff's, therefore mine as well, he's always kind of like the third or sometimes even seventh wheel. Basically, he doesn't have a girlfriend.

"I think I might be…do you think she'll be willing to barter now or is this something she might blackmail me with at such a time as it suits her purposes?" Tristan asked the room at large.

"Right now you have nothing I want, but thank you for being so amenable in helping me try out my new video camera. I think the picture quality is tremendous."

Apparently tonight, Jill is both the criminal and the spy. Mind you she didn't come from the kitchen. No, she came from upstairs...and we *never* saw her go up.

"Oh, hi Jillian," Pete said.

She ignored him. "Can we eat now? I'm hungry."

"What do you want on your pizza?" I couldn't help it.

"I don't want pizza, I want the meatloaf."

Out of all of us present, you'd think my sister would've already placed her order at the Bottle Shop for the best pizza in town after having borne witness to my dad's and Tristan's attempt to cook something edible. I say that with the utmost love and affection for both of them of course.

"Um…don't you think that's living dangerously?"

"Camie, I like living on the edge. Besides, it should be good."

"They put oatmeal in it though," I whispered.

I was teasing them before but I'm still thinking pizza. I'm also hearing Aerosmith's "Livin' On the Edge" in my head now instead of Sister Sledge, which is kind of a relief.

"O ye of little faith…"

Huh. If she's willing to give it a go, then I guess I should too. I'm just not excited about the idea of what my stomach will do to me…maybe I can get away with just a small piece if I fill my plate with vegetables. I should also make sure I have a couple napkins in case I can't get any of it down. Of course I had to hide a little giggle as an episode of *Seinfeld* involving mutton, napkins and Elaine being molested by dogs popped into my head.

O ye of little faith indeed.

At one point during dinner, which surprisingly wasn't bad—go figure...oatmeal in meatloaf—I was hard pressed not to climb on the table and do the Snoopy happy dance. I was, however, doing it in my head and quite vigorously at that.

"So what does everyone have planned for their Thanksgiving break?" My mom asked the four teenagers at the table who aren't related to her by blood.

"Sadly, I'm going to New Jersey with my parents to see my dad's family," Kate said, sounding utterly disgruntled.

"Which means I'm stuck having dinner at my dad's girlfriend's parents' house...thanks Katy." Kate threw a roll at Jeff in her defense. He really hates being away from her for more than even a few hours. Not that she enjoys time away from him, but still; he's a pouter.

"It's not like I wanna go, you know...I'm gonna be miserable."

"My family is spending Thanksgiving in Palm Springs this year," Pete said, ignoring the minor bickering that's going on between Jeff and Kate over their mandated holiday separation.

"What about you, Boy?"

This is when I started to get a little disgruntled myself and started to empathize with Jeff and Kate. Being what you might call desert-rats, my family—including some extended family—goes to the desert every year for Thanksgiving. It's a *ton* of fun. We all go in our motor homes and ride various pieces of desert vehicles like quads, dirt bikes, dune buggies, etc....but for some reason, I don't think riding around the dunes with my cousins and Jillian is going to be as much fun as it usually is as I will be sans hot boyfriend.

"I got nothin'. My parents were asked to take a flight to Tuscany (Yeah, Italy.) so they'll be gone most of the week," Tristan answered, sounding irritated. He also kind of threw a piece of his roll onto his plate to emphasize that irritation.

My mom frowned. "Can't you go with them?"

"Not this time. My passport expired last month and I sorta had other things on my mind so I forgot to get it renewed," he explained without saying that the "other things" on his mind last month were me.

Of course he made sure *I* knew what he was talking about by covertly pinching my butt under the table. It was totally unnecessary, like I didn't already know. Hell, most of the people sitting at the table played some kind of role in how we got together, including my little sister. Well actually, especially my little sister, seeing as how she operated as a double agent. And even if they didn't play a part, they all knew what Tristan was talking about but I didn't see him pinch any of *them*. I think he's just trying to get me to retaliate so he has an excuse to mess with me later on.

I was considering what form my retaliation would take when my dad said, "Well then, why don't you just come to the desert with us?"

I was stunned. I almost asked him to repeat himself because I thought there was no way my dad had just asked Tristan to spend four nights and four days with us in the middle of nowhere. I didn't have to ask him to repeat himself though.

"Kevin, I think that is a simply marvelous idea. Really Tristan, you shouldn't spend Thanksgiving alone and we won't take no for an answer."

I took one look at Tristan's face and although the expression he was wearing was something like innocent surprise, I knew from the way his eyes were sparkling that he'd just played my parents.

Then he pinched me again.

So now you can understand why I'm trying really hard not to table dance.

"Is there room on the trailer for my bike?" Huh. I didn't know he has a dirt bike. Then again, I shouldn't be surprised...bikes *do* have wheels.

"Aw, that sucks! This means I'm not gonna have my girlfriend *or* my best friend around for like five days...and Pete's gonna be gone...I bet Mike's goin' out of town too," Jeff muttered to himself while Tristan and my dad talked dirt toys.

After dinner was over and the dishes were done entirely by Kate, who'd placed a bet that dinner would suck and lost, my parents retired to the family room to watch a movie that none of us was interested in seeing, so we all played a card game called Bullshit. It's a game I've been playing since I was little and it's really fun.

The object of the game is to get rid of all your cards as they're played in order from smallest to biggest. However, if you don't have the right card on your turn then you have to pick up the pile, so what you're supposed to do is bluff. So say you're on threes and you don't have one, you would choose a random card from your hand and say "one three" and place it face down on the pile. Now, if someone calls you on it by saying "bullshit," you have to pick up the pile. But let's say you did actually play the right card and someone calls you on it incorrectly, well then *they* have to pick up the pile. There are all kinds of other ways to cheat, but you get the gist.

Jillian, Kate, and Tristan rock at this game. Kate does because she's gifted at being able to read people, and Tristan is because he's exceedingly sharp and he can *almost* always school his facial expression to look however he wants it to look, which is typically along the lines of being cocky, arrogant, or smug—I know the three are sort of like synonyms for each other, but there is actually difference between them, and he's very well versed in demonstrating that fact. Now, he doesn't know this, but I can usually pick up on his real mood by what his eyes are doing. Not always, but most of the time. And then there's Jillian who generally appears to be bored all the time. Well, she's good at it only because you can never trust her, so people tend to not call her on anything unless they have all four cards of the number she's on in their own hand. Also, she has an odd strategy. She'll play straight in the very beginning and then, whether she thinks someone's bluffing or not, she'll start calling everyone out so she ends up with a bunch of cards, which means there's a good chance she's never bluffing after that.

Anyway, the six of us were sitting around the kitchen table playing a game that encourages lying and cheating when Jeff cocked his head to the side like he was listening intently.

"Hey, what's this song called?"

"Lips of an angel," Tristan and I answered together. His eyes got just the slightest shade darker before he winked at me and went back to his cards. I got goose bumps and went back to mine.

"It's based on fact," Jillian and Pete commented in unison.

That had me looking up again.

Jillian's eyes slowly lifted from her cards to look at Pete—whose eyes never left his cards once—like she could've been mildly impressed…*or* mildly irritated. I'm not sure which but because he flew into her radar, if I were Pete, I'd think twice before doing a lot of bluffing tonight.

"Why?" Kate asked.

"Oh, well I swear to God my dad was singing it to someone the other night on the phone…not literally, but he might as well have."

"*What?* To *who?*" Tristan asked, sounding pretty surprised.

Like me, Tristan knows his music and that particular song is about what you might call a long lost love and the ramifications of when that person suddenly calls out of the blue and Tristan's surprise, come to find out, is more than justified.

"That's just it, I have no idea. I was studyin' for that chem test we had on Friday..." Yeah, I know. I have a hard time picturing Jeff studying too. "...and Denise was asleep in the living room when my dad's cell rang and when he answered it, he asked 'honey' why she was crying. No shit, he called whoever it was honey… Anyway, then he started to whisper about how it was really good to hear her voice but he had to be quiet because Denise was sleeping right there. It was bizarre so when he got up to go out back, I followed him into the kitchen so I could eavesdrop through the open wind—"

"Atta boy." I inwardly rolled my eyes at the pride in my sister's tone.

"What else did you hear?" Kate asked with a look of confusion on her face.

You see, we're all kind of surprised and/or confused by this because Jeff's dad, Grey, has never been married. Not even to Jeff's mom, whom I recently found out died shortly after Jeff was born. However, Grey has been with his girlfriend for something like two years and from what I've been told, he really seems happy with her. So happy in fact, Jeff was actually thinking he might marry her.

"Well, that's when it got even weirder…it was hard to follow because I could only hear his side of the call and he was still talking low, but when he stopped pacing in front of the window I heard this part really clearly, he said, 'Well I didn't move on, why do you think I never got married?' Then he started pacing again but I think he told her that he didn't want her talking to him to cause problems for her or something like that, and then all of sudden he got kinda excited or agitated I guess and asked loud enough for me to hear him 'Wait, what are you telling me?' so then after another minute he said something about how he'd never stopped loving her and for her to call him when they could both talk freely."

"Holy shit, man, you're right…he may as well have just played that song into the fuckin' phone," Tristan declared.

"I know, right?" Jeff agreed and looked at the rest of us for confirmation.

"Why didn't you tell me about this earlier?"

"Honestly Katy, I totally forgot about the whole thing until it came on the radio just now."

"I just can't picture it…he actually said he loved her?" Kate asked, sounding not just confused anymore, but baffled.

"Yeah. That he never *stopped* loving her."

"Wow. Do you think he's cheating on Denise?" Pete asked.

"No, I don't think so. It sounded like he hadn't talked to whoever she is in a while."

I'm thinking that if what Jeff said of that conversation is true, I'm inclined to agree with him. I don't think his dad is cheating.

Not yet anyway...

About the Author

Jenn Cooksey is a Southern California girl born and bred, and proudly boasts being a member of Grossmont High School's alumni. She currently resides in the 7th Ring of Hell (aka; Arizona) with her husband (whom she married on a dare while in Las Vegas), their three daughters, and more pets than she has the patience to count. Aside from her husband and one cat, everyone living under the Cooksey's roof is female. She's sure her husband will be not only be awarded sainthood when he kicks the bucket, but that Jesus will welcome him into heaven with a beer and a congratulatory high-five. She also believes that Bacon should be capitalized. Always.

You can learn more about Jenn and her books at:
www.jenncooksey.blogspot.com
and www.goodreads.com
Or follow her on Facebook at Jenn Cooksey Novels
and on Twitter @Jenn_Cooksey

Made in the USA
Lexington, KY
07 February 2015